Critical praise for

RUTH AXTELL
MORREN
and her novels

THE HEALING SEASON
"The author expertly creates an endearing story
that will both encourage and delight the reader."
—*Romantic Times BOOKreviews*

DAWN IN MY HEART
"Morren turns in a superior romantic historical."
—*Booklist*

"Morren's tales are always well plotted
and fascinating, and this one is no exception.
4 ½ stars."
—*Romantic Times BOOKreviews*

LILAC SPRING
"*Lilac Spring* blooms with heartfelt yearning and
genuine conflict as Cherish and Silas seek God's
will for their lives. Fascinating details about
19th-century shipbuilding are planted here and
there, bringing a historical feel to this faith-filled
romance."
—Liz Curtis Higgs, bestselling author of
Grace in Thine Eyes

RUTH AXTELL MORREN

The Rogue's Redemption

Steeple
Hill®

Published by Steeple Hill Books™

STEEPLE HILL BOOKS

Steeple
Hill®

ISBN-13: 978-0-373-78600-8
ISBN-10:   0-373-78600-X

THE ROGUE'S REDEMPTION

Copyright © 2008 by Ruth Axtell

www.SteepleHill.com

Printed in U.S.A.

For Melissa, my editor. Thanks for being my champion since the day you discovered *Winter Is Past* through a contest. You're the first one to read my completed manuscripts and the one whose comments and reaction I always look forward to and treasure.

and

To Allison, my critique partner, who gets to read the "work in progress" with all its warts. You always have an encouraging word to say. I'm truly grateful for all your insights and suggestions. They are invaluable in making the final product shine.

For love is strong as death…
—*Song of Solomon* 8:6b

Chapter One

Gerrit's gaze wandered over the crowded salon and he wondered yet again why he had come to this masquerade. Something about a bet made late last night with some fellows from his regiment.

He surveyed the crowded room as he had all evening, feeling no inclination to talk to anyone. The London ton, his world—or so it had been. It was all foreign to him now. Peopled by fools dressed in nonsensical capes and masks, as if one couldn't tell who was who and who was dallying with whom.

"My dear, that's the Duke of Weatherspoon," hissed an older feminine voice to the cloaked figure next to her. They had moved to stand just in front of Gerrit, close enough for him to hear them in the noisy salon.

Gerrit observed the pair of women in their masks and dominoes—one short and dumpy, the other tall and statuesque.

"He's coming our way! Smile!" the older, shorter one

entreated the taller. He recognized the peremptory tone as belonging to Mrs. Bellows. Was she still around? He'd known her when he'd first entered London society as a youth. Disdained wherever she went by the ton, known as a notorious social climber, she was barely tolerated by her betters, and that was only because she clung to a few people who allowed her to attend their parties. Little had changed in the years he'd been away. Little but himself.

He swallowed another mouthful of his drink. Mrs. Bellows's presence was only further evidence he was in the wrong place. A barometer was no more certain of predicting a storm than Mrs. Bellows in gauging the bad ton of a party.

Mrs. Bellows nudged her companion. "He's looking your way!"

Gerrit snorted into his drink. She was at it again, "introducing" a young lady. That inevitably meant the young lady suffered some severe social impediment.

He followed the direction of Mrs. Bellows's fan. Sure enough, the Duke of Weatherspoon was walking in their direction, the crowd bowing and scraping before him like a bunch of peasants. The duke's dark blue cape was thrown over one shoulder, revealing a perfectly cut coat with a lustrous white waistcoat beneath. Although tall and stately, he was beginning to show a rounded paunch.

As he approached, Mrs. Bellows stepped directly in his path, spreading her skirts in a magnificent curtsy. The duke and his colorfully garbed retinue were forced to stop. Gerrit watched in amusement, curiosity suspending his boredom. Weatherspoon was known as very high in the instep, but half the fun of a masquerade was the liberties people took with one another—pretending not to recognize each other and addressing them more freely than they would normally dare.

"Sirrah, there is a certain young lady desirous of making your acquaintance this evening."

"Indeed, madam?" he answered in a languid tone, bringing his quizzing glass up to the eyehole of his black mask and examining her as if she were some particularly gruesome creature.

"Most assuredly, your grace." She nodded for emphasis.

"Very well, if it will allow me to pass." He sighed audibly, provoking titters among his party.

Mrs. Bellows grabbed the tall young lady by the elbow and brought her forward. Gerrit felt an instant of sympathy for the girl as he watched her stumble, then quickly right herself, being freed from Mrs. Bellows's grasp in the process. She bent her knees in a smooth curtsy. "I am pleased to make your acquaintance, your lordship."

The titters grew louder.

She had a slight accent. Yankee?

"Oh, your grace," Mrs. Bellows gushed with a knowing wink, "my young charge is overcome by your exalted status, but I'll have you know she is a young lady of impeccable character—"

"Hoping to snag a title," a lady by the duke's side added in a low, mocking tone.

The young lady drew in a sharp breath and moved back a step, then stood rigidly straight.

Mrs. Bellows continued to chatter away as if she

hadn't heard the remark. Gerrit wouldn't have been surprised if she hadn't. "If you'd care to see her pretty countenance unmasked, she will be attending the Treadwells' ball on Thursday. And she goes riding every forenoon in the Row…"

These last words were said to the duke's departing figure. He'd barely given her a nod of dismissal before moving on with his entourage. "A pleasure I find myself able to forswear," came floating back to them, followed by outright laughter from the duke's party.

Bunch of sycophants. Since he'd been back from the Continent, Gerrit found his tolerance for these arrogant titled lords nonexistent. What had they done while so many of Britain's manhood had spilled their blood on foreign soil?

Gerrit tossed back the rest of his drink and turned to eye the hapless Yankee heiress once more. For an heiress she must inevitably be. Mrs. Bellows only took on those clients who made it worth her while.

"My dear Hester, I do believe he liked you."

"If that is the way the British show their favor, I'm hard-pressed to imagine their disapproval."

Humor laced her low, cultured voice. Gerrit found himself intrigued by the lady behind it. It couldn't have been easy to be so summarily dismissed by that pompous fool of a man whose only distinction was having been born with wealth and a title. He admired the aplomb of someone who could brush off the incident so easily.

"Oh, don't regard it, Hester. The duke is a funny man." Mrs. Bellows patted the young lady's hand. "You'll see, he is sure to be at the ball on Thursday.

Now, we just have to make sure you have the right gown, and he'll be smitten."

"I feel a bit of a headache. It must be this crowded room. Would you mind very much getting me some refreshment, Mrs. Bellows?"

"Of course not, my dear. Why didn't you speak sooner? I'll have it for you in a trice. Are you sure you'll be all right here by yourself? I'll only be gone a minute."

"I shall be fine. No one has spoken to me yet, so I'm sure I'll be left alone while you are absent."

"Are you quite certain?"

With a few more reassuring words from her charge, Mrs. Bellows bustled away.

Gerrit watched her disappear into the crowd before taking a step forward to stand in the place she'd vacated. Noticing his move, the young woman turned her caped head and their glances met.

Hazel eyes stared back at him through the wide holes of her half mask. They were the color of a dark pond that reveals deeper shades behind its mottled green surface.

He tried to tear his gaze away, but found himself helpless during those seconds. There was a directness in her regard, which he wasn't used to in a woman. He detected no coyness or false modesty there. Instead, her eyes told him more than words that she knew exactly who she was and pretended no more. He envied her that knowledge; what he wouldn't give to start with a clean slate and be able to look people straight in the eye.

Drawing in a deep breath, he ignored the command of common sense that told him to flee from her presence. Instead, he inclined his head a fraction.

He read the first uncertainty in her eyes, as if she wasn't sure the proper protocol to follow, very much aware that the arbiter of taste, the worthy Mrs. Bellows, was conspicuously absent. He wanted to shout to her, *Run, run while you still have the chance! I'm a wolf in sheep's clothing, known to devour little innocents for breakfast.*

Instead, he smiled that charming smile to which countless damsels from highborn to low had willingly succumbed over the years. "Although we haven't been properly introduced," he told her softly, "permit me to address you. A masquerade allows a certain license not normally observed in polite society."

"I see," she answered in matter-of-fact tones. "Are you also a duke?"

He appreciated her wit. "Alas, no. A mere soldier."

She tilted her head a fraction, considering. "A redcoat."

He chuckled. "Two strikes against me, I see."

"I must remind myself repeatedly you are no longer the enemy."

For someone who had been feted and admired since his return to England following Waterloo, it was deflating to be viewed as the defeated foe. "I suppose the overthrow of the tyrant Boney is viewed differently across the Atlantic."

"Our immediate threat was in the guise of redcoats encroaching our border from the north. Do you know they even invaded our city?"

"And which city is that?"

Her chin lifted a notch. "Bangor in the District of Maine."

"Ah…a namesake of our Welsh city."

"No. Actually it was named for a hymn."

"I see," he said. "In truth, I didn't know of the invasion. I was too busy keeping track of our campaigns on this side of the Atlantic to follow what was going on in the Colo—" He coughed. "Excuse me, in the United States."

"Yes, we won our independence, you know."

"I was aware of the fact. It was before my time in His Majesty's army, however."

"Would that have made a difference?"

He stared at her. She was laughing at him. In her quiet, dignified tone, she was making sport of him. He looked down at his empty glass. "Who is to say?" he murmured.

"Thank goodness for the peace treaty then," she countered lightly.

He chuckled again, raising his glass to her. "Otherwise, we might not be meeting here tonight."

"We haven't yet been introduced, have we?"

"A mere technicality. I am acquainted with your Mrs. Bellows, although I doubt she would give me a recommendation."

She pursed her lips, making their soft fullness all the more appealing. "Are you so very bad?"

"I have no title, unless you count a military one, and less fortune. I doubt you've sailed across the Atlantic for less."

She neither admitted nor denied the assertion. Instead, her focus continued on him. "You are a soldier. Are you decorated?"

Her questions were as direct as her look. Was it merely the mask that made her so bold? "I doubt my medals would recommend me, since they were gained killing your allies. I suppose I should be thankful I was never in the Colonies, so I can claim no Yanks on my conscience."

"Perhaps you would not have lived to tell the tale."

He laughed, a heartier laugh than he'd enjoyed in a long time, and enjoyed watching her lips curl upward, almost reluctantly.

"Perhaps not," he admitted cheerfully, setting his glass down on the tray of a passing waiter.

"What rank are you?"

"Recently promoted to major."

"Almost as good as a duke," she murmured.

He found himself laughing a second time. She had fine lips, he conceded, soft red, wider on the bottom, finely bowed above. Her skin, what was visible beneath the mask, was smooth and a shade darker than was fashionable.

She was also tall, coming up to his mouth at least, unlike most ladies, who barely reached his shoulders. Her build was slim, from what he could ascertain under her lightweight cape.

"By the by," he said, taking out his snuffbox from a waistcoat pocket, "a duke usually prefers to be addressed as 'your grace' rather than 'your lordship.'"

He heard another intake of breath and watched as a slow suffusion of red stained the lower half of her cheeks.

"Well, that only makes one more blunder on a shockingly long list. I doubt I'll have the opportunity to beg *his grace's* pardon," she added.

"What, don't you think he'll show at the Treadwells' ball?" he asked.

Her eyes twinkled in reply and he found himself enjoying the company of someone who could laugh at herself.

"I would wager the duke will not show at the Treadwells' ball. I am sure dukes do not make a habit of being seen anywhere near a Treadwell."

"Especially young, wealthy, unattached dukes. They would have a horror of the Treadwells," he confirmed for her.

"I suppose you know the intricacies of London society?" Her tone held a trace of wistfulness.

"Inside and out. I enjoyed a season or two before joining the Coldstreams and shipping off to the Peninsula."

"How fortunate for you." Again, he had the suspicion she was mocking him.

"That depends from which side you are looking at it."

She tilted her head sideways. "What are the possible angles?"

He looked down at his blue-enameled box, a gift from a young demoiselle in Paris for those weeks he'd spent in her company last summer after the liberation. "There is the duke's exalted view. Avoiding fortune hunters, fighting the inevitable tedium of a life of leisure…"

"How difficult for him."

"Then there is the less exalted view of the third son of a minor baronet." He grinned. "Some days it's fighting off the creditors, others it's fighting off the parental pressure to marry an heiress. Younger sons are the bane of their mamas, I vow. So have a care."

She frowned. "Is that a warning?"

He shrugged. "Do you need one?"

"I don't believe so."

"Are you so sure of your safety? There are quite a number of impoverished, unattached members of the ton floating around these days."

"Are there indeed?"

"Yes. A wealthy young lady must beware. She presents quite a catch for some of them, even if she hails from the Colonies."

"*Former* Colonies, I believe you meant to say." She laughed, an infectious, joyous sound. "They would have to pass Papa's inspection. I pity them."

"Is he so formidable?"

Again, that slight tilt of her head, like a bird knowing it could fly away at any moment. "Let us say, he is not easily fooled."

He clucked his tongue. "People can be very cunning when the stakes are high enough."

"Papa is very astute. He looks at a man's heart."

He felt a sudden chill at the simple words. How would he fare if his own heart were laid open to examination? "That is a daunting thought." He surveyed the company before them, wondering where the officious Mrs. Bellows had got to. He spied her struggling to make her way across the crowded room. "Tell me, are you in London in search of a title?"

"Not particularly. Do I look as if I am?" she asked. He detected only curiosity in her voice, no coyness.

"Those who engage Mrs. Bellows's services are usually known to be fond of a title."

"Oh." She sounded nonplussed. "Papa merely wanted

someone to take me about London before we return home."

That was a first. "I see. So, no interest in vying with the London misses for a duke? I hear a collective sigh of relief from the wings."

She laughed again. "Is competition so fierce for—how did the lady put it?—snagging a title?"

"Competition can be cutthroat. Mamas and their daughters spend countless hours discussing strategies for catching the attention of the latest young earl or duke on the Marriage Mart. If they suspect another of encroaching on their territory, they'll stop at little to thwart her."

"Oh, my." Her eyes sparkled, and he was caught once again by their fascinating depths. "It sounds like a challenge."

"You like a challenge?"

"At times." She sighed. "However, Papa is not easily impressed by a title. Quite the reverse, I should imagine."

"A pity. You'd be a prime target for someone with a lesser title, say a baron of good repute but very little means, who'd find a young lady of…" He hesitated, eyeing her.

"Substantial means, but no breeding, attractive?" she finished for him.

"Precisely," he answered, amused at her frank admission. Before he could say anything more, she asked him, "Are you, like my esteemed companion, hired on by the month to provide discreet introductions for wealthy tradesmen's daughters?"

"I should think not!" he retorted before realizing she was again poking fun at herself and not at him. "I suppose anything's possible for the right price, but I haven't as yet had to stoop so low."

"I do beg your pardon," she said quickly. "I hadn't meant any offense."

"I am flattered that I appeared as one who has free access to every fashionable address in town, but alas, I am the last man you'd need in your camp if your plan is to snag a respectable title."

"Why is that?"

"If your name is linked to a rakish reprobate like me, you'll have it tarnished faster than—" He had no chance to finish his sentence, as Mrs. Bellows came panting up to them, her ample bosom heaving.

"Oh, my dear, forgive my delay. I could scarcely make my way to the dining room, there was such a crush. And then I ran into Mrs. Palmer. I haven't seen her since her godson's christening—" The words died on her lips as she noticed Gerrit.

He smiled, realizing she probably recognized him behind the mask. Time to pay the piper. It had been an amusing few moments. More entertaining than any he'd spent among the ton since his return from Belgium.

The tall officer bowed towards Mrs. Bellows. "Madam, I have been keeping your young charge company but will now excuse myself and leave her in your capable hands." Mrs. Bellows could do no more than stare open-mouthed at the dark-haired, masked gentleman. He turned to Hester. "It was a pleasure to chat with you a few moments, a pleasure I would gladly partake of again. You say you ride in Hyde Park in the forenoon?"

She nodded, dazed. Before she could add anything, he was gone, his dark cape disappearing among the throng of other capes.

"Whah? Who?" Mrs. Bellows turned to Hester, the cups in her hands momentarily forgotten, her mouth working but seeming incapable of forming any words.

Hester reached out and took one of the cups of punch from her. "I didn't catch his name."

"Oh, my dear, I'm sorry, I shouldn't have left you alone. The nerve of him, daring to address you in that familiar manner—"

"He wasn't familiar at all, just friendly." Which was more than she could say for anyone she'd met in all the hours of standing on ceremony this evening. Well, "met" was stretching the facts. She hadn't actually met anyone at all, until the officer with the humorous tone of voice and twinkling blue eyes had taken the liberty to address her.

"Young gentlemen are becoming entirely too bold these days. It's the war, you know. So many *émigrés,* so many rude customs brought home by our soldiers…"

"He was a soldier, as a matter of fact."

Mrs. Bellows's kohl-rimmed eyes widened. "He was? An officer?" Her tone sounded hopeful.

"A major, I believe he said." Hester took a sip from the cup.

"A major?" Mrs. Bellows's tone had gone from censorious to admiring in the time it took for Hester to swallow her punch. Not as refreshing as cold spring water, but it would have to do.

"I wonder who he was…" Mrs. Bellows, her wits collected, turned to catch a departing look at the broad-shouldered man making his way through the press. "He looked awfully familiar…" Her voice trailed off.

"He said you know him."

She turned back to Hester. "He did? I thought I recognized the voice." She tapped a finger against her chin. "He appeared quite tall. Dark-haired, wouldn't you say? Although it was hard to tell with the hood."

"Yes, his hair is dark." Black, she could have told her. Thick and straight. With eyes as blue as cobalt.

"The Marquis of Haversham's eldest son?" Mrs. Bellows mused. "No, he is in Italy. He isn't that tall, anyway. Chester Ravenscroft's second son? No, he spends all his time in Brighton these days… He said he was an officer. Did he happen to mention which regiment?"

"I don't recall…he might have mentioned something. We didn't speak for long." His regal bearing was definitely soldierly. If he'd told her he was a duke, she'd have believed him.

"Pity you didn't inquire." As Mrs. Bellows continued naming the officers of her acquaintance, Hester sipped her punch and followed the man as he wended his way to the other side of the room. At the exit, he turned and looked back. For an instant, it seemed as if his eyes met hers. Then he raised a hand and gave a small salute in her direction.

She raised her own hand, but before it reached more than partway, he disappeared through the double doors. She couldn't help but feel a twinge of disappointment, as if the only person alive had gone from the room, leaving solely the dry and lifeless.

Silly girl, she chided herself, turning her attention back to her punch. She had only found him interesting because she was so heartily bored with the kinds of activities Mrs. Bellows had organized for her since her father and she had arrived in London scarcely a sennight past.

At that moment her father joined them. "Well, how is everything? Are you enjoying yourselves?"

Hester smiled, trying to muster up the enthusiasm to match his. He was trying so hard to please her. She needn't have worried. Mrs. Bellows immediately launched into a description of their successful evening.

She sometimes wondered if Mrs. Bellows saw the world through a different view than the normal person. The picture she was painting for Hester's father was quite contrary to how Hester would have described it.

Her father smiled. He was such a handsome man, only in his mid-forties, tall and straight, his light brown hair brushed back off his high forehead. His golden brown eyes crinkled in amusement at all he heard and saw around him.

"You'll have a flock of young gentlemen calling tomorrow the way I hear," he said, turning his attention to Hester.

She hid a yawn behind her hands.

"Are you tired, my dear? We could leave now. I've concluded my business."

He had spent the evening in the card room, talking with the gentlemen. His only interest in these social events was drumming up customers for his timber business.

"Do you have many appointments for tomorrow?" she asked him.

"Yes, I'll spend the morning down at the docks. We'll need a full hold of cargo for our return voyage."

"Oh, may I not come with you?"

He smiled indulgently at her. "You are here to be feted and courted. Your dear mama would tan me alive if she knew I was taking you around doing business while you're here in London."

Her smile disappeared. It had been the same since they'd arrived. Nothing but dress fittings, shopping expeditions and a dull round of teas mainly attended by women Mrs. Bellows's age, while her father sold his cargo and negotiated a return load.

"Very well, Papa, I'll find some way to amuse myself until you come home."

"Don't forget, we must take tea with the Blaisdells in the afternoon," Mrs. Bellows said. "And we must look at your frocks for the Treadwells' ball…"

But Hester was no longer following Mrs. Bellows's thread. She was wondering if the mysterious major with the amused voice would indeed seek her out in Hyde Park on the morrow.

Chapter Two

By midmorning the next day, Hester left the townhouse they had rented for the month. Her father had been gone since early morning, and Mrs. Bellows wasn't due to arrive until mid-afternoon. Hester had several hours all to herself. The first thing she did after a leisurely breakfast and bath was to dress in her riding habit. Ned, one of Papa's sailors, met her in the mews to accompany her for a ride in the park. She wasn't such a simpleton as to go out alone, even though she was used to doing so at home.

Her father had drilled into her head the dangers of the London streets since the day she'd disembarked from the ship.

When they arrived at Hyde Park, they headed for the deserted Rotten Row. She'd been here in the late afternoon when the lane was choked with carriages and riders. At this hour, the vast meadows and wooded parkland surrounding her were empty but for a few riders and some grazing sheep.

She cantered hard, enjoying the muffled sound of the beating hooves against the soft dirt of the riding paths. She inhaled deeply of the warm smell of summer's vegetation. If she were at home now, she would probably be riding through a field, or weeding the garden or breathing in the sharp, fresh scent of sap in her father's vast lumberyards.

She spied a black charger cantering toward her, the ground beneath her vibrating with its pounding hoofbeats. She pulled on the reins of her own mount and slowed. The black horse was magnificent, tall and sleek. Its rider was a redcoat. Her heartbeat quickened, remembering the major from the evening before.

She'd had a hard time getting him off her mind as she'd lain in bed last night. He was different from any man she'd ever met—sophisticated and self-confident, full of a humor that drew one toward him. He gave her the sense that he was very much a part of the fashionable world, yet as alien as herself.

As horse and rider drew nearer, she noted the soldier had the same broad-shouldered build as the major. He brought his horse to a walk as he approached her and Ned, where they had stationed themselves at the edge of the path.

The officer lifted a hand to the brim of his cocked hat, the gesture reminding her of his salute the previous evening. In that moment their glances met.

She knew those blue eyes. They were as amused as they'd been behind their mask last night. She hadn't honestly expected him to show up in the park this morning. Could he have really done so deliberately?

He pulled his horse to a stop. It danced a few steps sideways but he held it well in control. "Good morning," he said.

She felt an inward swell of anticipation as she recognized the voice of her mysterious stranger and took in his unmasked features. Strong, well-proportioned, like the rest of him. Just when he'd become "hers" she couldn't precisely say. He was certainly handsome, better looking than any man she'd ever beheld, in fact.

"I would address you by name, but fear I am still in ignorance. Perhaps I should have stayed long enough for Mrs. Bellows to introduce us."

"How do you do, major? My name is Hester Leighton. Lately from Bangor, Maine," she replied.

He acknowledged the introduction with a smile which formed a dimple in each smooth-planed cheek. "Major Gerrit Hawkes, lately from the Continent."

"You fought against Napoleon." He had said something about that last night, and she'd thought a lot more over his words after he'd left.

He inclined his head.

"Were you at Waterloo?" It was a name she'd grown familiar with since arriving in London.

"Yes."

He didn't elaborate and she wondered if soldiers disliked being asked about their battles. She glanced down at his chest, noticing the insignias and medals. She blushed now at her impertinence the evening before. Clearly he'd fought with distinction. Anyone who'd fought at Waterloo was a national hero. That much she'd learned.

"Would you care to continue riding?" he asked.

She almost forgot about Ned, but he spoke up behind her. "Begging your pardon, miss, but hadn't we best be returning?"

"It's all right, Ned. Major Hawkes and I met last evening."

Major Hawkes nodded to Ned before wheeling his horse around and spurring him on. Hester was left to decide whether to follow him or not. With a last glance at Ned, she nudged her mount on, leaving Ned to do the same.

After riding for some ten minutes, the major slowed again, this time to an easy walk.

"You ride astride," he remarked.

She'd forgotten that detail in her interest in the major. She must have shocked him, although he didn't sound shocked. "Where I live, it's hardly remarked upon. That's why I come out to the park in the morning, when there's scarcely a soul about. I wouldn't get very far if I rode sidesaddle along some of the trails I've been on," she added.

"Rugged terrain in—where did you say—Maine?"

"Yes, some of it."

"What is the country like?"

She pursed her lips. How to describe a land so different from England? "More trees than people."

He burst out laughing. "I'm hard-pressed to imagine such a landscape, and I've seen many landscapes. What do you think of London then?"

"There seem to be more people than air to breathe."

He chuckled. "Wait until everyone's back in town."

"Back? Why, where has everyone gone?"

"Off to the country. August is accounted a dead month here in town. Most people go to their country estates," he explained.

"Does everyone have a country estate?" What a strange notion.

He shook his head. "Hardly, only the exalted landowners. See how important a good match is?" His teasing tone was back.

"Well, we have countryside galore around Bangor, so we have no need to marry for it."

"In England land is a much-coveted commodity. It's only in the hands of a few, so you must marry into it to lay hands on some of it."

"Do you have any family?" she asked him after a bit.

"Two older brothers and a sister."

"And your sister, is she older or younger?"

"Older as well."

"So you're the baby."

His amusement deepened. "Once, I suppose. I daresay I've seen more than all of them combined. I don't know what that makes me, but I think it puts me out of infancy forever." He ended on a somber note.

"I'm sorry." She realized he must be referring to the war. "I didn't mean to make fun."

"Not at all. How about you? Brothers? Sisters?"

"Two sisters, one brother. All younger," she said before he could ask.

He raised a black eyebrow. "So you're the mama?"

"Sometimes. I think that's one reason our real mother insisted on this trip. As she put it, for me to enjoy being a young lady without having to worry about what my siblings were up to."

They turned down an avenue lined with evenly spaced trees. She marveled that there weren't any plantings so uniform where she came from. "I haven't seen you riding in the park before," she said, when he remained silent.

"I don't usually come at this time of day."

"Do you have drills and reviews?" She didn't know much about military life, especially here in England. Back home, there had been border wars against the British and uprisings from the Indians in times past.

"I am still on medical leave," he answered after a moment, as if reluctant to divulge any more.

She glanced at him more closely. "You were wounded at Waterloo?"

"Most of us who survived were."

"We've heard people talk about it. It sounds as if the fighting was quite fierce," she said softly.

"Yes." He lifted his arm slightly. "Mine was a mere trifle. A shot in the arm. It's practically healed, just a bit stiff."

"I'm sorry you were wounded, but I'm glad it's getting better." When he made no reply, she decided to change the subject. "I usually come riding earlier, but it was a late evening last night."

He smiled in acknowledgment. "Did you stay for the unmasking?"

"No. We left soon after you did."

"Is this your first visit to London?"

"Yes. My first trip across the Atlantic. My father

is British, and I suppose he wanted me to see his native land."

"Ah."

She smiled. "A bit of polish wouldn't come amiss."

His blue eyes surveyed her. "Are you in need of polish?"

"Even by frontier standards. Some would say I am a bit…wild."

"Indeed?" He gave her a funny look, one that sent a blush heating her cheeks. But he didn't pursue the topic. "Tell me," he added after a moment, "what have you seen of this fair city since you arrived?"

She went on to list the various monuments and exhibits she'd been to. "As you saw last night, Mrs. Bellows is introducing me to London society."

"I hope you don't judge London society wholly by what Mrs. Bellows shows you."

She patted her mare's neck. "I admit she is perhaps not the most highly placed name in society, but that is not particularly important to me. I have no wish to be presented at court."

He raised a black eyebrow. "I thought that was every girl's desire."

"I have heard too many shocking tales of your Prince Regent to think it an honor to have to curtsy to him."

"I concede your point. However, I shudder to think your impression of society will be formed solely by the parties where your Mrs. Bellows is welcome."

She sighed, acknowledging his observation. After a bit, she said, "I feel a bit sorry for Mrs. Bellows. She lost her only son in the war, and her relations seem ashamed of her. I don't think her husband left her much, so she is forced to present her card to visiting foreigners."

"You are quite astute for your years."

She turned down the corners of her lips. "You make me sound like an infant."

"You must be all of eighteen."

"You aren't very knowledgeable about young ladies, are you?"

He looked amused. "Some would argue the contrary. Howbeit, I have been away from London society for some time, so perhaps my discernment has dulled where young misses are concerned. Well, you can't be *younger* than eighteen, so you must be older. Nineteen, twenty?" When she continued shaking her head, he continued, "One-and-twenty?" He raised an eyebrow in disbelief. "Two-and-twenty?"

"You may stop your guessing game now."

"Does that mean I have hit upon your age, or that you don't wish me to continue guessing?"

"You have hit upon it. I don't suppose you will tell me your age now so we shall be even?"

He shrugged. "I am six-and-twenty."

"My, you are ancient compared to me."

"I feel ancient at times."

Once again, his tone was sober, and something in her wished to comfort him.

But he changed the subject before she could reply. "So, you have taken pity on the unfortunate Mrs. Bellows and will let her milk you dry while she touts the merits of the mediocre society she presents to you. You realize she eyes all wealthy Americans as fair game?"

"What is the good of having money if you can't use it to help people?" She lifted her chin defensively, not sure if she liked the humor in those blue eyes. "Why are you looking at me like that?"

"I tremble to think of you among the hungry wolves of the ton. They'll fleece you in a trice."

She shrugged. "They'll have Papa to contend with. He's quite a Yankee."

"Meaning?"

"Thrifty, ingenious, a hard bargainer."

"I see. So, you will sail home on the winning end of any marriage contract?"

"I doubt there will be any marriage contract. What I have seen of your British gentlemen leaves little to recommend."

He threw back his head and laughed, and Hester felt glad she could dispel the shadows from his eyes. "Heaven help us. In all fairness to our gender, I don't think you've seen enough to come to such a dire conclusion."

"I've seen a fair variety."

"But hardly the cream of the crop."

"It sounds as if you have entrée into these exalted realms."

He shrugged in turn. "More so than Mrs. Bellows."

She tipped her head in acknowledgement. It occurred to her that she hadn't enjoyed herself quite so much since docking in England.

Major Hawkes gestured with his whip. "I'll tell you what. I'll arrange for a few introductions for you and— your father, is it?" At her nod, he continued. "I'll whisper a word in my elder sister's ear. She is quite active in the right circles, those where the most eligible young gentlemen and ladies go to see and be seen each season when seeking to be paired up."

She didn't know whether to feel affronted or grateful. Did he really think she was solely bent on making an eligible match? She leaned forward to pat her mare's neck. "You needn't go to any trouble on my behalf."

He chuckled, as if reading her thoughts. "No need to get your dander up. It's no trouble at all. If you receive a call from Lady Stanchfield, you needn't receive her."

She raised an eyebrow. "*Lady* Stanchfield? Well, why didn't you say so?"

She enjoyed watching the edges of his eyes crinkle in humor. "The very one. My eldest—and only—sister. She went to all the right parties and caught herself a viscount, and her dowry was only a thousand pounds."

"Indeed?" Was he speaking seriously or in cynical amusement?

"Who is to say that a dowry-laden young lady from the former Colonies could not do better—catch herself an impoverished duke or earl? But only if she is seen at the right parties."

She scanned his face, trying to read his intention. He couldn't really be serious. "Pray, why should I want to do that?"

He shrugged. "I'd hate for you to leave our shores with such a low opinion of Britain's manhood. We did just win a war, you know, and are accounted the most powerful nation on earth at present."

"Which makes it all the more shocking you could never best your former Colonies," she countered.

"True enough. Now, would you have me speak with my sister, or would you prefer to continue under Mrs. Bellows's sole tutelage?"

She spurred her horse back to a canter, resisting the temptation to tell him she didn't need his help. No need to be prideful. Perhaps the Lord had a purpose for her in the upper circles of the so-called haut-ton. Or at least an escape from Mrs. Bellows' parties. "Very well, show me England's finest," she called back at him with a smile. "I'll let you know if they are worth their salt."

With those words, she rode ahead, leaving it up to him if he would follow her or not.

Late that evening, Gerrit sat in the backyard of the Cock and Crow Inn on Fleet Street. The name was appropriate, given the nature of the evening's entertainment.

"There he goes! Come on, Daggart, kick him in the chest! Thattaboy!" shouted the rooster's owner from the side of the pit in the dirt yard. The crowd around Gerrit added their encouragement as one rooster stuck his metal gaffs into the other.

Gerrit leaned forward on the wooden bench, forcing himself to watch the bloodied birds poking and jabbing at each other. Just as they would fight to the finish, he would endure it to the end. More than for the sake of collecting his winnings, he needed to prove that he was man enough to last.

The time before, he'd had to get up halfway through and heave up his dinner in a dark alley. Now he gripped his fingers into his knees, refusing to believe he'd become as weak-stomached as a child. Where was the man who'd charged into every battle, the bloodlust high, to fell as many Frenchmen as his Brown Bess had allowed?

His attention back on the fight, Gerrit saw that the losing rooster still had a lot of juice left in him. Though he'd lost an eye and his feathers were torn and bloodied, he continued pecking at the strutting Daggart.

Glad he'd at least put his money on a winner tonight, Gerrit rubbed his hand along the rough stubble of his jaw. He had to bring home some blunt. He could just hear Crocker's old woman scoldings if he came in empty-handed—or worse, with another pile of vouchers.

He'd forgotten how expensive London could be. His army pay scarcely covered his lodgings, and the quarterly income from his father was hardly enough to sustain a gentleman's existence.

Gerrit sighed. He'd have to give up his nightly rounds of amusements for at least a fortnight. The situation was almost enough to drive a man to marry an heiress. Almost.

An agreeable young face and personality came to mind. He'd felt a sort of kinship during their two conversations. Bits and pieces kept recurring during odd moments of the day, before he'd laugh at his own foolishness. He and Miss Leighton could have nothing in common—a redcoat and a Yank! A gentleman's son and a tradesman's daughter.

"He's got him now! Pull at his other wing, Daggart!" The yells intensified as the losing bird looked more and more bedraggled. The onlookers were now standing, waving their arms and stamping their feet.

"Huzzah! Huzzah!" cried the military crowd. Others took up the chant.

Gerrit rose more slowly to his feet. Victory was in sight. The cock, as if sensing it, seemed to grow more vicious. His stick legs jabbed the sharp curved blades strapped to them at his opponent's body, causing more feathers to fly. Gerrit's mind began to play the same tricks on him as on prior occasions.

Bursts of gunpowder and glimpses of screaming faces flashed before him, alternating their reality with the fighting cocks in front of him, till he no longer knew which was real and which was imaginary.

He rubbed his temple, desperate to stop the images. He would stay until the end. A few more minutes and it would be over.

"He did it. My Daggart did it!"

The men around him shouted the rooster's name and thronged forward. The loser's limp body was tossed onto a rubbish heap. Gerrit remained where he was, standing but bowed forward facedown, his hands supported by his knees. He gulped in the air.

"Anyone for a second round?" The rooster's owner marched around the yard, his rooster led by a string. "No one yet's beat my Daggart."

His breathing returned to normal, Gerrit straightened. After collecting his winnings, he left the yard with enough for a round of cards. With any luck, he'd be home with his pockets full this evening.

He looked up and down the thoroughfare. He could always catch a game of faro at the King's Crown or vingt-et-un at the Black Bull.

* * *

Many hours later, the sky pale blue on the horizon, Gerrit sat on his bed, his batman tugging at his boots.

Thud went the first one as it hit the floor, the noise barely penetrating his fuzzy brain. *Thud* went the second, and suddenly Gerrit found himself thinking once again of Miss Hester Leighton.

A self-possessed young miss with a warm undercurrent beneath those laughing eyes.

He shook his head groggily to stave off the image of the young lady in the park. No more maidens for him. He'd sworn off innocent young damsels after the last fiasco.

"Are you all right, major?"

He squinted at Crocker. "Fine…jus' fine…" he mumbled as he was helped off with jacket and waistcoat. "No—nothing an heiress wouldn't solve." He laughed at his own witticism.

"What's that you say?"

"Nothing…at all…" His hilarity increased.

"There now, major, you mustn't carry on so. We'll manage somehow. We always have."

"That we have, haven't we, Crocker?" He grinned at the older man with the crooked nose and thick dark eyebrows that always made him look as if he was scowling.

The coins jingled in Gerrit's pockets when Crocker took the jacket from him. He lifted an eyebrow. "I'd say someone had a bit o' luck tonight." His batman dug into a pocket and brought out a fistful of coins. His thin lips split wide in his leathery face. "What was it tonight, sir, the cards or bones?"

"You can thank a tough rooster named…what was his name?" Gerrit rubbed his head. "Dempster? Daggart! Yes, the stalwart Daggart, for bringing me luck tonight."

"Ah. A man can grow rich with the right bird. Much better than the luck of the faro table."

"Satisfied?" Gerrit asked, falling back on the bed in his shirtsleeves.

Crocker counted the coins. "Twenty crowns and some. It'll do to keep the duns at bay. But we'll need more'n this if you insist on entertaining every soldier in your company."

"Hos-pi-ta-li-ty." Gerrit's mouth had a hard time around the syllables. "That's what it's called."

"Hmm. What's it called when we land in the sponging house?"

"Sleep…that's what I need right now." Gerrit rolled over and buried his face in the pillow. Crocker could be worse than a wife at times.

"You sleep, sir." Crocker shook the coins in his fist. "You earned a good night's rest. I'll find a safe place for this and on the morrow we'll see who's to be paid." He shoved the money into his own pocket and hung Gerrit's jacket on a chair back. "Well, I'll be off then to my own bed."

"Right-o," Gerrit agreed, no longer following Crocker's conversation. As usual he had drunk too much. He kept telling himself he could make it through a night clear-headed, but the warm fuzziness that grew with each sip, and the promise of a temporary escape from his thoughts, was too much to resist.

The click of the door latch told him Crocker had

left. Silence filled the room like a familiar presence. Oh, for one blessed night's uninterrupted sleep. Dark, deep oblivion was all he asked. No dreams, no images... no memories.

Even as his thoughts became more disjointed, the face of a French boy stared at him in astonishment. Just as Gerrit's bayonet had stabbed him, his sky-blue eyes seemed to ask, "Why did you have to kill me? Why couldn't you simply wound me?"

But Gerrit's thrust had been too deep, too sure. His commander's orders had been clear. Keep the gates closed against the French. Hold the château, whatever the cost. But the French forces had gotten younger and younger with each passing year.

The lad couldn't have been more than fifteen.

Maybe Gerrit had been mistaken, as he had this morning with Miss Leighton's age. Maybe the boy had in truth been twenty or five-and-twenty. Gerrit let out a laugh that came out a groan.

The boy's smooth cheeks hadn't lied. Ruddy-faced and soft. Gerrit remembered when his cheeks had been just like that. When he'd been fifteen—careless and carefree, just discovering his charms with the opposite sex. Knowing he had years ahead of him in which to frolic. Nothing serious was expected of him for the time being, certainly not as the third son. An eventual career in the military—that or the cloth—but no, hadn't his older brother, Michael, already taken orders? That left only a military career.

No such frivolity for the young French cadet. No more years in which to play before facing the harsh realities of life.

Gerrit had searched for him after the battle, turning over every wounded, mutilated body in his path, both redcoat and blue. He'd finally found him, lying there in the courtyard of the château, not far from the gates Gerrit and his men had held against the French forces.

He'd identified him by the soft moans at his feet. He'd been half-buried by another French soldier, a full-grown man. Gerrit had rolled him off the boy with his boot. The man's mouth gaped open, the dark eyes staring blankly ahead, the saber wound at his neck already coagulated and turning black.

Gerrit crouched down at the boy beneath him. He was still alive! He cradled his head and felt his soft, silky brown curls between his fingers, incongruously like a girl's. His hair was the color of hazelnuts. What was he doing on a battlefield knee-deep in blood? The fuzz on his pale cheeks was barely discernible. Gerrit searched for his wounds, but the stain on the front of his blue jacket was large and already stiffening. The boy's long, golden eyelashes fluttered open. Gerrit's heart began pumping in hope.

"Maman?" His blue eyes searched Gerrit's hopefully before the life began to ebb from them.

Gerrit clutched the front of the boy, as if the movement could stave off the draining of his life force. And then he was gone.

Why had he lived just long enough for Gerrit to find him, before dying and leaving Gerrit with the indelible impression of his beseeching eyes?

Gerrit loosened his hold on the boy, laying him back down on the ground and closing his eyes.

Non, ce n'etait pas Maman. No, it wasn't his mother.

* * *

"You're not bamming me, are you?" Gerrit's sister, Delia, Viscountess Stanchfield, set her cup of coffee back on her breakfast tray and gazed at Gerrit in amused disbelief.

He shrugged, not wanting her to make more of what he was asking for than was warranted. "All I'm requesting is you introduce a young American lady to the right circles." He leaned his head back against the satin upholstery of his sister's settee to ease the throbbing between his temples. He really shouldn't have undertaken this visit so early in the day.

"'American' and 'lady'—can the two terms be used together?" Without waiting for a reply, his sister gestured with the butter knife at the food on her tray. "Are you sure I can't offer you some breakfast? Mrs. Hart's scones are the best in London."

"Thank you, no. Nothing appeals to me at the moment."

"Foxed again last night? You do look a bit green about the gills." She eyed him beneath her lacy nightcap. "Well, at least a cup of coffee will brace you." She held up the silver pot.

As she poured her own cup of the steaming black liquid, he relented. "All right, I'll take a cup as long it's strong."

"Strong as a donkey's kick."

He rose to take the dainty porcelain cup offered him. "Thank you." When he'd returned to his seat, he continued with the topic he'd come to discuss. "If you meet Miss Leighton, I'm sure you'll agree she is presentable enough."

"Miss Leighton? Is she of the Leightons of Surrey?" Delia's voice perked up as she spread marmalade over her scone. "Delicious," she murmured, closing her eyes after the first bite and nestling against the mound of pillows at her back.

"I have no idea which branch she hails from. All I know is she has enough of the blunt to tempt some fortune hunter to come sniffing 'round her heels." He sipped the coffee, gratified to find it was hot and bracing.

"Why not do some sniffing yourself?"

"She's not my type," he answered immediately, even as his mind conjured up her tall, lithe figure in the forest-green riding habit she had worn in the park.

"I haven't seen you in so long I've forgotten what sort you favor."

"Let's just say I like a woman who's experienced and knows what she wants."

"It sounds like you need a married woman."

He looked down into his cup, wanting no reminders of the last occasion with a married woman. What had he been thinking to rekindle what had clearly been over long ago with Lady Gillian? He replaced the cup in its saucer. "Anyway, this visit is not about me, but about Miss Leighton."

"An American, you say? How novel. I can't say I've ever been acquainted with one personally, though one does hear of them. She probably doesn't know how to hold her fork and knife properly and drops her *H*s."

"Oh, she's couth enough," he said with a shrug. "Though who knows about the rest of her family. She's probably attached to a barbarous clan of uncivil, illiterate relatives. Her father, by her own admission, is a hard-driving tradesman."

Her sister shuddered. "As bad as that? I can scarcely picture it. You with your fine manners ensconced in the bosom of money-grubbing Yanks."

"I agree, it wouldn't do," he said with a grin. "I may be a scoundrel and wastrel, in debt up to my teeth, but I have my standards."

"We shall just have to find you a nice English miss with the proper pedigree…"

"It's best if I don't marry at all. The whole fortune-hunting picture holds little appeal."

She waved a pale hand at him. "You must get over your scruples. Everyone in our circle marries for money to some degree or another. Look at how well things turned out for me."

"How is Lord Lionel these days, by the way?" he asked, preferring to steer the conversation away from himself. "I don't seem to run into him much since I returned to London."

"He hardly comes out of White's. You two just don't move in the same circles anymore." She frowned at him over the rim of her cup. "I hear you are hanging with a pretty reckless crowd…the Life Guards and Horse Guards. You know, there is a world apart from your military cronies."

"Is there?" He preferred not to enter into any disagreement with her about the merits of the society she moved in and that which he moved in.

She gave a toss of her lacy nightcap. "Very well, be

as inscrutable as always. Now, let's talk about your Miss Leighton."

He was relieved the topic was coming back to the reason he'd paid this early morning visit to his sibling.

"Well, at least her name sounds respectable. So, what is in it for you if you aren't interested in her yourself?"

"Nothing."

She looked skeptical.

"Upon my honor," he insisted, attempting to convince his sister as much as himself. "She knows no one in town and is floundering a bit. You'll never believe it. Her father hired Mrs. Bellows to introduce her."

Delia's pretty gray eyes widened. "Is that old hag still around?"

"My thoughts exactly. She's not only still around, but as pushy as ever." He shrugged. "All you need do is send Miss Leighton an invitation to your next party. The girl is young and passably pretty. She'll find herself a suitor in no time." And be beyond his reach.

"You really don't care?"

Gerrit passed a hand over his eyes. The coffee had done nothing for his throbbing temples. "Why should I? She's a young chit, much too innocent for me."

"Very well." She thought a moment. "I know. I'll ask dear Alexandra to invite her to her rout on Friday. All the best people will be there. She's holding it after the theater to coincide with Convent Garden's opening for the season. Are you going?"

"I wasn't planning to. What are they playing?"

"Oh, just *A Beggar's Opera*. Would you like me to save you a place?"

He considered, then shook his head, thinking of things he'd rather do than sit through a melodramatic presentation of song and dance. "No, thanks. I'll meet up with you later at Alexi's."

"Very well." She thinned her lips, clearly disappointed with his refusal. "At any rate, make sure you are there around midnight so you can introduce me to your little American."

He nodded.

"It will be perfect." She sat up, pushing the breakfast tray away from her. "Everyone will stop by Alexi's after the show. I can introduce her to some of the most eligible beaus. Too bad it's not the season. Do you know how long she's to be in London?"

"Haven't a clue." He remembered how crowded one of those affairs could be. "A rout can be a bit intimidating to a newcomer."

"Is she so very green? Don't tell me she's just out of the nursery. What a bore."

"Not exactly. She's two-and-twenty."

Delia pursed her lips. "That's a bit old still to be unmarried. What do you think is wrong with her?"

He thought back to the fresh-faced young lady with a directness of speech and manner and a competent way with the ribbons. "Nothing, apart from being American. I don't know how much of society she's seen over there. She talks of her home as the frontier."

"A barbarian, how delicious." Delia's eyes lit up. "Has she been living among the savages? It sounds so very exciting. Oh, wait 'til I tell Alexandra. I shall go around as soon as I'm dressed." She reached behind her mound of pillows and tugged on the embroidered bellpull. "What fun. Introducing a young lady to society. I've never done that before. Does she have a decent wardrobe, d'you know? What about her hair? I could recommend a good lady's maid to her…"

He remembered the tawny brown of her hair beneath her bonnet. Unlike most ladies, no curls had framed her oval face, but her straight locks had been pulled back, showing to greater advantage her fine cheekbones. "Don't tell me you're planning to parade Miss Leighton around as a novelty? I think not…although she does strike me as an original."

"That's even better. Does she say outrageous things?"

He regarded the tip of his boots against his sister's jade-green carpet. "Nothing scandalous, she just has a very honest and frank way of expressing herself."

Delia laughed. "That could have dire consequences. What if we all went about saying exactly what we thought? No, it wouldn't do."

"She's not mean-spirited. I would venture to say she's a breath of fresh air in a very stale environment."

His sister raised a finely shaped eyebrow at him. "Are you sure you're not interested?"

He shook his head. "Even if I were, I wouldn't do anything about it. I've sworn off innocents for good."

She gave a laugh of disbelief. "Since when?"

"Since the last one." Before she could ask for specifics, he added, "Too many complications. Irate brothers, fathers…uncles…husbands…"

"Husbands?" Her cup paused halfway to her mouth. "Since when do wives number among the innocent?"

"When they don't play by the rules of the game, and they happen to have husbands who are in love with them."

She leaned forward, her eyes brimming with curiosity. "I must hear more of this."

"Never mind." He drained his cup, the cold dregs tasting bitter on his tongue. "How is Reggie, by the by?"

Her smile froze and she set down her own cup without taking a sip. He could tell she didn't like the question by the deliberate way she set down the cup and saucer on the tray. "He's fine as far as I know. Why?"

"No reason. Just thought I'd ask. Haven't seen the old chap in a few weeks."

"He's not old and if you haven't seen him, it's because you are frequenting those low-life taverns, by all accounts."

"Well, give him my regards, when you do see him. Now, back to Miss Leighton. You'll look after her at the rout?"

"Of course. It will give me something to do. London is so dismal this time of summer with almost everyone out of town. Where is your young lady staying?"

He thought of this new knot. "You know, I never did find out. No matter, I shall be sure to see her at the Treadwells' tomorrow night and can find out for you then."

"The Treadwells?" She wrinkled her nose. "Since when are you so hard-up for society?"

"I'm not. I told you, Miss Leighton has been at Mrs. Bellows's mercy."

She dropped a finger against her chin. "Oh, dear, as bad as that. Well, help is on the way."

Gerrit rose and came toward her. "I knew you'd understand." He bent down and kissed her brow. "Well, I must be off."

"Good luck in not getting snared by the young American yourself, although, who knows, she might just be the answer to all your problems."

His hand paused on the door handle. "The least I can do is save her from myself."

With Delia's laughter floating after him, he opened the door just as the maid arrived.

"Where are you off to now?" his sister called out.

He turned and winked. "To wangle myself an invitation to the Treadwells'."

Chapter Three

Hester gave the young gentleman a wan smile as they came together in the dance, then stepped back from him as the music continued its lively pace.

She was hot and bored. The young Mr. Sedgwick with his prominent teeth and eyes had latched onto her as soon as Mrs. Bellows had introduced him, making sure she knew he had "five hundred a year."

She had come to know what that meant. It seemed ever since she'd arrived in London, eligible gentlemen were not described by what they did—he's a farmer, he's a lumberer, he's a first mate aboard the *Alice Mae*— but by how many pounds sterling he would receive yearly as soon as his sire passed away.

What a strange land where men were not measured by what they did for themselves, but by whose name they carried and whose unearned wealth they would one day spend.

As soon as the dance ended, Mr. Sedgwick escorted

her back to Mrs. Bellows, but instead of leaving them, he graciously offered to bring them refreshment.

"How thoughtful." Mrs. Bellows beamed at him. "A little lemonade would be delightful."

Hester stood fanning herself as she looked around the spacious and well-lit room. The furnishings around her outdid anything she'd ever seen. She'd always thought her parents' home comfortable and tastefully furnished, but it looked rustic and old-fashioned compared to the elaborate decor here.

Pale-pink walls were topped by creamy white stucco carvings of urns, palm fronds and fruit. Greek statuary was placed at intervals along the walls and crystal chandeliers hung low from the ceiling.

Mrs. Bellows' glance followed the young man's back as he left to fetch their refreshments. "Mr. Sedgwick is a most distinguished gentleman. He has five hundred a year, you know," she whispered loudly behind her fan.

"Yes, you told me." Hester continued scanning the room. Groups of foursomes had arranged themselves for the next set, a quadrille, and when the music started up, Hester amused herself watching them, tapping her fan against her palm in time to the music. She was thankful she knew most of the country dances, although she was glad she was standing this one out. The quadrille had just been imported from France. It hadn't yet come to Bangor, so she was unfamiliar with its intricate steps. At least it wasn't the scandalous German waltz, another new import.

She smiled to herself, imagining her acquaintances,

Ned, Tim, Nicholas, or much less, her younger brother, Jamie, behaving as gracefully as the elegant men she now watched.

But she did enjoy listening to the measured strains coming from the full accompaniment of instruments at one end of the room, rather than a simple fiddler playing his heart and soul out.

"Here you are, Mrs. Bellows, Miss Leighton." Mr. Sedgwick handed her a cup, his gloved hands brushing hers in the exchange.

"Thank you, Mr. Sedgwick," she murmured, looking down to escape his obsequious smile and wondering if he would trail her all evening like a slimy snail. She swallowed a giggle, thinking how she would describe him to her sisters in her next letter.

"I vow, there's Mrs. Talmadge." Mr. Sedgwick bent lower, forcing Hester to take a step back. "She shows a good deal of countenance after making a cake of herself over Lord Wilbur at Somerset House the other night."

"What did she do?" Mrs. Bellows edged closer to him, her nose quivering like a hound on the hunt.

Hester turned away from her companions, her mother's Scriptural teachings against gossip too ingrained. Her attention wandered back to the quadrille, but before it reached the end of the room, it was arrested by a bright scarlet uniform.

Major Hawkes leaned against a satin wall, his arms folded across his chest, his gaze directly on her. Her heart flip-flopped. When had he arrived? The next instant he straightened and began heading toward her.

Ignoring the erratic rhythm of her heart, she took the

time to observe him. He was certainly an imposing figure. Were all the redcoats as splendid as Major Hawkes? His scarlet waist-length jacket was trimmed in lots of gold braid and buttons. A gold sash that crossed the front displayed a shiny gold badge with a silver star in its midst. A gilt gorget framed his high black neck cloth. Long legs encased in snug white trousers and tall black boots completed the uniform.

Was it that, which made him seem larger than life? Hester had never seen such a splendid uniform. When the redcoats had invaded Bangor, her father had sent Hester and her younger siblings, along with their mother, out to a cabin they had in the woods, so she had never caught a glimpse of them, only heard the awful tales once she'd returned.

Her mother would say the man was too handsome for his own good.

She raised her eyes to find his deep blue eyes looking straight into hers. She drew in her breath at the sense of connection she felt with this foreign soldier who, as late as last winter, had been considered an enemy.

"Good evening, Miss Leighton." He bowed his head over her hand. How had it come to be so completely enveloped in his white-gloved one? Her throat felt dry, her breath short.

"Mrs. Bellows." He had already turned to her companions and Hester was free to study his profile. Everything about his features was perfect, from the high forehead to straight nose and strong jawline. His black hair was neatly trimmed and brushed away from his face.

"Gerrit Hawkes!" Mrs. Bellows brought her hands up together in delight. "Is it captain?"

"Major," he corrected quietly.

Her eyes widened. "Major! Indeed, I've heard of your heroism at Waterloo."

His blue eyes met Hester's once again, a brief shadow flickering over them. Undoubtedly mention of the battle was painful to him. She glanced down at his arm, remembering his wound.

"Have you met my young charge, Hester Leighton, from America?"

"Indeed I have," he replied. "At the Featherstone's masquerade the other night."

"You were the mysterious officer!" Mrs. Bellows' gloved hands came up to her rouged cheeks. "I was up all night going over all my acquaintances with sons in colors. I never guessed it was you. I didn't realize you were back in London. I imagined you in Paris or Vienna since the Peace."

"Our company was sent home for rest and recuperation."

"Oh, dear, you weren't wounded, I hope?"

"Nothing serious. Nothing to preclude me from enjoying the delights of London." The light returned to his eyes, again meeting Hester's and she felt the bond between them deepen.

Mrs. Bellows fairly twittered. "Oh, I'm glad of that! I hope we may see you at many of the coming events. Miss Leighton is eager to see the sights of our fair city…"

Hester continued studying the major, or more accurately, her reaction to him. She couldn't fathom it. When he turned to her and asked her for the dance, she acqui-esced, deciding she must get to the bottom of this odd sense of communion with a gentleman she scarcely knew.

He offered her his arm, a dimple deepened by his smile. "We meet again, Miss Leighton."

Was he teasing her, or did he feel it, too?

She strove for lightness. "I'm surprised to see you tonight. I had the impression the other evening the Treadwells weren't quite the thing."

"Did I give you that impression? If so, I beg your pardon," he said, leading her toward a set that was forming.

Now she knew he was laughing at her—or at himself, but she didn't mind. As long as the haunted look was erased from his eyes.

"If you saw some of the places I frequent, you'd realize what an improvement this gathering is." His low voice rumbled in her ear as he leaned close to her.

She felt her cheeks grow red at his sudden proximity. What would he consider worse than the Treadwells? She tried to picture what his life was like but could not imag-ine anything beyond the moment. Even Mrs. Bellows and Mr. Sedgwick had ceased to exist.

Thankfully, the quadrille had ended and a simple country dance was forming.

"Do you know this one?" Major Hawkes asked as they found their places in the two rows. "It's called 'Dainty Davy.' Is it danced in America?"

"Yes, I've danced it." She felt reasonably confident of her ability to perform the figure. The caller would help with any variations in the way the dance might differ from the one across the Atlantic.

The first bars of music began, giving her no time to say anything more. She curtsied lightly as he bowed to her.

He was a superb dancer, and she wondered what he would say of some of the vigorous movements that passed for dance steps by the young men of Bangor. She hoped she was graceful enough to do justice to his partnering.

Under his smooth leadership, she began to fully enjoy herself. She'd always liked to dance, but had scarcely had an opportunity since arriving in London.

During one of the figures, where he took her hand and accompanied her up the row of dancers, he smiled at her. "Actually, I came this evening expressly looking for you."

She stumbled. "You did?"

He led her back to the formation with expert precision before replying. "I did." Again that smile that made her wonder what he found so amusing.

She had to wait for an explanation until the dance steps brought them close enough again. This time they had a few more seconds to talk as they waited for the lead couple to perform the figure. "I wanted to advise you that you will be receiving an invitation for a rout given by the Duchess of Wakefield."

"That sounds quite grand." Would he be there?

"It can actually be quite dull, but it will give you an opportunity to meet my sister, Delia. The Duchess is a bosom friend of hers. My sister would love nothing better than to take you under her wing and introduce you 'round." They parted again at the allemande.

Hester had to wait for a few more dance figures before she could talk to him again. "What about Mrs. Bellows?"

"What about her?"

"Doesn't she have the job of introducing me?"

"Does she?" He looked across her shoulder in the direction of Mrs. Bellows. "Is that young gentleman you were standing with an example of a possible suitor? Let me guess…he's a solicitor with two-hundred pounds a year." The major quirked an eyebrow at her.

"Five hundred." Laughter bubbled out of her, and she put a gloved hand to her mouth. "I suppose that's not done," she said.

"Laughing during the lead outsides? No, it's not the norm. I told my sister you were an original."

"A what?" It made her sound like a circus animal.

"It means immediate notice in our jaded society. People will leap on you in their search for some novelty to distract them."

"They will be sorely disappointed when they find I'm nothing but an ordinary person." Once again they stood facing each other.

"Maybe what's ordinary in your realm is extraordinary in theirs."

As they repeated the figures, Hester found herself more at ease. During the promenade down the middle and back, she said, "You speak as if you didn't belong in this society."

"Perhaps not anymore." He turned away from her to make his way back to his starting position.

She pondered his reply. What had changed him? She glanced at his broad chest, noting again the star-shaped medal. The war, of course.

He stepped up to her in the next figure. "Where are you and your father staying? I need to let her grace know so she can send you an invitation."

"Number fifteen, Curzon Street." She laughed. "Is that an unfashionable address?"

"Quite respectable." A gleam of approval shone in his eyes. "Near Chesterfield House."

"Yes. It's around the corner. It quite dwarfs every other house on the street."

"Have you let a house?"

"Yes. Papa found it through his agent in London."

He didn't engage her in any more conversation after that, and she was glad, preferring to give herself fully to the music. It was a long and lively dance, and by the time it ended, Hester was warm and breathless.

Major Hawkes bowed to her, then offered her his arm once more. She tucked her hand around the crook of it, feeling the strength beneath her fingers. She was glad to see him leading her the long way around the room. "Is Papa invited to this rout as well?"

"Naturally."

"He won't embarrass the exalted company of dukes and baronesses?" she asked with an innocent look.

"Not if he's an original."

"Oh, he's an original all right."

"What's his name? For the invitation," he added.

"Jeremiah Leighton. *Mister.*"

"How simple."

"Everyone in America is simply 'mister.'"

"I must remember that…if ever I'm in America." His tone implied that was an unlikely event. She felt a twinge of hurt that a person would dismiss her country out of hand—and a sudden pang, realizing she'd never see the major again once she'd returned home.

"What is a rout like?" she asked, preferring to change the topic.

"A roomful of people with barely enough space to move. Not to worry, I'll introduce you to Delia and she'll take care of you."

So, he did intend to be at the rout. Her heart kicked up its rhythm at the thought of seeing him at least once more.

Hester bit her lip, seeing Mr. Sedgwick still hovering beside Mrs. Bellows. She was torn between hoping Major Hawkes would not excuse himself immediately and embarrassed that he would be subjected to Mr. Sedgwick's stupidity and Mrs. Bellows's foolishness.

Hawkes gently disengaged his arm from hers. "Thank you for accompanying me. You dance charmingly," he said.

She smiled, wondering if he was merely being kind.

Before Hester could reply, Mrs. Bellows began introducing Mr. Sedgwick.

Major Hawkes inclined his head. "Work in the city, do you?"

"Yes."

"Barrister?"

He shook his head. "Solicitor at Barnes and Jenkins."

"Very good." Hawkes's eyes met Hester's, and she had to struggle to hold back her laughter.

"A lucky guess," she murmured behind her fan.

"What was that?" Mrs. Bellows asked.

"Nothing, ma'am, just breathless."

"Of course, dear. What a lovely couple you two made on the dance floor."

The major inclined his head. "Thank you. The credit belongs entirely to my partner."

Mrs. Bellows tapped him on the arm with her fan, an eager glint in her eye. "Nonsense. There's nothing like a uniform to give a gentleman a dashing appearance."

"Appearances are funny things…" Despite the lightness of his tone, his eyes were bleak. Before Hester could think how to reply, he was bowing. "Well, I must be off." He took Mrs. Bellows's outstretched hand, then turned to Hester.

"Until Friday evening." His blue eyes held hers a moment before letting go of her hand.

Once more, Hester was left to watch his departing back as he made his way across the salon. She remembered his words about coming expressly to seek her. It seemed he had spoken the truth. Had it been solely to deliver his sister's invitation, or had he wanted to see her, too?

Her mind began conjuring up the rout. Would Papa agree to go? Would Mrs. Bellows accompany them? She cringed at the thought. What would the major's sister be like? Haughty and proud, or amusingly indolent like her brother?

Would the major dance with her again? She had executed all the dance steps without faltering. Would there be dancing at the rout? She wished now she'd asked the major more questions about it.

Mrs. Bellows tapped her fan against Hester's arm. "Have a care, my dear. You've caught the major's eye."

It sounded like a warning. "What do you mean?"

"He's known to be a *rake*." She whispered the last word and looked around as if afraid someone would overhear. "But oh, what a handsome one he is, to be sure!" She snapped her fan open and fluttered it before her face. "Even my old heart still trembled when he turned those blue eyes on me."

Mr. Sedgwick cleared his throat.

Mrs. Bellows ignored him. "*And* he's a war hero."

"He was at Waterloo," Hester offered, hoping to draw out more information while distrusting the older lady's words.

"Oh, my yes, and many more battles before that. Let me see, I remember him when he first came to London, before he obtained his commission. Oh, the heads he turned! Then he got his colors as an ensign in the Coldstreams, a most elite corps, you know. Before he'd hardly made the rounds of London, he was off to the Peninsula. Fought under Wellington. Very distinguished career." She nodded her head, threatening to topple the purple toque that sat above her gray curls.

"But have a care, my dear," she repeated, her rouged face drawing closer. "They say he's broken more hearts than he's killed French."

Hester turned away, not wanting to hear any more. That was what she got for listening to gossip. She would not judge the major on hearsay. As Papa would say, a man should be judged by his deeds.

The major was as good as his word. Two mornings later, Hester came back from her ride in the park to find a gilt-edged invitation awaiting her on a tray in the entrance hall.

Miss Hester Leighton was written in ink across the front of the folded paper. Curious, she took it up and broke open the seal.

You are cordially invited to a rout at Hampshire House, Grosvenor Square, on Friday, August tenth, at nine o'clock.

It was closed with a long, curling signature, which Hester made out as Alexandra Pennington, Duchess of Wakefield.

She fingered the thick paper. It was her first invitation to a real London society event. What would her sisters and childhood friends back home think of this? she wondered, bringing the folded sheet to her chin.

Would she fit in? Would her dress be fine enough? Mama had had some dresses made up from the magazine pictures brought back from London, but they were undoubtedly already out of fashion.

Would Major Hawkes be there? Would his sister truly befriend her?

These questions revolved around her mind a dozen times a day until the moment she and her father alighted from their hired carriage at the well-lit entrance of the stately mansion called Hampshire House.

They ascended the red carpet covering the sidewalk to the front entrance, where they presented their invitation to a footman at the door and were admitted to a grand foyer.

Hester drew in her breath at its large proportions. It was bigger than any house she'd ever seen. The ceiling was at least two stories high and a double staircase curved around to another floor. It, too, was red-carpeted.

"Shall we enter the lion's den?" her father asked with a smile.

She smiled back, as impressed by his appearance as she was by her surroundings. Her father looked so handsome tonight with his black coat and knee breeches and white waistcoat. She wished Mama could be with them.

"Doesn't look like many people are here," he commented as they began to climb the marble staircase.

It was true. She saw no one else about except for a footman standing guard at the entrance to another room.

This room was even more impressive than the foyer. Large gilt-framed paintings lined the walls. The gilt was repeated at the ceiling molding. The ceiling itself was decorated with painted oval panels of clouds and delicate blue sky, cupid-like figures and other angelic beings floating between them.

She tightened her hold on her father's arm and walked slowly with him around the room, gazing around and above them. Their heels clicked against the shiny parquet floor with its geometric pattern. The room was empty, except for velvet-upholstered chairs arranged at intervals along the sides and tall urns or Grecian statuary on marble pedestals interspersed between them.

"Where is everyone?" Mr. Leighton asked in bemusement when they had circled the room once.

They exited back into the hallway and entered another empty room. This one was smaller than the first and carpeted, but also lined with paintings. They spent some time examining the various landscapes and still lifes.

"I feel as if I'm at the British Museum," Mr. Leighton

said after a few moments. "I wonder if we got the date wrong. Maybe the party was for tomorrow night."

Hester withdrew the invitation once again from her beaded reticule. "No, it states right here Friday. Besides, the doors were open and the footmen received us with no question. Perhaps we're early, although it does say nine o'clock. What time is it now?"

He removed his gold watch from his pocket. "Half-past nine," he said, then snapped it shut again.

The room led into another. From there they found themselves in a long hallway lined with portraits.

Her father surveyed the length of paintings. "If I am correct, this is what is known as a portrait gallery." Once again they began a slow promenade.

Hester studied the ruff-decorated men and women in their stiff black clothing and even stiffer expressions. "Do you think they're all family members?"

"I expect they are."

When they reached the end, they turned around to walk back along the other side. Here, an occasional window broke the procession of portraits. They paused at one to look out. They could see a torch-lighted garden below, laid out in formal beds enclosed by dark green hedges.

Her father chuckled. "When I was a young lad in London, I wouldn't be allowed anywhere near such a place. The watch would have run me out of the neighborhood long before I'd get anywhere close."

"Like Lazarus and the rich man?" Hester asked with a smile.

"Something like. Except I'm still on the earth and could probably buy one of these mansions if I so desired."

"You can also take the message to the rich man's brothers."

He glanced at her, as if taken aback. "I don't know about that. I don't think he—or she, in this case—would listen any more than the rich man did in the parable."

"Is that a reason not to try?" she asked, wondering what kind of faith the major had.

Her father shook his head. "No, no...of course not." They continued walking the silent corridor. They retraced their steps and discovered new rooms with ornate furnishings and paintings, only occasionally coming upon a footman carrying a tray somewhere or standing at attention.

"Well, someone has clearly got it wrong," her father said in exasperation. Before she could stop him, he marched up to a footman and demanded, "See here, this rout—or whatever you want to call it—is it for tonight or isn't it? It's—" he snapped open his watch again "—ten o'clock and nary a soul to be seen."

"The rout is this evening," the man answered with no trace of expression on his face.

"Well, when does it start?"

"Guests do not usually arrive until approaching midnight."

"But the invitation states nine o'clock, doesn't it?" He turned angry eyes toward Hester.

"Yes, sir," she answered at once.

"That is correct," the footman affirmed when her father turned to demand an answer from him. "But most guests don't come until the theater lets out. Some will trickle in at eleven."

"Confound it! I've had enough of this. If I'd wanted to look at pictures tonight, I'd have gone to a gallery. Come along, Hester," he said, already stalking away.

Hester hurried to catch up with him, knowing it was useless to persuade him to stay. Once her father made up his mind about something, there was little one could do to change it. How she wished now that they'd brought Mrs. Bellows. Then Papa might allow her to stay with the older woman, at least until midnight.

She gave one last look of longing down the splendidly empty corridor, picturing it filled with elegantly clothed ladies and gentlemen. If only they could have stayed a bit longer. There would be no chance of seeing Major Hawkes now.

She wondered why he hadn't told her to disregard the time stated on the invitation and not arrive until midnight? Had he assumed she knew the ways of the London ton?

Chapter Four

Gerrit took a careful sip from his glass and glanced at the cards pasted onto the enameled board on the table in front of him. After studying them some seconds, he looked at the deck sitting in front of the dealer. If only one's mind had the ability to envision which card would turn up next. What a priceless talent that would be!

Alas, he must be content to study the beads on the casekeeper to the dealer's right one last time. Two beads at either end of the metal rod indicated two aces had already been played. He lifted a couple of chips from his pile and placed them on the ace of spades on the layout in front of him.

Beside him sat a well-fed earl, a sergeant of the Guards, and a lieutenant from Gerrit's company. The men placed their bets on the thirteen cards laid out before them on the board. A few coppered their bets—predicting that their cards would lose. Gerrit debated a few seconds then decided against it. He had a few chips on the ten of spades, the queen of spades, and now the ace.

The banker glanced around him. "All bets are down?"

At the nods and grunts, he flicked the top card on the deck in front of him upward. Gerrit felt that familiar rush of anticipation—the same sensation as when he ordered the charge of his company. Who would come out alive? Who would come out a winner and who a loser? Only the Fates knew as they laughed from the sidelines.

The banker, a youngblood named Fickett, placed the card on his right in a growing pile. The four of clubs came up. The thick-necked earl who'd flatted the four seemed unmoved that his bet had lost. He had good reason, having already won a significant pile that evening. The next card would determine the winner.

The card came up and the dealer placed it on the pile to his left.

It was the nine of hearts. Gerrit swallowed. One pip short of winning. At least the turn was a stalemate for him. His chips could remain in place until the next deal. Again, the men on each side of Gerrit placed or moved their chips on the enameled board. The losers paid up their lost bets, the winners collected theirs from the dealer. It all took less than a minute. Gerrit sipped his drink, remaining otherwise motionless.

The dealer turned up the next card on the pile. Gerrit breathed a silent sigh of relief when it was an eight of spades. The next card came up and went into the pile on the left. It was the five of diamonds.

His bet was unaffected. His chips remained on the

ten, queen and ace. He took another sip, hardly feeling the gin flow down his throat anymore. Fickett, looking barely out of the schoolroom, but with enough blunt to hold the bank, was smiling at Gerrit as if he hadn't a care in the world. He should be sitting at White's or Brooks's—not in a third-rate tavern's backroom parlor.

The evening had started out well for Gerrit when he'd entered the game of faro. He'd won enough to break even, though not to come out ahead by much. But for the past half hour, going through two packs of cards, he'd lost steadily. It was as if the very cards were against him, determined to turn up wherever they would hurt him most. If he placed his chips on a two, it would come up to the right of the banker, if he coppered his bet, the card would come up on the left, making him a loser in either case.

Fickett began the next turn. Gerrit watched as the two cards were flipped up. This time the four of diamonds was dealt on the losing pile.

Gerrit began to hope his luck had changed. The deck was more than halfway dealt. The counters clicked on the spindle, as the dealer marked which cards had been played into which piles.

Gerrit studied them, knowing soon they would be to the end of the pile and he would bet on the sequence of the last three cards. Just before the dealer called the turn closed, Gerrit moved his chips from the ten of spades to the four of spades, judging it unlikely that another four would be played.

He wiped the sweat from his brow with his sleeve, finding it hard to concentrate anymore. He'd long ago removed his jacket and waistcoat. Had the king of diamonds been played yet? He struggled to recall but every suit and rank formed a jumble in his head.

He must concentrate. But something kept teasing the edge of his thoughts, distracting him like the moth around the candle flame in front of him. He pushed the question to the recesses of his mind. There'd be time enough after he recouped his losses. Just one more hand.

The four of hearts was played onto the losing pile.

How could that be? Gerrit glanced from it to the casekeeper, a rack which looked like an abacus. Only two fours had been played. And now the four of hearts made three. He moved his pile of chips off the four and gave them to the banker, scrawling the amount on an IOU. He'd long since run out of money.

The heap of vowels sat by Fickett like a flimsy stack of onion skins ready to blow away at the merest breath. If the numbers they represented would only scatter as easily. How much did they total now? He'd lost count, preferring to focus on regaining his losses by night's end. He gave a barely perceptible nod when the waiter approached with a fresh glass of gin.

He took another swig from his glass. Vile drink, this gin, but it was all they drank in these taverns. As the deck grew smaller, so did his pile of chips. He knew he should get up and leave, but was unable to move. He had to see it out to the end. The turn came down to the last three cards, the two of clubs, the seven of hearts and the ten of diamonds. Gerrit bet everything on the sequence he believed would come up: seven, ten, two. If he won, the dealer would pay four-to-one on his chips.

The two of clubs came up first, then the seven and lastly, the ten of diamonds.

"Worse luck," Edgar, his lieutenant mumbled, as they settled their bets.

"Don't worry, the tide could turn on the next one," the beefy earl said as he collected his winnings with an energetic will.

But Gerrit shook his head, having no more to bet that night. He'd probably have to hock something to pay off this debt. As he totaled his vowels to the dealer, he found himself owing him five hundred pounds. How had it grown so rapidly?

"By Jove, that's a beautiful stepper you've got below." Fickett flashed him an enthusiastic smile as he accepted the IOUs from Gerrit's hand. The boy undoubtedly had unlimited credit at home.

"Thanks, she's been with me a few years." Gerrit drained the last of his drink and rose from the table. His limbs felt stiff from sitting so many hours.

"I bet she saw some battles." The earl donned his coat and picked up his fat purse.

Gerrit rolled down his sleeves and fastened his cuffs. "Steady as a rock in all of them." Where in all of creation was he to come up with five hundred pounds? He didn't think he had anything of that much value. He wanted to laugh at the absurdity. Crockett would have his hide for sure this night. How many times had he told him to stay away from the faro table?

He could hear his voice now. *Play whist if you must, but don't lay odds on faro. You'll lose your shirt if you do.*

If his shirt was of any value tonight, he would have

played it. What was it about playing that, once he started, he felt compelled to see the game through, always hoping for better luck at the next turn?

"Royal has saved Gerrit's life more than once," Edgar told the earl. "Once when Gerrit was wounded and was just hanging by his stirrups, Royal knew enough to leave the battle and carry her master back behind the lines. She's never lost her master."

Fickett slapped his gloves against his palms. "I'd love to own a horse like that. Did you see my pair of grays? By Jove, they're tops. Won every race I've run 'em in."

"Yes, they're a fine pair." Gerrit had noticed the pair of horses when the young gentleman had come dashing to a stop in his high-perched phaeton in front of the tavern. Gerrit had remarked to Edgar that they'd last the young swell but a short while if he treated them like that every night.

As they turned to leave the room, Fickett thumped Gerrit on the back. "I say, I have a capital idea. I'll tear up your vouchers in exchange for your horse."

Gerrit stared at him, hardly believing what he'd heard. Was the boy serious, or did he know Gerrit had his pockets to let and no way of paying his gambling debt?

The others all began to speak. "That's a good offer. You'd better take it, Hawkes. Royal's a fine mount, none better, but you can get a fine mount for two hundred. Top-of-the-line."

Gerrit looked at the vowels stuffed in the young man's pocket. "I have a better idea," he said, a thought forming in his mind even as he spoke. "I'll race you for those IOUs."

The young man's eyes gleamed.

"If Royal beats one of your grays, you tear up my vowels. If your horse beats mine, I owe you the money plus," Gerrit wet his lips, knowing there'd be no turning back once the words were uttered, but feeling that same sense of invincibility he did whenever he placed a bet, "Royal is yours."

The man thrust out his hand. "By Jupiter, you're on!"

The two shook hands, the young man trembling with eagerness, Gerrit keeping himself reserved. If he lost, he'd probably have to flee back to France.

The men hurried out the door, impatient for the race to begin. Edgar turned to Gerrit, concern in the lieutenant's eyes. "Are you sure about this, sir? You've had Royal a long time. I'd hate to see you part with her now."

Gerrit grinned at him. "Who's going to part with her? You said yourself what a splendid horse she was."

"Yes, but you saw his grays. They're racers. Besides, are you in any shape to race?"

"In no worse condition than he is," he said with a glance at Fickett, who had stumbled in his haste down the stairs.

When they stood on the street, the sky was already beginning to lighten with the dawn.

"Where shall we race?" They looked up and down the deserted length of the street.

"Too bumpy and slippery," Edgar judged the dark cobblestones, shiny with the light mist that had fallen through the night.

"What about the Mall? We're not too far and it's light enough now."

"Yes! The length of the Mall. We'll cross St. James's and determine the length of the course there."

"Two furlongs easily. That would make a splendid race." Fickett and his companions, who had joined them from the tavern as soon as they'd heard about the race, nodded in agreement.

Gerrit, leading his horse, and accompanied by his fellow officers, left the York Street tavern and walked past the barracks toward the park. It took only a few minutes to arrive at the long promenade. Tall, slim trees planted at evenly spaced intervals created a wide alley down the length of the Mall.

One of the young men volunteered to ride to the end. "I'll mark the finish line."

"You go with him," Gerrit instructed Edgar.

"Yes, sir."

The men shouted when they reached the end of the Mall. The usually crowded promenade was empty of all except their group.

Gerrit sat atop Royal and patted her neck. "Don't let me down, old girl. I need this win." He felt better in the cool dawn air. He looked down the broad, tree-lined corridor, envisioning the moment of crossing the finish line. The morning was foggy, but not enough to impede their race.

"Gentlemen, to your marks," one of the gentlemen shouted. At the words, Gerrit and Fickett leaned forward on their mounts. The horses, as if sensing the tension in their riders, snorted and fidgeted, pawing at the hard-packed earth.

"At the sound of the gun, you're off," the man on the sidelines told them. They each nodded.

The man lifted his pistol and Gerrit braced himself for the noise. A second later the explosion rent the early morning air. Gerrit dug in his spurs and Royal was off. The pounding hooves thudded through Gerrit's body and up to his temples. The wind whooshed past him. He leaned forward into it, holding the reins, digging in his knees.

"Come on, girl, come on," he urged, holding his course steady with a light pressure on the reins. He didn't look to the other horse, but focused ahead on the invisible line between the two men standing there beneath the tall, shady trees.

The damp earth kicked up around them and he could scarcely hear the shouts of the men. He had no idea if he was ahead or behind or even with his opponent.

As soon as it had begun it was over. Edgar came running up to him. "Congratulations! You beat the gray by a handspan. By Jove, that was a fine race." He slapped Gerrit on the back as soon as he'd dismounted.

As the excitement of the challenge ebbed, Gerrit began to feel sick. He had drunk too much and eaten little. The short gallop had shaken his insides like a spinning wheel.

Fickett held out his hand, no animosity visible on his face. "What a piece of horseflesh! I'm still willing to buy her from you. Name your price."

"She's not for sale." Gerrit turned to Royal and smoothed down her sweaty neck. "Just cancel my faro bets and we're even."

"I'll give you eight hundred for her," the youth insisted.

"No." Gerrit turned to the others. "But I'll stand you all a drink at the nearest tavern."

The men cheered.

He gestured across the park. "The Rose and Lion is sure to be open still. It's not far from the Horse Guards."

Edgar walked beside him, the fine gravel crunching under their boots. "I didn't think you were in any shape to race a horse in the dark over an unmarked course. You're one lucky devil!" The lieutenant shook his head. "I don't know how you pulled it off."

"'Pon my word, I hardly do myself. Perhaps because Royal was more in control than I."

"Eight hundred quid. That's a hefty sum."

When they arrived at the tavern, Gerrit tossed a coin to a lounging boy to take Royal. "I'll double that if you rub her down, feed and water her."

The taproom was nearly empty, only one patron stretched out, snoring on a wooden bench by the large fireplace.

"A round of your finest!" the sergeant shouted toward the bar. When no one appeared, they all raised their voices. Finally a man in a white apron, his hair mussed and his eyes blinking as if he'd just been roused from sleep, emerged from the back.

"What'll it be, sirs?" he asked them as if it was a normal occurrence for a loud group of gentlemen and soldiers to appear at the crack of dawn.

"A round of your finest ale," Gerrit ordered.

"And some hot soup!" another one added.

"You heard it. Be quick about it," Fickett bellowed, thumping the bar with his fists.

The men settled around a long table, stretching out their legs and loosening their neck cloths, their talk returning to the race. A young maid hurried in to light the candles in the wall sconces.

She stooped in front of the grate and began to sweep out the cold ashes in preparation for laying a new fire. As Gerrit watched her, he suddenly remembered.

Miss Leighton. The rout.

He swore under his breath.

Edgar nudged him. "What's the matter?"

He shook his head. "Nothing. Just remembered an engagement."

Edgar gave him a sly wink. "Never mind. You'll be able to smooth things over with your winnings."

Before he could agree about his oversight, the barkeeper returned with a tray loaded with pewter mugs and slammed it down on the table. The foamy amber liquid sloshed forth.

Edgar stood up as soon as everyone had grabbed a tankard. Holding his high, he shouted, "To the best, bravest major in His Majesty's Guards!"

They raised their tankards toward Gerrit. "Hear! Hear!"

"To Royal!" added Fickett.

"To Royal!" they all repeated, banging tankards.

The serving maid returned with a tray of soup bowls, followed by the barkeeper with a tureen of soup. Gerrit sipped at the tepid ale, needing something to clear his mind and wash the taste of gin from his mouth.

Neither his companions' hilarity nor the tasty soup was enough to dispel his irritation at his own forgetfulness. Had last night been Friday already? How could he have forgotten the rout? He'd promised Miss Leighton to introduce her to Delia. He knew from experience how crowded a rout could be, so he hadn't much hope that the two ladies had been able to find each other without him.

Without finishing his soup or ale, he stood.

"Where're you going? Have some more ale!" The sergeant held up the pitcher to him.

Gerrit shook his head. "Have it yourself." After settling the bill with an IOU, Gerrit headed for the stables.

After a few hours' sleep, he'd go around to Miss Leighton's and leave a note of apology.

Or should he just forget her? The thought took hold. He'd been spending entirely too much time thinking about her. It was better she see what a worthless cove he was, before any real harm was done.

The last thing he desired was for a young innocent to develop a *tendre* for him. He was the last man to be trusted.

The sound of curtain rings screeching across their rods awakened Gerrit. A second later, daylight bombarded his eyelids as he cracked them open.

Crocker set a tray on the bed. "Good afternoon, sir. I brought you a nice hot pot o' coffee."

Gerrit eyed his batman deciding whether he could muster the energy needed to throw him out of the room. He probably couldn't even manage flinging the tray to the ground, he realized, testing his limbs. They felt like lumps of cold porridge.

"What…are…you doing here?" he groaned, falling back against his pillows.

Crockett smiled at him, bringing his beaked nose downward and his eyebrows together in an evil-looking grin. "Just following orders. You told me to always get you up before three."

Gerrit ignored him, knowing it was useless to get the better of his man in the shape he was in. "What time is it?" he asked through a yawn.

"Just passed two o' the clock. Now, why don't you sit up before this coffee gets any colder?" Crocker gazed down his nose at him. "I'd say you could use a good cup or two. What happened last night? Get run over by a dray?"

Gerrit eased his body up against his pillows, which Crocker obligingly placed behind him. His own odor assaulted him. By George, he reeked of stale smoke. A wash and shave was what he needed, he decided, running a hand across the bristles on his cheeks. A good dunking in some water should also help his sluggish head.

Crocker laid the tray on his lap. "So, anything of interest happen to you last night?" He poured the coffee from the dented pewter pot into a cup and handed it to Gerrit.

The prior evening was a haze of indistinct images. A young lord…faro…

Better not enlighten Crocker about that.

Had he won or lost? He dug in his memory. Maybe an inspection of his pockets would be quicker.

A horse race. Yes, he'd won a horse race. More of the bits fell into place. "I recall winning a horse race. And betting lots of money," he added.

"Did you now? 'appen to know if you won or lost?" Crocker was a great fan of the turf.

"I won."

Crocker went immediately to his coat pockets. After

turning them inside out, he looked at Gerrit in puzzlement. "Where's the blunt then?"

Gerrit took another sip of coffee, a longer one as he let the strong, hot liquid linger in his mouth before swallowing. He might manage getting out of bed after all. "I don't have any."

"No winnings? What kind of a race is that?"

"The winnings were more in the line of a cancellation of debt." The details were becoming clearer.

Crocker looked long and hard at him. "I see. And what debt might that be?"

"Faro, as I recall."

Crocker went about the business of batman. He picked up a brush and attacked Gerrit's coat with long, vigorous strokes. Gerrit knew the routine whenever his man was cross with him. Crockett made a great show of inspecting Gerrit's boots before putting them by the door. "They'll need a good blacking. Horse manure, bits o' straw, mud..."

Gerrit continued drinking his coffee and debating whether his stomach was up to the two pieces of slightly burnt toast that lay on the plate. He would just have to put up with Crocker's sulks for the next hour or two. By this evening, he'd be his old self, ready to go out and do some of his own carousing.

He glanced out the window. The fog had lifted, leaving a hazy hot day by the looks of it. "What time did you say it was?"

Crocker made an elaborate show of taking out his pocket watch and snapping it open. "A quarter past two." He narrowed his eyes at Gerrit. "Where is your own watch, by the way? Haven't hocked it, have you?"

Gerrit screwed up his eyes and tried to remember. "I don't recall. Has it been missing long?"

"About a week. I'll just have to check with Farley."

The mention of the pawnbroker reminded him of something else. "See if he still has my silver cuff links."

"Yes, sir. Now, be you needing anything more, *sir?*"

When he started sounding like a real servant, Crocker was truly miffed.

"Hot water. Lots of it."

"Yes, sir."

The door banged shut behind him as Crocker left with boots in one hand, dirty linen in the other.

As Gerrit shaved and bathed, he thought about how he should spend his day. He'd check in at the Horse Guards' barracks and see what might be going on. He didn't think there were any reviews until the following week. He stared down at the sleeve of his uniform. He really should order a new one for parades and reviews. This one was beginning to show its wear, and the others were in worse shape.

But first a ride. He wanted to check on Royal. What a fine mare she was. He'd bring her a treat then take her out for a canter. Fresh air, even the hot, dusty air of an August afternoon, could only benefit the two of them.

Gerrit spotted Miss Leighton riding in an open carriage along the path by the Serpentine. He drew his horse up, seeing the unmistakable face of the young American in profile as she sat opposite an older gentleman.

Once again the memory hit him. He'd forgotten the rout. He'd decided against calling on her. And then when he'd awakened, everything from last night had been sketchy at best. Sudden shame constricted his neck and flushed his face. Since when had he begun feeling shame over a missed appointment with a fair damsel?

Since he'd returned to England after Waterloo, remorse seemed to dog his footsteps. First with Lady Gillian and now with this young Yankee. What was becoming of the old, carefree Gerrit?

The young French soldier's face flashed in his memory. It had started with him.

It had started with a cadet. Like an invisible fist punched in his gut, the realization hit Gerrit. Only military discipline kept him from doubling over in his saddle.

"It's all right, my lady," he said, patting the mare's withers. Keeping Royal prancing in place, he considered, unsure of his next move. Only two options presented themselves: forward or retreat.

"Go on." He communicated his intentions and the horse advanced.

He would not retreat.

He approached the slowly moving carriage and doffed his cap. "Good afternoon." He bowed to both occupants, noting the absence of Mrs. Bellows.

Miss Leighton turned. "Major Hawkes." She gave him a slight smile, as if unsure how to proceed. This only caused him to feel his failure more acutely.

"May I present my father? Papa, this is Major Hawkes. I told you about his sister, Viscountess Stanchfield."

A pair of brown eyes scrutinized his face. "Major Hawkes."

"Major Hawkes, this is my father, Mr. Jeremiah Leighton."

Jeremiah Leighton. The name was formidable enough. Hester's description came back to him: thrifty, ingenious, a hard bargainer. Gerrit put his hand to the brim of his hat. "An honor, sir."

"Hmm," was all the man said. "You've been on active duty?"

"Yes, sir. On the Continent," he added quickly, lest the man think he had been involved in the action across the Atlantic.

Leighton echoed his thoughts. "We saw a troop land on our shores. But we soon routed them."

Gerrit inclined his head. "Well done, sir." He glanced toward Hester. Was he being weighed in the balances by her sire?

Hester gave him a small smile. At least she didn't appear angry.

"You are British, sir?" Gerrit asked, deciding to go on the offensive himself.

"Not anymore," he growled out. "American and proud of it."

"Very good, sir." He had to refrain from smiling at the man's belligerent tone.

"I travel for business," he said. "I don't mind making money off you Brits."

"I'm sure the feeling is mutual. Thankfully, the blockades are over."

"Your ships sunk more than one good merchant vessel of mine until we sent our privateers after yours."

"Yes, I've heard about your privateers."

"You seem to have led us on a wild-goose chase last night."

"I beg your pardon?"

Miss Leighton's voice intruded. "The rout. Did you attend?"

Here it came. He turned his attention to her. "I must apologize for not attending. I—something detained me at the last moment." How many times had he used that vague excuse with women he was trying to put off? "I hope you found my sister."

"I don't think she was in attendance. I don't think anyone was."

He frowned. "What do you mean?"

"We were there at nine o'clock sharp as it stated on the invitation," her father answered for her. "Not a soul in that empty palace. Waited around for more'n an hour and nothing. What kind of joke was it supposed to be?"

Gerrit looked down. It was worse than he'd imagined. "I'm sorry. I should have explained. No one shows until eleven or so. After the theaters let out." He added, "or the opera. My sister mentioned she would be there at midnight." He wondered what Delia had thought when he hadn't been there. He'd have to make his apologies to her now as well.

"I'm sorry she wasted her time then. We were long gone," Miss Leighton said.

He gazed at her, wondering what she thought of him now and realizing he cared about her opinion. "I'll talk to her. I know she will be heartbroken not having met you. She'll invite you to something else."

"You needn't bother," her father spoke up before

Miss Leighton could say anything. "We're busy enough as it is. Good day, Major—" he paused only long enough to let Gerrit know he had to search around for his name "—Hawkes."

The man's tone was final. Gerrit touched his fingers to his brim. "Good day, Miss Leighton, Mr. Leighton." He stayed unmoving as they drove away. He would have to find some other means of making amends.

It would undoubtedly entail lots of flattery along with a gift to Delia in order to persuade her to send the Leightons another invitation. Well, if there was one thing he knew how to do, it was coax a woman.

Chapter Five

Hester sat beside Major Hawkes at his sister's dinner table. She glanced further down the long table to her father, sandwiched between two brilliantly dressed women. One had him in what appeared vivacious conversation, her ostrich plumes waving up and down when she nodded to make a point.

Hester smiled to herself and turned back to take a spoonful of the blancmange placed in front of her. She had lost count of how many courses she'd partaken of.

"What do you think of a London dinner party?" Major Hawkes's soft voice came to her.

She turned her head toward him and found his amused gaze fixed on her. The vivid blue of those eyes against the almost blue-black of his hair never failed to startle her.

She managed a shy smile. "Overwhelming."

"This is a small gathering, you know."

"Is it?" There must have been at least two dozen

people ranged down the length of the table. "I can scarcely imagine a large dinner party."

"However did you get your father to accept my sister's invitation?"

Her smile deepened. "That was not so difficult."

"No? I thought he seemed a bit put out about the rout."

"He was, but he never stays angry long. Besides, I don't think he had the heart to turn down your sister's kind invitation. She wrote us a very nice note."

He glanced down the table at his sister. "Delia can be very charming."

"It was thoughtful of her to include us in tonight's party."

"Oh, she loves to entertain. The more the merrier." The major lounged back in his chair and eyed Hester. "I'm relieved to hear your acceptance was never in doubt."

She gave him a sidelong glance. "I didn't say that exactly."

He quirked an eyebrow. "What was the impediment to your accepting this invitation?"

She remembered the careless way he'd told them he hadn't even been at the rout. "I wasn't certain if we *should* accept."

"Why wouldn't you want to accept?" His rich blue eyes were focused on her mouth.

She brought her napkin up to it, wondering if there was a drop of pudding on her lips. "I wasn't sure if it was worth our while to meet more of your distinguished class. What I had seen at the rout hadn't unduly impressed me."

He chuckled. "You didn't miss anything, by the way,

by not staying. Routs are vile things, crowds of people just standing around to be seen. They greet each other then proceed to the next group."

"You should have told me that before we went."

His lips curved upwards, dimpling his cheek. "Told you? Why, then you'd never have gone."

She shook her head at him, but couldn't help smiling. "Don't you ever take anything seriously?"

"Never in peacetime," he answered. "I find life a cruel joke." He waved a hand around them. "How about you? Don't you find the antics here amusing?"

She considered, her gaze roaming over the gathered assembly. They did look a bit pompous, their dress and their behavior extreme by her standards. She turned back to the major. "Life is much too serious for me to laugh at the behavior of others."

"What is so serious about it?"

"The salvation of souls. That's a very serious affair. Nothing to joke about."

"You're one of those Evangelicals." His voice held amused disbelief.

She said nothing, disliking the mockery of his tone.

His glance strayed over the table again. "I pity you here. You will feel like a fish out of water."

"Perhaps." She'd felt like a fish out of water since arriving in England. "They are souls, like any others." At least she'd been trying to tell herself that.

His gaze returned to her, his blue eyes searching hers, all amusement gone. "Do you want to know why I didn't come to the rout?"

"If you care to tell me."

"I clean forgot it." There was neither teasing nor mockery in his tone.

"Why are you telling me this?" Was she so easily forgotten and he not a man of his word?

"You have a funny way of making a man want to come clean and confess all his sins." He paused, his look remaining intent. "That could be a dangerous thing."

She felt on the edge of a precipice, unsure what he meant, and prayed for the right words. "Not if it means the beginning of true friendship."

He gave a soft laugh. "Can there be such a thing between a man and a woman?"

"Of course there can, when there is the love of God between them."

His eyes flickered away from her, and she wondered if her answer had disappointed him. Just then a footman came between them to clear away their used dishes. When a clean cover had been laid before them, the major turned to her once again. "Tell me, have you ever been up St. Paul's dome?"

"No, where is that?" she asked, relieved to hear his friendly tone.

"In the City. On a clear day, you can get a bird's-eye view of all London and the country around it."

Hester was intrigued. "I should like to see that."

"Good. Maybe I can persuade your father to accept my escort."

Her heart plummeted. "I don't know if he'll agree to another wild-goose chase."

He grinned. "Have no fear. My memory is much better in the daylight hours."

* * *

Later that night, when Hester and her father had returned to their town house, Hester stood outside her bedroom door and broached the subject of St. Paul's on the morrow. The major had formally asked her father's permission, but the older man had been evasive with him.

Her father frowned. "I don't know if I like the idea of your spending time in the company of these fashionable people. I know they can be quite immoral."

"The viscountess seems very respectable to me. Besides, if Mrs. Bellows is with me, what harm can there be?"

He shook his head. "I don't know… I can't accompany you tomorrow. I can't say I like your Major Hawkes any better upon second meeting, either."

"But, Papa, you've hardly spoken with him on either occasion. You've always taught me not to judge a person too quickly."

He sighed. "That's true. But I've also lived a few years longer than you and am used to dealing with many men. One becomes adept at summing up a man's character in a short time."

"He's been nothing but kind and gentlemanly. It was through his intervention with his sister that we received her invitation. Mrs. Bellows has explained to me that it takes only one such invitation from a member of society to open the doors to others."

"I know your mother and I decided it was time you saw a little bit of the world, but now I wonder if this is the right type of world." Her father fixed his brown eyes on her. "Tell me, what is your opinion of the major?"

"He's a fine person." She smiled. "He makes me laugh." She remembered how lonely that first week in London had been. "He's been a godsend."

"As long as you don't have your heart broken by his type."

"What do you mean by 'his type?'"

"Spoiled, careless of young women's feelings, and used to getting his way with the ladies through his charm and good looks. I'll bet he uses that uniform to advantage in this pursuit."

"Oh, no, he's nothing like that! He's warm and caring." She refrained from telling him about Major Hawkes's admission that he'd forgotten the rout. No need to add fuel to her father's fire. When he made up his mind about someone, he could be obstinate. Unfortunately, he was rarely wrong.

"Humph," was her father's only reply. "Have a care."

"There's hardly any danger of my heart's being broken. I don't think—" she looked down, hesitant all of a sudden to voice what was most on her mind "—I don't think he's saved."

"That doesn't surprise me… What does surprise me is that you should give someone like that the time of day."

"But, Papa, isn't that precisely what we should be doing?"

Her father made no reply to that. With a final sigh, he turned toward his own bedroom door. "Have a care, dear Hester, is all I can advise you. Have a care."

* * *

After the last dinner guest had departed, Gerrit sat on a settee in his sister's boudoir, watching her remove the jeweled pendants from her ears.

"So, where did Lionel go off to?" he asked through a yawn.

"Brooks's or White's. Or maybe that new one, Watier's," Delia replied to his reflection in the mirror.

"Well, he proved amiable tonight at least."

"Yes," she said, easing the kinks from her neck as her maid undid the clasp of her necklace. "He was in good form. He even remembered your protégée's name and actually said a few nice things to her father." She turned to say something to her maid, who then departed. "I've asked her to bring us both a glass of punch. How does that sound?"

"Like the perfect end to a successful dinner party." He stretched his legs out on a low black-lacquered Chinese table before him and crossed them at the ankles. "I thought she was to become *your* protégée."

Delia cocked an eyebrow at him in the glass. "Is it all settled then?"

"You tell me. What did you think of Miss Hester Leighton?"

"Charming, I'm sure." She looked down at her hands as if she wanted to say more.

"Go ahead."

Her eyes met his. "Nothing. I just wonder what you saw in her. Miss Leighton is nice enough, I grant you, but nothing extraordinary. Just another young deb. I'd have thought she'd have more spice, more flair to catch your eye."

Gerrit smiled but said nothing. Miss Leighton's "flair," was evidently too subtle for his sister to perceive. His sister was flamboyant and attracted the same types around her.

"Well, her understated personality notwithstanding, will you take her on?"

"And what about you? Are you sure you're not interested? You know Father wouldn't be happier than if you'd announce your engagement to an heiress, no matter where her money came from. They worry about you, you know, with the war over. Officers are being decommissioned all over the place. What will you do now?"

He shrugged, continuing to smile. "I'll make out."

"But doing what? Do you think you'll be sent abroad?"

"There's always India."

She shuddered. "I do hope not. I'd like to see my baby brother now and again. You survived those years on the Peninsula. I'd rather you didn't gamble on your life anymore, at least for the time being."

He made no comment.

"Miss Leighton's dowry doesn't tempt you in the least bit?" she persisted.

"Miss Leighton hails from solid Puritan stock. What would she ever see in a dissolute rake up to his ears in debt?"

She tilted her head at him. "Oh, I don't know about that. You've got your looks. And your Waterloo medal."

"Looks don't last." He glanced down at his chest. "And a medal? Yes, that's a real asset. D'you know, for an American, that's actually a strike against me?"

"Never!" She looked outraged. "Well, I suppose so… But we're at peace now. Don't tell me Miss Leighton is one of those rabid patriots that will never forget we were once at war?"

He chuckled. "No, I don't think so. Her own father is British."

"Well, he at least was presentable. Quite a distinguished looking man, actually. I hardly had a chance to talk to him but he seemed to know how to hold a knife and fork at any rate. Anyway," she continued more briskly, "I wouldn't discount your medal. It's an entrée. You who fought at Waterloo are the toast of London right now. You've got to use that asset while it lasts. Look at me, I didn't land a wealthy viscount just on my looks and dowry alone. I had to use every ounce of wiles I possessed."

"Yes, and look what it got you…"

"It got me wealth and privilege. Any door is opened to me. I don't have to hear Father or Mother with their endless talk of limited funds and retrenchment and letting servants go. Lionel lets me lead my own life. What more can a woman want?"

When he said nothing, she asked softly, "How are you for funds?"

"Oh, treading water, as always, but what's that to the point?"

"I'd give you something if I could, but things are a bit tense with Lionel on that score lately. He got my last dressmaker's bills, and there's a little matter with a small gambling debt."

He shook his head. "You needn't tell me." He shifted on the settee. "Truly, I don't need any assistance in that quarter at the moment. If I get desperate enough, I shall rethink the heiress option. But for the moment, I shall remain a free man."

Delia laughed, as he knew she would, glad to have distracted her. "I'm planning a house party," she said, changing the subject, though continuing to observe him.

"A house party? How delightful."

"I invited Miss Leighton. Do you think she'll enjoy it?"

He looked up at the ceiling as if considering. "I imagine she'll add a whole new element."

"I shall compose a list with at least a half-dozen eligible bachelors to invite. Would you like to approve it?"

His glance met his sister's as he kept his smile in place, knowing how discerning his sister could be. "As long as you keep away that stodgy old company that's usually there to entertain Lionel."

"Well, I have to have a few of his cronies if I'm to keep him happy." She looked down at her fingernails. "So, shall I bother inviting you?"

His fingers tightened on the satiny ebony of the sofa arm. Better to decline. "Whatever would I want to do there? I can only remember being bored to distraction at Thistleworth. Lionel with his sole interest in hunting."

"That's precisely why you should come," she insisted. "To ensure Miss Leighton is suitably entertained."

He knew how easy that task would be for him. All too easy. "What about those bachelors?"

"Well, I haven't secured their attendance yet. Besides, you know how eligible bachelors can be—either too supercilious to look at any available female, or too silly for words. You could help keep them in order."

He snorted.

"Please, Gerrit, for me." She gave him the look he knew she'd used to entangle Lionel.

It was better to stay away from the refreshingly honest Miss Leighton no matter how appealing a short flirtation appeared to him. He feigned a groan. "For you, dear sister, I would sacrifice anything, but there are limits to what one can decently demand of one's own flesh and blood."

She pouted and turned away from him. "Very well, be as self-centered as always. I hope you end up falling hopelessly in love with Miss Leighton and she turns you down flat."

He chuckled, though he didn't bother to contradict Delia. There was little danger of losing his heart to Miss Leighton—or anyone. Whatever heart he had, he'd lost long ago. Somewhere between Ciudad Rodrigo and Waterloo.

As to Miss Leighton, after his conversation with her this evening, he knew he must steer clear of her. He didn't need the additional sin of corrupting a pious young lady on his conscience, especially one whose direct way of looking at him stirred a need in him, as he'd told her, to confess every misdeed.

Why, for pity's sake, had he invited her to tour St. Paul's the next day? He was playing with fire and he didn't feel at all confident of his ability to keep from getting them both burned.

Chapter Six

The next day, Major Hawkes walked between Hester and
Mrs. Bellows in the square fronting St. Paul's Cathedral.

"Why, it's massive!" Hester stared up at the giant
pairs of ribbed pillars lining the cathedral's facade. "I
get dizzy just looking up."

"You'll get even dizzier looking down from the top."

She turned to him, hardly believing what he'd told
her last night about climbing to the top of the dome.
"Can a mere building really be so high?"

"Come along and I'll prove it to you." He lightly
grasped Hester's arm on one side and Mrs. Bellows's
on the other and led them up the wide steps into the
cathedral.

"We haven't any churches like this where I live," she
whispered, instinctively lowering her voice when they
entered the cavernous interior.

"No? There are so many splendid cathedrals all

across Europe, one grows used to seeing them, isn't that so, Mrs. Bellows?"

"Oh, I don't know if one quite grows *used* to seeing them," the older lady replied. "And I haven't traveled the way you have, Major."

"Every village across Spain and France seemed to have its cathedral," he said in a careless tone.

"I think, like Mrs. Bellows, I wouldn't grow used to seeing something so grand," Hester said. They had stopped near the entrance and stood looking down the long nave toward the altar. "This puts me in mind of Jesus telling the disciples that not one stone would be left upon another of their beautiful temple in Jerusalem."

The major chuckled. "This cathedral has already been destroyed a few times in its long history."

She looked at him in surprise. "Truly?"

"The latest was in the Great Fire which took much of London with it."

"And this magnificent structure replaced it?" They resumed their tour, their heels clicking on the black-and-white diamond-patterned stone floor.

"Yes. It was rebuilt by Sir Christopher Wren."

She drew in her breath at the length and breadth of the colonnaded nave before them. The stones were white and seemed to glow from the light streaming in from the arched windows high above them.

"It is a lovely building, is it not, my dear?" Mrs. Bellows said, turning to look all around her.

"Lovely," she murmured, preferring to simply stare. When they reached the dome, she craned her neck up to view the soaring expanse above them. Light flooded the interior from the row of windows all along the circumference of the base of the dome. "It's like no church I've ever seen."

"It was Wren's masterpiece." The major's hushed tone was in keeping with their surroundings.

"I can well imagine. How could anyone paint those murals so far up?" she asked, gazing in wonder at the pictures far above them.

"Using all kinds of scaffolding, I suppose," he said in amusement. "You haven't seen the Vatican?"

She glanced at him with a shake of her head. "The only churches I've seen are small wooden structures called meeting houses, and we don't even have one of our own yet in Bangor."

"So, do you want to get a closer look?" His blue eyes held a challenge.

"Do you mean go up there?" She hadn't really thought it possible the way he'd described it the evening before.

"See the gallery all around?" He pointed above them. "There is someone up there already, probably another tourist."

"Oh, my dear, it's too far a climb," Mrs. Bellows shook her head, her voice sounding worried.

Major Hawkes turned to her. "My dear lady, this is the sole reason Miss Leighton came with us today. Would you deny her the opportunity to see this grand city laid out in all its splendor?" He took the older woman by the arm. "Why don't you sit over there in that cozy corner of this cathedral and rest your feet for a few moments while I show Miss Leighton the grandeur of London?"

"Why, all right. I could use a little rest…" Hester

heard her voice dwindle in the distance as the major led Mrs. Bellows to a stone bench in the south transept. In a few moments he was back.

"Come, we haven't much time," he told her with a grin and quick motion toward Mrs. Bellows. Hester followed him, finding his smile irresistible.

He took her to an opening near the transept. Stone steps led upward. "How far is it?" she asked as they mounted the first step.

"This leads to the first gallery, the one you saw from below. It's called the Whispering Gallery."

"Why is that?"

"If you whisper something against the wall on one side, it will be heard directly across."

"How can that be?"

"Something to do with the acoustics of the dome. It does work. We can try it."

Hester was quite out of breath by the time they arrived at the gallery which circled beneath the dome.

Hester paused at the entrance, a hand to her chest. "Oh, my."

"Scared?" He glanced back at her and held out his hand when she still hesitated. She took it, needing to hold on to something. His larger hand held hers securely and she felt immediately safer. She stepped over the threshold onto the narrow gallery.

On one side of her, only a few feet away, stood a thin iron railing, the only barrier between them and a sheer drop to the bottom of the cathedral. Gingerly, she trod the worn stone floor beneath her, doubtful it would hold her.

The major walked on the outside. After a few footsteps, he paused and led her to the edge so she could look below. She gripped his strong arm more tightly, feeling dizzy looking down.

"What a difference from all the way up here." Down below she could see the diamond-patterned floor and the beautifully carved wooden altar. She couldn't see Mrs. Bellows from where they stood. She drew in her breath as she looked around and above her. They were still well below the base of the dome. All around her were golden grayish frescoes.

She remembered what the major had told her. "Shall we try to whisper to each other?"

"If you wish." He indicated the stone benches lining the sides of the circular gallery. "You sit here and I'll walk to the opposite side. Then you can whisper something to me."

When he had reached the other side, he waved and sat with his ear against the wall.

She copied his position then thought a few seconds. What could she whisper to him? It came to her all of a sudden.

She cupped a hand against the cool stone and whispered, "For God so loved the world that He gave His only begotten Son." Then she looked across to him. He motioned for her to listen.

She did so. A second later she heard the verse being quoted back to her. She looked at him in amazement. How could it be possible for him to have heard her and sent her words back to her?

She forgot her fear of heights and began walking toward him. He met her halfway.

"I can't believe you heard me! And that I heard you!"

"Yes, it is rather amazing. I first came here as a school-boy and we used to think it a lark to whisper back and forth to each other. Except we didn't quote Bible scriptures."

"What kinds of things did you whisper?"

"Oh, all sorts of naughty things which seem very tame now." His eyes twinkled. "Are you game to go higher?"

She felt her excitement growing. "Higher? Can we truly?"

"I told you, we can get a whole view of London. Come along."

"What about Mrs. Bellows?"

"What about her? She can't very well stop us from down there."

Hester laughed and followed him. The stairwell was now a narrow circular stairs with only a single iron railing to hold on to. Her legs began to tire.

At last they came to a small doorway leading to the outside. When they passed through it into the sunshine, Hester couldn't believe she was standing so high above the world. She gripped the stone balustrade, which came up to her chest. Hardly daring to look directly down, she preferred to stare across at the city laid out before them. "Are we on the dome?"

"Yes," he answered beside her. "We're at the very base." He pointed upward. "We can climb even higher to the cupola."

"This is quite far enough for me," she said with a nervous laugh.

"Don't grow fainthearted on me now. Let's walk around a bit and I'll show you some of the sights."

"All right," she replied, glad of his hand on her elbow.

When they stopped farther along the balustrade, Hester clutched her bonnet against the breeze and gazed in awe.

"Well?"

Below them, for miles she could see the tiled roofs of the city. "It's magnificent. I can scarcely imagine so many people living in one space."

"Many believe it's the greatest city in the world."

She turned to find his gaze on her. "Do you think so?"

He shrugged and turned back to the vista beyond. "I've seen enough of other cities to weigh its advantages and disadvantages."

"The Thames looks like a silvery thread," she said pointing to the river flowing south of them. They looked beyond it to Southwark.

"That way lies Greenwich and the sea," he indicated.

"The people and horses look like ants down below." She shivered, glad of the thick stone balustrade between her and the drop downward. "How can you walk so carelessly up here? I feel all shaky inside."

In reply, he suddenly heaved himself onto the balustrade and leaned halfway over the side.

She gave a little scream. "What are you doing?"

He merely grinned at her, leaning farther out and looking down.

"Have a care," she admonished, inching her way closer.

"It's not such a far drop on this side, only to the roof below."

She peered down, her heart pounding the farther out she edged. Beneath lay the slate roof of the transept. She imagined Mrs. Bellows sitting quietly underneath it somewhere. "I don't think a person would survive a fall even to there."

He considered, following her gaze. "Don't you?" The next second he had jumped back down to the walkway and brushed his hands off. He lingered at the spot, his hands spread out on the stone surface. "You know, this is wide enough to hold a man...if he should stand upon it."

The colonnaded balustrade was about a foot and a half wide. The mere thought of standing on it made her shiver. She looked at his face, not liking his tone. It was as if he were suddenly far away from her, entranced by the stone beneath his palms. "What a silly notion. Why would anyone want to do such a thing?"

He shrugged and turned to her again. She breathed a sigh of relief at the hint of humor in his eyes. "For the challenge of it, I suppose."

She frowned. "Why should anyone want to risk certain death when there is so much to live for?"

"So much to live for... Tell me, Miss Leighton, what are you living for?"

Her eyes were caught by the deep blue of his, several shades deeper than the expanse of sky around them. How to explain to a person who had seen too much death and destruction the reason to live? "I have a race to run. Until it is over, I shan't be deliberately putting my life in harm's way."

He smiled and straightened away from the balustrade. "Rest easy. I don't suppose I shall either...at least not today."

"I should hope not! Or ever." Hester stepped away

from the edge with a sense of relief. Although he'd been funning, the major's attitude continued to disturb her. What was *he* living for? "You've been in danger many times."

"Many times, but I've eluded death every time. A few wounds only." He sounded almost bitter.

"I think each one of us is appointed an hour of death," she said in an effort to comfort him.

He drew her gaze away from the scene below. "Do you?"

"For those of us in Christ, it only signifies the shedding of this outer body of ours. Our spirit lives forever and we have the hope of a new, incorruptible body."

"An incorruptible body—now there's a thought." With a sigh, he pushed himself away from the edge. "Come, let's walk around and you can see another side of the city."

Hester followed him, glad he seemed back to his old self.

"That's Ludgate Hill leading to Fleet Street," he said, indicating a heavily traveled thoroughfare farther along.

She followed the line of his finger. As her gaze wandered into the distance where the buildings ended and the greenery began, she noticed the wavy horizon of trees. "I never imagined hills around London. Everything here seems so flat."

"That's Hampstead and Highgate."

"What's that large building there?" she asked, when they'd arrived back on the eastern side of the dome. "It looks a little like this one with its light colored stone."

"That's the Bank of London. You might say it's the cathedral's twin."

"How do you mean?"

"The church and the bank—London's twin bastions of power."

"You don't think much of the church," she commented.

"What little I've seen of it, no."

She said nothing more, but listened as he pointed out more monuments. Then he fell silent and they both gazed at the panorama. She wondered if he was as loath to return below as she was—but for different reasons. Was he still thinking of risking his life, while she contemplated the grandeur of God's earth?

Hester lifted her face to the cooling breeze on her cheeks, concern for the man beside her weighing on her heart.

"You're a curious girl, Hester Leighton."

She turned to him, startled to find him observing her. How long had he been doing so? At last his thoughts had shifted from death. Her cheeks grew warm at his continued study. She remembered her father's warning. "How do you mean?"

"You give a man a feeling of safety. You don't know how strange it is for me to say that to a woman. You spoke last night of a man and woman being capable of friendship." He gave a rueful laugh. "I can almost believe we could be friends."

"Why is it so hard to believe? I know lots of boys back home I call my friends."

His smile deepened. "Yes, boys. But boys grow into men."

The silence between them lengthened. Hester felt as if all she would have to do was take one small step closer and she would feel his lips on hers.

Her gaze dropped to his mouth. It looked firm yet soft. She'd never been kissed before. Never wanted to…until now.

"What are you thinking?" His low voice drifted into her awareness.

She pulled her gaze back up to his. Instead of mockery, she found it curiously intense. "I've never had an amorous friendship before."

"Is there such a lack of gentlemen in the Maine Territory?"

She shook her head slowly, unable to tear her eyes away from the tender amusement she read in his. "Quite the contrary. In fact, I believe there are more men than women. Papa knows them all. The young men who work for him are always coming to the house."

"I doubt they're coming to see your father." His voice was low and teasing. Was he flirting with her? The boys Papa brought home were too mindful of his presence to dare to flirt.

"I'm not so vain to think they are coming to see me alone. I have sisters."

"I think you underestimate your charm." The humor slowly faded from his eyes and once again, he was looking at her in that way. Before she could make up her mind what she wanted, he stepped away from her. She felt in those seconds that he had drawn away more than physically. Tapping his fists lightly on the balustrade, his gaze fixed on the city below, he spoke. There was nothing teasing or seductive in his tone now. The words were halting as if he had difficulty formulating them.

"I…haven't much of value to offer you, let alone to a wealthy and devout young lady from the—er—former Colonies, but what I have, I offer you." He half turned to her and held out his hand. "My friendship."

Hester stretched out her own hand and felt it engulfed by his. What did the Lord intend with this new friendship? She sensed the major's deep need, but had little idea how she could help him. The Lord would have to guide her step by step.

Gerrit returned to St. Paul's late that night, this time accompanied by a loud group in uniform. They'd come from their usual round of public houses, where Gerrit had done his best to obliterate the image of the innocent maiden he'd spent the afternoon with. He hadn't realized quite how innocent she was until she'd stood inches from him, her soft lips parted and said, "I've never had an amorous friendship before," as if she were telling him she'd had the measles as a child. Simple candor. She had no idea how to flirt. And, for all his vows to stay away from her, he'd had to exercise every ounce of self-control not to kiss her.

Now, he stood where he had been hours earlier with Miss Leighton as they'd gazed over London. He smiled, unable to help remembering how pleasurable he'd found her company.

The breeze was sharper and cooler than it had been in the afternoon. The lights of the city twinkled for miles around them, although it was still twilight.

A young corporal's voice intruded Gerrit's thoughts.

"All right, gentlemen, the bet is this. Twenty crowns for whoever can walk along this balustrade for twenty paces without falling off." At the last words everyone burst out laughing, knowing a fall would be fatal.

"A crown a foot!" Laughter followed.

Gerrit had proposed the challenge in the taproom. Here, in the dimming light, Gerrit looked below him. The cathedral's straight sides fell more than a hundred feet before coming to the roof of the transept and nave. From there a body would doubtless bounce off and continue falling the remaining hundred feet or so to the ground.

"All right? Who'll be the one to take the challenge?"

Shaking away the glimpse of such a horrific end, Gerrit stepped forward. The idea had seemed such a lark. He'd remembered Miss Leighton's fright when he'd leaned over the edge, at first just to tease her.

Now, as he stared down at the gloomy abyss, the idea grew on him to test himself. His glance strayed to the darkening sky, the first stars beginning to twinkle. Perhaps, too, it was a direct challenge to whoever held the reins of life and death. How far must he go before his breath would be snuffed out like the thousands of young men buried in anonymous fields across the Continent?

The soldiers around him began to chant their huzzahs. It reminded him of leading a charge into battle. It seemed the louder the roar of their voices, the more they could dismiss their fear.

Giving himself no time to back down, Gerrit took the bottle of champagne offered him and lifted it to his lips. The sharp, fizzy liquid flowed down his throat, strengthening his resolve. When he'd drunk his fill, he flung the bottle over the side, and they heard it smash against the roof tiles far below. Would his body follow, arms and legs flailing like a rag doll?

. With a nod to his lieutenant, he indicated he was ready. Edgar stepped forward and gave him a hand up.

A wave of lightheadedness swept over him. Gerrit remained crouched atop the stone balustrade, his hands gripping the rough surface, and cursed himself a fool. The huzzahs began again. Daring to look at the men on his left, he saw a ring of shiny faces, their cheeks exerted with their shouts. He might die a fool, but not a coward. Resolved to see it through, he took his hands away from their support. With one, he grasped Edgar's.

Slowly Gerrit rose to his feet. Once standing, he waited a few seconds to steady his legs, which felt woozy from the champagne.

He let go of Edgar's hand, knowing he was letting go of his last lifeline. At all accounts, he must not look down. He instead focused on the man who had gone to mark the end of the course. Taking a few deep breaths to clear his head, Gerrit stretched his arms out to keep his balance and took a step forward.

Only nineteen to go.

Easy, he told himself, just one foot in front of the other, just as he had done when scaling the walls of the French fortress at Ciudad Rodrigo. Only then, he hadn't been drunk and his perception had been sharpened by the sense of mission.

The breeze pushed against him and he was aware

once again how easy it would be to topple over. Images danced before his eyes. Battle explosions, lights of other cities, laughter, drinking companions, women, their faces all a blur. He struggled to maintain his focus on the man at the other end. One boot in front of the other. Only ten paces to go.

He breathed out. The image of falling over the side and ending up with his skull split against the roof like the champagne bottle hovered at the edge of his mind.

Five paces to go. Three, two…

"Hurrah! Hurrah!" broke out all around him when he reached the soldier.

"Double if you make it back!"

Repeat the insane feat? As he stood, another shouted, "Fifty quid!"

The men took up the chant. "Fifty quid for a return!"

He chanced a glance at Edgar, who shook his head. The gesture was enough to decide him. Once again Gerrit held out his hand and Edgar was forced to help him turn around on the narrow surface. Gerrit's eyes swept the length of the return journey. One false step and it would be all over. Why should he risk it again?

Because he had nothing to live for, and every reason to die. With a deep breath, he took a step forward.

Fall. Fall. The chant sprang up in his mind. How far could his luck hold? The shouts of the men grew louder even as they seemed to be coming from farther and farther away. He was alone with the sky, the narrow ledge beneath him and a great chasm to one side.

Halfway to his destination, one foot slipped on the stone. For a timeless few seconds, Gerrit flailed his arms about, certain it was his end. But a part of him fought to live. *Dear God, help me!*

Blind panic crowded everything else. Then miraculously he regained his balance. He risked a glance to the side. Not one man spoke. Fear was written on every face. Edgar still held out his arms as if to catch him had he fallen. Gerrit managed a grin and small wave of his hand. The men broke out in wild shouts.

He began to walk again.

Hardly aware of crossing the remaining space, he found himself at the end. The men grabbed him up on their shoulders and marched him around the narrow walkway.

"Our hero! Hawkes! Waterloo's finest!" A champagne cork popped off and Gerrit grabbed the neck of the bottle handed up to him, its white foam spilling over his fingers. He gulped down the liquid, experiencing the heady victory and relief of surviving another battle.

One more bloody massacre of human flesh. Once again, he'd cheated death of its grasp.

When would his luck turn? he asked the night sky again. How many challenges would be too many?

Chapter Seven

Hester arrived at Thistleworth Park on a Friday afternoon with Mrs. Bellows. Her father had been unable to attend the house party but had met with Lady Stanchfield and her husband to ensure that his daughter would be well looked after.

A few miles beyond the village of Sunbury, they came to the lodge and gates of Thistleworth. Hester peered down the long tree-lined drive, seeing no house in sight.

Their hired chaise-and-four rode over the dirt lane for what seemed a long time. She glimpsed lush green pastures sprinkled with sheep and cows through the thin line of trees. At last they turned on to a gravel drive and began to cross a small bridge.

"How delightful. Look at the swans!" Hester craned her neck out the window and pointed. Willow trees draped their fronds into a large pond with a small island at its center.

"My dear, we've arrived."

Hester turned to look out Mrs. Bellows's side and drew in her breath at the sight of the large brick mansion fronted by tall white columns with a pointed turret at each corner. "It looks like a castle from a storybook!"

Mrs. Bellows agreed. "It's magnificent, isn't it? One of the finest Tudor mansions in Middlesex. Oh, it's been renovated extensively in the last century and is quite commodious, so you needn't worry. You are fortunate that Major Hawkes took such a liking to you, dear. His sister is very well positioned."

Hester ignored the older lady's comment. She had heard or seen nothing of the major since their outing to the cathedral, although the next day the viscountess had called on her. Hester had taken a liking to the vivacious lady at once, and hid any disappointment she felt over the major's absence.

A large fountain splashed a cascade of water in the center of the clipped front lawn as their coach drew to a stop in front of a wide set of stairs. A liveried footman came immediately to open the door and lower the step.

Several other carriages stood in the curved drive and confusion reigned over the next several minutes as footmen signaled the guests. They gave their names to one, who signaled them to follow a maid before turning to give instructions about their luggage. Hester didn't see her hostess anywhere.

They followed the maid across a wide courtyard at the top of the steps.

"Is there always so much mayhem at a house party?" she whispered to Mrs. Bellows.

"Oh, dear yes. Lady Stanchfield's are famous since

she married the viscount. Though always an exclusive guest list. Of course, she's known for her hospitality, so there will never be fewer than a dozen people, most likely more. You should see it during the hunting season when the viscount brings his friends along."

Mrs. Bellows continued her description as they followed the maid across a wide room filled with marble statuary and sculpted ceilings, and up a carpeted staircase. Hester said nothing, too interested in looking about her.

Uniformed maids and footmen passed them, their young faces looking harried.

The maid opened a door and they followed her into a room filled with gilt furniture. Soft thick carpet muffled their footsteps.

After an inspection, Mrs. Bellows nodded at the maid. "We'll do very well here."

As the older lady directed the girl to bring them some refreshment, Hester removed her bonnet and wandered to one of the windows. How soon before she could explore the grounds? She unlatched the window and leaned against the stone rail.

She breathed in the scent of mown grass, glad to be alone for a few moments, away from Mrs. Bellows's chattering.

Lush forests edged the wide lawns. In the distance a flock of sheep grazed in one field, while in a grove of cedar trees she glimpsed a stone structure like a temple. Appealing shrubbery-edged walkways invited a person to wander through them.

She turned back into the room and picked up her bonnet. "I shall be back in a bit. I'm going for a walk."

"But, my dear, you can't—you mustn't go alone."

Before she could utter more protests, Hester opened the door and stepped into the hallway. At the look of shock on the older lady's face, Hester almost relented. "I shan't be gone above half an hour. You needn't worry."

"My dear, wait. It's simply not done—"

Leaving the older woman's words floating behind her, Hester closed the door and hurried down the hall, trying to retrace her steps.

It wasn't as difficult as she'd supposed. She simply walked against the trail of footmen, maids and guests making their way upstairs. Finally, she was outside and away from the confusion of the arriving guests. She circled the house and made her way to the gardens she'd seen from her room.

She needed to be alone before facing the other guests that evening. If they were anything like the ones she'd met in London up to now, it would be like braving the first snowstorm in winter, feeling the sting of snowflakes against her exposed cheeks. Only Major Hawkes and his sister had expressed any warmth to a Yankee. As soon as anyone else had perceived she was from the former Colonies, their aristocratic bearing became as cold and hard as one of the thick icicles hanging from the eaves of her house. She needed to remember who she was and what her life was about, she reminded herself.

Raising her face in the warm afternoon sun and closing her eyes, she prayed. *Dear Lord, You are my all in all. You give my life purpose and meaning. I thank You*

*that You've brought me so far and shown me so many
things. Help me remember I am Your vessel. I am here
neither to awe this company of the fashionable world
nor to be awed by them. I am here to reflect Your glory
alone.*

Feeling better, she followed a gravel path which led her
to the small lake she'd spotted from the coach. She entered
the shadowy area under the willows and stood there
watching the swans swim silently by. She sat down on a
stone bench. Her thoughts returned to Major Hawkes.
Despite his offer of friendship, he had not called.

Perhaps he'd proven his friendship by sending his
sister instead. Hester smiled, remembering the hard time
her father had had in the face of Lady Stanchfield's
charm. In the end, he hadn't been able to refuse his permission for Hester to come to Thistleworth. She wondered whether it had been easier for him when he'd
asked pointblank if Major Hawkes would be in attendance and had been told that Gerrit would remain in
London because he found house parties "dull."

Hester sighed. Try as she would, she had not been
able to erase the major from her thoughts. He remained
an enigma to her. He was more dashing and handsome
than any man she'd ever met. The young men of her acquaintance, although not much younger in years,
seemed boys in comparison. Was it his admitted sophis-
tication with women? Or was it his years in combat,
facing death each day?

When in his company, she sometimes felt she was
merely an amusing girl…and yet she sensed he needed
amusing. She had caught glimpses of another man be-

hind the laughing blue eyes, a man who was trying to flee something or forget something.

She would gladly do anything in her power to make him laugh. And she desired with all her heart to be the friend he needed. But it didn't seem she would be given the chance. She bowed her head and began to pray for him, the way she had been praying for him since the night they'd met. Most of all, she prayed for his soul. She sensed he needed to be made whole.

She breathed in deeply, praying for herself as well. *Lord, give me the grace to be only a friend and nothing more.*

That evening, after an interminably long dinner, in which Hester was seated between two of the most empty-headed young gentlemen she'd ever met and across from Mrs. Bellows, she sighed with relief when the ladies at last rose from the table, leaving the gentlemen to their port.

Her relief was short-lived. Once in the drawing room, she found no lady approached her. Those she gave a tentative smile to turned away as if they hadn't seen her. She finally found a vacant chair by Mrs. Bellows. But the woman was already in conversation with the only other elderly lady present. Most of the guests seemed to be married women Lady Stanchfield's age.

At home this would not have presented a problem. The conversation would span generations. Hester would probably be helping to watch their children as the married women talked. Here, not a child was to be seen. She wondered where they were all hidden, and she spent a few minutes amusing herself conjecturing their where-abouts. Maybe they were all bound up in one of the towers at either corner of the great house, fed only bread and water until they turned eighteen and were then pre-sented fully grown to the company.

Or perhaps they had all been kidnapped and were being held for ransom by an evil ogre in some dark cave.

She'd been reading too many of those gothic novels Mrs. Bellows had given her. She glanced at her chap-erone, glad the older woman at least had found a com-panion of similar age. Hester half-listened to their conversation.

"My dear, they say he sleeps with a pair of pistols beside him," the heavily jeweled lady said.

"*Loaded* pistols," Mrs. Bellows added with a signifi-cant nod.

"Think of the danger to poor Annabella. And now that she's enceinte, to the child!"

"It's unthinkable. He may write beautiful poetry but he is mad."

"But Miss Milbanke was even madder to marry him. She was after Lord Byron for years and was not satis-fied till she had landed him."

Another group of ladies talked on the other side of Hester.

"The case has gone to assizes!"

Shocked gazes turned to the speaker, an elegantly dressed woman only a few years older than Hester. "He's brought a crim.con suit against the Earl of Glastonbury. Think of it, my dear, a poor curate accusing an *earl!*"

The women laughed at the absurdity of such a thing.

"What cheek! What does he hope, aside from the scandal? He'll probably lose his living and his wife in the process."

"I'm sure Glastonbury will produce a whole flock of witnesses in his favor. He'll outspend the curate before the month's up."

"Poor fool…but then no one likes to wear the horns…"

More laughter followed.

Hester rearranged her skirts, trying to appear as if she couldn't hear every word. She had no idea what crim.con meant but it certainly appeared to involve gossip of the worst kind.

What would her mother do in her place? Like as not reprove them in the gentle way she had. Hester had seen her do it more than once when her visitors wanted to gossip about one of their acquaintances.

Seeing all the women around her deep in their conversations, Hester finally rose and took a turn about the room. There were certainly enough furnishings and ornaments to claim her attention for a while.

After inspecting every tapestry, painting and inlaid table the length of the room, she came to one of the French doors leading to the rear terrace. The half-opened door invited her. Torchlights had been placed all along the garden paths.

She debated the propriety of exiting into the warm night and following one of the paths. One foot was already out the door when she spotted a couple in the shadows of an arbor. Where had they come from if all the gentlemen were still at the dinner table? The lady's laughter floated up to her before the couple disappeared down one of the lanes. Hester turned away, unwilling to come upon anyone unawares.

She finally arrived at a pianoforte at one end of the room and began flipping the pages of a music book upon it.

Lady Stanchfield came up behind her. "Do you play, my dear?"

"Only passably," she answered immediately, afraid she'd be asked to perform.

"What a pity."

"It's a lovely instrument."

Lady Stanchfield's face brightened. "It's a Stein. From Austria," she added when Hester said nothing.

"It's beautiful," she repeated, stroking the shiny cherry veneer and realizing how much she missed playing.

"Please feel free to indulge us in a song. Don't worry if you're not an expert. Most of the company are too preoccupied to pay you any mind. Lady Devon will probably sing us an aria or Mrs. Summerton play us something later in the evening when the gentlemen rejoin us, but for now we're content to indulge in a good gossip."

Hester hesitated, but as her gaze wandered over the large gathering of brightly gowned and plumed women, she realized Lady Stanchfield was right. No one was paying any attention. What if she played a song she was familiar with?

She sat down and asked the Lord for a song. As her fingers hovered over the keys, she thought about a tune she frequently performed at home. She touched the keys, playing the first bar. Then she began to sing.

O come and dwell in me, Spirit of Power within...

She forgot about the people around her and the hymn became her own prayer for the coming days.

I want the witness, Lord, that all I do is right, according to Thy mind and word, well-pleasing in Thy sight.

At the end of the piece, her hands came to rest and she looked up into the room, as if she had been away and was now reentering it. Everyone was still talking. No one even looked her way. Encouraged by the anonymity, she began to play another hymn. The words of the song refreshed and strengthened her, reminding her of what her life was about. She was transported back home, in the company of other believers and the work they had in common, bringing their witness to those in need.

When she tired, she arose from the instrument. Seeing Mrs. Bellows still in lively conversation and her own seat taken, Hester found, after some searching of the crowded salon, another vacant chair quite removed from her chaperone.

"Really, my dear, this is not a church," a dark-haired woman wearing a very low-cut gown said to her. Before Hester had a chance to reply, she turned back to her companion.

"As I was saying, *un petit soupé* is one thing, but her behavior was flagrant. One must be discreet in these affairs."

"Or at the least, carry things off with a certain *éclat.* Remember Millicent with that cicisbeo of hers, that consumptive-looking young man who seemed more her page boy than a paramour?"

The women tittered behind their fans.

"But when she began increasing a few months later," the lady continued, "he proved to be more able than just someone to fetch and carry for her."

The other woman shook her head. "As I recall the gossip finally drove her to the country to rusticate until the birth."

"She was a fool. It's a wonder her husband didn't send her abroad."

Hester sighed and snapped her own fan open. As she waved it desultorily back and forth in the stuffy room, she asked herself how she was going to survive the next fortnight. She not only had nothing in common with these older women, their morals were completely contrary to hers! If her mother were here, she'd know how to behave, what to say....

The euphoria of the hymns evaporated and Hester felt a wave of homesickness so powerful she had to bow her head against the assault.

Gerrit felt relief once he knew Miss Leighton was safely away at his sister's. His part was done. His sister would take on Miss Leighton's social agenda. Temptation was beyond his reach.

He ignored the little voice which kept whispering questions to his mind in the intervening days. How was the young Yankee getting on? Was she fitting in? With all her duties as hostess, was Delia able to take her under her wing? House parties could be a deathly bore at best...or a time of amorous assignations at worst.

I've never had an amorous friendship. The naive admission circled round and round in his mind at the thought of the worthless coves his sister was likely to invite. Had he sent a lamb to the wolves?

At that moment, Crocker came into the room, his

brow furrowed, his head shaking from side to side as if his horse had lost the Derby.

"What is it?"

Crocker eyed him. "Your pockets are to let."

"Is that all?"

"This time you're done for. The duns are at the door, insisting on some blunt."

Gerrit felt his pockets. "All I have are a few coppers. What happened to my last winnings?"

Crocker snorted. "You mean of a fortnight ago? What'd you think we've been living off in the meantime?"

He looked down at the floor between his feet. It was true, he'd been having a streak of bad luck lately.

"There's only one thing to be done." Crocker's voice sounded like he was condemning Gerrit to the noose. "You'll have to leave town. Lay low for a spell."

Gerrit lifted his head. Leave town? Suddenly his spirits lifted, feeling he'd been given a reprieve. "Pack our things."

"Right away." Relief eased his batman's leathery features. "Where're we going?"

Gerrit stood and headed for the door. "Didn't I mention? My sister's holding a house party at her place in Sunbury."

As soon as he arrived at Delia's, Gerrit went in search of Miss Leighton. Being told by the butler that she was at the shooting range, Gerrit left the house before he'd even greeted his sister, and headed toward the stables. Why this pressing need to see a young lady he'd scarcely met a fortnight ago? Ignoring the question and heeding only the drive within himself, he reached the stables with a rapid pace.

He heard Miss Leighton's laughter before he saw her. He'd recognize that joyous tinkle even after a year, he realized. It filled him with a gladness completely out of proportion with the circumstances.

She stood with her back toward him, a bow poised in her hands, her head tilted to one side as she took aim. Beside her stood a bevy of young men, all intent on the target ahead.

The arrow flew straight and true and landed just at the edge of the bull's-eye circle.

"Bravo, Miss Leighton! Well done!" the gentlemen congratulated her. Gerrit recognized several of the young men. "Yours is the closest," Lord Matthew Astley said. "We declare you the winner!"

Gerrit approached Miss Leighton.

"I see you've found amusement at my sister's house party."

She spun around, her mouth spreading in a smile, which he couldn't help returning. "Major Hawkes!" There was no subterfuge in her look, only gladness. In those seconds, he experienced a depth of pleasure he hadn't felt in a long, long time.

"Hawkes! What are you doing here?" Gerrit ignored Astley as his glance skimmed over Miss Leighton, re-acquainting himself with her appearance. Her tall, slim build was elegant, even in the creased muslin frock. Her straight, light brown hair was pinned carelessly back in a knot, with several wisps swirling around her face. Her bonnet had fallen back and hung only by its ribbons around her neck. Everything was natural and unadorned, yet oddly charming to his jaded eye.

"When did you arrive?"

His gaze returned to her eyes, deep pools of that variegated combination, neither brown nor green. "Just now."

"You've missed a delightful house party."

"Have I?" His glance strayed to another gentleman approaching with a sheaf of arrows in his hand.

"What say another round?" Lord Billingsley suggested.

Delia had succeeded, after all, in rounding up eligible bachelors. The Marquess of Billingsley was considered the catch of the season. Gerrit eyed the tall man with the carefully arranged blond curls, who was worth at least five thousand a year.

"If you wish," Miss Leighton replied, her eyelids demurely lowered to the young lord.

"So, you finally decided to grace your sister's party." Astley held out his hand.

"Yes." He'd known Astley since his school days. "I see you've had a chance to get acquainted with Miss Leighton." He struggled to keep his voice neutral. Where were the other young ladies? What was Miss Leighton doing unaccompanied in this crowd of ravening wolves? Where was Delia? Or, for that matter, Mrs. Bellows? Feeling the blood rise to his face, he wanted to go and demand an explanation of Delia. If he weren't so scared of leaving Miss Leighton alone.

Astley chuckled. "We are pitting our skill against hers. Did you realize she was such a marksman?"

"No, indeed." Gerrit turned his attention to the target in an effort to calm himself.

"Care to try your skill, Gerrit?" Billingsley asked, his regard insolent as always. "After all those Frenchmen you killed, doubtless our skill will prove no competition." His tone suggested otherwise.

Gerrit shrugged. "Why not?"

"Major Hawkes is a crack shot," Astley told Miss Leighton.

Her smile widened. "All the better. We need someone to show us up." Her words seemed genuine and Gerrit felt a slight easing of the tension between his shoulders.

They lined up at the targets. By the time they'd each taken three turns, it was clear Miss Leighton's skill hadn't been exaggerated. Only she, Billingsley and Gerrit remained in the running.

Gerrit wiped the perspiration from his forehead. It was dastardly hot in the full sun of the mid afternoon. The woolen collar of his uniform jacket chafed at his neck. He'd dearly love to jump into his sister's lake and go for a swim.

He took up his last arrow, fit it in his bow and took aim, thinking it would be an easy win. One of his arrows was already within the center circle, the other just on the edge. Miss Leighton's were only slightly farther apart.

As he got ready to let the arrow go, he had a sudden, split-second image of the French cadet. It didn't matter whether it was the shimmering heat against the painted target or the fact that Gerrit was stone-cold sober, that fleeting vision was enough to thwart his aim. His arrow landed in the circle outside the bull's-eye.

"Worse luck," Billingsley said with a thin sneer.

Billingsley took his aim next. Neither of his shots

had been as good as Miss Leighton's or Gerrit's. Nor was his third.

Miss Leighton took her position. She lifted the arrow and fit it against her bow. Not a sound disturbed the warm air around them.

She looked as cool and statuesque as an Indian princess.

The arrow flew through the air and landed smack in the middle of the target.

The men burst into shouts.

"Well done, Miss Leighton. Where did you learn to shoot like that?" Billingsley edged in front of Gerrit. Like a swarm of hungry beasts circling their prey, the other gentlemen ringed around her. The worst part was that the prey seemed wholly unaware of the danger she was in.

"Well, we live surrounded by Indians, you know," she joked. "Besides the fact we've been invaded by you British. We had to learn to defend ourselves." They all laughed heartily.

Astley looked over at Gerrit. "It must have been Major Hawkes's off-day. He's usually an excellent bowman. Maybe you're up to swords today. What of it?" He turned to Miss Leighton. "Hawkes is famous for his swordsmanship. How about it, Gerrit, not too tired after your ride from London?"

Gerrit shook his head. "I'll pass on this occasion." He didn't need another humiliating defeat. He still wasn't over the last sword fight he'd had in London with an irate husband. To top it off, this silly little loss of attention with the bow. Before he knew it, he'd doubt his own skill.

Miss Leighton looked at him in concern. "I'm sorry, Major. We shouldn't have forced you into this target practice. You don't look quite yourself. Are you sure you're all right?"

"I'm fine. You're just a better aim," he said, forcing a careless smile.

Her frown deepened. "Nonsense. I won't believe that until we've had another go. I'll warrant you are tired and just won't own up to it."

Before he could answer her, she turned and went to put her bow away. Gerrit watched Billingsley accompany her. Well, his sister had done as he'd asked and it seemed to be proving a success. He slapped at a gnat hovering around his face, feeling more out of sorts than a short ride from London in the heat would normally warrant.

Gerrit stuck around a while longer, unwilling to give evidence that he might be tired or that the miss had upset him in any way. The group decided to hold a shooting contest. Gerrit bowed out, ignoring the part of him that wanted to show Miss Leighton his prowess with the weapon. The other part, which feared an even greater defeat, declined the invitation.

Once again, they were all astonished at Miss Leighton's skill. This time it was she and Billingsley who were tied at the end. Billingsley beat her when they aimed for a card stuck to a fence post at fifty paces, but it was only by a couple of inches. She nicked the edge of the card, and he blasted it off the post.

Well, he'd had enough. "I'm off," he told the company with a wave, "It's too hot to stand here sweltering."

"Back to the house?" one of the men asked. "You only just got here."

"I'm going to get cleaned up. It was a dusty ride from London."

"You rode Royal?" Miss Leighton asked at once, approaching him.

"Yes." Her velvety skin was more golden than the last time he'd seen her. Any other young lady would be mortified, but Miss Leighton didn't seem aware of her looks. She pushed impatiently at a strand of hair that fell across her cheek. Gerrit stifled the urge to smooth it back for her.

She walked with him to the end of the field.

"You're here all by yourself?" Gerrit asked.

She gave him a puzzled look. "What do you mean?"

He indicated with a motion of his head. "It hasn't escaped your notice you're the only female?"

She laughed in disbelief. "They're a bunch of overgrown schoolboys—just like the ones back home."

"They might behave like overgrown schoolboys at times, but they're full-grown men. Have a care, Miss Leighton."

She gave him an indulgent smile. "You sound like my father."

That was a first for him. Did he sound that old? "Where's Mrs. Bellows?"

"Oh, it's much too warm for her out here. She's probably having a nap."

He nodded. "There are no other young ladies who'd care to accompany you?"

Her lips pursed, but she only shook her head.

"Come, Miss Leighton, surely there must be at least one young lady available."

She put on a bright smile that struck him as false.

"Well, there isn't. You shall see for yourself tonight. I won't keep you from your rest. It was nice to see you again, Major Hawkes."

She turned away from him and returned to the group of men.

He sensed the last question had upset her. He turned away from the laughing crowd, determined to get to the bottom of things.

Chapter Eight

By the time Gerrit descended the stairs in search of
his sister, he felt more like a commander with a plan
of action than a man running away from his creditors.
A bath and change of uniform had done wonders. He
wandered up and down the long terrace overlooking
the lawns and gardens as he waited for the other guests
to congregate, wondering all the while where Miss
Leighton was.

Spying his sister entering the drawing room, he
opened one of its French doors and entered.

"Gerrit! Why didn't you tell me you were coming
today?" She rushed over to him and he bent down for
her kiss.

"I wasn't sure myself until this morning."

She glanced up at him with amusement. "Why the
sudden change of heart?"

"As my batman put it, 'London's getting a bit hot for
you.' He told me I'd better make myself scarce for a while."

"Low in the water, are you?" She patted his cheek. "Well, maybe you can recoup at whist while you are here."

He chuckled. "At a penny a trick? Is Lionel still as strict on placing betting limits as he was the last time I was here?"

She nodded, walking toward the sideboard. "What can I offer you?"

"Nothing for the moment. I shall wait for the others."

She arched a brow over her shoulder. "Abstaining?"

"No, though I'm sure you'll appreciate if I'm on my best behavior. You wouldn't want me upsetting your guests." He strolled over to a japanned cabinet and made a show of examining the books behind the brass-grill-work doors. "By the by, how are all the young men you've invited behaving?"

"Very well, up to now, but I think they respect Lionel's presence. Of course, we never know what they are going to be up to from one day to the next. Did you see your Miss Leighton?"

"I saw Miss Leighton with a throng around her."

Delia smiled. "Yes, she's become quite popular with the Corinthian set. They are dazzled by her athletic prowess. You told me she was an original, but you never said a thing about her being like honey to bees.

"Every young man—and those not so young—is vying for her attention either on the shooting range, at the archery target or on horseback."

He remembered his own less than stellar performance at the archery range and shook his head, amused now at his clumsiness.

"I even heard something about a footrace," she added,

then frowned into her drink. "I don't believe they've attempted boxing."

"I should hope not." He folded his arms and faced his sister. "I noticed Miss Leighton had no chaperone."

Delia considered him. "Since when are you interested in preserving a young lady's reputation?"

He pressed his lips together, irritated at her teasing. "Since I asked you to look after her. I do feel a certain responsibility to her father."

"My heavens, aren't we a stickler for propriety all of a sudden?" She gave him a speculative look. "To what do we owe this sudden about-face?" Apparently expecting no reply, she went on. "I must say she's behaved herself with all decorum. I invited every desirable young gentleman I could claim acquaintance with but…I hope I haven't overplayed my hand."

He frowned. "What is that supposed to mean?"

"It means I hope her tomboyish ways don't make them all forget she's an eligible young lady and not one of the boys."

"She did seem unaware of their admiration." As long as things remained merely friendly. Unfortunately, he didn't trust the lot of them.

At that moment, the topic of their conversation entered the room.

Miss Leighton looked quite transformed. Her hair was neatly dressed in a coronet above her head and encircled with tiny flowers. Her pale blue muslin gown looked light and airy. A silk band of ribbon was tied around her neck as a choker. She wore no jewelry, which he found strange for a wealthy Cit. Indeed, she looked the perfect picture of a young English miss. Gerrit swallowed, regretting having declined that drink.

Delia beckoned with her hand. "Come in, child."

"I didn't want to interrupt anything." When she remained standing, Delia went forward, cutting off Gerrit's own impulse.

"No worry. We're just whiling away the time waiting for the others." Delia smiled. "As a matter of fact, we were discussing you."

Led by his sister, Miss Leighton came to where he stood, asking with a shy smile, "Me? What could there be to discuss about me?"

Gerrit couldn't help smiling back, feeling the tension in him ease. She seemed to have no idea she might catch someone's eye.

"Oh, whether your manly pursuits might not cause the gentlemen to forget you are a young lady," Delia explained.

Miss Leighton looked at his sister as if the notion had never occurred to her. "I must admit I hope that to be the case."

Now it was Delia's turn to look surprised. "Why ever so?"

"It makes things so much simpler."

At Delia's look of inquiry, Miss Leighton explained, "It prevents any foolish *tendres* from developing. I wouldn't want to hurt anyone's feelings."

Gerrit couldn't help laughing, the remaining tension easing from him. Miss Leighton might be an innocent, but she had a practical bent to her nature. Poor Billingsley…

"But, my dear, I thought you were here precisely to

receive such attentions. Don't any of the young gentlemen appeal to you as more than just sporting partners?" Delia looked so crestfallen, Gerrit had to intervene.

"Maybe your selection of youngbloods leaves something wanting."

Delia glared at him. "Nonsense. The finest crop of young gentlemen of impeccable ton are here at my house party."

Hester turned to her immediately. "I'm sorry, I didn't mean to imply I don't like any of the gentlemen."

Delia brightened. "So there *is* someone who's caught your eye!"

"Not at all. I meant they are all very nice."

"I think we should come up with another topic of conversation," Gerrit suggested.

Miss Leighton bestowed on him a grateful smile. It gave him a curious feeling, as if he were her ally, and he remembered his words to her on top of St. Paul's about being friends.

"I hope you're recovered from your journey." He read genuine solicitude in her hazel eyes.

"You make it sound as if I'd crossed the Atlantic. It was a mere two hours' ride from London."

"Still, in this heat, that can take a toll," Delia said before turning her attention back to Miss Leighton. "You look fetching. What will you have, lambkin?"

"Just some barley water if you have any."

"Certainly." She signaled to the footman who had entered the drawing room with a tray laden with glasses. She turned to Gerrit with an innocent look. "Will you also partake of some barley water?"

He grinned at her. "Barley water sounds just the thing." If nothing else, he must keep his wits about him this evening.

With a shake of her head, she gave their orders to the footman. "You and Miss Leighton put us all to shame."

Soon other guests began arriving. Within moments, Miss Leighton had a bevy of young swells around her. Gerrit smothered his irritation, then left her and sauntered about the room. He was no schoolboy to be part of a young lady's entourage.

He stopped to address an acquaintance or two. After a while, he noticed that most of the women were Delia's age and married. When he paused a moment by his sister, he remarked on this. "All your old school friends seem to be here."

"Yes, many are, why?"

"You didn't think to invite some ladies Miss Leighton's age?"

"Oh, that. Yes, I did think about it, but decided against it."

He waited, eyebrow cocked, for an explanation.

"You said to invite lots of eligible young men. I didn't want to bring in a bunch of debs as competition. I wanted to keep the field clear for your protégée."

His gaze wandered over to Miss Leighton. Billingsley certainly seemed attentive. "You didn't think she'd stand up to the competition?"

Delia shrugged. "Who's to say? But knowing how the game is played, why stack the odds against oneself? Trust me, I have your Miss Leighton's best interests at heart."

"I wish you wouldn't keep referring to her as 'mine.'"

He didn't know why it bothered him, except that he didn't like to claim possession to anything these days. He was not to be trusted, least of all with a living soul.

"As you wish."

He didn't like the way she continued to eye him. "When are we eating anyway?" he growled. "I'm famished."

She signaled to the butler, then turned back to Gerrit. "Let me find Lionel, so we may begin assembling for dinner. He's probably holed up in the library with some old crony, drat the man."

Gerrit lounged against a wall, awaiting instructions, knowing he'd be one of the last in the procession. Curious to see who was to accompany Miss Leighton, he turned to look for her.

One of the many young bucks—they were indistinguishable to Gerrit with their golden locks or dark tresses combed back à la Brummell—had lined up with her. He shoved a hand through his own straight hair, disgusted with himself for being put out. He was too old and far too world weary to let himself be rattled by the mating game as it was played out in the ton.

He was paired with a buxom dowager, someone's widowed mother. Was Delia afraid he'd seduce anyone under sixty?

Gerrit hid a yawn several times throughout dinner, wondering if he would be able to endure the next few days. He was seated in between the wheezing dowager on one side and an older gentleman, who was only interested in telling him how many gamecocks he had landed in the day's hunt.

The elderly matron had no conversation beyond how beastly hot the weather was behaving and could he please pass her plate down to the waiter to get her whatever dish was at the other end of the table.

His glance strayed to Miss Leighton for about the hundredth time that evening. She was seated farther up the long table. Obviously her dowry made up for any lack in rank. Mrs. Bellows had whispered loudly to him that it was twenty thousand.

Twenty thousand should buy her a proper husband with no one inquiring too closely after her pedigree. His sister had placed her between Billingsley and another young gentleman. The two men seemed to spend a good amount of time keeping her amused. Billingsley's gaze straying to her neckline. Gerrit strained his memory trying to remember what he knew of the fellow. Not much more than an indifferent scholar and a good athlete. An older fellow—was that Georgie Hanscom? looking awfully jowly—sat across from Miss Leighton, eating heartily and joining in their lively conversation.

Gerrit eased back in his chair. Suddenly balancing on the balustrade of St. Paul's dome seemed preferable to sitting out the rest of this dinner. He'd have to get Delia to seat him in more interesting company tomorrow. Would her suspicions be raised if he requested Miss Leighton as a seating partner?

When the ladies excused themselves and the gentlemen were left with their port, Gerrit wondered if the conversation would take a turn for the better.

"Tell us about Waterloo." Georgie Hanscom leaned his ruddy face close to Gerrit as he poured himself a tumbler full of cognac. "Is it true they were looting the corpses on the field as soon as the battle was over?" He took a generous swallow of the brandy and smacked his lips.

Gerrit eyed the man's fleshy lips still moist from the cognac, remembering too late this was why he avoided these social circles and stuck to the company of fellow officers at the taverns. "I heard something to that effect."

"Of course it's true!" A man farther down banged his tumbler on the damask cloth. "Haven't I got a saber from a French officer to prove it?"

"They were offering soldiers' fingers preserved in vinegar when I was over in Brussels," Billingsley drawled, leaning back in his chair.

Gerrit looked down at his drink, pondering the merits of dashing it in his face. Waste of good cognac, he decided.

The man with the saber continued, his face growing red with enthusiasm. "I was in Brussels the night before the battle. We knew something was up when the duke had to rush out in mid-ball. You should have seen the panic in the city," he chortled. "Everyone on every sort of vehicle from chaise-and-four to farm cart, piled with belongings, headed north. Ladies riding amidst squawking fowl, crying babes. It was a sight."

Georgie wiped the perspiration off his forehead with a crumple linen napkin. "Do y'think Boney's down for good this time?"

Gerrit simply stared at him.

Billingsley swirled the cognac in his glass, "How long were you in the war, Hawkes?"

Gerrit eyed him, measuring his intent. "Since I enlisted five years ago."

Georgie waved a plump beringed hand in front of Gerrit. "Tell me, Hawkes, how were the ladies in Spain? See your red coat and say *'Si, señor'* every time?" He giggled, a high, girlish sound, a lascivious sheen filming his bulging eyes.

"And the French demoiselles, *Oh là, là!*" The overfed young man laughed at his rendition of the French.

Gerrit glanced down to the head of the table where Delia's husband and his cronies sat drinking and talking hunting in lower tones. His palms felt clammy and a thundering had begun to beat in his ears. He felt only an inch away from grabbing Georgie by his shiny jowls and squeezing until he began to feel the fear of real combat.

To what purpose? To give these toadies more fodder for the gossip mill? *Hawkes has gone over the edge.* He could hear their snide remarks. *Poor old duffer. It was the war, you know.*

He looked down at his hands and slowed his breathing, trying to focus on the words around him. The talk became bawdier as the men got deeper into their cups. From discussing the French women, they moved on to the ladies of the house party. Gerrit remained silent, telling himself he'd been no different from these baby-faced young men sweating in their ornate waistcoats and high collars before he'd left for the Peninsula. Now all he saw were the similar-looking young men he'd left mutilated and rotting in the mud on the battlefield.

It had never affected him during all those campaigns prior to Waterloo. Perhaps it had been the relief of surviving yet another battle, or the driving need to turn the tide of war and set Spain free of Napoleon. Or, had it merely been the oblivion of heavy drinking and wenching between battles? Until Waterloo.

"Now, there's a particularly fine morsel..." He caught the words of another young dandy. "She's young and as innocent as a babe, I'll wager."

"Miss Leighton—*l'enfante sauvage* from America," another offered with a laugh.

Gerrit's heartbeat began to thud like a dull kettledrum.

Billingsley swished his glass at them and drawled, "I'll wager you twenty guineas I'll be the first to steal a kiss from her."

Gerrit clenched his fingers around his glass. Easy, he told himself. By tomorrow they'll have forgotten this folly.

Astley leaned forward. "I'll stand you twenty it won't be done for a week." All at once, their end of the table erupted as everyone tried to place a bet.

The man boasting the French saber thumped his glass on the table. "A hundred quid you can't get below the neck."

Before he could do anything foolhardy, Gerrit shoved back his chair and stood. Without a word he headed for the door.

"Hey, Hawkes, where're you off to? Aren't you going to wager?" Ignoring their calls, he left the room.

How many times in the past hadn't he joined in similar crude bets? Why then did he feel an overwhelming urge to attack anyone who so much as touched Miss Leighton? Why did she matter so much?

Was it merely because he was responsible for her being here and he didn't want to see anything untoward happen to her? Or did he think he could in some way atone for his unforgivable behavior in the past with Lady Gillian? He stopped, the thought having come unbidden.

The perspiration beaded his forehead. The affair with Lady Gillian was in the past. Why think of it now?

He resumed his walk, striding rapidly down the corridor toward the drawing room. He could hear the muffled sounds of women's voices through the doors and he slowed, debating whether to enter. The door opened at that moment and Miss Leighton herself came out. She turned from closing it behind her and started when she saw him.

"Major Hawkes, I didn't see you there."

He stood looking at her, uncertainty paralyzing him. The men's words returned to him, and he could feel the fury return at the thought of their pale, manicured hands touching her anywhere.

Her brow furrowed. "Is something amiss?"

He relaxed his features with an effort. "Why do you say that?"

"I don't know. You are looking at me so strangely…" She smiled. "As if you'd never seen me before."

He attempted to return the smile. "Perhaps I haven't, not like this, at an English house party. You're very far from home, are you not?"

"Yes, but I'm becoming accustomed to it somewhat." She peered at him, her dark eyes clouded with doubt. "Are you sure nothing is the matter?"

"Absolutely nothing. I was just debating whether to brave the lion's den and enter the drawing room before the other gentlemen left the dining room."

She smiled in relief. "Then, I'm glad I ran into you. I was just going up."

He frowned. "So early?"

She looked away from him. "Yes, I usually leave before the gentlemen return."

Had any of those scoundrels already—"Why?"

His sharp tone drew her attention back. "Oh…they're always the worse for drink."

Without having intended to, he said, "It's a bit stuffy in here. Would you care to take a turn on the terrace before you retire for the evening?"

When she hesitated, he added, "I can assure you I'm sober."

An immediate smile touched her lips. "It's not that. I trust you."

The simple words sent a spear through him and he wanted to shake some sense into her. "Are you sure you can?"

"Of course. We're friends, remember? Come, let's walk. It's been a while since I saw you."

She put her hand through his arm and he automatically covered it with his, then drew it away rapidly as he realized what he'd done. Miss Leighton's words continued to reverberate through his mind. *I trust you.* It came to him then how much he wanted to be worthy of that trust. He struggled to regain a light tone. "How do you find the English house party?" he asked.

She sighed. "Entertaining for the most part."

He pondered the significance of that sigh as he held one of the doors open for her. "You haven't been bothered by any of the gentlemen, have you?" He examined her face in the semidarkness of the torch-lit terrace.

"Oh, no. They're perfect gentlemen. Of course, I would never be so foolish as to find myself alone with one on a dark terrace like this," she added with an impish smile.

He felt captivated by that smile. "How am I different?" he managed, a pulse thudding in his temple and his mouth dry.

"You said it yourself. We're friends. Friends respect each other and are not a danger to each other."

He nodded, unable to formulate any reply to her statement, when all he wanted to do was take her in his arms. But her words stopped him more securely than a dozen chaperones.

"How was London?" she asked as they walked the length of the stone terrace.

He kept a space between them and endeavored to follow the change of topic. "Hot. Deserted."

"I trust you'll find more enjoyment here in the country."

"I see you've become popular with the young dandies but I don't see many young ladies. Have you missed company your age?"

"A little. I've kept quite busy though, and I write to my own sisters most every day describing the life here, so that makes me feel as if I'm not so far away from them. They've been very good about writing to me, too."

He stopped and looked out at the darkened gardens, torches outlining the paths. "I noticed a few of the gentlemen being quite attentive to you…Astley…Billingsley…"

She laughed. "The only reason the gentlemen keep

company with me is because I enjoy doing what they enjoy doing, nothing more."

Was she truly oblivious to the men's attraction? "Are you sure it's only that?"

"Well, since I am the only unmarried lady under the age of thirty, there is that attraction as well, I suppose." Humor laced her words. "But never fear for my virtue, dear sir. Beneath all their funning, they are quite a proud group of young gentlemen. They'd have to be in rather desperate straits to lower themselves to marrying a woman whose father is in trade."

He winced at the truth of her words, realizing he'd harbored the same prejudices himself. Since when had he gone from thinking her a cit to thinking he was unworthy of her? "You don't sound too broken up about it."

She laughed. "Glad is probably more accurate a description."

He raised an eyebrow.

"I'd hate to think I was breaking anyone's heart if I found myself having to turn him down."

Relief filled him like a warm posset. He turned to lean against the balustrade. "You are a most singular young lady. Most would be sending every sort of lure to snare one of the gentlemen around the dining table tonight."

"In that case, a visit to a house party entails some risk to a young gentleman of fortune," she said in amusement.

"Untold risk," he agreed. "But you would be in some danger yourself. I'm sure quite a few would be swayed by your twenty thousand and not mind at all being captured."

"Twenty thousand. Goodness. Who told you that?"

"Mrs. Bellows."

She shook her head. "I should have known."

"Don't worry. Everyone's worth is always discussed on the Marriage Mart."

"And how much are you worth?"

"Not only are my assets nil, but I am actually a liability to any young lady aspiring to marriage."

"That must keep you safe from any dangerous lures."

He chuckled. "That's one way to look at it. My sister would look at it as an almost insurmountable obstacle for securing a good match for me."

"Is she so keen on your being married?"

"Oh, yes. Since I returned from Belgium, she considers finding me a suitable wife one of her moral obligations."

"In that case I am all the more grateful that she's taken the trouble to introduce me to society."

"Oh, she likes nothing better than to have a few projects going at the same time. This time last year she was busy fixing up one of my elder brothers with his wife, as well as a cousin of ours."

"Was she successful?"

He nodded. "Oh, yes. My clergy brother was hooked up with a very proper young lady worth five thousand. She'll make an admirable curate's wife. And my cousin was matched with a widower with two children. At eight-and-twenty she was in danger of being left on the shelf, and he was sorely in need of a mother for his babes, so the two should suit."

"It sounds as if you need to have a good eye for a person's financial needs and situation in life to make a good matchmaker here in England."

He looked down at her with an indulgent smile, glad for the renewal of the camaraderie he had experienced with her in London. He felt on much safer ground. "I hope you don't let the prospects tempt you. I assure you the results can be disastrous. My sister's successes were pure luck."

"Oh, never fear. I would never want to play match-maker with someone."

"How are matches made in America?" he asked, curious about the world she came from.

"Mainly, people just fall in love."

He smiled. "How deucedly simple."

She laughed. "It would appear rather simple, wouldn't it?"

"No concerns over whether a man can provide adequately for his wife, or whether a woman's lack of fortune will weigh a man down?"

"Well, as there is work for any able-bodied man, and a woman as his helpmate provides a home for him, it works out quite advantageously for both."

"No idle gentlemen there?"

"I have never seen one."

He gazed up at the mansion before him. "Tell me, are your parties in Maine anything like this?"

She smiled in the semidarkness. "Nothing like this."

"What would you be doing this evening in Bangor?"

"Let's see. Some young people might drop by." She folded her hands on the rail. "Both gentlemen and ladies. We'd roast popcorn over the fire, depending on the time of the year. We'd play music and sing. In summer I'd walk to singing class held once a week. Those are always fun. If the party were at my house, we might open up some room and have a little dancing. Papa and Mama would bring out refreshments."

He listened to her, soothed by her description of a land where everything sounded so wholesome and simple.

"Sometimes we tell stories," she continued. "I love hearing Papa's stories of when he was a young man in England. He was quite poor, you know."

"I surmised something of the sort."

"Why did you become a soldier?"

He raised an eyebrow. "That's a change of topic."

"You don't like talking about yourself, do you?"

He shrugged. "What's to talk about? As a younger son, there were only two or three avenues open to me—the military, the cloth or the law. My oldest brother inherits my parents' estate, you see. My next older brother chose the church and he's found a living up in Nottinghamshire. That left only two roads for me. Having no head nor patience for the law, I chose the more active career."

"You certainly have made a successful soldier."

He looked at her steadily. "I've been trained to kill people. It's my only skill."

She drew in her breath, and he could tell he had shocked her with the terse words. To lighten the mood, he added, "By this afternoon's performance, I wouldn't be surprised if you doubted even that."

"Oh, I'm sure you're very good at what you do. You wouldn't have been awarded those medals nor reached your rank if you weren't."

He looked up at the dark sky. "Oh, everything in England can be bought."

She shook her head at him. "There you go again. You refuse to take credit for any good in you."

"If there *is* any good in me, I haven't found it yet."

He turned to her and found her staring at him, a look of sadness in her eyes.

He gave an abrupt laugh. "Don't pity me, sweet Miss Leighton. I'm not worthy of even that."

Giving her no chance to reply, he shoved himself off the balustrade. "Come, let me take you back inside. The night's grown chilly."

Why had he told her those things? The next thing he knew, she'd have him opening up completely, letting her see how vile he really was.

Hester wondered what kept Major Hawkes at his sister's house party. His laconic attitude, his careless stance all denoted boredom. He participated in the games—horse races, shooting and all kinds of feats of prowess, and excelled at them all, convincing her he had indeed been tired that first afternoon. She was certain he would have won the archery competition otherwise. But though he was in the thick of things, he gave the impression of being on the fringes of the company.

Hester cheered him on whenever she herself did not participate. She was glad Mrs. Bellows knew little of her athletic activities. With the weather so hot Mrs. Bellows rarely ventured out, for which Hester was ever thankful.

She couldn't forget their conversation the first evening on the terrace. She wanted to reach the man who'd revealed a quiet desperation beneath the humorous facade, but with the same dexterity he displayed on the playing field, he deflected any further attempts she made. She noticed he never talked of the war, no matter how often it came up in the conversation around them.

She looked forward at each day's end to those few moments when he met her outside the drawing room as she was about to retire. As he had the first evening after his arrival, sometimes he invited her for a stroll upon the terrace. Other evenings he merely walked her to her room and bid her a brief goodnight.

As she had the first evening, she always sensed he'd been waiting for her when she exited the drawing room, but she was afraid to ask, lest by her question she break the tenuous connection they had in those few moments alone. For she felt the connection was indeed fragile. Perhaps because the major had no romantic inclinations toward her, Hester thought his reasons for seeking her company might be more complicated.

Hester hadn't told a soul about these brief interludes, except in her letters to her mother, where she'd asked her to pray for the major. She instinctively knew few would understand. They would construe their friendship as romantic and warn her of the dangers, as Mrs. Bellows had the night of the dance.

Hester sensed the major needed something deeper from her and she was content to wait until it should be revealed.

Chapter Nine

A few days after Major Hawkes's arrival, Lady Stanchfield organized an excursion to a nearby abbey. Some of the company rode on horseback; others, especially the women, went by carriage. Because Mrs. Bellows was to venture forth on this outing, Hester had to plead with her to allow her to go with those riding on horseback.

"I'm used to riding long distances. I can't bear the thought of being crowded in a stuffy carriage."

"It's not done, a young lady without her chaperone."

"But it's a whole party. There will be plenty of ladies with me."

"But they are all married ladies."

"They can be my chaperones," Hester pointed out.

"You won't be able to wear one of your pretty frocks, but must don a habit. You'll get there all mussed and hot."

Hester suppressed a groan. She couldn't understand these British conventions. "I shall be more hot and uncomfortable if am confined in a closed carriage."

"But it's so unseemly, cantering about when you can sit demurely in a carriage."

Finally, she enlisted Lady Stanchfield's help to convince Mrs. Bellows to allow her to ride.

It took about an hour to assemble the whole company by late morning. Hester stifled her impatience at the women who needed to fetch this and that. She wished the horseback riders could go ahead of the carriages, but Lady Stanchfield was the organizer of the event and would have no one start before the whole group was ready to move.

Hester glanced back over her shoulder. Major Hawkes was in the rear on his beautiful mount, Royal. Once again she had the sense that he was there as an observer or watchman, and not a participant. His glance crossed hers and he acknowledged her with a brief touch of his fingers to the brim of his hat.

He was so handsome in his uniform. He was the only soldier present. The other men seemed soft in comparison to him.

"Miss Leighton, how glad I am that you chose to ride horseback." Lord Billingsley brought his mount up alongside hers.

She forced herself to smile. Although he was pleasant enough, she couldn't help feeling hemmed in whenever he was about. He seemed to appear constantly at her side. She sometimes wondered if that was the reason Major Hawkes rarely approached. Did he think Lord Billingsley was courting her?

She dearly hoped not. Nothing could be further from the truth. She'd never received a proposal of marriage and wondered how one turned a proposal down gracefully.

"It's too beautiful a day to be in a carriage, even an open one," she replied to him now.

"Too true. Tell me, Miss Leighton, have you ever been to an abbey before?"

"No, we have no abbeys in America."

"You're in for a treat. This one is a veritable ruin, sure to please any young lady addicted to gothic novels. You'll be able to imagine every ghostly terror taking place in such a place after dark."

"Since I am not addicted to gothic novels, I doubt the abbey shall have any such effect upon me. Excuse me, Lord Billingsley, but I must address myself to Lady Stanchfield." With those words, she nudged her horse toward the front of the line of riders where she saw Major Hawkes's sister.

When they arrived at the ruins an hour later, the party broke up into smaller groups to wander about the towering stone structure and its surrounding grounds.

"This is truly the picturesque," one of the ladies in Hester's group exclaimed, stopping before an arched window. They admired the splendid view through it of sloping green lawns and scattered forests.

"I would say rather it is the sublime," one of the gentlemen countered.

"Oh no, absolutely not." She motioned with her hand. "Note the wild abandon of the greenery against the sky. I insist, it is nothing but the picturesque."

"Nay, my lady, the majestic effect of the sky and trees denotes the sublime."

The two continued to debate the merits of the scenery a while longer. Hester stopped listening to them.

"And what do you think, Miss Leighton? The picturesque or the sublime?" Major Hawkes's low voice asked behind her.

She turned with a smile of delight. "I haven't a clue."

Lord Billingsley was quick to edify her. "The picturesque refers to the resemblance of a landscape to a painted scene. The sublime to the transcendent greatness of the scene. I myself would vote for the picturesque, wouldn't you say, Hawkes?"

The major didn't answer but cocked an eyebrow at Hester, who shrugged. "As for myself, I couldn't tell you. We don't call landscapes either picturesque or sublime in Maine. They are all quite magnificent without any need of labels."

"Are they perhaps all wild and savage?" Billingsley inquired. "I confess I am unfamiliar with that geographical area."

She raised her head toward the bright blue sky and puffy white clouds moving across it, trying to describe what was so familiar and yet so far from her now.

"We have mountains and forests, rivers and the bluest lakes you can imagine. The ocean, too, but that is a little farther away." She breathed deeply, remembering the scent of pine and fir. "The trees soar as high as spires to the sky."

"Are they anything like the forests you see before you?" Billingsley swept his arm over the panorama.

She followed his gesture, comparing the lush, plump curve of trees in the hazy distance. "No, not at all alike. Our forests seem never ending. The trees cover the mountains, and if you are at a high point, you can see miles and miles of trees like waves upon the ocean."

She turned to find Major Hawkes observing her. "It sounds truly sublime, indeed," he said softly.

She nodded. "I suppose it is. The way God created it and little touched by man. That is changing, however. Men are constantly going into that forest and cutting down the tallest trees and transporting them over the lakes and rivers and shipping them across the ocean to places like England."

"Come along everyone," Lady Stanchfield called to them. "The servants have laid out a luncheon beneath the trees."

Hester walked with Lord Billingsley on one side and Major Hawkes on the other. Soon some other gentlemen joined them and they sat together on a rug. Hester had never attended such a luxurious picnic. Waiters bent down with silver trays to offer her delectable sandwiches, their crusts trimmed off; golden pastries, their edges perfectly crimped; and fruit tarts, their colors vibrant against the pale china.

Her father could probably buy all these luxuries ten times over, and yet it would never occur to her family to put on such a display.

After the sumptuous meal, they walked some more. Hester swallowed a sense of disappointment when Major Hawkes wandered off by himself. A short while later, she saw him walking with one of the older women, and she felt a moment's twinge, thinking how sophisticated this titled lady from London undoubtedly was. She would surely know how to distinguish the sublime from the merely picturesque. She would know how to date this ancient ruin looming over them.

Hester was left to evade Lord Billingsley. She jumped at the chance when a party of young gentlemen proposed hiking to a nearby creek. They ended up taking off their shoes and stockings and wading in the cool running water.

"Let's see who can cross the rapids without falling in," one of the men proposed.

Hester joined those attempting the crossing, while the rest lined the creek bank, shouting their encouragement.

Hester made it halfway across with no problem. As she hesitated a few seconds, looking for a foothold, she glanced back to the bank. Major Hawkes, the lady at his side, stood high on a ridge by the abbey, watching them. How juvenile she must appear to them.

Well, she hadn't come here to try and hook Major Hawkes, so she might as well enjoy the day, she chided herself. She gave them a quick wave before turning her attention back to the stones.

There was a shout ahead of her as one man lost his foothold and fell in. Uproarious laughter greeted his mishap.

"You clodpole!" shouted Billingsley.

Soon more had fallen in and they began to splash those who were still dry. By the time Hester made it back to the bank, she was more than a little damp, but she was laughing as hard as the rest. The water felt refreshing on such a warm day and she knew her habit would soon dry in the sun. She looked around for the major, but he was no longer to be seen. She stifled the sense of regret, realizing she mustn't let foolish notions get the better of her.

* * *

Gerrit felt worn out. For days, he'd been doing his best to keep his eye on Miss Leighton, while trying to keep his vigilance from becoming apparent to anyone else, least of all Miss Leighton herself. He'd observed her in all kinds of antics a respectable young English miss would never dream of—from climbing trees to galloping astride—but through it all, she retained an innocence he knew wasn't feigned. He could see how the other men thought otherwise, however, and he knew it was only a matter of time before one of them crossed the bounds of propriety.

Although Billingsley no longer referred to his wager, Gerrit knew it wasn't forgotten by him or any of the other gentlemen. He knew enough about how these things worked to know Billingsley must act soon before the others began ribbing him for his failure.

But keeping Miss Leighton constantly in sight without hanging around her like one of her puppies, was wearing work. The most crucial times came in the evenings. If Gerrit had been in his lordship's shoes, that would be when he'd make his move, after dark when Miss Leighton made her solitary way up to her room.

But it was like playing ring-a-rosy, trying to anticipate when she'd retire. Gerrit drank little, needing to keep a cool head about his shoulders.

The worst part was the temptation to prolong his evening strolls with her. He fought this urge, knowing to give in would be dangerous. The last thing he desired was to join the ranks of Miss Leighton's admirers, much less have her develop a fondness for him. Thus he permitted himself only a short stroll on the most pleasant evenings and kept her busy with questions about her own life in America, offering little about himself.

Was his reticence out of pride or fear? He preferred not to analyze it, knowing only he didn't want Miss Leighton discovering the real Gerrit Hawkes.

Gerrit surveyed the guests around him. It seemed everyone had turned out to watch the footrace.

The young gentlemen were milling about in a group near the starting line. Among them stood Miss Leighton. After his first moment of shock, seeing her in a pair of men's breeches, he'd found it hard not to smile. From a distance she looked like a slim lad, until she turned and he saw the braid down her back, reaching almost to her hips.

"Gerrit, why aren't you here amongst us? Not scared of being beaten, are you?" Astley called out.

"I wanted to give you a sporting chance," he called back.

Amidst their shouts of derision, he only smiled and waved.

His sister came up to him. "Seriously, Gerrit, why aren't you running? I know you could easily beat any of them out there."

"I have no inclination to be part of a stampede."

"I suppose you have nothing to prove to any of the company here?"

"You suppose correctly."

"Did you see Miss Leighton?" she asked with a smile, directing her gaze to the young woman. "I don't know how she gets away with such scandalous behavior.

I know of no other young lady of the ton who could undertake the activities she has and come out seeming even more pure and innocent than any of us."

"Perhaps because she is."

"You know, I do believe you're right." She shook her head, her tone indulgent. "When she told me she'd secured a pair of breeches to run in, I vow I was quite envious!"

"I think they become her."

Delia laughed. "I find I quite agree with you. Maybe she'll set a fashion." She turned away from him, her canary-yellow parasol twirling on her shoulder.

In truth, Gerrit had decided at the last minute not to race, because he'd much rather watch Miss Leighton run. He was secretly hoping she'd win and show up all those overweening dandies who fancied themselves Corinthians.

Delia's husband directed the men to their places. At his nod, the butler fired a pistol into the air.

The runners were off. It was then Gerrit noticed Miss Leighton ran barefoot. She was swift, her long legs eating up the turf. She reminded him of a young colt running free. Her braid flew out behind her, her eyes narrowed in concentration, her hands balled into fists.

She quickly left the majority of men behind. The course was one-hundred yards and the only contest was between her, Astley and Billingsley. But Miss Leighton beat them both, seeming to take a final leap across the finishing ribbon a hair ahead of Astley.

Gerrit smiled, seeing the grim look on Billingsley's face.

After that there were more races, one of which had

to be run backwards. The crowd roared with laughter as the contestants kept falling atop each other.

Delia presented the winners with ivy crowns the women had woven the day before.

As the crowd thinned out, individuals squaring their bets, Gerrit lingered at the edge of the lawn. Spotting Miss Leighton alone, he sauntered over to her. For once Billingsley wasn't hovering. Probably gone off to sulk.

"Congratulations," he told her when he reached her.

She smiled up at him. He felt captivated by her smile, the way he did each time. It reminded him of a time in his boyhood when he still knew how to take delight in things.

"Oh, it was really no contest. *You* didn't participate."

He shrugged. "What makes you think I could beat anyone here?"

"You're taller than the rest, for one. That and the fact that you're used to marching for miles. You appear very fit, major."

"Not as fit as I once was." Too much debauchery over too many nights, he refrained from adding.

"Why don't we determine the real outcome now?"

"The real outcome?"

"I mean, let's race now." She glanced around. "Everyone's gone."

"You mean you against me?" What was her aim?

She nodded. "That's right."

"You won your race fairly and squarely. You needn't pit your skills against mine."

"I'd like to. I like to run."

"You silly child."

"Hardly that." She half-turned from him. "Well, if

you are afraid I'd be a poor loser and cry and carry on like some of the young gentlemen today…"

He laughed. "You noticed. I don't think Lord Billingsley was too pleased at being shown up by a young lady."

She joined in his laughter. "He'll get over it by dinnertime, I imagine. So you'll run one race with me?" Her look was so eager, he didn't have the heart to refuse.

"Very well, if it will make you happy."

"Come on. Here's the starting line. Let's do the first race."

"If we must." As he spoke, he removed his jacket and laid it carefully on the grass. He debated removing his boots, but then shook his head at his own folly. Did it really matter how he ran? He wasn't about to compete with a child.

Before he knew what she was about, she'd put two fingers to her lips and issued a shrill whistle. One of the stable boys turned back from where he was heading toward the stables. At his look, she nodded and waved him over. When he arrived, she told him, "Now, Tom, I want you to say, 'On your mark,' then 'go' when you see us lined up and ready, just like Lord Stanchfield did earlier. Think you can do that?"

"Yes, miss, 'course I can."

"That's wonderful." She gave the lad a smile that would warm any man's heart, then turned to join Gerrit at the imaginary starting line.

The moment the boy shouted "Go!" the thrill of the race took over and Gerrit ran his hardest. It was only when it was over that he realized he'd come in before Miss Leighton.

"There, didn't I tell you? You beat me by a good two yards. Congratulations." She extended her hand to him, her smile as pleased as if she had won the race herself.

As he took her slim hand in his, his gaze traveled the length of her. Her braid was disheveled, her face was overheated and she positively glowed. Her lithe, erect stance made the rough garments gain a strange appeal. Gerrit swallowed, realizing he'd never have given her boyish figure a second glance in the past. What was it about her that suddenly gave him such a jolt of awareness? There was something about her spirit—its freedom, its absolute lack of artifice—that enthralled him.

"You were just tired from your earlier exertions," he said, hardly aware of what he was saying.

"Fiddlesticks. If you don't believe me, we can race again tomorrow."

He pulled her braid and laughed. "Very well. I won, and we'll have done with it. Satisfied?"

She agreed and bent down to pick up his jacket.

He took it from her and the two started walking across the lawn together.

"Soon, my brother, Jamie, will beat me the way you did. I'm so used to racing ahead of him, but I've heard he's shot up in stature during the time I've been away."

He heard the affection in her voice. "Do you miss him much?"

"Oh, terribly. I miss all my family. But I shall go back soon."

He felt a sudden tremor. What would it be like when she was gone—and he'd never see her again? He shook aside the thought. She was just another—albeit somewhat more original—young lady whose memory would be effaced by next season's crop, each group disappearing into the anonymity of matrimony.

That evening, Gerrit was late leaving the dinner table. One of the young men had cornered him with a long discussion of beating the odds at faro. When he finally managed to break away, he glanced at his watch. He hoped Miss Leighton had waited for him.

As he left the dining room, a footman handed him a note. He broke it open and glanced at the signature. Miss Leighton's. He scanned the contents. It said only that she was fatigued "from the races" and had already retired to her room.

Gerrit had never seen her handwriting, so he had no idea if she'd really penned the note, but he smelled a rat. He was rereading the note as he walked toward the drawing room, but now he turned and headed back to the dining room.

Billingsley was gone. He couldn't remember when he'd seen him last at the table.

Gerrit went back into the corridor, his anger rising at the man's audacity. He checked his usual meeting spot, but Miss Leighton was not there. He hesitated then headed out to the terrace to peer into the drawing room to see if Miss Leighton had indeed already left. He daren't risk being delayed by anyone if he entered the drawing room himself.

When he'd didn't see her with the ladies, he walked back to the corridor and looked down the length of it.

She was not at their usual meeting place. He crumpled the note in his fist.

Should he go up to her room or look for her elsewhere? If she wasn't in her room, he'd lose precious time. But perhaps she really was tired. Perhaps at that very moment Billingsley was escorting her to her room, meaning to take advantage of her up there, where no one was about.

Gerrit couldn't risk it. He turned and ran toward the stairs, cursing the size of his sister's house.

Hester exited the drawing room, already anticipating seeing Major Hawkes. She had to swallow her disappointment. She so looked forward to these few minutes in his company. To think she'd miss the pleasure this evening made her realize how much she was growing used to seeing him.

Instead, she was surprised to see Lord Billingsley lounging against the wall, his arms folded. He straightened as she entered the corridor.

"Good evening, Miss Leighton."

"Good evening, my lord. Are the gentlemen already finished?"

"Not quite. They'll be at their port for a while yet."

She looked at him, wondering what he was doing there.

"I was waiting for you," he said before she could ask him.

"For me? Whatever for?"

"I came to fetch you for Hawkes. He asked me to look for you here, as you're wont to leave the assembly of ladies around this time."

She frowned, finding it strange the major would mention something like this to anyone. Was he a particular friend of Billingsley's? She hadn't noticed any closeness between the two.

"He's gone to get a spyglass. He asked me to bring you outside. There's a curious phenomenon in the sky he'd like us to see."

"Oh, really?" Her interest immediately perked up. That sounded like something the major would do.

"Yes, indeed. Come along, we can exit out through the terrace."

"Very well. What kind of phenomenon is it?" she asked, hurrying along beside him.

When they reached the terrace, she was disappointed not to see the major right away. "Where is Major Hawkes?"

Lord Billingsley pointed toward the lawn. "By the small temple. It's a good vantage point the way it's situated on a slight rise."

The two made their way along the gravel path. Hester wished Major Hawkes had come for her himself. She normally would never accompany a gentleman out at night down a secluded path.

When they reached the circular, colonnaded temple, there was still no sign of Major Hawkes. Hester turned to the marquess. "Where could he be?"

"Oh, he'll be along. Probably trying to scrounge up that spyglass."

She turned away from Billingsley, unsure how to behave with him. She knew he was a flirt and she'd never encouraged him, but in the broad daylight he'd always seemed perfectly harmless. She certainly wasn't going to enter the small temple alone with him.

"It's a beautiful night," she said, trying to enjoy the warm evening atmosphere. She looked up at the star-studded sky. "I wonder what Major Hawkes saw. Oh!" She jumped as she felt Lord Billingsley's hand on her shoulder. "I didn't realize you were standing right there."

He didn't remove his hand from her shoulder, but instead used it to propel her around to face him. "I've been waiting for a moment alone with you."

"W-whatever do you mean?" Suddenly his hand felt like a heavy iron. She swallowed, realizing her mistake in coming out alone with the marquess. Would the major be here soon? She peered into the dark shrubbery. Or had it all been a ruse? Her heart began to thump at the realization.

He chuckled, a low noise in his throat. "I think you know perfectly well what I mean."

She took a decisive step back from him, her mind in a whirl. How was she to defuse the situation? Was he intoxicated? "I have no idea what you mean. We see each other every day."

"But not alone…and not in the semidarkness."

"I am not in the habit of being alone with young men in the semidarkness or elsewhere," she answered tartly, knowing she mustn't show any fear.

"Oh, no? What do you call your nightly trysts with Hawkes?"

"How did—" The question died on her lips. Had he been spying on her? "Those are different."

"Different? A well-known rake like Hawkes and a

young lady, strolling alone on the terrace. Hawkes wouldn't be able to help himself."

"Major Hawkes and I are simply friends. There is nothing improper in our short walks together. And they're certainly not trysts! And moreover, I don't see what business they are of yours." She could feel herself getting more and more incensed at the thought that she had been spied upon.

"When I find myself attracted to a young lady, I make it my business to know the competition." He took a step toward her again, but she refused to back down from him.

"Well, you can rest easy. Major Hawkes is no competition. We are merely friends." At all costs, she must keep him talking.

"That does ease my mind."

"I think I put that badly. The fact that Major Hawkes and I are friends doesn't mean I am seeking the attention of any other gentleman."

He reached out his hand and touched her face.

"Lord Billingsley, I must ask you to keep your hands to yourself."

"I find I cannot help myself."

"Of course you can. If you do not keep your hands at your sides, I must warn you I shall return to the house immediately."

"You shatter me." As he spoke, he took her in his arms and brought his face down close to hers. "My, but you're a tempting armful."

Hester pushed against his chest. "Lord Billingsley, you must stop this nonsense this instant!" She pushed harder, but he was immovable. "You are no gentleman!" she said through gritted teeth.

His laughter was deep. "The fault is yours. You make me forget myself."

She moved her face this way and that, trying to dodge his kisses, but he was persistent. His breath smelled of brandy and his whiskers burned her face. Oh, why hadn't she thought to take the pistol her father had given her, along in her reticule?

"My lord, I told you you must stop this unseemly behavior immediately!"

"And I continue to tell you I am helpless to stop."

"You are a gentleman, Lord Billingsley, and must behave as such."

"But you bring out the beast in me."

As his mouth came down to hers, she managed to free one of her hands enough to bring it back. The next second it cracked against his cheek.

Billingsley cursed and brought a hand up to his face.

"I am sorry to have been forced to do that, but you brought it upon yourself—"

Before she could finish, he grabbed her roughly by the arms. "Why, you little tease—"

Chapter Ten

Gerrit raced back down the corridor from Miss Leighton's room, having found no one there.

Swearing at the length of the hallways, he finally reached the wide stairs and took them two at a time. Where could Billingsley have taken Miss Leighton?

Outside, of course. Isn't that what Gerrit himself would do if he were planning to seduce a young lady at a house party?

He reached the terrace and scanned the length of it. Not a soul. His panic mounting, he descended the shallow steps to the gardens. There could be a million places a man would take a young lady. But would Miss Leighton be foolish enough to follow him? Yes, she would. She was such an innocent. His mouth dry, he imagined the worst.

He raced down the path, his boots crunching on the gravel. They couldn't have gone far, his common sense told him. Miss Leighton wasn't so naive as to venture too great a distance from the house.

Slowing down, he forsook the gravel for the well-trimmed lawn and strained to hear past the evening sounds. A soft breeze rustled the trees and crickets sang by the pond.

"No!"

Gerrit froze at the sound of a woman's cry. Miss Leighton! Adrenaline flooded his veins and he took off in the direction of the voice. Reaching the small temple he pushed past the shrubbery surrounding it. There before him, two figures were locked in a struggle.

In two strides, Gerrit was upon them. Grabbing Billingsley by the shoulders, he hauled the marquess off Miss Leighton and threw him onto the ground.

"What the—"

"You'd better learn to listen when a lady tells you to stop."

Billingsley got up with a groan, dusting his clothes as he did so. "What in blazes do you think you're doing, Hawkes? You have no right to interfere in my amorous affairs."

"Don't speak of Miss Leighton as if she's a light-skirt, or you'll find yourself with more than just a dusty jacket."

Billingsley grunted. "Coming to claim what is yours? Sorry, old boy, but Miss Leighton has made it clear the field's wide open. To use her words, you and she are 'merely friends.' So, I'll thank you to stay out of what doesn't concern you." Before Gerrit could forestall him, Billingsley swung out his fist and connected with his jaw.

Gerrit's face jerked back, but he recovered immediately.

"Why you—" Ignoring the pain, Gerrit assumed a

fighting stance, crouching low. For the next few minutes, the two fought it out. Although Billingsley was strong and a skilled boxer, he was no match for Gerrit, who had learned to fight in all kinds of situations where the only rule was kill or be killed. With a strong hook to his gut and a knee to his groin, he wrestled the marquess to the ground and slammed his head against the turf. When Billingsley cried, "Enough!" Gerrit sat back, straddling him.

Seeing the wind knocked out of him, Gerrit finally stood. "I suggest you get yourself to the kitchens and request a slab of meat to put on your face, if you don't want too many questions tomorrow," Gerrit told him, fingering his own sore jaw. "And you'd better make it clear to the others that you lost the wager."

Once more Billingsley pulled himself to his feet, more slowly this time. "Confound you, Hawkes, for spoiling a man's fun." Without even looking at Miss Leighton, he limped from the enclosure.

When Gerrit was sure he was gone, he turned to Miss Leighton. "Did he hurt you?"

She stepped up to him. "No, he just frightened me." She reached out a hand but stopped just short of his face. "Are you all right?"

"I'm fine," he replied, looking at her from head to foot to make sure she spoke the truth. Now that the danger was over, he felt a strong awareness of being alone with her, a distance from the house.

She took a step closer to him and peered at his face. "Are you *sure* you're all right? You two were at it quite furiously."

He shrugged and attempted a light tone. "Apart from a few bruises which will make their appearance by tomorrow, I'm fine." He smiled. "I planted him a few good facers. I don't know how he'll explain those to the company."

"Thank you for…coming to my…aid," she said softly. Her smile was sweet, her gaze filled with gratitude.

He half-turned from her, rubbing the back of his neck to keep from touching her. "Think nothing of it. I'm just glad I got here in time."

"Yes, I am, too," she said with feeling. When he said nothing more, she asked, "What did you mean by 'losing his wager?'"

Gerrit hesitated, regretting that she'd heard that. "Billingsley and some of the other youngbloods placed wagers that…he would be the first…to steal a kiss from you."

"What?" She stared at him, her eyes wide.

It sounded even more vile in the retelling. He looked away from her, ashamed that he'd even been a witness to it. "It happened one evening after dinner. You said it yourself, the gentlemen have a few too many brandies and forget they're gentlemen."

"You said Lord Billingsley thought he'd be the *first!* What kind of woman do they think I am?"

When he said nothing—having no way to defend their behavior—she shook her head as if trying to puzzle it out. "I thought Lord Billingsley was a gentleman! That they all were."

He found her innocence both endearing and alarming. What would have happened if he hadn't come to Thistleworth?

She clutched her arms tightly around her midriff.

"Are you cold?"

She shook her head.

He took a step toward her. "You're trembling."

"Just the reaction, I suppose."

"That's understandable." After a few seconds, he said quietly, "You must have a care whom you go on solitary walks with in the evening…or anytime, for that matter."

"He tricked me! He told me you had sent him and that you were waiting out here with a spyglass to show us some 'curious phenomenon in the sky,'" she quoted with a short, bitter laugh.

"He's a clever fellow. You'd best be more cautious around him in future. Endeavor never to be alone with him."

"You needn't tell *me* that! Believe me, I have tried my best to evade his company."

"He doesn't give up easily."

She gave a firm shake of her head as if putting the event behind her. "He couldn't have hurt me anyway."

"Oh, no?"

"I'm protected."

"Protected?" He glanced around the enclosed shrubbery. "By whom, may I inquire?"

"By the Lord."

He gave a snort. "Isn't there a scripture somewhere about not tempting God? Being out alone with a gentleman falls into that category, I would think."

"I told you, the marquess tricked me."

"So, when was the Lord going to put in an appearance to save you this evening?"

"He sent you, didn't he?"

It was his turn to stare at her. "Believe me, the Lord wouldn't choose me to guard a young lady's virtue."

"But you did, didn't you?"

He shook his head, charmed in spite of himself. "You green girl." He didn't know whether to be angry or worried about her misplaced faith in him. At that moment all he could think was how easily he could take advantage of her. The thought sickened him. To distract himself, he challenged her, "And what if I hadn't come along?"

"'Though He slay me, yet will I trust in Him,'" she replied softly.

"What is that supposed to mean?"

"It's what Job said of the Lord. It comes down to trust."

Trust. That word again. No young lady had ever been safe in his company. They were all fair game as far as he'd been concerned.

"How did you know to find me here?" she asked.

"I didn't," he replied quickly, glad for the change in topic. He explained about receiving the note. "I smelled something fishy right away. You see, I've been watching Billingsley for a few days, wondering when he was going to make his move."

"'Make his move?'"

"The wager," he reminded her. "He had to prove himself soon to the others, or they would start to roast him."

She shuddered in revulsion, which made him feel as dirty as the men involved. How many times hadn't he participated in similar challenges?

"Why didn't you just tell Lord Billingsley to stop such a wicked plan?"

"He'd have laughed me to scorn."

"You were afraid of being laughed at?"

"It wasn't so long ago I'd be the one suggesting such a stupid bet myself. I knew it would do no good to try to stop them. I figured I'd have better luck keeping an eye on him…and you."

She pondered his words. "So, you've been looking after me all these days?" She didn't sound angry but curious.

He felt uncomfortable under her close scrutiny, as if she were seeing more than he cared to reveal. Why hadn't she focused on what he'd just told her, that he'd made similar wagers in the past?

"Is…that why…you've been meeting me in the evenings?" she asked slowly.

He nodded. *In part,* he added to himself.

"So you are my guardian angel." She smiled, as if receiving a revelation which pleased her.

Again he snorted. "The sooner you get that silly idea out of your head, the better off you'll be." Knowing how dangerous her situation grew as long as she remained outside alone with him, he said, "Come, I'll take you back inside."

"All right," she said but made no move.

As he drew closer to take her arm, he asked, "Are you certain you're all right?"

She nodded, facing him. He stood so close to her, he could see her chest rising and falling. What was she thinking? What did she see in his eyes? Suddenly, he found himself helpless. Leaning down an inch…then two…he brushed his lips against hers.

She felt sweet and yielding.

He ached for more. With a supreme effort he withdrew from her a fraction. "That should show you."

"Show me what?" Her voice was a soft breath against him.

"That I am the last man you should trust."

"Why shouldn't I trust you?"

He sighed. "Because I am no better than Billingsley. Probably many times worse."

Despite his warnings, all he could read in her gaze was complete faith in him. He groaned inwardly. *No, don't let her develop some kind of hero worship of me.*

He blew out a frustrated breath, rocking back on his heels. "My dear, innocent Miss Leighton, I am a soldier of fortune and a wastrel of the worst kind. Never forget that. If your wise sire were here, he would warn you to flee from my kind."

"I think you're wrong." With that statement, which expressed the same sort of confidence she had when talking of her Lord, she touched his cheek with her fingertips. Then she let her hand drop and turned from him. Before he could react, she began to leave the shrub-enclosed area. Gerrit followed her, thrown more off-balance by her brief touch than he cared to admit.

They walked back to the house without speaking. At the terrace, he opened the door for her, and she looked up at him. The light from the doorway spilled onto her face. He was caught by the hint of wonder in her eyes. He had the sense that he could do anything with her and she would acquiesce willingly. Such a responsibility filled him with a sense of dread.

"Come, it's getting chilly," he said, more abruptly than he'd intended.

When they finally reached her room, he waited while she opened her door and made sure the room was unoccupied.

"Thank you again for rescuing me," she said, standing at the door. "I shall never forget it."

He searched her face, hoping she would be able to put the terrifying incident behind her—and forget his kiss. "Don't worry about Billingsley. He'll probably give you the cold-shoulder for a few days, but he'll get enough ribbing from the other fellows to have to act the good sport."

She shuddered. "I can hardly believe they will all be discussing me like that."

Unable to help himself, he reached out and touched her on the cheek with his forefinger. "Men are dangerous creatures not to be trusted. Never forget that."

She shook her head, making him all the more aware of the softness of her skin. "Not *all* of them."

He broke the contact. "I'm one of the vilest." Without another word, he turned and made his way back down the corridor.

He returned to the terrace to ponder what had happened. He could kick himself a thousand times over for that kiss. In one moment of carelessness, he'd ruined everything.

In his book there were only two kinds of women: wenches and ladies. Miss Leighton didn't fall into either category. He didn't quite know where to place her, much less qualify the feelings she was arousing in him. He'd yearned for women before; he'd been on the hunt many times in the past, stopping at nothing until he obtained what he wanted. But then his interest waned and he was off on a new chase.

Why the hesitation where Miss Leighton was concerned? Why not go after what he wanted? He hadn't let innocence stop him before.

An image of another young lady rose in his mind. Gillian Edwards. Even now the memory filled him with revulsion at his own despicable behavior toward her.

But it was too late to right past wrongs. He'd just have to live with the kind of man he was. And keep as far away from Miss Leighton as he could.

But now in the warm night, Gerrit was helpless to stop his imagination and longing from having free sway. He remembered the exquisite softness of her skin and her yielding lips and felt like a parched man in the desert.

That brief kiss had been a mistake. A terrible mistake. More for him than for her.

Lord Billingsley's shocking behavior was eclipsed from Hester's mind that night by the greater impact of Major Hawkes's kiss.

Hester lay awake in her bed a long time reliving it. She touched her own lips, remembering the soft texture of his and the whiff of the spicy, masculine scent of his cheeks.

So, this was what all the excitement was about, what so many poets devoted pages to, what drove so many individuals to periods of apparent insanity….

She could begin to understand it—the way her heart warmed at the mere sight of the major, how her heartbeat quickened when he came to take her for their evening walk, how she perked up at the sound of his laughter and blossomed under the teasing look that came into his eyes at certain moments. Why, she'd come to think he was the most fascinating and kind man she'd ever met… and even felt a conviction the Lord had brought him into her life. She could now understand it…this thing called love….

The next morning, as she prepared to descend the stairs, her thoughts reverted to Lord Billingsley. She wrinkled her nose. How she wished she could avoid him altogether. A perfect gentleman one moment, a monster the next. She remembered Major Hawkes's words that men were dangerous creatures. She knew men were powerful. She had seen enough of their feats in the logging industry back home. She knew they frequently drank too much or brawled. But she had never experienced the direct loss of respect from one for a lady.

She bit her lip. She knew there was a certain type of woman—a few who inhabited the waterfront taverns in Bangor—who wouldn't mind the kind of behavior Lord Billingsley had exhibited last evening. But those women were the exception. She'd never known a gentleman to behave so to a *lady*.

Once again, she thanked the Lord for Major Hawkes's timely appearance. She didn't doubt for a moment that the Lord had sent him. To think he'd been looking out for her all those days. She touched her fingers to her lips, marveling once again at his kiss.

So different from Billingsley's. So tender and…gentlemanly. Yet she'd sensed behind it, a passion held in check. What would it be like to be kissed with abandon by him? She shivered, but not with revulsion as she had over the marquess's kiss. She smiled. The major had tried to warn her afterwards that he was worse than Billingsley. She wanted to reassure him. She hadn't objected to his kiss in the least. She'd even felt a momentary pang when it was over so quickly.

She frowned. Why had the major been so adamant in making her believe he was as untrustworthy as Billingsley? She'd pondered his words quite some time in her bed last night. He seemed intent always on making himself appear in the worst light to her. A gentleman could not return so decorated from war and be the base fellow he claimed.

She'd just have to continue showing him that she did trust him.

The memory of his kiss gave her the courage to venture downstairs and face the company. Major Hawkes would be there. She smiled again. His kiss had been exquisitely sweet—like maple sugar poured on new fallen snow.

Instead of seeing Major Hawkes as she wished, Hester ended up wandering around the large house after breakfast, at loose ends. Her hopes of seeing the major had been dashed early. She heard at the table that he had gone off with Lady Stanchfield's husband on a shooting party. The men would probably be gone all day. She found it strange since he hadn't joined the hunting expeditions up till then.

After Billingsley's behavior, and the major's information that several of the young gentlemen had discussed her and placed wagers on Billingsley's success or failure, Hester felt no inclination to join the young gentlemen who'd remained behind.

Unfortunately, she had no desire to be in the ladies' company either. With the exception of Lady Stanchfield, they all treated her like some innocent beyond help. The day loomed before her. She paused at the landing, debating her options. A walk, a book?

Deciding she'd take a book out to one of the sheltered gardens to read, she headed for the library. With most of the men gone hunting, she knew she was safe from unwanted male company in the gardens. During the daylight hours, at least, she reminded herself with a shudder.

Book in hand, Hester stood on the terrace, shading her eyes from the sun. Once again, she'd forgotten her parasol. Mrs. Bellows would scold.

Hmm…where to go? Her eyes skimmed the top of the temple visible above the trees. She grimaced, remembering her tussle with Billingsley the evening before. She looked in the opposite direction, then smiled. The rose arbor. It was a lovely private spot, filled with benches and shaded with the lovely pergola redolent with the scent of roses.

Clutching the book more firmly to her chest, she headed down the steps in that direction. She couldn't help looking behind her several times to make sure she wasn't being followed, but she saw no one but a lone gardener. Breathing a sigh of relief, she entered the first arched trellis. The fragrance of late-blooming yellow climbing roses assailed her as she passed under it.

Oh! Her hand went to her mouth, stopping the silent exclamation.

Directly in front of her, at the far end of the enclosed garden, stood Lady Stanchfield locked in an embrace with a gentleman. Embarrassed at having intruded on a private moment between husband and wife, Hester began to back out. Just as she was remembering that Lord Stanchfield was not at home, the couple separated a fraction.

The gentleman first spied her across the small garden. Staring daggers at her, the middle-aged man, whom she vaguely recognized as one of the guests—a Mr. Delaney—swore as he disengaged himself from Lady Stanchfield. For a second, Hester stood motionless, unable to take in what she was seeing.

Then she turned, wanting only to forget the tableau. Before she could disappear back through the arbor, Lady Stanchfield began running toward her.

"Hester, wait!"

Hester turned back a moment, her hand still clutched to her mouth. She lowered her hand and tried to compose her features. "Forgive me. I hadn't meant to come here. I really—I mean, I'm sorry, I—I really must go—" She fled the garden, ignoring Lady Stanchfield's renewed pleas to come back.

Hester was in no shape to talk about what she had seen, not with one of its perpetrators. She let out a choked sound as she raced away from the area. What could Lady Stanchfield possibly say to her to offer an explanation?

What a naive fool she'd been! Hester held her middle, feeling sick. Sick with what she'd seen and wishing she'd never seen it. Major Hawkes was right. She knew nothing of the world.

"Hester, please…please wait! I can't run as fast as you. You must listen to me, please!"

Hester finally stopped, unable to harden herself against Lady Stanchfield's cry. She stood watching the other lady finally catch up to her.

Lady Stanchfield was panting heavily, and Hester had a moment's alarm. What if she swooned? She'd have to fetch Mr. Delaney. The thought terrified her.

"Are you all right, my lady?"

The lady just nodded, still unable to speak. "You… are…so…swift," she finally managed between gulps of air.

Hester remained silent until finally, with a last sigh, Lady Stanchfield's breathing slowed. She grasped the shawl around her shoulders more firmly with one hand. With the other she smoothed down one side of her hair.

"I must look a fright."

Hester felt the heat flood her face, realizing how Lady Stanchfield had gotten so mussed.

"My dear, I am *so* sorry you had to see that."

"I didn't see anything," she began, then realized that would be a lie. She amended, "Please forget I saw anything."

"I—" Lady Stanchfield waved a hand as if floundering for how to proceed. "You're so young and innocent. Please don't think so badly of me."

"I'm thinking nothing at all," Hester continued, hearing her own voice coming out stiff and prim. Oh, what could she possibly say? How could she condone what she'd seen? Why was Lady Stanchfield making her confront it? "Excuse me, I must go. I—" she lifted her book, hardly knowing what she was doing "—I was just looking for a spot to read. I must go and find some place." *Some place where I'm sure to run into no one,* she wanted to shout hysterically.

Before Lady Stanchfield could stammer any more apologies, Hester turned once more and hurried off. Thankfully, this time her hostess didn't attempt to follow her or call her back.

Hester ran only far enough to be out of Lady Stanchfield's sight. But she didn't find another spot to read. Instead she made her way back to her room. She breathed a sigh of relief to see the room she shared with Mrs. Bellows unoccupied. She didn't know what she'd have done if she'd had to endure the lady's chatter at that moment.

She flung herself on her bed and buried her head in the pillow. Why had she come to this awful house party? She didn't belong here. Her father had been right. These people were no sort of Christians. They were rich and spoiled and believed they could follow their own set of rules.

If she'd believed last night's run-in with Lord Billingsley had been an isolated incident, she'd been wrong. It had been only typical of the world in which she found herself.

Her visit to England had been not at all what she had envisioned. She'd imagined lots of new gowns and sightseeing. What she had never imagined was the kind of people she would meet. She sometimes wondered if they would have seemed less strange if she'd gone to Africa or China.

Naturally, she had expected a different mode of doing things. After all, her parents had told her enough of England to understand that what Americans did and ate, how they dressed and even spoke, would differ somewhat from their mother country.

But what she had run into since Mrs. Bellows had begun to take her around to parties and routs and assemblies—and what she'd felt even more strongly since Lady Stanchfield had invited her to this fashionable house party—was a different mode of behavior. She'd sensed a deeper, ofttimes subtle, undercurrent in the people around her, as if they thought her slow and backward.

Outwardly she might dress as these ladies dressed. She might be a few years' younger—but she knew lots of women of various ages back home—and she might speak their same language, yet she felt like an entirely different creature.

She remembered snippets of conversation between the guests, little of which she'd understood. She so often felt that there was a double meaning to their words. They would laugh at each other's remarks when what had been said appeared completely innocuous to Hester. No wonder. Everything appeared quite clear to her now.

That's why she had spent so much time at sports with the gentlemen. She felt their conversation more straightforward, even if what they spent most of their time at was placing wagers on each others' prowess at the different activities. Her parents and most of her acquaintances wouldn't approve of the betting, but she still had found their language and behavior more direct.

Until last evening.

Even though she'd been honest when she'd told Major Hawkes that she'd never truly worried for her safety—she was too close to the Lord not to trust Him— the event with Lord Billingsley *had* shaken her. More than what liberties he had taken—or could have taken— with her, was the confrontation with his wickedness. For he had been wicked to try to overpower her when she'd clearly not welcomed his advances.

Hester rarely came face-to-face with real evil and it always startled her when she did. It made her realize how truly sheltered her life was.

Oh God, what am I doing here? Why did I come? Why didn't I heed Papa? I need to go back to London. I want to go home. She rocked herself back and forth on her bed, wishing she could be transported immediately back to her safe home across the Atlantic.

But then she'd never see Major Hawkes again. The thought brought her up short. He was the only bright spot among the Philistines she found herself amidst. *But he came from their world,* a small voice in her head reminded her. It was his world, too. *But he was different,* she argued. *He was nothing like them.*

She felt to the core of her being that she had been meant to meet him. But could there ever be a future for the two of them? Sitting up in her bed, a pillow clutched to her chin, she stared at the dust motes in a streak of late-afternoon light.

She had been brought up to seek God's will above

all. Since her birth, her parents had prayed for a godly man for her eventual husband, and she'd looked forward to that day, in anticipation of the one God would have for her. She swallowed, realizing Gerrit Hawkes could have very little part in that landscape. Suddenly everything in her life seemed out of kilter.

She needed help. That much was certain. Scrambling off her bed, she went to the dresser and took up her Bible. She needed to hear from the Lord. Surely he had a purpose for bringing her to England and having her meet Gerrit Hawkes.

Chapter Eleven

That evening Gerrit entered the drawing room with some trepidation, wondering how he would find Miss Leighton. He regretted a thousand times his behavior of the evening before and was afraid he would see some expectancy in her eyes, or worse, some hurt.

He'd taken the cowardly way out today; he'd left the house. Knowing that Billingsley was in the hunting party put his mind at rest about Miss Leighton's safety at home. The man sported a good-sized bruise high on his cheek, and as Gerrit had predicted, he'd been asked about it quite a bit. When the marquess hadn't been forthcoming, the men had begun teasing him that it was the lady who'd given him the injury.

Luckily, Gerrit's own bruise along his jawline hardly showed. As he scanned the drawing room, he saw no signs of Miss Leighton. Strange, she was rarely late. He saw Mrs. Bellows and decided to inquire about her charge's whereabouts.

"Oh, Major Hawkes, how dashing you always look in your regimentals. How was the hunt today? We missed the gentlemen but I'm sure you were all having too grand a time to give a thought to us."

"We had some success," he managed to interrupt. "You'll probably be tasting some pheasant and woodcock at the table in the coming days."

"Oh, I do so love a roast pheasant." She fluttered her fan in the throes of anticipation.

"By the by, I don't see Miss Leighton."

Mrs. Bellows shook her head. "Oh, the poor dear. She said she would stay in her room this evening."

He frowned at the older woman. "Indeed? Is she ill?" Had Billingsley harmed her more than she'd let on?

"Well, I don't rightly know," she answered, pursing her lips. "She didn't complain of any ailments, although I will say she looked a bit pale and seemed subdued." She gave a smile. "I told you we ladies were pining your absence today."

He smiled wanly, wishing he could know for certain what was wrong with Miss Leighton. Could she be avoiding Billingsley—or him?

"I'm sure she'll be quite all right after an early night. She's not used to the late hours of a house party," Mrs. Bellows prattled on. "I had the maid prepare her an infusion of pennyroyal and take her a little toast. Good against a touch of melancholia. Perhaps it is a religious melancholia. She was reading her Bible again…although she assured me she was quite well."

"Thank you, Mrs. Bellows. Please send her my well

wishes for her speedy recovery when you see her again this evening."

"Of course, my dear major. I'm sure your wishes will do the trick. She's quite fond of you."

Gerrit swallowed, not wishing the confirmation of what he was most afraid of. Was she really unwell, or was she just avoiding the company? Melancholia? He couldn't picture Miss Leighton melancholic. Well, he'd have to bide his time until the morrow and see how she appeared—or more precisely, how she reacted to his presence.

He toyed with the idea of going back to London. That would probably be best, he decided. Yet, he was reluctant to leave as long as Billingsley remained at Delia's. The young lord had avoided Gerrit during the entire hunt. Gerrit sighed. He'd just have to have a word with him after dinner and gauge his state of mind.

He knew if he were in Billingsley's shoes, he wouldn't give up on a lady he had his eye on just because of a first refusal on the lady's part. He was skilled in the art of wearing down a woman's resistance.

If Billingsley was worth any of his reputation as a dandy of the first stare, he would be just as persistent with Miss Leighton. This was precisely what worried Gerrit. What if he weren't around the next time to rescue her?

Late that night, when the men were in their cups and hadn't yet risen from the table to join the ladies, Gerrit stood from his place and sauntered over to where Billingsley was regaling some fellows with his exploits at the hunt.

Gerrit pulled out a chair and straddled it. "How's the bruise?" he asked.

Billingsley gave him a cold look, but shrugged. "Your concern overwhelms me."

"Tell us again how your lovely face got so battered?" Astley inquired from across the table. "You fell in the tub, you say?"

"No, wasn't it when you couldn't find your way back to your bedchamber last night and stumbled on the stairs?" The other men roared with laughter.

"The question is, was it Miss Leighton's room he hailed from or another?"

"Perhaps it was Miss Leighton herself who milled him down," Gerrit offered.

"That's a good one!" one of the men said, and the table erupted in a round of guffaws.

"I can just picture it. She opened her door and there stands his lordship in his silk dressing gown, candle in hand, asking the way to the library. The next thing he knows, she's drawn his cork. Never saw it coming, did you, old fellow?" another man asked with a slap on the back.

"If she's as good with her fives as she is with the bow and pistol, you're lucky your nose isn't broken."

Billingsley gave Gerrit a look that promised they would have words later, and that they wouldn't be pleasant ones.

Gerrit hardly cared what Billingsley's opinion of him was. What concerned him was his opinion of Miss Leighton. If he couldn't make it clear to Billingsley in private that her virtue was not to be toyed with by word or deed, he'd have to take matters further.

When the others were leaving the dining room for the drawing room, Gerrit stopped Billingsley with a touch on his elbow.

"A word if you please."

"There's nothing I'd like better," he said, his jaw hard. It would have had more effect if it didn't look so mottled by a bruise.

Once on the terrace, Billingsley faced Gerrit. "I'll thank you to stay out of my business and leave your clever remarks to yourself."

"I consider it my business if they involve Miss Leighton."

"Fancy her yourself, is that it?"

"That's not your concern. She's an innocent, and as such, it's beneath you to compromise her virtue."

"That's a fine thing coming from you."

Gerrit swallowed back his growing anger. It would be much simpler to have another round with him instead of trying to appeal to his better nature.

"Be that as it may, I'm telling you to stop slandering her character among the male company. She's done nothing to you except show excruciating patience with your inept advances, and it shows poor sportsmanship to try and get back at her by talking of her as if she were available to anyone."

Billingsley made a show of taking a pinch of snuff from his box. After inhaling of it deeply and sneezing into his handkerchief, he rocked back on his heels, trying to stare Gerrit down. "As I see it, you have very little control over what a man says—"

Gerrit grabbed his cravat, cutting off his words.

Billingsley's snuff box dropped with a clatter to the stone pavement.

"If you can't control your speech, then I'll have to make sure your mouth isn't in working order." Gerrit squeezed the neck cloth tighter until he could see Billingsley's face turning redder and his eyes begin to widen with entreaty.

"Don't trifle with Miss Leighton. I've killed more frogs than you've years on you, and I wouldn't hesitate to add one more corpse to the pile." With a shove, he let him go. Billingsley flailed his arms but to no avail. He landed with a thud on his backside. Gerrit would have found the sight of his ridiculous position amusing if he had had any inclination to laugh.

"Leave her alone, Billingsley. Are we clear on that?"

At Billingsley's nod, Gerrit turned and strode from the terrace. He didn't have much faith that his threat would do any good. He rubbed his own sore jaw, wishing again that he'd never left London. Now, he'd clearly have to stay to the bitter end, at least as long as Miss Leighton and Billingsley were residing under the same roof.

Since when had he become a protector of female virtue?

If the idea weren't so ludicrous it would be as laughable as Billingsley on his rump.

Tomorrow he'd have to find Miss Leighton and see for himself what her feelings toward him might be. If there was any hero worship, he'd have to make sure to quash it.

Of the two encounters, he feared this next one the more.

* * *

It was much later, when he was finally retiring, that Gerrit was faced with another encounter. His hand was on the doorknob of his room, when a female figure detached itself from the shadowy corridor. He hid his annoyance, wondering if it was one of Delia's friends looking for male companionship.

A second later he breathed a sigh of relief when he recognized Delia. "What are you doing there in the shadows like a specter?"

She didn't smile.

"What is it, love?" he asked. "You look scared."

She closed her eyes. "I'm lost, Gerrit." She bit her lip and closed her eyes.

"What happened?" He turned to her and put a hand on her shoulder. "Come, it can't be as bad as that."

She reopened her eyes. They were red and swollen. "It's worse."

"Tell me."

"I can't talk here."

"Let me see if my room is unoccupied." He opened the door and shone his candle in. The fellow he shared the chamber with hadn't come up yet. "Come in and tell me what's happened."

Delia entered and he closed the door behind her. "Now, what is so dire that you must be skulking in dark hallways?"

She walked to the center of the small chamber and spoke without turning around. "Miss Leighton came upon Reginald and me in the rose garden."

"So, what is so unusual about that?"

Delia swung around to him. "She *saw* us!" When he still didn't react, she added, "Embracing!" She gave a harsh laugh. "Believe me, even your innocent Miss Leighton couldn't misconstrue that type of embrace."

"What did she say?" he asked, trying to imagine how Miss Leighton might react to the sight of a passionate embrace between a married woman and her lover. After all, she was far from the jaded members of the ton into which she'd been thrust.

Delia gave a choked laugh. "What could she say? She was clearly shocked. I ran after her. I had to. I couldn't let her go without knowing what she might do."

"And?"

Delia shook her head. "I think she was too stunned to say much of anything. But what will happen when she's had a chance to think about it? She wasn't at dinner this evening." Delia looked at him, her eyes beseeching. "What if she goes to Lionel?"

"Oh, come now, she wouldn't do that. She hasn't said more than two words to your husband this whole time. She's not very well going to go up to him and tell him, 'pardon me, but I caught your wife in a compromising position.'"

"It's nothing to joke about. If Lionel ever had any proof, he'd throw me out."

"Does he really believe you've been faithful to him all these years?" he asked with a touch of wry humor. Although he didn't interfere in his sister's affairs, he knew her marriage was a loveless one.

"I've never given him any reason to suspect me. I've been very discreet."

Gerrit made a sound of disbelief, but at her hurt expression he relented. "All right, so he has no reason to suspect anything. Why be so worried now? I'm sure Miss Leighton would never do anything to prejudice you. She might not approve of your conduct, but she wouldn't go running to your husband."

"I can't be sure of that." Delia pulled out a handkerchief from her sleeve and wiped at her eyes. "You never know. What if Miss Leighton feels it her moral duty to inform my husband? I know she's quite religious. Why, all she plays on the pianoforte are hymns. What if—"

Gerrit reached out for her. "Shh. She'll do nothing of the sort. Now get those silly thoughts out of your head."

"Oh, Gerrit, I'm so scared." Her lower lip trembled and her eyes began to well up with tears again. "I know it's wrong the way I've conducted myself, but I…love Reggie. Lionel is so cold…so distant."

Gerrit wrapped her in his arms. "There, there, I know that. You'll make yourself sick with worry. Do you want me to talk with Miss Leighton?" He tried to picture that and hadn't a clue what he would say.

Delia's head came up immediately from his chest. "Would you? I know she'd listen to you."

He twisted his lips into a smile which came out more a grimace. "Very well," he answered, hiding the reluctance he felt. "Now, stop fretting about it and try to get some sleep. I'll seek Miss Leighton out tomorrow and see what I can do."

"You're such a dear," Delia murmured from his chest. "I knew I could count on you."

"What did Reggie say when he saw Miss Leighton?"

asked Gerrit, wishing he could have seen the old chub's expression.

"He was livid, of course."

Gerrit stifled a laugh. Typical. "Isn't he worried about Lionel?"

"Of course he is, but he was so furious at Miss Leighton's intrusion that he didn't think about that at first. He wanted to throttle the girl, as if it was Miss Leighton's fault that she had come upon us. Poor thing, she was just trying to find a secluded spot in which to read."

Gerrit chuckled then sobered as he pictured Miss Leighton in a secluded spot in the vast gardens, just ripe for Billingsley to pounce.

He sighed. Now he had two females to look out for. When had he gotten himself into such a whisker?

The next morning, Hester attended church with Mrs. Bellows. When she saw Lady Stanchfield in a pew at the front of the church, she felt even worse than she had the previous afternoon. Immediately she scolded herself; maybe Lady Stanchfield was there in a spirit of repentance. But no matter how much she observed her during the service, Hester didn't detect anything to point to a change of heart. She sat beside her husband, the two were even sharing a prayer book.

Nor was the sermon of a nature that would inspire repentance. Hester's mind wandered as she thought about why a woman as nice as Lady Stanchfield would be unfaithful to her husband. What little she'd seen of Lord Stanchfield didn't endear him to her, but still, he seemed a typical man of his class. As if she knew what that was, she chided herself. The more she saw of the English aristocracy, the less she understood of them. They seemed a rule unto themselves. Yet here they were on a Sunday morning, following the same Scriptures she and her family lived by.

Hester tried to look around her, but she didn't see Mr. Delaney. In fact, she didn't remember ever having seen him attending before. At least he wasn't a hypocrite.

After the service, she didn't know where to go. If she went outside, she risked coming upon some lovers' tryst. If she went out to the stables or archery ground, she'd likely run into Lord Billingsley. She hadn't seen him since his attack two evenings ago, but she knew she couldn't avoid him forever.

Oh, this was ridiculous. She wasn't going to hide in her room on such a glorious day. She picked up her book and left the house, determined to find some solitude in the vast gardens of Thistleworth Park. There couldn't be that many couples looking for a meeting place. Making sure once again that she wasn't followed by any unwanted male, Hester finally ended up at a sheltered garden surrounded by yew hedges. Bypassing the stone bench, she opted for the soft, green grass and leaned against the bench.

She was deeply engrossed in her book, when she heard a masculine voice above her.

"You have hidden yourself well, Miss Leighton."

"Major Hawkes!" she glanced up and saw him towering over her. His handsomeness always took her breath away, but now it was tinged with the knowledge of what those masculine yet soft lips felt like grazing hers.

"I have spent the last hour in search of you."

Her heartbeat quickened. "You have?" She wondered what the reason might be. His kiss? His sister's conduct? She felt the color rise to her cheeks for both causes, and put the memories aside, preferring to suppress them altogether for the moment. The latter was too disturbing, the former—well, she hadn't come to any conclusions yet on how her new feelings for the major would affect their friendship.

"Yes. Do you mind if I have a seat?" he motioned to the stone bench.

"Of course not. Please do," she hurried on, suddenly shy.

"Would you prefer to remain on the lawn or come join me here? I could just as well sit down there with you."

She glanced down at his light colored breeches. "Oh, I wouldn't want you to get grass stains on your…" Her voice faded away in embarrassment. She had learned that in London society ladies didn't speak of men's "unmentionables." If she were at home with her brother, she would not hesitate to speak plainly.

"Have no fear, Miss Leighton." Before she could stand, he came to join her on the grass. "I have sat on much rougher terrain in my uniform."

"Of course. How silly of me."

"Not silly at all. We are at a house party where decorum is of the utmost consequence."

His deep blue eyes were twinkling at her and she smiled tentatively back.

"Speaking of decorum," he began after a moment.

Hester looked up from the book she'd been in the act of closing. Was he going to mention their kiss?

This time it was he who looked down at his loosely clasped hands. "I wanted to speak to you about…my sister."

She stared at him. Her mind couldn't help conjuring up the scene she had interrupted the afternoon before. "Did she send you?" she asked softly.

He met her gaze once more, his eyes searching hers. "Yes, in a manner of speaking."

"But why?" She felt a reluctance to talk about what she'd seen.

He gave a wry smile. "She's terrified of what you might do."

Hester struggled to understand his meaning and finally her eyes widened in horror. "You mean she thinks I might tell someone?"

"I told her I was sure you wouldn't tell a soul."

"Of course not!"

"That's my girl," he said with a gentle smile, which warmed her more than she'd ever imagined a man's smile could. Then she remembered what they were talking about and she sobered, turning her face from his. "I just want to forget I ever saw anything."

"Of course you do. But it's not always possible to forget what one has seen, is it?"

Although the words were lightly spoken, his tone was tinged with sadness. She turned to him slowly, realizing he must be thinking of the war. As she shook her head in agreement, he smiled with understanding. "So, what now?"

"Now? What do you mean?"

"Will you despise my poor sister?"

"Oh, no! Of course not—" she began and then stopped as she realized her feelings for Lady Stanchfield *had* changed.

"But things are not the same, are they?"

She nodded, glad he understood. "It's the same with Lord Billingsley. I always found him a rather tiresome, pompous gentleman, yet harmless enough, but now…" She couldn't help the shudder that ran through her. "I'd be happy never to see him again."

He chuckled. "Unfortunately, the man is a shameless leech. He won't leave Thistleworth unless Delia throws him out. Now there's a thought…" He rubbed his chin, considering.

She laughed. "Please don't have Lady Stanchfield do anything so drastic on my account."

"Delia is awfully worried you'll think less of her."

Hester turned away from him again. "Your sister has been so kind to me. Since I arrived in England, only you and Lady Stanchfield have truly made me feel as if I'm worth knowing." She smiled. "Your sister is not many years older than I, yet she persists in calling me child and lambkin and behaving as if she's a mother hen and I'm the baby chick." She looked down at her lap and smoothed away the blades of grass she'd plucked earlier.

"Yet my own mother would never—would never—" She couldn't even say the words, the concept was too shocking.

"Commit adultery?" Gerrit finished for her.

She raised her eyes to meet his gaze. The words sounded so severe, bringing their sinfulness into stark relief. She couldn't even reply to Gerrit. The words made her understand that she hadn't misconstrued the scene in the rose arbor. No matter how she might like to explain the scene away in an innocent way, it was clear Lady Stanchfield was breaking the seventh commandment.

"What was worse," she said almost in a whisper, "was seeing her at church this morning with Lord Stanchfield. They looked as content as—oh! It doesn't bear thinking on!" She shook aside the scene from her mind.

Major Hawkes said nothing for a few moments. Then, "Do you know how Delia came to marry Lord Stanchfield?"

She shook her head.

"My parents arranged it. She was nineteen and had already enjoyed one season. My parents, with four children close in age and no great income, didn't want to finance another London season. Those are quite costly, you know. We grew up not far from London. A season in town entails renting a good house in a respectable neighborhood, hosting any number of parties, purchasing a whole wardrobe for those offspring being presented. Then with the cost of my commission in the army and my brother's studies at university, well, things were a bit strained for a while."

"I understand."

He smiled faintly. "Possibly not, but no matter. When Lord Stanchfield began to leave his calling card and show a marked preference for my sister, my parents jumped at the advantageous match. Not only was he titled, but more importantly, he had a substantial income and family seat. My sister would be set for life. My sister had no real choice in the matter."

"How awful for her. I hardly know Lord Stanchfield."

"You've probably observed him enough to see that he's an insipid fellow with little to recommend him but a love for hunting and fishing with his drinking companions. As long as my sister provided an heir for him, he was content to ignore her existence." He shrugged. "And since that blessed event has not yet occurred, nor may it ever occur as the time goes by, Delia's place beside her husband is in no way assured."

"But you said he pursued her. He must love her."

He shrugged. "Love? How long does that sentiment last once a couple has exchanged their vows?"

"A lifetime."

"You sound convinced. What? Are there no unhappy marriages in the Maine Territory?"

She frowned, thinking of the marriages she knew besides her parents'. "The husbands and wives of my acquaintance seem content enough. Leastways, they don't go around revealing their problems to others." She tilted her head, picturing her parents' circle. "Mrs. Smith is a bit bossy, and everyone says Mr. Smith is henpecked, but he doesn't seem to mind.

"There are a lot of second marriages but it's not because the first marriage was unhappy. People are often widowed and a widow or widower doesn't stay single long. They usually have young children to raise, and there's always someone willing to share the load."

"Do so many die young?"

She nodded. "A fair number. There is sickness—fevers and such. We have few doctors."

"Marriage seems like a risky business there. You've seen much death?"

His question caught her off guard again and she took her time to mull it over. "I suppose so. I hadn't thought about it in those terms." She looked at him. "You have seen much death as well."

He nodded but said no more.

"During the war?" she ventured. She sensed he would say more so she remained silent but after a few moments when he'd said nothing, she turned the subject back to what they were talking about previously. "At least in Maine people marry for love, even the second marriages."

"One can't live off love."

"But to marry anyone—to agree to share a lifetime together for mere monetary considerations! It's not right. It's so mercenary. And look where it ends. Look at your sister's plight!"

He nodded. "Very true. On the other hand, she could have married a penniless young gentleman who stole her heart and be living on the fringes of poverty, with a half dozen children to feed. Instead, look at what she enjoys." He waved his hand at the green bower surrounding them.

"At what price?" Hester murmured.

He leaned back with a sigh. "If I ever want to live with half this comfort, I must some day conform to my parents' wishes and pick out a future wife from the crop of heiresses presented every year at court."

Hester looked at him in disbelief. "I can't imagine your marrying against your will."

"Believe me, I have fought it until now, but some day I may have to pay the piper, in this case whichever creditors are the most pressing." He grinned. "But if I must marry for money, I shall go about it on another plane entirely from Delia. Instead of being led like a lamb to the slaughter by my parents, I shall take full control."

Her eyes widened. "How so?"

"I shall go about it methodically, like planning a military campaign. For starters, I will assess the terrain and select the least attractive female on the Marriage Mart, the one whose papa was most desperate to be rid of her to a charmingly worthless fellow like myself for a substantial price."

She couldn't help laughing at his description, hardly believing he could be speaking of something as important as his marriage.

"She would be so grateful to me for offering for her, that she'd never give me any trouble and let me go my merry way."

She shook her head at him. "I don't think any woman would be happy with that arrangement."

He eyed her, the look in his eyes belying his facetious words. "You think not?"

"Certainly not."

"Ah, but we would conclude a straightforward bargain where no emotional entanglements would hinder things."

"How wonderfully romantic," she replied, her tone dry.

"But eminently practical."

"Why don't you marry me then? I'm an heiress," she said before she could consider her words.

Seconds of absolute stillness followed as his blue eyes met hers. She didn't flinch, but held her chin high, wondering what was going on behind his steady gaze.

Then the moment was broken with a gesture of his hand and an indulgent smile. "I could never ruin a good friendship with marriage. Besides, you've forgotten my advice already. You must fix your focus on firstborn sons. They are the only ones who count."

She chose her words carefully, adopting his light tone. "You are most likely right. We would never suit."

He brought up one knee and rested his elbow on it. "And why wouldn't we suit, wise child?"

"For one thing, my future husband needs to be a man of God. I could never marry a man who is not saved."

"Saved from what? Eternal perdition?" His tone was teasing.

"Yes," she replied with utmost conviction.

Gerrit looked into those hazel eyes and felt a chill down his spine. At any other time—even those moments when he faced death in the thick of battle—he could have laughed in her face. But not today.

Why did it seem with each day he had been home that he was indeed already sentenced and condemned?

"Oh, there's no one to save me from that," he countered, keeping his tone carefree under her scrutiny. Why was it that he always had the feeling those eyes saw more than he cared to reveal?

"Yes, there is. His name is Jesus."

He shook his head. "My dear, I'm afraid I'm beyond the pale of even His mercy."

"There's no one beyond His mercy. God's love for us is stronger than death."

A love stronger than death? The words shook him. There was nothing stronger than death.

Chapter Twelve

Gerrit returned to London two days later. He didn't care if the duns in London beat down his door. He didn't care how deserted or hot the city was. The emptier, the better as far as he was concerned. He didn't care if Delia felt abandoned. He'd done what he could. If that slowtop Reggie didn't behave more discreetly, it was his own fault if they were discovered.

Before leaving, he'd informed Delia of Billingsley's behavior, and she, as hostess, had quietly asked him to leave the house party. That taken care of, Gerrit was free to quit Thistleworth. Quit it he did, at earliest dawn before any of the guests were up. He felt like a thief on the run, hating himself for his cowardice where Hester Leighton was concerned, but helpless to behave any differently.

He knew he must not see Miss Leighton again, for her own good.

The fact that he was at times actually tempted to

pursue her terrified him. More than anything, he didn't want to end up hurting her. He prided himself on the fact that he still had *some* ethics left. But he also knew he was a weak man, given to indulging his every whim, especially when it came to women, games and drink.

However, the more time he spent in Miss Leighton's company, the harder it was becoming to hold onto those few shreds of scruples and not turn his charms full force on her. He was an expert seducer; he had enough conquests to know he would succeed, no matter how many religious convictions she claimed. Stronger, more experienced women had succumbed to his lures.

He considered his amorous history, not with pride, but in a realistic assessment of the risks to the young, innocent woman.

Why *not* pursue Miss Leighton? a tiny voice asked. As she had so frankly stated it, she was an heiress, and an heiress would keep the wolves from the door, even if her money had no power to save his soul.

Like a strong magnetic pull, the idea drew him. What was it about this girl that threatened to captivate him as no other woman in the British Isles and across the Continent of Europe had and whose attraction he fought with everything he possessed?

It was more than her freshness and innocence. He'd enjoyed that before. It was more than her pretty face and pleasing personality. He'd known such women by the score—more beautiful and vivacious. Was it perhaps the look he'd sometimes catch in her eyes, a sort of pensiveness, as if she were discerning who he really was deep in the recesses of his black soul?

He was tempted at those times to give in to his desires and pursue her, to meet the challenge he read in her gaze. It was as if he wanted to win her for the sole purpose of discovering what her look really meant. Somehow he suspected that even after he'd captured her and was ready to claim his victory, she would have the last laugh. Those variegated brown eyes with their greenish depths, would laugh as if to say, "You thought you'd fooled me, that I was too naive to know what I was getting, but you didn't fool me. I knew exactly who you were."

He'd see then that she had perceived all along what a base, worthless fellow he was. She'd uncover his history, and then concede that even her Savior would want nothing to do with Gerrit.

He shook his head at the folly of his thoughts. She was a mere chit of a girl. What did she know of men and the world? Look how Delia's behavior had shocked her.

Miss Leighton was an innocent. He was sure of it. How he'd love to test his theory by stealing another kiss—not a bare skimming of lips. No. This would be a soul-searing kiss that would brand her forever as his.

One real kiss would prove just how innocent she was. But he'd held back up to now from crossing that threshold.

Why was he trying so hard to spare her? Or was it himself he was desperate to spare?

After Major Hawkes left the house party, Hester found Thistleworth Park a dreary place. At least Lord Billingsley had also departed. Neither had bid her goodbye and she wondered if they had left together. She felt Lord Billingsley's departure a good riddance, but couldn't help feeling a sense of hurt at Major Hawkes's lack of any farewell.

Had he left because of her silly words about marrying her? She'd thought the awkward moment had passed satisfactorily, but perhaps she had frightened the major. Perhaps he thought she was falling in love with him, and his leaving was a gentle way to discourage her sentiments.

Or maybe he hadn't thought of her words at all afterwards. He was a man of the world, as he kept trying to tell her, and doubtless had left many engagements pending in London.

But the life of leisure and self-indulgent amusements among the vast and beautiful rooms and grounds of Thistleworth had lost their charm for Hester, and once again she only felt a desire to end her visit as soon as decently possible.

She avoided Lady Stanchfield and felt awful for doing so, but she couldn't help herself. She had no idea what to say to her, and each time she saw her or Mr. Delaney, she felt sick inside. Thankfully she saw little of him, and when she did, he stared through her as if she were a stick of furniture.

Lady Stanchfield was different. After Major Hawkes had spoken to Hester, Lady Stanchfield had approached her in a diffident manner. Hester had felt so awkward that she'd been extra polite, but this seemed only to create more of a distance between the two of them.

In an effort to put Miss Leighton completely out of his thoughts, Gerrit went in search of alternative female companionship. That had always worked in the past.

A few days after his return from Thistleworth, he left a tavern after a game of dice with his lieutenant, Edgar, and headed to Haymarket. The two men sauntered down the street eyeing the women who lounged against the buildings or loitered on the street corners. It wasn't long before Gerrit saw what he wanted. As he paused beside the pretty blonde, she let her shawl fall off her shoulders and sported her charlies for him. She was all he favored in a woman, lush and curvaceous.

She eyed him up and down. "Care for some company, captain?"

Although her cheeks and lips were rouged, her features were still young and fresh. "You're a bonny lass. Have a friend for my companion?" He indicated Edgar with a gesture.

"Always willing to oblige." She waved down the street, "Tess!" In a moment, another girl joined them. She was similarly clad in a diaphanous gown, which left little to the imagination. She sidled up to Edgar. "You're an 'andsome pair o' gents in your regimentals."

"You're a fine-looking piece yourself," Edgar told her, patting her generous hips.

"Where're you off to this fine evening?" the first girl asked Gerrit.

He reached for a ringlet of her blond hair and twirled it around his forefinger. "I had no particular destination in mind. Any suggestions?"

She leaned closer to him. "I'm not particular. If you've no place to go, there's always St. James's down the road."

He chuckled. "I fancy a soft bed myself rather than a park bench. Care to come along to my rooms?"

"I'd enjoy nothing more."

Seeing that Edgar was already walking off with the other woman, Gerrit hailed a hansom and gave the jarvey his address. Inside the coach he immediately proceeded to kiss the wench, seeing no reason to delay gratification. It had been too long.

"You don't sound like a London girl," he said as he caressed her.

"I come from Lancashire—oh," she giggled against his mouth. "I like that." She moved to accommodate him more.

"Been here long?" he murmured.

"Only three months…"

He'd been right in his cursory assessment. Fresh from the country. Less chance of disease. He'd protect himself in any case. One experience with the clap in his younger days had been enough to last him a lifetime.

After they arrived at his lodgings, Gerrit lit a lamp in his sitting room while the girl divested herself of her shawl. Crocker was nowhere to be seen. All the better. His batman was probably engaged in similar activities of his own.

The girl wrapped her arms around him from behind. "Patience, my girl, until I finish with this lamp."

She only laughed and slipped her fingers into his hair.

He replaced the glass on the lamp and turned to her. "You are a naughty girl."

"It's not always I get to lay 'ands on such an 'andsome gent." She smoothed her hands down the sides of his coat sleeves. "And an officer. Are you a Waterloo man?"

"Mmm," he murmured, silencing her words with a kiss.

She returned his embraces, her body melting against his.

Even as he kissed her and held her, he felt a strange waning of any desire for her. He renewed his efforts, telling himself it was merely the lateness of the hour, or perhaps the fact that he'd been abstemious for…most of the summer, it seemed. He'd lost track of how long it had been.

Since the disaster with Lady Gillian. The memory drew him up short.

"I feel thirsty." He pulled himself away from her slightly. "Care for a drink?"

"I'm parched," she said, outlining his lips with her fingertip.

Gerrit poured them each a generous goblet of wine. He felt the need for the invigorating drink. He took a long swig, wondering why the prospect of an attractive, willing female held so little allure. After another swallow, he set the pewter cup down. "Come, sweetling, it's time to satisfy your host."

"I'd love nothin' better," she said with a laugh, downing the rest of her glass and wiping her mouth with her hand.

Gerrit led her to his bedroom. The girl lay back on his bed, beckoning to him with her arms outstretched. He lay down alongside her, waiting for his initial desire to rekindle. She pulled him close and kissed him, obviously using her skills to entice him. To no avail.

After several equally fruitless efforts on each one's part, Gerrit lay back away from her, still no closer to fulfilling his end of the bargain. He felt a strange torpor, as if his limbs no longer belonged to him. What had happened to him? For the first time in his life, he hadn't been able to perform.

The girl laid her hand across his chest. "That's all right, luv, nothin' to worry yerself about. It 'appens to plenty o' coves. No need to get upset."

"I'm not upset...merely pensive," he said, draping an arm over his eyes. Wishing he could just be rid of her, he eased away farther on the bed. Had he drunk too much this evening? That must be it.

"I remember a gent, tried so hard but nothin'. 'Ole night long 'e was at it..." She chuckled. "Then there was Mr. Marleybone. I remember 'is name cause 'e was sweet on me and kept me a few weeks. There was a spell when he couldn't manage it neither..."

A spell? Gerrit rubbed his eyes. This was one *night,* hardly a spell.

"Now this other toff, never did know 'is name. Most don't give their names. Well, 'e swore by Dr. Berrychill's Elixir. But it didn't work that time."

"Thank you for regaling me with your stories," he said, rising from the bed. "You are most informed, I'm sure, but you needn't bother. This was just a momentary aberration."

He put on his dressing gown and belted it tightly. "I merely drank too much, slept too little last night...was distracted..." How many nights hadn't he drunk more and still bedded a woman?

Was he getting old? Did a man lose his prowess already at six-and-twenty? He'd have to ask Crocker, who was in his forties. Yet he'd never heard Crocker speak of having a problem.

The girl finished adjusting her gown and stood looking for her shawl. He spied it in the sitting room and fetched it for her.

"I'm sure you're right, luv," she told him as he draped it around her shoulders. "I told you, it 'appens to the best o' men."

"Yes, so you said." He dug into the pocket of his jacket for some coins. "Here, you go. That should make up for your trouble."

"Oh, no trouble at all, captain. I quite enjoyed myself," she replied with a sly smile. "Come, look for me anytime ye want to 'ave another go. The name's Esty. I'm usually at Haymarket. 'Twould be my pleasure to accommodate ye anytime…day or night," she added with a saucy wink.

"I'll be sure to remember that."

She waved at him. "Don't forget, 'appens to the best o' men."

Well, now it had happened to him.

Gerrit lay back on the bed, his arms folded behind his head, pondering this new knot in his life.

The next afternoon—Gerrit deliberately chose afternoon, a time when he was well-rested and sober—he looked up a female friend from his former days in London.

She was still as beautiful and amusing as he remembered. They spent the first hour reacquainting themselves with each other over tea.

The next hour proved not as entertaining, as Gerrit again tried every way he knew to bestir himself, with no success. This time he couldn't tell himself it was because the woman in question was a common street wench with little attractions. This lady was not only beautiful, but expert in the ways of pleasing a man.

"Darling, Gerrit," she told him, smoothing his hair back off his forehead, "it's nothing to be concerned about. I'm told it happens to every man once in a while."

He shushed her with a fingertip. "Yes, to the best of them, I've heard." He quirked an eyebrow at her, "You say you've been told. I take it that means this is the first time it's happened in your—er—presence?"

She considered. "Yes, I believe it is. But don't worry." Her smile was languorous. "I shan't take it personally. Now," she said more briskly, as if knowing instinctively that he didn't want to dwell on the topic, "how about coming with me to the Little Theatre tonight?"

"I think not. I have an engagement with some of the Guards," he lied, knowing it would soon be true enough.

As he rode toward Whitehall later that day, he tried to put the past two days out of his mind. They were merely isolated incidents, nothing more.

As soon as he returned to a steadier routine in his life, things would get back to normal. Thankfully, he was taking command of his regiment once again. Keeping more regular hours, cutting down on the drinking, getting regular exercise should do the trick.

He nudged Royal forward, eager to meet with his commander at the Horse Guards.

Delia returned to London in early September. Soon Viscount Stanchfield would be headed north for the hunting season. So, she wanted to do some shopping in town before she was isolated in the wilds for a month.

She was annoyed with her baby brother. Gerrit had up and left Thistleworth with only a note. He'd clearly left poor Miss Leighton pining.

However strained their own friendship had become, Delia was grateful the girl hadn't betrayed her. Neither by a word nor gesture had Miss Leighton hinted to a soul about the viscountess's little indiscretion in the garden. So Delia hated to see her sad countenance over that worthless Gerrit. After he'd abandoned the party, Miss Leighton no longer joined the gentlemen at their outdoor games. She spent all her time either reading by herself or sitting beside Mrs. Bellows, helping her with her needlework. Delia shook her head. It wasn't right.

Thus, as soon as she was back in town, Delia sent a note to Gerrit asking him to come to tea the next afternoon. As she sanded the note, she thought how it wouldn't be a bad thing for Gerrit to settle for someone like Miss Leighton. Besides the obvious advantage of her dowry, there was something sweet and constant about the girl. She'd be a steadying influence on that rattle of a brother of hers. And if he was too much of a slowtop to see it, well, Delia would just have to help him along.

After she pressed her seal into the wax of the note, she took another sheet of paper and began her invitation to Mr. and Miss Leighton.

Gerrit read Delia's note and tossed it aside. Tea at four. So, his sister was back in town. He wondered about Miss Leighton. Delia made no mention of her.

How had she fared after he'd left Thistleworth?

Gerrit strolled to his window and pondered the question that had never left the perimeters of his mind since his departure.

Needing to find out, he headed to his sister's for tea.

When he arrived, he found both Mr. Leighton and his daughter seated in his sister's salon, sipping tea. They were not the only guests present, so Gerrit couldn't talk privately to either Miss Leighton or Delia. After greeting his sister who scolded him for absconding from her house party, he made the rounds of her crowded sitting room. When he reached the Leightons, he nodded to the father.

"Good afternoon, Mr. Leighton."

The older man furrowed his brow at him as if trying to remember who he was.

"This is Major Hawkes, Papa," Miss Leighton said softly beside him.

"I remember. Major." Leighton gave a brief nod of his chin.

"I trust you are finding London to your liking."

"It's profited me."

Gerrit inclined his head and said no more, preferring to turn his attention to the man's daughter. She was a sight for sore eyes in her yellow sprigged muslin, with matching ribbons in her straw bonnet.

He bowed his head over her hand. "It's good to see you again, Miss Leighton."

She said nothing. He peered again into her eyes, which continued studying him. Was she angry? Hurt at his abrupt departure? "How was your journey back?" he asked, hoping to elicit something, he didn't know what, from her.

"Without incident." Although brief, her words held no animosity.

"I'm glad. And you are well?" She seemed more than well. She seemed like a breath of fresh air in the stuffy city. There were no signs she had been pining for him. He should feel relieved.

"I'm very well, thank you." She hesitated a second. "And you?"

Was there more behind her simple words? "I'm fine." *Drowning, but fine.*

With nothing more to say, he was forced to nod once again and move on to the next guest. After that, he had to content himself with sitting across the room and observing the woman whom he'd been unable to get out of his thoughts even though he'd removed himself far away from her presence.

She sat quiet and erect, replying whenever spoken to. Delia did try to include her and her father in the general conversation, but it was difficult for her as hostess to do much more than throw an occasional question their way, when they did nothing to contribute to the talk.

Gerrit couldn't help but smile. Mr. Leighton said no more than "yes, ma'am" or "no, ma'am" to Delia's questions. Gerrit knew how uncomfortable these gatherings were for Miss Leighton. He pictured how wild and free she'd been on the grounds of Thistleworth. As he watched her now, he relived that fortnight at his sister's house party. Had his presence there made it more tolerable or less for Miss Leighton? Had she been sorry to see him leave or glad?

He didn't regret leaving. He knew it had been the best—the only—thing to do.

When Miss Leighton and her father rose to go, Gerrit got up immediately and followed his sister to the door to take his own leave of them.

After a brief exchange of nods with Mr. Leighton—the man clearly hadn't warmed to him at all since the disastrous rout—Gerrit turned to Miss Leighton and held out his hand.

"It was good to see you again," he began, even as he hated the sound of the insipid phrase that didn't begin to describe what he'd felt upon seeing her.

She gave him a small smile. "I've missed you."

The words were his undoing, more fatal than a gunshot. They were spoken so simply and with such evident sincerity that they ripped through every reason he'd created for staying away from her.

Without having any prior intention of doing so, he found himself asking, "Is it still your custom to ride in the Park in the forenoon?"

His words seemed to throw her. She hesitated a few seconds but then nodded. "Yes. It's my favorite part of the day."

Her quiet words didn't diminish the enthusiasm of them, and he was struck again at how much *he'd* missed her. "Perhaps I shall run into you."

"I rather think not. I am out quite early, usually by eight."

That *was* early, but her immediate assumption that he wouldn't show challenged him. On the other hand, she'd been specific with the time. Clearly, she was leaving it up to him. The early time of day would give him a chance for a quick ride to the park before he had to be at the Horse Guards' Parade Grounds.

"You never know." He bowed over her hand. "Good day then."

"Good day."

Reluctantly he let her hand go and turned to leave, feeling a sudden pang. He really didn't want to be out of her company.

He felt her gaze on his back until he was out the door.

As soon as he'd left Miss Leighton's presence, Gerrit told himself to stay away. He repeated the same thing to himself all evening long.

He'd gotten what he'd wished. He'd seen that she had survived Thistleworth; she'd come away unscathed, in fact. If he were to judge by her appearance, the place had agreed with her. She looked positively refreshed. Soon, she'd be heading back across the Atlantic with her father. She would make out fine in the remaining time in London under Delia's and Mrs. Bellows's wings. His part in the drama was over.

Yet, the next morning, he was up at seven, shaved, washed and breakfasted. By a quarter to eight he was out the door with plenty of time to get to Hyde Park.

Drat! He'd forgotten to ask her which gate she used. Taking a chance she would follow a similar route as when he'd last seen her, Gerrit headed his horse in that direction. It was but a short while later that he spotted a rider in the distance, followed by another. The place was almost deserted at that hour. He breathed a sigh of relief, realizing only then how fearful he'd been of missing her.

"Good morning, Miss Leighton," he greeted her when he came abreast of her. He raised his hat to her, then to her groom. "Ned. How are you?"

Miss Leighton gave him a wider smile than the one the day before. "You remembered his name."

"Why shouldn't I?"

She laughed, a sound of pure joy, and he wondered if it was for him or merely for the beautiful morning, or because they were both alive and in each other's company.

Her eyes sparkled at him. "Why indeed?" Without another word, she took up her pace once again along the riding path. Gerrit followed suit, nudging Royal forward with his heels.

Hester kept her horse at a canter, preferring to ride than indulge in conversation. She'd rather not dwell too deeply on how happy—a word hardly adequate to describe what she was feeling—she'd felt when she'd seen Major Hawkes on the riding path.

In the days after his departure from Thistleworth, she'd had time to realize how foolish her awakening feelings for the major were. She'd observed enough of his sister's way of life and that of her friends to see how little she belonged to their world.

Would the major's world be any different? Of course not. Hadn't he himself striven to make her see that? If she'd wanted to disbelieve it, it was only because of her foolish fancy. Didn't the Lord teach clearly not to be un-equally yoked with another? Even her mother had frequently cautioned her in her letters to guard her heart.

But Hester's growing resignation that her feelings must be put aside had taken a drastic reversal the moment she'd seen Major Hawkes in his sister's London drawing room. To see him this morning in the Park, to know he'd made the effort to come out so early to see her filled her with such joy that she could hardly contain it.

She didn't fool herself that his sentiments were any deeper than they'd been at his sister's house party. If they were, he wouldn't have left the way he had, without even a farewell.

Deeply grateful, nevertheless, for this temporary gift of his company, she determined to enjoy it to the fullest and not think too closely of the moment when it would have to end. For now, she was content to ride and laugh with him as they talked of inconsequential things.

From that morning followed a week of early-morning rides. The major met her each day at the same place, except Sunday, when she'd told him she'd be going to church. They never prearranged it; upon parting, the major would simply say that maybe he would "run into her again." Hester saw him at no other functions, although plenty of invitations appeared in her mail since her return to London. These she attributed to Lady Stanchfield's patronage.

To keep her mind off the future, she kept her calendar full, taking Mrs. Bellows with her on her calls. Although Hester couldn't help looking for the major at each ball or rout, it was in vain. Often, he would ask her about her activities, and she amused him with anecdotes.

One morning when they rode as far as Kensington Gardens, the major suggested they dismount a moment to view the ducks gliding along the Basin. Walking along the edge of the water, he turned to her. "Delia says you've taken London by storm. She tells me all the young ladies want to emulate your popularity with the gentlemen."

She gave an inelegant snort, not breaking her easy strolling gait. "All they have to do is gain some skill at athletic games…and never find themselves alone with any one gentleman."

He glanced over at her. "Have any more of them been making a nuisance of themselves like Billingsley?"

She shook her head. "Not at all, but then, I am more careful now…thanks to you."

"Have you seen the marquess?"

"I catch sight of him now and again, but I steer clear of him." She giggled. "And he of me. I don't know if seeing each other is more painful for him or for me."

He smiled back at her, and she was captivated by that smile that dimpled his cheek and reached deep into his eyes. "I daresay the memory is something that will forever cause him mortification."

The two remained silent a few moments. She was startled by the major's question when he next spoke. "Surely among the cream of London's crop you have found one young gentleman worthy of your notice?"

She hesitated. "No-o," she finally answered.

"You don't sound too definite. Surely there is one?"

She could feel her face grow warm under his scrutiny. She turned back to her horse. "Major, you're incorrigible." Ned helped her remount. As she guided her mare back onto the path, she called over her shoulder, "You won't be satisfied until you have me married off to an Englishman, will you?"

He laughed and saluted. "I'm nothing if not persistent."

She joined in his laughter, although it was a bitter-sweet sound to her ears, and nudged her horse into a trot, feeling the Major watching as she rode away.

After that conversation, Gerrit had to ferret out the truth. He had to find out who had managed to win Miss Leighton's affection. He began to fling out names of young bucks at her and to each she would laugh and shake her head, which only challenged him the more.

As they sat on the banks of the Serpentine, throwing sticks into the dark water, he brought the subject up again. "I bet you have finally managed to snag that title and are too ashamed to tell me."

"I'm sorry to disappoint you, but no titled gentleman has offered for me. Papa and I must swallow our disappointment." She gave an exaggerated sigh. "Mama will be devastated. She had her heart set on my marrying a lord. A mere baronet would have served the purpose."

He forced a jovial laugh. "There's still time. Whole fortunes have been determined on an evening's round of cards."

"Your confidence in me is flattering, but I fear not one of them will marry a mere cit." She shook her head sadly.

"That has been no impediment to a number of lords and baronets. Even a mighty duke has been known to succumb to the allure of a fortune." He snapped his fingers. "I know. I can set about ruining a titled gentleman for you at an evening's game of faro, and by next week, he'll be asking for your hand."

She fell silent a moment until he wondered if she had taken him seriously.

"By next week, time may have run out."

He looked at her, wondering now whether she was the one serious or still playing their game. "Why is that?"

She turned away from him and stared out at the water. "Papa told me this morning he's ready to sail back to America."

Gerrit swallowed. How could one simple sentence have the power to tear at the fabric of his existence? His carefully controlled nonchalance? His devil-may-care attitude?

She was watching him now, that steady measuring gaze that always threatened to see too much. Gerrit tooled his features to reveal nothing of the gaping chasm opening up within him. Yet try as he might, he couldn't tear his gaze from hers.

He saw something so pure in her eyes that it scared him. It wasn't the desire, wanting or grasping he was familiar with, just a profound depth of feeling, which asked nothing in return.

What could she read in his eyes? Desire? Want? Or just a profound need? Nothing pure, all selfish and self-interested.

"When are you leaving?" he finally asked, pulling away from her gaze and concentrating on the murky pond in front of him.

"By next week sometime."

When he said nothing, she added, "Papa has concluded the bulk of his business. It only remains to load the final cargo."

"Yes, quite." He gave a deep sigh and looked at her again. "And his other business? Finding a suitable husband for his eldest daughter?"

She gave a choked sort of laugh. "Oh, that. Well, he can't have everything."

He narrowed his eyes at her, convinced now she must feel heartbroken over someone.

"Surely there is one young man of the ton you favor." He strove for lightness. "As I said, I can still bring you a duke to heel."

"Your concern is flattering, but I fear such a husband wouldn't suit me. I could not respect a man who wooed me solely for my fortune."

"Of course you couldn't." He kept his smile in place, imagining what it would be like to lose Hester Leighton's respect. A deep dark hopelessness engulfed him.

"I really should be getting back," she said, rising to her feet and shaking the skirt of her riding habit.

He stood at once. As they walked back to their mounts, he asked, "Are you looking forward to going home?"

Before mounting, she turned to him, her hand on the pommel, "Yes, in many ways. But I can hardly bear the thought of never seeing you again."

Once again, he was riveted by her direct gaze. This time there was no misinterpreting it. It was a woman's love he saw in her eyes. He knew enough of the senti- ment to recognize it.

He swallowed and before he could stop himself, said, "I can scarcely imagine it myself." His voice came out half-whisper, cracked, low and unsteady, but she didn't seem to notice. Her eyes filled with tears, until one, then two began to overflow and run down her cheeks.

He felt as if someone had punched him. How his body strained to close the gap between the two of them and crush her to himself!

But he refused to let go and give in to his baser instincts. If he did, he knew he would regret it, and more importantly, so would she.

For she would eventually see, in the not-too-distant future, past his facade and would come to despise him. He would know firsthand what it would mean to lose Miss Leighton's respect. He didn't think he could survive that.

At least now she thought of him as an amusing companion, a dashing soldier…a friend. It was the best he could hope for.

So he took out his pocket handkerchief, the one Crocker had handed to him this morning, neatly folded and starched, and patted the tears from her cheeks.

"Will…you continue to be my friend?" she asked in a small, hesitant voice.

He smiled, feeling tenderness well up inside him, a sensation he thought never to feel again. "I shall always be your friend." That, at least, he could promise.

"And forget this silly schoolgirlish display and treat me as before?"

He put away his handkerchief, damp with her tears. Later, at his leisure, he could take it out and put it against his mouth. "It's not silly, and of course we shall continue as before." What kind of an insensitive brute was he? But it could be no other way.

Her eyes still glistened. "You were my only friend in London."

His heart squeezed at the simple, sweet declaration. "A privilege I regard highly." Keep the tone light.

She smiled a watery smile and he managed a smile in return.

"Now, up you go," he said softly. "You mustn't be late for your next engagement. There is no telling how many dukes will be awaiting you."

As the days grew closer to her departure, Hester's anguish also grew. She prayed and paced her room, but deep inside she didn't know how she could leave without letting Gerrit know how much she loved him. Maybe the reason he never shared his feelings with her was that he felt unworthy because of their differences in fortune. She did not want that to be the reason.

As far as spiritual matters were concerned, she was still in a quandary. How could she leave him when she still felt he needed so much more than the society he was in could offer him? Where was he expected to hear about the Lord among the company he kept?

She broached the subject with her father. She'd always been able to talk to him about anything, but this time, he replied curtly that "Major Hawkes is typical of the society which spawned him—spoiled, indolent, in short, the last man I'd want my daughter to lose her heart over." Hester bit her lip, shocked at her father's vehemence. This was not the merciful man she knew, who had helped many an unfortunate to start over and make something of himself.

Hester was surprised, yet heartened, to see Major Hawkes at a ball a few nights after their ride in the park. She felt as if the Lord had answered her prayer, giving her another chance to talk to him. She'd let his nonchalance put her off in the park. But now, she felt the evening would bring her courage.

With her father on one side and Mrs. Bellows on the other, she didn't know how she would get a moment alone with the major. He didn't approach her immediately, yet whenever she glanced across at him, she noticed him looking her way. He didn't dance. As at that dance so long ago, she had the impression he was there expressly for her.

Finally, when Hester was getting desperate, afraid her father would suggest at any moment that they should leave, Major Hawkes came up to her as a new set was beginning. After greeting both her father and Mrs. Bellows, he asked her for the dance.

"Yes, I should like that," she replied, trying to tell him with her gaze how glad she was to see him.

As he was leading her out to the dance floor, she turned to him on impulse. "Major Hawkes, would you mind very much if…if we didn't dance?"

He lifted a brow in question. "Are you unwell?"

Her eyelids fluttered downwards. "No, not at all. It's just, I was wondering…" She looked up at him. "Might we…take a stroll in the gardens instead?" There, she'd been bolder than she'd ever been with a gentleman. She waited, hearing only her thudding heart.

If he felt any surprise, he didn't show it, but murmured, "Of course. Come." He took her arm and weaved through the crowd. She wondered if her father were watching her and how she would explain it to him afterwards.

They walked in the cool night air. She didn't ask where he was taking her nor did she notice where they were going. She felt no fear or hesitancy the way she had with Lord Billingsley. All the contrary, she felt safe and protected.

They stopped and only then Hester bothered looking around. It was a sheltered space, away from the noise of the ballroom. The major led her to a stone bench.

"It was a bit stuffy in there, wasn't it?" he asked after they were seated.

"Yes, very."

When he said nothing more, she took a deep breath, glad for the semidarkness to hide the flush of her cheeks. "All this time you've gone over any potential suitors— you've poked fun at them, you've described their attributes and faults to me. Why haven't you ever courted me yourself?"

If her question took him aback, he made no show of it, but answered almost immediately, "Because you are good and I am evil."

She stared at him, struck by his directness. "Don't be silly. You are always hiding behind that mask of rake, but I've seen nothing except kindness in your behavior toward me."

"What does the Good Book say? What has light to do with darkness? You think I'm harmless." He sighed, rubbing the back of his neck. "How little you know of me." He held out his hands, palms up in a gesture of frustration. "Don't you understand how many men I've killed with these? They're covered in blood. So many young Frenchmen killed. For what? So that I can enjoy an idle, useless life here in the London salons?" He turned away from her with a bitter laugh.

"But that was in battle. You fought honorably to defend your country—"

He turned back to her angrily. "Honorably? Tell that to the scores of young men not yet twenty years of age who lay on those battlefields."

How could she reach him and help heal the pain he carried? "You did what any good soldier would have done."

"Precisely. A good soldier maims and kills, and after he's beaten his enemy, he plunders his wealth and uses his women." His eyes glittered in the dim light. "Or perhaps you can understand this scenario more clearly. Like Billingsley, I took up a challenge once to seduce a young lady.

"Unlike you, she wasn't even of age. She was only seventeen. But none of that mattered. I wanted her and would let nothing stand in my way."

Hester swallowed, suddenly knowing she didn't want to hear the rest. "Why—why didn't you offer for her?" The question was out before she could stop herself, driven by the need to know in spite of her fear.

"She was of the finest pedigree and had quite a fortune. Her parents would never have countenanced a match with me."

"But…if you loved her?"

"That had little to do with anything. I merely fancied

her." His lip curled in a sneer. "The chase is all that matters to most men, my dear sweet innocent. So, I did everything in my power to seduce her."

When she said nothing, but continued to stare at him, wanting so much to believe in a good ending to his tale, he continued. "I took her most valuable possession."

She blinked, her heart racing. Was he really saying what it sounded like? Could he really have done such a vile thing?

"Do you not understand me?" He leaned down to her and grabbed her arm in a bruising grip. "I took the one thing more valuable to her than her name and all her wealth."

"Why?" she whispered, knowing there had to be more.

"Simply because it amused me at the time."

"C-couldn't you make it right?" she stammered out, feeling sick.

"Of course I could have, but I chose not to. I preferred becoming a soldier and seeking glory on the battlefield."

"But you came back. Couldn't you have married her then?"

He gave a harsh laugh. "I'd clean forgotten her existence and enjoyed countless women in between." He looked away from her, as if the next part filled him with more shame than the first part of the story. "*She* had not forgotten *me*. She'd given me her heart and I could still have taken it." He glanced back at Hester and now she read pain in his eyes. "You see, she still loved me, scoundrel that I was."

"So…why didn't you make things…right?"

"Because she was already married."

At Hester's sharp intake of breath, he continued, a hard smile stretching his lips. "Probably an arrangement by her parents. The joining of two old, prominent families. But for some inexplicable reason, despite all my unfaithfulness to her, she still fancied me and offered herself to me. Her marriage wouldn't have stopped me, of course—"

"What did stop you?" she pressed on, knowing there was more.

He shrugged. "Divine providence?" He gave a mirthless laugh. "No, I suppose you could say it was her husband. He was an honorable man." He looked down, letting go of her arm. "A gentleman. The type of which I had never met before. This man defended her honor in the most quaint, time-honored way. He fought for her. And won." He sighed, a long, drawn-out sound. "Do you see what I am now? I'm nothing but a bloody rogue. I pick and choose women as I go along, then discard them when I'm tired of them. Billingsley is a gentleman beside me."

Hester sat bowed down on the bench, her hands lying loosely in her lap. She didn't know what to say, what to think. These things couldn't be true of the man she knew. The man she'd given her heart to. But one glance at his bleak face told her it was all true.

It was that very expression of despair in his eyes that touched her heart and eased the pain and shock of his confession. It gave her hope that he was a man desperately in need of forgiveness. Slowly she stretched out her hand toward him and touched his arm, striving with the light touch to show him he was not beyond redemption.

But he moved away from her as if her touch burned him. "Don't. Through these weeks of knowing you, the only thing that has kept me going is the knowledge that I haven't dragged you down with me. Please grant me the illusion that I've exercised some long-hidden scruples where you are concerned." His voice was a hoarse plea.

She wanted with all her heart to comfort him.

He stood and stepped away from the bench. "Go away from me, Hester. Run as far as you can!"

She stood. "You're wrong. You are not beyond hope. You've treated me honorably. All you need is to let the Lord know you repent of your past and He will grant you forgiveness."

He glared at her, his eyes dark and fearsome. "Haven't you heard anything I've said? Leave me! Leave me and save yourself!"

She took a step toward him, but he put up a hand as if to fend her off. She took an involuntary step back.

He let his arm drop. "Goodbye, Miss Leighton," he said wearily. Then he left her. She heard his footsteps echoing on the pavement. She brought her hand to her mouth to stifle her cry. The tears began to flow. He was gone. She knew she'd never see him again.

Chapter Thirteen

Although Hester went to the park at the usual time the following morning and the one after that, Major Hawkes no longer came. She hadn't expected him to, but still she hoped.

She looked for him at all the society events she attended. Every time she spotted a bright red uniform jacket on a taller-than-average form, or a head of black hair, she stood on her tiptoes and craned her neck to get a better look, her heart beating with anticipation, but it always turned out to be someone else. Another dashing officer, but not as dashing nor as handsome as Major Hawkes.

Although she'd known since he'd left Thistleworth that her love for him was hopeless, she couldn't help falling into a despondency and a quiet sort of desperation as each day ticked closer to her departure. She read the Bible and prayed in earnest for the major's soul, for the time that he would realize he was worthy of love and forgiveness as a being formed in his Creator's image. She also asked God to do something with the feelings in her heart that refused to go away.

Oh, Lord, purify this love. I know I mustn't desire him as my husband…not in the state he's in, but oh, God, I love him so much. How am I going to bear never seeing him again?

She'd delve into the Word and seek the Lord's strength, the way she'd been taught by her parents and her pastor and those elderly ladies of prayer whom she'd looked up to all her life.

She found her greatest solace in Psalm 119. *Blessed are the undefiled in the way, who walk in the law of the Lord… O that my ways were directed to keep Thy Statutes! With my whole heart have I sought Thee: O let me not wander from Thy commandments….Thy word is a lamp unto my feet, and a light unto my path. I have sworn, and I will perform it, that I will keep Thy righteous judgments.*

She had always loved God's Word and wanted more than anything to continue obeying it.

At breakfast, Hester picked at her eggs with her fork, as she'd done for the last three days. Her father looked at her over his newspaper, his eyes reflecting concern behind their spectacles. "You seem to have lost your appetite, my dear. What's ailing you?"

She moved the congealed egg around her plate. "Nothing," she said scarcely above a whisper.

He didn't look convinced. "It would have nothing, by chance, to do with a certain redcoat, would it?"

Her glance flickered up to her father's. "What do you mean?" Was her heartache that obvious?

The ruffle of his paper was the only sound in the room. He looked at the two servants standing at attention against the walls. "Please leave us."

When she was alone with her father, he said, "Are you sad because you must say goodbye to your attentive major?"

She swallowed. "Yes. How—how did you know?"

He shrugged, a twinkle showing in his brown eyes. "Because I care about you. He's been 'running into' you in the park every morning, hasn't he?"

"Yes. We haven't planned on it. It just happens." Ned must have told her father. She looked into her porcelain chocolate cup. "He's my…friend."

"I believe your 'chance' meetings have been innocent, at least on your part. I've trusted you to use good judgment. That's why I haven't forbidden you nor said anything until now." He sighed deeply, sitting back in his chair. "I hope he hasn't pressed you to become more than a friend." His tone was ironic when he used the term friend.

"Absolutely not." She thrust her chin out a fraction. "In fact, he's done quite the contrary." She looked down, remembering all the self-effacing remarks he always made. "I would say he's done everything in his power to convince me he is no good for me."

Mr. Leighton pursed his lips. "I see. It's more than I would have given him credit for." He fingered his unused silverware, aligning the utensils against the edge of the table. "I had him investigated."

Hester stared at her father, her mouth agape. "Papa, how could you do such a thing!"

He dismissed her accusation with a wave of his hand. "Because I love you. It's what I would do for any of my children or family members. Your Major Hawkes is no more than I supposed when I first talked to you about him."

"He's a brave man, a decorated soldier—"

He shrugged. "He may be all that. But he's also in debt up to his ears and he shows no promise to make anything of himself now that it's peacetime. Officers are in excess at the moment, so unless he gets himself appointed to some European court in some diplomat's entourage, or gets himself to one of Britain's far-off Colonies, there's not much future for him here.

"From the little I saw of him, he appeared spoiled and too handsome and charming for his own good. Look how he behaved in that whole rout debacle. He never showed the least remorse. No, my dear," he ended with another sigh, "he's not the man I would see you settle down with."

She looked at her plate. She'd always dreamed of having her father's approval the day she fell in love with her future husband. It tore her heart apart to think there was such a divide between the two men she loved most. "Everything you say may be true," she began slowly, remembering the major's terrible confession. "But I love him, Papa. I see something good in him, something worth saving." She looked across at her father.

"We are all worth saving," he answered gently. "Our Redeemer paid too high a price for any to be lost. But that doesn't mean it's your task to save the major, nor do I think he wants to be saved." Her father spoke in that soft, kind voice he had always used when discussing something with her he knew would be difficult for her to accept.

Her lips trembled and she could feel the tears welling in her eyes. She dashed them and pressed her mouth tight, hating herself for breaking down. She wanted to be able to discuss things sensibly with her father, to make him understand what she'd seen in her weeks in the major's company. But now he'd only behold a sentimental young woman unable to see realistically past her calf love.

She stood. "Well, you needn't worry, Papa. The major has already said his goodbyes to me. We shan't be seeing one another any more, and in a few days you and I will be on our way across the Atlantic, far from him."

"Hester—" her father began, but Hester turned away from him and headed to the door.

"It's all right, Papa. I shall be fine."

Once out the door, she ran out to the back to the mews, where she would meet Ned for their accustomed ride in the park.

During her entire outing, she breathed in the smells of late summer and tried her best to impress every image in her mind. Memories of their early-morning rides would soon be all she had of Major Hawkes, and she didn't want to forget a single image, a single word…the major's teasing smile, the way he held the bridle of her horse when she dismounted, or spoke a gentle word to Royal, the elegant way he carried himself, his courtly behavior, so different from any man she'd ever met.

* * *

Gerrit visited the London docks to find out which was Jeremiah Leighton's ship. The *Sally Ann.* Must be named after his wife…Hester's mother. He wondered briefly what that woman was like, the one who'd probably most influenced Hester to become the woman she was. Was she as true and faithful to her husband as Hester seemed destined to be to the one she'd eventually spend the rest of her life with?

He shook aside the thoughts, his heart sinking afresh. After making a few inquiries he found out exactly when the ship was scheduled for departure. The day after tomorrow near dawn, with the tide.

If he could just hold out until then, Hester would be safe. Every morning when he'd awoken at seven, he'd had to fight a battle with himself not to go to the park. Instead, he'd dressed—lying in bed was impossible— and headed directly for the parade grounds and begun his drilling exercises earlier than usual with the few men who were assembled at that hour.

He'd ignored every invitation his sister sent him, her every note, knowing exactly what she was up to.

Only two more days and Hester would be free of him.

He turned and left Limehouse Dock.

On the night before Miss Leighton's departure, as soon as his military duties were over that day, Gerrit headed for the nearest tavern, as he had been doing every night since he'd found out the ship's schedule.

The only way he knew to keep away from Miss Leighton in his free time was to get good and drunk so he'd be in no condition to see her. He no longer tried to substitute another woman, terrified he'd prove another failure in that area.

Edgar came by and sat down beside him. "What's up these days? Rolled up more than usual that you have to hide out from your creditors?"

He grunted into his tankard, preferring for him to believe that.

"The boys are complaining you've become a bore. They miss the old Hawkes who wouldn't back down from any wager."

He turned to his lieutenant. "What did we come back for?"

Edgar stared at him until he understood his meaning and just shrugged. "The war is over. No one here at home will ever understand what it meant, but who cares? We've got one another. That's all that's important." He gave Gerrit a slap on the back before turning to a passing serving girl. "Another round, d'you hear!"

Hours later, Gerrit left the tavern. He wasn't even drunk, having spent the last few hours passed out on a bench. He couldn't even remember the evening behind him. He shivered in the predawn gloom. The sky was thick and gray and a fine drizzle fell.

There'd be no sun lighting this morning's eastern sky. Without meaning to, he headed for the river. He needed to check the course of the tide so he'd know when Miss Leighton's ship was weighing anchor.

He walked down the Whitehall Stairs to the river's edge. The watermark was high so the tide wasn't yet on the ebb. He took out his pocket watch. It wouldn't be long now. With the morning's sobriety, he could no longer run away from the reality of Miss Leighton's departure. In truth, the fact hadn't left him the entire evening.

He stared at the leaden water, flattened by the drizzle. His life resembled that murky gray depth. Nothing but a dreary rhythm with no purpose.

His gaze wandered eastward once again but he couldn't see beyond the bend at Somerset House.

Suddenly he turned and bounded back up the stairs.

Hester leaned over the ship's railing, watching the barrels and boxes being brought up the gangplank. What a dismal morning to be departing England. Raindrops plopped onto the dark Thames. The rain didn't stop the activity on the quay, however. People crowded the wet stones; boxes and crates were piled high at the edge. Sailors shouted orders from the deck of the ship.

Normally a ship's departure would have excited her. She loved to watch them arrive and leave from the Bangor waterside. This morning the hustle and bustle only reminded her of the fact that it was her own leave-taking, which meant never seeing Major Hawkes again.

Soon the tide would begin to recede. With each wave, her father's ship would take her farther from these English shores. She watched the flotsam bob up and down on the black water. The cries of seagulls and the shouts of sailors filled the air.

"It won't be long now, miss," her new maid said at her side. Hester looked over at the young girl named Meggy and gave a wan smile. Her father always visited the poorhouse and hired on both sailors and anyone else he saw fit and able, whose character he judged to be decent, before making his homeward journey. He promised them a fresh start and opportunities of land and employment in the new world, and never lacked for willing workers.

Meggy was only about fourteen and seemed eager to leave London. A few weeks ago, Hester would have shared her feeling. Well, it *would* be nice having a friend on board ship. And in a few weeks, she'd see her family again and sleep in her own bed and breathe in the scent of her beloved fir and pine.

Hester glanced once again at the crowd down below on the quay. Her heart jumped. Could it be? Or were her eyes playing a cruel trick on her?

She peered hard through the rain toward the back of the crowd. He came into focus. The tall, rugged figure standing head and shoulders behind some bystanders. His dark cape hid his uniform, but his bicorne was unmistakable. She nearly cried out in her joy.

He'd come! He'd come to see her after all! Hester grabbed up her traveling skirt and backed away from the rail in the direction of the gangplank.

"Miss, where you be going?" Meggy called after her.

"I need to go ashore," she shouted behind her shoulder.

"Oh, miss, we be leaving soon!" Meggy hurried after her. "You best not."

But Hester wouldn't have been able to stop if the ship had already been in motion. "There's time. I'll be back in a trifle, I promise." Without another word, she pushed her way past the sailors making their way on board, pushing large barrels before them. She was the only one going downward.

Another voice—a sailor's—shouted out, "Come back, Miss Leighton. Where're ye off to?"

"I'll be right back. I see someone!"

"Have a care or you'll miss the ship!" another shouted after her.

"I will. Tell Papa I've just gone down on the quay." Then she ran the last half of the gangplank, ignoring any further warnings. When she got to the dock, she had to push through the crowd.

"Major Hawkes! Major Hawkes!" He'd seen her and began pushing against the people toward her. She was panting by the time she reached him.

At last! She stared up at him. In those few seconds she took in every inch of his features. The brim of his hat dripped with rain. His jaw was shadowed with the black stubble of his beard and there were shadows under his eyes, but his blue eyes were the same as always as they searched hers now.

"You came," she breathed. And then she was in his arms, not aware of who had made the first move, not caring, only knowing how wonderful it felt to be crushed against his damp cloak, his strong arms wrapped around her, her face pressed against his chest. She breathed in the scent of him, the dank fog, the salt sea, the remainders of tobacco from wherever he'd been that night, the damp wool. And she knew she'd never forget this mingling of scents.

At last she separated herself from him just enough to look up into his face once more. That dear, beautiful face. Never had he looked so handsome to her, even though he looked a far cry from the polished officer she was accustomed to seeing. His eyes were bloodshot, she noticed, his unshaven cheeks haggard.

"You came," she repeated.

He pulled a glove off one hand and brought it up to her face, stopping just short of touching her cheek. Finally his forefinger skimmed her skin so lightly she hardly felt it.

"Yes. I…I couldn't let you go…" He cleared his throat, as if he was having trouble with his voice. His lips twisted in a grimace of a smile. "I didn't want you to think so badly of me…after all."

"I could never think ill of you," she whispered, her heart so light it nearly floated. "Don't you know that?"

"I couldn't let you think I didn't care about you," he continued as if she hadn't spoken. "I've never had a friend such as you."

He explored her cheek gently with his fingers as he spoke.

"I'm glad. I knew you cared…a little," she told him, her face leaning into his touch.

His warm hand cupped her cold cheek at last. She closed her eyes, reveling in its warmth.

"I care about your happiness," he said in a low, rough voice.

She opened her eyes and stared into his, trying to discern what he was telling her.

"Some day, when you're a little older…and happily married to some worthy young man and have lots of children at your feet, you'll look back to this time and thank the good Lord that He saved you from this wastrel."

She was shaking her head as his meaning became clearer. He hadn't come for her, but to bid her a final farewell. She could feel the tears filling her eyes and spilling over her cheeks.

"Dear child," he whispered, wiping one away and bringing his finger up to his mouth to taste it.

"You speak as if you were so ancient, as if your life is half over," she said, trying to figure some way of refuting what he was telling her.

"I am and it is." He wore such a sad smile. "I feel all dried up inside—as if I'd been all used up." He brought a handkerchief up to her cheeks and wiped away the dampness. "You mustn't cry. I can't bear it if my being here causes you more pain."

"Your coming here brings me joy, but your saying goodbye fills me with grief. I…I'm so afraid I'll never see you again." Her lips began to tremble.

He shushed her with his fingertip. "You have to go back to your family, your life… You are too good for this place."

"I'm not 'good!'" she cried, her fingers clutching his cloak.

"Yes, you are. You are all that is goodness and light. The people here have been too blind to see that."

"I'm not like that," she insisted, half laughing, half crying, despair filling her as she realized what she hadn't before, that this really was the end.

"Don't ever change," he continued softly, his hand once again cupping her cheek, his thumb pad stroking it. "Maybe then, when I think about you, all the way across the ocean, it will help me to stay the course."

"Don't speak that way," she said, not caring that she was openly crying now.

"Hester!"

They both turned as they heard her father call from the foot of the gangplank.

"You must go," the major told her. When she made no move, he gave her a little push away from himself.

Hester put her hand to her mouth. Why must she choose? The two men she loved best were at opposite ends of the quayside.

"Go, Hester," the major urged her. She took a step back from him, and reluctantly disengaged from his embrace.

He gave her a little salute.

There were so many things she wanted to say to him. *Write to me. Come to me! Ask me to stay! I love you!* But she said none of these things. Instead she reached out one last time with her bare hand to his stubbly cheek.

"Remember that Jesus loves you."

His only reply was a twisted smile, which smote her heart. It showed her he would give anything to believe that but was unable to.

"He has called you friend," she told him. "I call you friend. Goodbye." Though there was much longing in her heart to remain, she finally turned away and began her slow trek back to the ship. Her father was standing only a few yards away, but he didn't approach her, letting her come to him of her own will. She gave him a grateful look for not having interrupted her time with the major.

Now he only took her arm silently and helped her back up the gangplank.

"Goodbye, my friend," whispered Gerrit to Hester's departing back.

He didn't leave the quay until Hester had reboarded

the ship. He stood watching until he saw her tiny figure high above him, leaning against the rail. He knew when she'd spotted him, although neither one waved to the other.

He waited until the first sails were unfurled and he heard the shrill sound of the boatswain's whistle. Slowly, aided by the departing tide, the great ship began to move. The rain had stopped and a light breeze filled the foremasts.

He knew Hester watched him as he watched her until the ship disappeared at the bend at the Isle of Dogs and the East India Docks.

"Goodbye, Hester," he whispered to the foggy air enveloping the now empty quay.

"Time to get up, sir."

Gerrit mumbled something and turned away from the stern voice.

Next he was roughly shaken.

"What the—"

"Up and at 'em," Crocker said firmly, as he had each morning at what seemed only a few minutes after Gerrit's head had touched the pillow.

Gerrit rubbed his face, wanting only to bury it in his feather pillow and disappear back into sleep. But his faithful batman was already thrusting a cup of coffee at him. Gerrit pulled himself up, every muscle sluggish, and took the cup in a hand that had a slight tremor to it.

As he sipped at the strong hot drink, he watched Crocker get his shaving things together.

"All right, sir, get yourself over here so I can make something of that ugly mug o' yours."

Gerrit set the half-empty cup on the bedside table and stretched. He felt a hundred years old. With a shudder, he stood and, picking up his cup again, ambled over to the chair Crocker indicated, knowing it was only with Crocker's prodding that he was able to face each day as the commander of a troop.

As soon as he sat down, a hot towel was wrapped around his face. Then lather covered his whiskers and next Crocker's sharp razor was scraping away at the previous day's growth.

"You know you can't keep this up," Crocker began as he wiped the razor against the towel draped over his shoulder.

"Keep what up?" he asked, his eyes closed, knowing full well what Crocker was about to say. He was amazed the man had kept quiet until now, although every morning and every evening he'd eyed him with that look, which said more than a shake of a head.

"You know perfectly well what I'm talking about it, so don't treat me like a flat. You can't get jug-bitten every night and stay out till the wee hours, then expect to be at drill by eight the next morning."

"I seem to be doing fine."

Crocker gave a loud humph as he scraped the razor down Gerrit's jaw, just missing his earlobe.

"Watch you don't slit my throat."

"Why not take you out o' your misery and be done with it?" was his only reply.

They spoke no more. Gerrit stood and splashed cold

water on his face. After he'd washed the rest of himself and donned the freshly pressed uniform Crocker held out to him, he felt once again that perhaps…just perhaps, he could get through one more day.

To what purpose, he didn't know.

"Well, I'm off to the parade grounds," he said to his man as he was ready to leave.

"Maybe you should take a fall off that horse o' yours and break your neck. Put us *both* out of our misery!"

Gerrit chuckled and closed the door after him.

Knowing Crocker was right didn't help Gerrit change his ways.

Since Miss Leighton's departure, he found he couldn't face his free time alone. As soon as his duties of drilling and reviewing his troops were over, he headed to an out-of-the-way tavern, having no desire to be with any one of his former drinking companions, and began to drink. It was the only way he knew to blunt the edge of his memories and to avoid thinking of the future. Even the next day was too daunting to face.

It was only in the hours after midnight that he was able to stumble home and collapse in bed. Sometimes, he miscalculated. He'd thought his mind was sufficiently benumbed, but when he lay in his bed, the images would come. Hester, Lady Gillian, the French cadet…every bloodied soldier on the battlefield…all colliding on the panorama of his mind until he thought he'd go mad.

He tossed and turned on his bed, wanting to shout for it to stop, but knowing nothing would help. He clutched his temples and buried his head in his pillow to stifle any sounds. Finally he'd have to rise, although his body protested with fatigue, and go to his table and pour himself another drink with shaking hands. He drank like one parched, the liquid spilling down his chin.

Why don't you kill me, Lord, kill me and be done with it? His mute scream went unanswered, as he knew it would.

Scarcely more than a fortnight since Miss Leighton's departure, Gerrit stood at the same quay and looked down the Thames. This day was a crisp September afternoon, the sun bright against the water, enough of a breeze to cause a light chop to the waves.

He'd come to a conclusion the night before. Either Crocker was going to find him one morning drowned in his drink, or he could take the only salvation offered him.

He could go after Hester.

She was the only one who could save him. If she couldn't, then there was no hope for him. It was that simple.

He kicked at a piece of debris at his feet and watched it fall into the river. It bobbed a few seconds in place before it began to float down the river toward the sea.

Yes. He had to follow that same course. Leave England and head to America. Discover if it was possible to make a new start.

Putting his plan in place took more effort. As he sat that evening totaling his debts and figuring out a way to pay for a passage to America, he realized it was nigh on impossible.

On his next free day, he went to visit his father.

"Off to America?" he said, pouring himself a drink from a crystal decanter. He lifted it before Gerrit, but Gerrit shook his head in refusal. "No? Well, no matter."

His father took a sip. "Fine Madeira. Had it from a fellow in town last time I was there." He sat back in his armchair with a satisfied sigh. "So, tell me more of this venture. Duns after you? You could go to France, you know, now there's the peace. Fellow can live a decent life in Calais, I've heard, on a pittance."

"I'm going to sell out. Use the funds to pay off my debts. I may still be shy for my passage." He stopped short of asking his father for any help. He needn't have bothered.

"Sorry I can't help you with anything. In a bit of a fix myself at the moment. You know how it is."

Gerrit looked at his father, his once handsome face slightly bloated, the bags beginning to become more pronounced under his eyes, the black hair now streaked with white, but heavily pomaded.

"No, I didn't expect you to," Gerrit assured him. "Just thought to stop by and tell you and Mother my plans."

"Well, let us know when you're leaving. Maybe we can host a send off. Any excuse for a party will cheer your mother."

Gerrit left a short while later. After pawning anything of value—every miniature of any lady who had given him one, his gold watch and cuff links, he stopped short at his Waterloo medal. That should bring in some money from some collector, he admitted, weighing it in his hand. It was either that or sell Royal.

He sighed, having to face the prospect of giving up his horse. That turned out to be harder than all the rest.

Finally, he visited his sister to tell her the news.

Delia stared at him when he told her of his departure. Instead of crying out a protest as he'd expected, she reached out a hand and squeezed his. "I'm glad you've come to your senses."

He gave a grunt. "My senses?"

"Go after her. She's what you need."

He turned away from his sister. "I'd have to win her first."

Delia touched him on the elbow. "I don't think that will be so difficult."

"I won't come to her a ne'er-do-well or pauper."

She considered. "I see. You don't want things easy this time, do you?"

He shook his head.

She sighed. "I wish you Godspeed then."

He finally told Crocker.

"Are you mad?" were his faithful man's first words. His look of disbelief was almost comical.

"Most likely," he answered cheerfully. Since he'd sold everything of value, beginning with his commission, he'd felt a certain lightening of the heaviness that had seemed to weigh down on him since returning from the Continent.

Crocker scratched his head. "Well, when do we leave?"

Gerrit braced himself for what he must answer. "I'm going alone this time."

The older man looked at him. "You're serious."

Gerrit nodded.

Crocker's shoulders seemed to slump the tiniest bit. Then he turned away, busying himself with straightening a chair.

"I want you to have Royal."

Crocker swung around to him. "You're giving her up?"

Gerrit shrugged, having come to terms with the reality of it, and comforted by the fact that he could trust Crocker with his horse. "I want you to have her. You saved my life more than once on the battlefield…and now, these past few weeks…" Gerrit swallowed, his throat suddenly thick. He turned away from the older man. "Anyway, consider it barely a recompense for your services all these years."

Crocker was rubbing his face, as if still trying to digest what Gerrit was telling him. "But…but you could…sell Royal to pay off your debts."

"Those are taken care off. There are plenty of young gentlemen eager to pay a sizable sum for the glory of an officer's uniform in peacetime."

"But that money's your capital. What'll you use for blunt to start your new life in America?"

He gave a slim smile. "My wits, as always, I suppose."

Crocker fell silent a moment. "I sure hope the lady is worth all this."

Gerrit answered without hesitation. "She is. The question is, am I?"

Crocker approached him and squeezed his shoulder. "That's a much harder question for a body to answer about himself."

Gerrit sat down on his bed, suddenly feeling the reality of leaving all that was familiar. "I'm burning my bridges behind me this time."

"Well, they say America is the land of opportunities."

"Just because the Almighty saw fit to spare me on the battlefield and allowed me a few victories, doesn't mean I'll be any good in that wilderness over there."

Crocker sat down beside him with a heavy sigh. "I've been with you a long time, sir. Seen you do a lot of crazy things. Once the notion takes you to do something, there's none can stop you." He paused. "But, I daresay, many's the time that's what's saved the day on the Peninsula—when you dared what no one else would. If you ask me, you've got what it takes to make a go of it off the battlefield, in that new land."

Gerrit smiled, appreciating Crocker's kind words. He shook the old man's hand, squeezing it gently in his. "I pray you're right."

The morning he left, Crocker was the only one he allowed to see him off. As promised, his family hosted a party for him the evening before, and when he'd left it, he'd had another send-off by his military comrades at a tavern, until dawn had tinged the horizon.

Now he stood with his former batman in the gray light of morning. It had been almost a month since Miss Leighton's departure, and the air was chillier, the breeze stiffer.

Crocker, his arms folded tightly against his chest to ward off the cool, said, "Thanks for arranging things with your sister to board Royal at her stables and to give me a job as groom."

"Think nothing of it. She was more than happy to do it."

"Who knows, maybe I'll prefer serving horses to serving men."

Gerrit grinned. "They'll be a darn sight more grateful, I'll warrant."

Crocker eyed him, not bothering to contradict. He cleared his throat. "I took the liberty of packing some writing paper in with your gear. Once you're settled in, drop me a line occasionally just to let me know you're still alive."

Gerrit nodded.

"Just send it to your sister's address for the time being."

"Don't expect any news for a while." Gerrit hesitated. "If you never hear anything, it means I'm dead…or that I failed."

"You're not going to do either, sir, so I expect word some day." He glanced up at the ship Gerrit would soon be boarding. "You certainly didn't give me trouble with packing. You're hardly taking a thing with you."

"I haven't need of much."

Crocker eyed him with approval. "I must say, you look just as fine in a gent's togs as in an officer's."

Gerrit fingered the cloth of his new greatcoat. "It feels funny not to be in uniform anymore." He felt naked in some ways.

"By the way," began Crocker, "I didn't see your Waterloo medal—nor any o' them for that matter—when I packed your things. Hope you gave them to Delia for safekeeping."

"I took them to Farley, as a matter of fact."

Crocker stared at him open-mouthed. "You hocked them! Are you loose in the haft? If you have no use for 'em, maybe your future grandchildren might have a thing or two to say about your throwing away the most honorable thing you ever earned!"

Gerrit looked away with a sigh, not wanting to be reminded of what he'd done. "Well, many a fine gent who's never been near a battlefield will probably find good use for them. At least Farley seemed to think so. He gave me a good price. Enough to pay my passage at any rate, with a little left over for provisions."

Crocker shook his head at him in disgust. "You could have asked your family to tide you over."

Gerrit's father had made it clear to him how matters stood in that department. He had not applied to Delia, knowing how delicate things were with Lionel at the moment. And his brothers…one was too far away to visit and Gerrit wasn't close enough to either one to beg for funds. But he told Crocker none of this, just shrugged once more. "What's done is done."

Finally the two shook hands. "Don't forget to write me once you see your way clear," said Crocker. "You're more like a son to me—" His voice broke then and with an oath, he pulled Gerrit to him. The two embraced, Gerrit feeling as if he were letting go of his last mooring in a perilous sea.

Chapter Fourteen

Bangor, Maine Territory
December 1, 1815

The voyage from Liverpool, England to Bangor, Maine was not something Gerrit wanted to repeat—ever. In closed, dark quarters on a merchant ship crossing the "Western Ocean" as the sailors called it, through gales so fierce, the ship seemed ready to sink any moment and there wasn't a dry spot on the entire vessel, the voyage lasted a grueling eight weeks. It had been much longer and more harrowing than the crossing to Spain in his younger years, despite the threat of French frigates then.

Gerrit had never been so thankful as when the look-out shouted "land-ho" from the crow's nest. Shading his eyes and peering into the distance, the wind whipping at his greatcoat, Gerrit saw it at last—the slim edge of coastline.

It proved to be only an island. But soon they were

sailing past more and more islands, some only an out-cropping of rock and barren snow-covered turf, others larger and wooded.

As they sailed by the larger islands, Gerrit spotted small inlets, their harbors lined with boats of many sizes—sloops, schooners, dories—and a half-dozen white clapboard houses with black shutters and dark shingled roofs rising above them on rugged slopes.

The mainland appeared at last on the horizon. Gerrit looked at everything in wonder. Great gray rocky boulders, stony beaches, dark green wooded hills inter-spersed with snow-covered meadows and fields, an oc-casional farmhouse visible in the distance, or a bobbing boat moored at a private landing. Behind the large, white farmhouses, the many outbuildings were attached to the main house, creating the look of long buildings standing alone on the harsh landscape.

The ship navigated the mouth of a wide river and continued upstream. A sailor told him it was the "Pe-nobscot." The river wound its way from the rocky coast inland, past ever hillier terrain. Farmland soon turned to fir-covered mountains, just as Hester had described to him. The land was breathtakingly beautiful, like noth-ing he had ever seen, but it also looked primitive and lonely.

Soon, cleared land and farmhouses began reappear-ing. Several three-masted ships and two-masted schoon-ers edged the river as they approached Bangor harbor, with its companion town, Brewer, which Gerrit would call a village, visible across the river.

What caught his attention at these two harbors were

the logs. They floated in special enclosures at the river's edge, they were piled onto the quays, and they lay on the sandy banks opposite, where frames of ships' hulls stood in stocks.

He turned his attention back to his destination, the town of Bangor. It appeared more of an outpost to him. Although there were at least a dozen ships and schooners moored along its wharves and several brick buildings along its waterfront, beyond them the town soon disappeared into more fields and scattered farmhouses.

Where was Hester Leighton in this quaint setting? he wondered. He gripped the gunwale, more and more nervous with each passing minute.

Would she even remember him? Or was England some distant memory now? Was his coming here nothing but a fool's journey? The fears he'd fought to ignore during the many monotonous days and nights at sea now barreled him like a cannonade.

As soon as the ship was brought quayside, a small crowd of men gathered. Amidst shouts, ropes were thrown down and the gangplanks lowered. Confusion reigned as the cargo from Britain was unloaded. Gerrit took up his satchel. The time of reckoning had arrived.

His gaze scanned the area. He'd already learned that there was no hotel in town. The cheapest and most plentiful rooms were to be found right there at the harbor, nicknamed the Devil's Half Acre. They couldn't be any worse than the places frequented by seamen in London. He gripped his satchel tighter, making his way down the gangplank. For the first time in his life he was truly alone, answerable to no one.

Just as he stepped onto the Quay, a winch swung a netted cargo overhead. As it was lowered onto the dock, one of the ropes broke loose and the wooden crates within it began tumbling out.

A lone boy bent to lift a bundle, oblivious to the danger above him.

Dropping his satchel, Gerrit lunged toward the youth, hauling him away by the arm just as the crates came crashing down.

Men clamored around them and the split crates. "Are you all right?" came from all sides.

The boy, his eyes wide with fright, could only nod. Gerrit stared at him now, feeling his own cheeks drain of color. The young French cadet stared back at him from wide blue eyes.

Gerrit blinked, erasing the image. Of course it wasn't the same boy. He could see how he'd been mistaken. The two appeared about the same age—perhaps fifteen—with the same physique and coloring. As he stepped back, he saw the differences. This boy's face was slightly longer, his nose a trifle larger. Mostly, this boy was very much alive, his cheeks ruddy and full of health, not the ghostly white of a corpse.

This youth was tall for his age, reaching almost to Gerrit's height and his shoulders were broad. But he was still a boy, Gerrit could see from the scant whiskers on his cheeks. What continued to startle Gerrit was the color of his eyes. It was the same shade as the dead French boy's—bright and blue as the cloudless sky over Waterloo after the previous day's rain, which had turned the battleground into a field of mud.

"You s-saved me," the boy stammered.

"I just happened to be at the right spot at the right time," Gerrit replied, uncomfortable with the boy's look and tone of awe.

The boy glanced past him at the damaged crates on the wharf, and with the resiliency of youth, began to laugh. "I would have been as flat as a flapjack if you hadn't come along just then."

A smile tugged at Gerrit's lips, relief beginning to flood him, now that the danger was over.

"Are you sure you're all right, Jamie?" an older man asked, clapping him on the back.

Jamie? Where'd he heard that name?

"I'm fine, Ethan."

"We'd better tell your father."

Alarm filled his powder blue eyes. "No! Please don't. He won't let me come down here anymore if he knows what happened." Seeing the man's hesitation, he grabbed his arm. "Please, Ethan. You know how I want to go to the camp, and if he hears about this, he'll keep me home."

The man scratched his grizzled head, shaking it back and forth. "All right, I won't say a word…though I'm sure he's bound to hear about it from someone else."

The boy grinned. "Thanks. It'll at least give me some time to think how I can reason with him."

The boy turned back to Gerrit, a frown clouding his young features. "You won't say anything either, will you, sir?"

"I don't know. Who's your father?"

"Jeremiah Leighton. He owns the ship."

So…this was Miss Leighton's baby brother, the one she spoke of with such love. "No, I won't say anything."

The boy smiled in relief. "Thanks, mister." He shoved off a wool glove and stuck out his hand. "I haven't thanked you properly. Jamie Leighton, at your service. And I *mean* that."

Gerrit had to smile at his earnest tone, although he still had to fight his reaction to the boy's uncanny similarity to the young Frenchman. He clasped Jamie's hand in his. "Gerrit Hawkes."

"Glad to make your acquaintance. You sound British."

"That's because I am." Thankful his own name didn't seem to mean anything to Jamie, Gerrit disengaged his hand and stepped back. He wasn't ready yet to reveal his purpose here to this boy. "Can you direct me to a rooming house nearby?"

"They're all along the street behind here," the older man indicated with a gesture.

"Thank you. Well, I'd best be on my way." His tongue itched to ask about Jamie's sister, but he held back.

The boy, too, seemed to want to delay him with more questions, but Gerrit turned away with a wave. "I expect I'll see you around in a town of this size."

"Yes, I hope so." His voice sounded eager.

Gerrit strode quickly from the area and began to look for an available room. He ended up at a large tavern which several sailors had recommended.

It didn't take him long afterwards to find the offices of Jeremiah Leighton. It seemed Hester's father owned half the wharves and ships lining the banks of the Penobscot River.

He faced a square brick building, its brass plate etched with the straightforward name of Jeremiah Leighton Logging & Shipping on its shiny surface. Taking a deep breath, Gerrit opened the door, ready for his first real test in the New World.

The jingling of a bell above his head announced his entrance. Several clerks, working on stools at tall narrow desks, looked up. He approached the nearest, a young man who peered at him over wire-rimmed spectacles.

"May I be of service, sir?"

"Yes. I'd like to see Mr. Jeremiah Leighton if he has a moment. You can tell him—" he hesitated only an instant, still not used to his plain, civilian name "—Gerrit Hawkes is here to see him."

"Very good, sir." The young man set down his quill pen and slipped down from the stool. "I'll be back in a moment." He disappeared through a door at the rear of the room.

Good to his word, he came back a few minutes later. "This way, if you please, sir."

Gerrit followed him through the door, where the man left him, closing it behind him.

Mr. Leighton sat behind a wide, polished mahogany desk. He gave Gerrit no smile of greeting nor stood at his approach. His brown eyes measured him as Gerrit crossed the distance between them.

Gerrit debated extending his hand but thought better of it. Mr. Leighton would probably ignore it.

"Major Hawkes." Mr. Leighton sat back, laying down his pen. The creak of his chair was the only sound in the room.

"Mr. Leighton."

The older man didn't offer him the seat in front of the desk.

"What are you doing in Bangor…or is the answer the obvious one?" he asked dryly.

The man wasn't going to make it easy for him. Gerrit cleared his throat. "I've come to ask you for work."

Gerrit could see he hadn't expected that reply. Mr. Leighton pursed his lips and made a pyramid of his fingers. Finally, he said, "You want to work in my company?"

"That's right, sir."

"What do you know of the shipping or lumber business?"

"Nothing, sir."

Mr. Leighton rubbed his chin. "In that case, you'd have to start at the bottom."

"I'm prepared to do that."

Mr. Leighton eyed him up and down. "You might change your mind about that in a few weeks—*if* you last that long."

The silence hung between them.

"I'm only asking for an opportunity to prove myself."

"And if…by some unforeseen miracle, you manage to do that, what then?" The older man tapped his fingers together, the challenge clear in his brown eyes.

Gerrit lifted his chin a fraction. "If I succeed in proving myself to—er—*your* satisfaction, then I would like to ask for your elder daughter's hand in marriage."

Leighton nodded slowly, as if saying this is what he'd expected to hear all along. "You know what I think of you, Major?"

"I have a fair idea."

He harrumphed. "Whatever it is you think, you can double it." With a loud scrape of his chair, Leighton stood and leaned his fists against the desk. "I don't like you, Major, never have."

"I understand that...*sir,*" he added softly.

"You're the last man I'd wish for my daughter."

"I'm in complete agreement with you there."

The older man seemed taken aback for an instant. "I'm glad we can agree on one thing." Leighton came around the desk and stood face-to-face with Gerrit. "I've prayed to the good Lord for the future spouses of my four children since the day they were born. I want them to have the kind of marriage I've been blessed with—to a faithful, loving, godly partner. Do you have any notion about the kind of union I'm talking about?"

Gerrit swallowed, taken aback in his turn by the man's words. "I confess I've never seen one like that."

Mr. Leighton looked at him for an inordinately long time. "My instincts haven't failed me yet. And right now, it goes against all my instincts to give you this opportunity to destroy my daughter's future happiness." He sighed and turned away from Gerrit as if he couldn't stand being so close to him.

"You came back a decorated soldier from your war with the French. Obviously you can kill and survive." He made a dismissive sound. "It's easy to destroy. It's much harder to build something." He stared hard at Gerrit from under his heavy brows.

"I always give a man one chance when it comes to

working for me. Your medals must have meant something. Your attitude coming here today says something more. Now show me if you're any good at building anything. You have one chance to prove yourself to me, Hawkes. If you destroy it, you can leave this city… without my daughter. Do I make myself clear?"

Gerrit nodded. "To the utmost." He paused a fraction of a second. "Thank you, sir."

Leighton grunted. "You won't thank me in a few weeks."

Gerrit faced him down although inwardly he was quaking. "That remains to be seen."

Hester's father moved away from him. "You can report back here tomorrow morning at eight sharp. Ask for Henry. He'll put you to work."

With a nod, Gerrit turned to leave. At the door, he paused. "May I—" He cleared his throat, hating himself for his trepidation "—may I see Miss Leighton?"

Mr. Leighton was already sitting back at his desk. He looked down a second before replying. "My inclination is to say no, but this is a small town. She'll soon find out you're here and probably visit you herself. I'd rather you call on her openly and honorably like any—suitor." He seemed to swallow on the word as if it had a bitter taste. "You may come to our house for supper tonight. Six o'clock. Anyone will tell you where it is."

"Thank you, sir."

Gerrit left then, feeling the biggest hurdle of his venture was behind him.

He returned to the tavern. It was not the best inn he'd

been to but neither was it the worst. Most of all, it was warm, with a large fire going in the great room. He went up to the bar and requested a bath. The middle-aged woman who'd taken his money looked at him as if he had asked for champagne and caviar.

"The men usually have their bath on Saturdays."

"As I've just come from a voyage of two months at sea, I'd appreciate if I didn't have to wait until Saturday."

She pushed a graying ringlet away from her face, then turned to the door behind her. "Daryl!"

A towheaded youth appeared in the doorway.

"Haul up some hot water to this gent's room."

The boy stared at him a moment before nodding. "Yes'm."

As Gerrit walked toward the stairs, he noticed a tavern maid standing behind one of the rough-hewn tables, a rag in one hand. She stared at him boldly and put her hands behind her hips, thrusting out her chest as he passed. He only gave a nod and continued on his way, recognizing the look of invitation in her eye.

If she only knew how futile her attempts at flirtation were, she'd laugh him to scorn.

At least that was one area he didn't have to worry about failing in his test to win Hester Leighton. A sudden fear gripped him. What if he never was a man again on that score?

Hester looked up from the pillowcase she was embroidering, when her father came home from his warehouse.

After he'd greeted her mother with a kiss and some soft spoken words, he turned to Hester and her sisters.

They all looked up from their work and smiled their welcome. "Hello, Papa," came a chorus of female voices.

"Hello, girls. You appear very industrious," he said in approval.

"Did a ship come in today?" Katie, Hester's next-youngest sister asked, eagerness lighting her features.

"Yes, and I've a box full of lovely things from England sitting out in the hallway."

"Oh!" she and her younger sister squealed and hurried out of the room.

Her father turned a look of inquiry to Hester. "Does the thought of lace handkerchiefs and bolts of French silk no longer interest you?"

Hester shook her head with a smile. "I've scarcely been able to wear all the beautiful things you gave me when we were in England." *Nor had the heart to.*

He sat down beside her on the love seat. "A few weeks in London and you're jaded already. What a pity. I can no longer surprise you with pretty gifts and baubles."

Hester patted his hand, glad to have him home. She always enjoyed the news from the ships in port. And if there was ever a slight chance that someone might have sailed in from England who knew Major Hawkes... well, maybe someday his name would slip out in their conversation. She sighed as she put aside her sewing, knowing her secret hope was but wishful thinking. "You know you've never been able to tempt me with anything I'm obliged to sew."

He chuckled and continued to regard her with a thoughtful expression.

"What is it, Papa?" she asked.

He shook his head and shifted his gaze. "Nothing..." He turned to his wife, who sat in a rocker beside the Franklin stove set out from the brick fireplace. "We're having a guest for supper tonight."

Mrs. Leighton raised her head from her sewing. "Oh, who?" she asked with a smile.

"No one you know...except by reputation," he muttered. "A young gentleman," he added, with a sidelong glance at Hester.

Hester wondered who it might be. Her heart quickened. Maybe this time her dream would come true. But no, Papa was always bringing home young men from the office or warehouse. "Is it someone off the ship?" she asked.

"Yes...as a matter of fact."

Her mother knotted the end of her thread. "One of your employees from London? I hope he'll enjoy our simple fare. Perhaps if you'd invited him for dinner instead of supper..."

"Oh, he'll enjoy it fine. I don't believe he's coming for the food, at any rate."

Before either of them could ask him any more questions, he stood and retrieved the day's edition of the *Weekly Register* he'd brought with him when he'd come in. "This paper is not half-bad," he said, settling in an armchair on the other side of the stove, and unfolding it. "We're becoming a first-rate city, with our own newspaper. Now that all the blockades are finally ended, there's no limit to what we'll be able to bring in."

Hester knew better than to press her father when he changed the subject so decisively. If he wanted to surprise them, so be it. She picked up her embroidery with a sigh, hoping supper would be called soon, so she could put her work aside for the evening.

Her father peered over the paper. "Where's Jamie? I didn't see him at the office this afternoon. I hope he wasn't making a nuisance of himself down at the ship."

"He came in a little while ago. I put him to cracking some walnuts for after supper."

Her father nodded his head in approval and turned back to his paper. A short time later, when her mother rose to supervise things in the kitchen, Hester followed her. Together with their cook, Josie, and young Meggy, they finished the meal preparations. Hester helped Meggy set the table in the dining room, then went into the kitchen to cut the warm cornbread.

"The creamed cod is ready to be served, ma'am," Josie told Mrs. Leighton.

"All right. Let me call everyone to the table."

Just then, the front bell clanged. Her father entered the hall. "That'll be our guest, right on time." As Hester turned back into the dining room, he stopped her a moment, motioning to her mother and sisters to continue on in.

"You might want to answer the door. It's someone you're acquainted with." Her father's voice, instead of cheerful, was grim.

"Acquainted with?" *Who could it be?* She tried to remember the names and faces of the men who worked with her father, but she'd rarely been to his offices in London. The only one she'd seen daily had been Ned, and he sailed back and forth all the time.

Her father gave her a nudge. "Go on, don't keep him waiting in the cold."

She started, remembering how frigid it was outside after dark. "Aren't you coming, too?" she asked, when she realized he hadn't followed her to the door.

This was becoming more and more mysterious. Her father stood, still serious, in the doorway to the dining room.

She grasped the doorknob. Slowly she opened the door a crack, then a little wider. Gerrit stood in front of her, his face revealed in the lamplight. Gerrit! All the blood rushed from her head. Her eyelids fluttered down as the strength drained from her body.

"Miss Leighton!" As if from a great distance she heard his shout and then she knew no more.

Hester opened her eyes, blinking several times to focus. As she regained consciousness, she saw a ring of faces above her, all regarding her with anxious concern. She fixed her gaze on one face, the only face that mattered to her in that instant. *He was real!* She clutched at Major Hawkes's coat front, drinking in the sight of him. He was looking at her with concern, and more. Her heart swelled.

You've brought him here, Lord. Oh, praise You! Praise Your name forevermore! Her soul sang with joy.

All around her, her family was asking questions.

"Are you all right?" Major Hawkes asked her softly, his hold on her strong and sure.

She nodded. "What happened?"

His lips quirked upward. "You swooned."

How romantic! She'd never swooned in her life, she

wanted to tell him, but remained silent, preferring to gaze upon his handsome features and bask in the concern she saw in his beautiful blue eyes.

"Hester, dear, are you all right?" Her father's face hovered at her other side. She turned to see him crouched beside her.

"Yes, I was…so startled to see…" she turned back to the major "…Major Hawkes standing there."

Her father's face flushed. "I'm sorry, Hester. I should have told you. I didn't realize you'd have such a shock."

She scrunched her brows, trying to take in what he was saying. "You mean…you knew he was here?" Her gaze flew back to the major's and read consternation in his as well.

"You *didn't* tell her?" His voice sounded stern as he looked across at her father.

Her father ignored the major and answered her instead. "He showed up in my office today and I invited him to supper tonight." Instead of explaining further, he said, "Here, let me take you—" He moved to put his arm around her shoulder, but to Hester's delight, before he could do anything, the major tightened his hold on her and swung her up in his arms.

He turned to her mother. "Where can I lay her—is there a settee?"

"Yes, follow me." She led them to the front parlor.

Hester could have told them all that she was quite capable of walking. Instead she laid her head against the major's broad chest and listened to his steady heartbeat. She brought one hand up to touch him and felt his answering squeeze on her shoulder.

Oh, would that this moment lasted forever!

But then the major was setting her down and her mother and sisters were bringing pillows to put behind her head and a crocheted throw to cover her feet.

"What a peahen, Hester, to go and faint like that!" Jamie stood at the foot of the couch, but his eyes soon left her and focused on the major. "It's you!" His voice turned from scorn to awe.

Her father turned his sharp eyes on his son. "Do you know this gentleman?"

Jamie blushed and looked as guilty as if he'd been caught stowing away on one of his father's ships. "I— I—met him today as he was getting off the *Katherine Marie.*"

Major Hawkes took up the explanation. "Your son helped me get my bearings."

Her father gave a curt nod, but Jamie looked at the major with eyes bright with admiration.

Assuring herself of Hester's comfort, her mother now turned to the major. "Welcome to our home. My husband only told us we were having a guest for supper, and not that it was to be a friend of Hester's." She held out her hand. "I'm Sally Leighton, Hester's mother."

The major took off his glove and held out his own hand with a smile. "Gerrit Hawkes."

"*Major* Gerrit Hawkes, lately from His Majesty's army, the Coldstream Guards, I believe?" Her father's tone was sardonic.

Hester could see the thunderstruck look on the faces of her family members. Her youngest sister, Adele, brought a hand to her chest as if they were all going to be shot momentarily. Katie looked utterly disbelieving. Jamie's look of respect was turning into one of disgust.

"Just *Mr.* Hawkes," he said in the silence, "I've sold my commission."

Jamie was the first to find his voice. "You—you were a redcoat?"

"That's right." He answered quietly. "Before you ask me to leave your house, let me assure you I have no American blood on my conscience. I've only fought on the Continent."

Jamie's mouth worked as he tried to reconcile this new piece of information with his concept of redcoats. Hester's heart went out to him, knowing what he must be experiencing.

"Excuse their…amazement," her mother spoke with quiet dignity. "You must understand we've been invaded by the British, and for two years we watched them burn our ships and blockade our ports."

He turned to her. "I understand perfectly. That is why, if you wish me to leave, I shall do so." He bowed his head.

She took a step toward him. "If my husband has seen fit to invite you, then you are most welcome." She turned to Hester. "If you're feeling up to it, I suggest we all repair to the dining room before everything gets cold. Would you like me to bring you a tray, dear?"

Hester shook her head. "I'm perfectly fine now." She turned to Major Hawkes. She felt shy asking him, but was not about to lose an opportunity to have him near her, when she hadn't seen him in months. "Would you help me up?" She extended her hand.

He came to her side at once and took her hand in his

warm one and helped her stand. Once in the dining room, he helped her into her chair, and her mother indicated that he should take the one beside Hester's. Hester wondered what her mother thought of the major now that she was seeing him in person. Hester's letters had been filled with him during her time in London.

When they were all seated, her father bowed his head and began to pray, "Heavenly Father, we thank You for giving us this day our daily bread. We ask that You bless this food set forth before us. Help us to be mindful of those without, so we may share our portion with them. In Jesus' name, amen."

Hester glanced sidelong at the major and saw that he had followed her father's lead to bow his head and close his eyes. She wondered how her less fancy home and plainer fare would compare to the grand houses of England.

The dishes were passed around as her mother made excuses for the food. "You must come for dinner some day. We eat very simply in the evenings. And I know the food has grown cold."

"Everything is delicious," the major hastened to reassure her. "After weeks of ship's fare, I am doubly grateful for a home-cooked meal."

Her mother smiled at him. "Well, you are welcome to dine at our house whenever you like."

"Major Hawkes will begin working at the warehouse tomorrow."

Hester swung her head from the major to her father and back again. When had all this been decided?

"Indeed?" her mother said. "How nice. Have you,

like my husband in his youth, come to America to make a new beginning?"

"Yes, you could say that," he answered softly, his gaze meeting Hester's. She smiled at him, hope springing in her chest.

Jamie shook his head on the major's other side. "I can't believe you fought for the British."

"I never fought against your nation. I was busy fighting to liberate the Spanish people from the French invaders."

Her father put in from his end of the table. "We consider Napoleon a great man over here. Don't forget France was our ally."

"Many in Europe do," Gerrit answered coolly. "Even in England he has admirers."

"In the time he was in power, he did more than anyone to bring Europe out of the Dark Ages and spread the best ideals of liberty and equality of the French Revolution to the rest of Europe," her father continued.

"I suppose my opinion is colored by the thousands left slaughtered on the battlefields across Europe. To think one single man is responsible for wiping out an entire generation of Europe's manhood is quite…unimaginable, unless one had witnessed it," Gerrit ended quietly. He took up his water glass and swallowed.

The table fell silent.

Hester longed to touch the major in some way, to let him know that her family would grow to love him the way she did.

"Hester wrote to me how helpful you were to her in London," Mrs. Leighton said.

He gave Hester a sidelong glance, the familiar look

of amusement deepening the hue of his eyes. "My sister was the one who did the most to introduce your daughter to London society. Miss Leighton did the rest."

"Did you ever see Napoleon?" Jamie asked.

"No. He had left Spain by the time my regiment arrived. When we entered France, he was busy fighting in Russia. Then during Waterloo, I was busy defending an outpost."

"What's it like to face a column of the French?" Jamie persisted.

Knowing how skillfully Gerrit had always evaded her questions about the war, she was amazed to hear him answer, "It's terrifying."

"What regiment were you with?"

"I was in the first company of light infantry of the Coldstreams Guards. We were a flank company, which meant we would be at one end of the columns during an attack."

Jamie kept plying him with questions which Gerrit answered. By the end of the meal, Jamie seemed to have overcome his aversion to a redcoat at their supper table in the greater reality of having a real soldier—an officer—fresh from the battlefield at his side, able to give him a firsthand glimpse of warfare.

Gerrit wondered if he'd have a chance to talk with Miss Leighton alone. After all that time without seeing her, to have been able to hold her in his arms, however briefly, had been blissful. But now he itched to sit with her and talk and see what his coming here meant to her.

Although she'd seemed to be happy to see him, new

doubts began to surface. She seemed quiet at the dinner table. Her family, overcoming their initial shock at having a British soldier in their house, gradually grew at ease again. Jamie hammered him with questions of the war. Miss Leighton's two younger sisters asked him about London society.

"Is Lord Byron as handsome as they say? Has the Prince Regent really refused to address another word to Beau Brummell since the dandy insulted him, calling him fat? Did you meet the Czar of Russia last summer?"

The youngest sister, Adele, began flirting with him. She was clearly the beauty of the family, with her thick honey-brown locks and long eyelashes, which she was soon batting at him. When the family left the dining room to assemble over coffee and tea in the back parlor before the fire, she usurped her older sister's place and slipped down beside him on the settee. He looked with frustration at Hester who had to sit farther away.

"Tell me about St. James's Palace. Have you ever been presented at Court?" the younger Miss Leighton asked him.

"Ages ago, before I obtained my commission," he replied, his gaze trying to meet Hester's.

"Did you see the king, or was he mad by then?" Adele leaned closer to him, her blue eyes wide in inquiry. She had pouty lips which she seemed to know how to use to maximum advantage.

Gerrit inched back a fraction. "No, I didn't see him. He was spending most of his time at Windsor Castle by then. I was presented to Queen Charlotte and to the Prince Regent."

"Is he as wicked as they say? Does he have a string of mistresses?"

"Adele, come help me pour the coffee." Mrs. Leighton gave her youngest daughter a stern look.

"Yes, Mama." She turned to him with an apologetic smile. "Excuse me, Major, I shall be right back." With a flounce of her skirts, she rose and went to her mother.

Gerrit glanced at Hester, hoping she'd come to sit at her sister's now-empty place. She returned his look and smiled shyly, but did not get up to join him. Her absence brought new doubts. Had he been wrong about how happy she'd seemed to see him at her door?

He continued to wait and hope, forcing his attention to the polite conversation at hand. However, when Hester had still not come to sit at her sister's vacated place, Gerrit drained the last of his coffee and stood to bid them farewell. His body felt old and tired.

Mr. Leighton rose to see him to the door. Gerrit's heart sank. He turned to thank his hostess for the meal.

Mrs. Leighton gave him her hand. "I hope to see you again, major. My invitation stands. Please come by any time for dinner or supper. We always have enough for guests."

Bowing over her hand, he said, "Thank you, madam." Before Mr. Leighton could escort him, Mrs. Leighton turned to her daughter. "Hester, could you please see the major out?"

"Yes, Mama." She rose and came to him, her smile all that he could wish for. It lighted him in a place deep inside him.

Mr. Leighton cleared his throat. "You can report at

the sawmill tomorrow morning bright and early. I'll let the foreman know you're coming."

From the warehouse to the sawmill? Neither prospect sounded easy. Well, he hadn't expected a life of ease in the former Colonies.

He followed Miss Leighton down the corridor to the front door, where she retrieved his coat for him.

"I still can't believe it's really you, here in my own house. I'm afraid as soon as you leave, I'll wake up and find it's all a dream."

"I hope it's a nice dream and not a nightmare."

"How can you say such a thing? A nightmare was having to say goodbye to you in London and thinking I'd never see you again."

He dared reach out and take one of her hands in his, relieved that she did, indeed, seem to care for him. Perhaps she hadn't come to sit by him because she didn't want to appear forward in front of her parents. "Hester—may I call you that when we're alone?"

She curled her fingers around his hand and nodded. "I'd like it if you did."

He didn't ask her to call him by his first name. Above all, he didn't want to compromise her in any way. "I realized after you left—" he glanced away "—that nothing remained for me in England. You were its only bright spot and when you'd gone, everything was all gray."

When he risked looking her way again, her eyes were tender and filled with understanding.

"I came to America planning to work hard. I sold what little I had." He gave an unsteady laugh. "I hope what they say about America is true, that a man can make his fortune here."

"My father did."

He nodded. "I may very well not be half the man your father is."

She squeezed his hand. "You don't have to measure yourself against my father. To each man is given different talents, and I have no doubt that you have many."

"I thank you for your confidence in me. However, I don't want it to be misplaced. I don't want to promise you anything—nor do I want you to promise me anything." When she made to speak, he put a finger to her lips. "There's so much I would like to say to you— and to hear from you, but we mustn't do so now."

"My feelings for you haven't changed, nor will they," she said. Her eyes looked at him steadily, never wavering.

"That gives me hope. I know things won't be easy in the coming months." He looked down at their joined hands. "Your father was not happy to see me show up at his office. I'm sure he thought he'd seen the last of me in London. I have to prove myself to him."

"Was my father very hard on you?"

He gave a crooked smile. "Let's just say he's hoping I'll find the work too rough."

"Don't worry. When my father seems the toughest, that's when he cares the most."

"He cares about you."

"I don't deny that. But he also cares about your soul, Gerrit," she said his name softly, as if making sure it was all right to use it. He said nothing, neither giving his approval nor withholding it. He wanted more than anything to hear his name on her lips, but he didn't want her to put her faith in someone who might not be able to live up to her belief in him.

"Things will get better, I promise you," she continued. "Beneath his tough exterior, my father has a good heart."

He'd stick it out all right, he promised to himself. And not only to win Hester, he realized, but for himself. Leighton's words had challenged him and he wasn't one to walk away from a challenge. He'd had more than one military commander tougher than Mr. Leighton.

It's easy to destroy. It's much harder to build something…show me if you're any good at building anything. Yes, he'd stick it out, and not just to show Leighton what kind of man he was.

As if she'd read his thoughts, Hester said, "You don't have to prove yourself to my father or to me. You only need to find peace for yourself. And there's only One in Whom you will find that kind of lasting peace."

He had no answer for that. "I'll bid you good night. I'm sorry I gave you such a fright when I first arrived."

Her dark hazel eyes sparkled with humor. "A wonderful fright." She became serious. "I thank God that He brought you here. You may not understand this yet, but it was He who brought you to these shores."

"I hope you're right and that I haven't…well—" he shrugged unsure how to word his greatest fears "—done the most foolish thing in my life."

She brought his hand up to her lips and kissed his knuckles. "Don't worry. You've done the right thing."

"Good night, sweet Hester." How he wanted to close the narrow gap between them and kiss her lips. Reluctantly he let her hand go, knowing he would continue feeling the pressure of her lips against his skin for a long time.

She opened the door for him and he braced himself against the freezing air. With a final wave from the front steps, he turned and hurried down the dark path.

Chapter Fifteen

That night, Jeremiah Leighton came to sit at his wife's bedside. "What did you think of Major Hawkes?" He trusted his wife's judgment, but he also knew how persuasive the major's charm and looks could be to a female.

As if reading his thoughts, she laid down her Bible. "I found him delightful. A very presentable young gentleman. Modest, too."

He made a sound of disgust low in his throat as he loosened his cravat. "I wonder if there's a woman alive who finds the major displeasing."

His wife smiled indulgently. "You forget, Hester confided a lot more to me about the major in her letters home than she did to you. I feel as if I've known him almost as long as she has."

"Why didn't she say anything to me all that time in England?"

"I'm sure she knew your feelings about the man and knew you were already predisposed to judge against him."

"I told him I always give a man one chance to prove himself."

"I'm glad you told him that. I think the major has come here to take hold of that one last chance. Hester told me that he has spoken little of his war years, but that she senses he is very troubled by them."

He snorted. "At least he knew enough not to come prancing into Bangor in his full redcoat regalia covered with gold braid and silver badges."

"I'm glad he showed the patience of a saint in answering Jamie's questions, especially if he dislikes talking of the war."

Too restless to sit still, Jeremiah got up and began to pace over the fine Persian carpet. "The thing that troubles me is that we are talking of our daughter's future! It's all very well that the man has come all the way across the sea, fleeing his own demons, and seeking a new life—but is he the right kind of man for Hester?" He stood in front of his wife, imploring her.

She met his look with understanding. "We must pray for them both. I know Hester won't defy you if she believes that your assessment of the major is the correct one."

"You saw the way Adele—and even Katie—were smitten by evening's end. What happens when the other young ladies of our acquaintance set eyes on him? Who's to say Hawkes won't let his gaze wander further than Hester?"

"There is that danger," she agreed, her own gaze troubled. "But if he didn't fall for any English lady…"

He snorted again. "I've heard he left a string of

broken hearts—and worse—in England and who knows where else!"

He continued pacing a few more minutes, his hands clasped behind his back. He knew his duty, as his wife had pointed out, was to pray for Hawkes, but he didn't like the fact that, for the foreseeable future, his Hester and this man would be seeing each other on a daily basis. England had been bad enough, but here Hester was at much more risk. Knowing the major had come all the way to be with her, what wouldn't Hester agree to? And if she shackled herself to this man for life, and the man turned out to be a heartless womanizer—

He had to do something. Suddenly he stopped and snapped his fingers.

"What is it?" his wife looked up, keeping her place in the Bible.

He turned to her slowly. "I want you to plan a few sociables for the major. Invite every pretty young niece of ours and every other young lady we know to meet him while he's here."

She drew her brows together. "But I thought you didn't like him."

"I don't. But I want to see—and I want Hester to see—how he behaves when he's surrounded by every available female. Will he still stay true to our Hester? Or will he let his head be turned by a pretty face? If I know the man, he'll soon let his gaze wander farther afield."

"You want to trip him up. I don't know if that's worthy of you." His wife's gentle reproof would normally have convicted him. But this was his beloved daughter they were talking about.

"I'm doing it for our daughter's future happiness."

She nodded. "Very well. I shall do as you ask."

The next morning, although it was still dark outside, Gerrit showed up at the riverside mill at the appointed time. The air was bitingly cold, worse than the winters he'd spent on the plains of Spain. He was glad he'd bought sturdy work clothes before his voyage when he'd sold his uniforms.

Now he stamped his feet at the entrance of the saw-mill. Already men were busy at their tasks. A middle-aged man approached him across the sawdust-strewn floor, his face dark, his mouth bracketed by deep lines. "You Hawkes?"

"That's right."

"I'm Baxter, the foreman. Ever worked in a sawmill?"

He shook his head. "No, sir," he answered, his long-ingrained military habit of address kicking in.

"Well, come and let me show you what to do."

A couple of men were already placing a log beside a long vertical saw. The water-powered saw began its slow up-and-down movement, slicing through the log which had already had its curved outer edges chopped off.

After taking him around and explaining the various procedures, Baxter took Gerrit outside to where other men were wielding their axes, chopping the outer layers of the logs away.

The foreman handed him an ax, holding it just under the blade. "This can be your best friend or your worst enemy. Keep it sharp. Learn how to wield it, and you'll do all right here."

He showed him how to whack at the outer bark of the pine logs to leave the yellow pulp exposed and straight, making a four-square piece of lumber to be fed to the mill saw.

"The biggest and best of these logs will end up on one of your country's ships as a mast. That's why they need to be handled with care. The rest will be for board lumber and shingles."

Gerrit took the ax from him and attempted a few whacks of his own. He barely nicked the wood.

"You've got to put some muscle into it and develop a rhythm. Here, practice on this waste lumber." He pointed out a pile of lumber heaped haphazardly at one end of the yard.

Four hours later, his back aching in protest from the constant bending and stretching, his palms beginning to blister, his fingers frozen stiff, and his stomach growling with hunger, Gerrit finally had a few moments' rest when the men abandoned the mill for their dinner break.

Gerrit walked back to the tavern. He didn't recognize any of the other men from the mill, so he assumed they had their own homes to return to. As soon as he'd opened his mouth, and they'd realized he was British, he'd noticed a distinct cooling in their attitude. That, coupled with his own incompetence with the ax, didn't guarantee him much popularity with his fellow workers.

At the tavern, a few other men, mostly sailors from the ships in port, sat at the rough trestle tables in the taproom.

"Here's a nice hot bowl of barley soup for you, Mr. Hawkes," the same tavern maid he'd seen the day before came by and placed the thick bowl in front of him. She leaned very close to him as she reached to set down a small loaf of bread on his far side. "Just give me a holler if you need any more," she told him, her gold-flecked blue eyes looking at his mouth.

"Thank you," he said, looking down at his bowl.

A few minutes later, she brought him a pewter tankard.

"There aren't many guests here this time of year, I imagine," Gerrit said, curious at the quiet atmosphere of the tavern.

"Most o' the loggers are up country. Wait till spring, this place will be hopping."

"What happens in spring?"

"The river drive. The loggers all come back to town." She smiled and sat across from him, seeming in no hurry to leave. "They're a wild bunch after a winter in the woods. Then the port will be full of schooners again. Winter is too quiet around here. Nothing but a bunch of womenfolk snug in their houses. Too cold to do much except bundle indoors." She gave him a speculative look, leaning forward on an elbow and displaying her scooped neck for him.

Gerrit bent down to his soup once again. The last thing he needed to do was encourage an over-friendly tavern wench.

He quickly finished his food and drained the last of his ale. The serving maid had left him with an angry sniff when he hadn't continued the conversation. He stood now and looked down at his hands. Four blisters had appeared along the ridges of his palms. Well, soon they would form calluses, he thought with a shrug, before taking up his coat and heading back outside.

When he left the sawmill yard late that afternoon,

the sky was already dark. He saw the shadowy outlines of three horses standing in the street. "I was hoping you'd come out soon." Hester waved to him, laughter in her voice.

His fatigue forgotten, he hurried over to where she sat atop one of the horses. He smiled up at her welcoming face, framed by a warm bonnet and thick scarf. Her cheeks were red.

"Hello, Hester, what are you doing here?" He glanced over at the other rider. "Hello, Jamie."

"We've come to fetch you for supper. I knew you probably wouldn't come of your own accord, even though Mama gave you an open invitation." She held out the reins of the third horse. "I even brought you a mount. I meant to ask you about Royal. What did you do with her when you left England?"

He took the reins and swung himself up in the saddle. It felt good to feel a horse under him again. "I gave her to my valet, Crocker. He'll board her at Delia's and play groom at her stables for the time being."

"I'm glad Royal has a good home."

"So am I." He nudged the horse forward to ride abreast of Hester's mount. Jamie rode ahead of them. "Delia knows horses and keeps an excellent stable."

"Soon we'll be riding sleighs down this street," she said as they followed the road along the river, the churning sound of water loud in the darkness. "We haven't had much snow yet, but it won't be long."

"What do people find to do when they're snowed in?" he asked, remembering his conversation with the tavern maid.

"For the men, it's a busy time, going out to the forests and cutting next year's wood. We women always find occupations at home—there's wool to be spun, sewing, knitting." She glanced over at him and laughed. "I'm sure you're not interested in hearing all about that. It must sound awfully tedious to you."

He wanted to say that actually it sounded quite homey and comforting. He caught himself short. He must be changing. Only a short while ago, he would have found it sounding hopelessly beneath him. Now, what wouldn't he give for a warm home and hearth the way he'd witnessed the previous evening at the Leightons?

"More interesting to hear about are our sleighing parties and skating parties, dances, and singing school. I hope Papa won't work you so hard that you'll be too tired to attend these sociables."

They had left the busier part of the small town, and now the houses were scattered between wide fields. The sound of the river receded in the distance as Hester led them down another road, which he recognized as the one he'd walked the night before. The large houses and outbuildings resembled farmhouses more than town houses.

"What is the name of the river we were walking along?"

"That's the Kenduskeag Stream," she answered. "We have two main waterways in Bangor—that and the Penobscot River."

"Those names don't sound English."

"They're not. They're Indian. The first means 'place of the eel weir' in the Penobscot's language, and the second is 'place of white rocks.' It refers to a rapids further up the river between here and Old Town."

Everything sounded foreign and new. Would that he could make a new beginning in this strange land.

They reached the Leighton home and rode up the long drive toward the stables. One of the barn doors stood open and a warm light spilled out of it. Hester called out a cheerful greeting to a groom who came out to them. She relinquished her reins to him after he'd helped her down. Gerrit followed suit.

From the large barn, which housed a sleigh, a coach and a few wagons, along with several horses and cows, they entered a long shed. The smell of fir wrapped around him like a spicy blanket. Every inch of wall space was stacked floor-to-ceiling with cordwood. The wooden floor beneath him was littered with wood chips.

From the shed, they entered another area which looked like a pantry or buttery. They wiped their shoes on a rush mat and entered the warm kitchen. A cheerful fire burned in the large stone hearth.

He wondered for a moment if Hester's family would still welcome him. Would her father glower at him all evening?

Hester unwound her muffler. "Excuse me for taking you by the back way, but in winter, it's a lot nicer than walking through the ice and snow outside to the front door."

"Good evening, Major Hawkes." Mrs. Leighton turned with a smile from the massive fireplace lined with pewter plates along its mantel. She wiped her hands on her white apron before approaching him. "I'm so glad Hester managed to find you and bring you home. I hope our meal will make up for last night's cold fare."

He shook her hand, warmed by her friendly smile, so different from her husband's. "There's nothing to make up for. I appreciate the invitation to dine with your family. I hope I don't trespass on your hospitality."

"Please don't feel pressed to do so, but please come whenever you'd like." She turned to her daughter, who was removing her long, scarlet cloak. "Why don't you take the major's things and show him where he can wash up? Then you two can sit in the back parlor until supper. Your father should be there."

Gerrit grimaced as he unbuttoned his coat, embarrassed by his dirty work clothes. "I'm sorry, I'm not dressed for dinner. I came directly from the sawmill."

"Don't worry a thing about it. You won't appear any differently from Jamie. He's begun to work in the warehouse when he's not at his studies."

Gerrit nodded, feeling only slightly comforted. Mr. Leighton surely would be in his well-tailored coat and stock. It wasn't easy having to appear as a laborer to a self-made man, whose origins were as common as a sailor's. He sighed, wondering how long he must endure this testing. He saw no end in sight, and he'd only just begun.

The evening passed very pleasantly, and his negative thoughts were pushed aside as he enjoyed the company of Hester and her siblings. Mr. Leighton spent most of his time before supper reading his paper, although Gerrit caught him observing him from time to time. The meal was again filling and hearty. He was developing a taste for this new vegetable called pumpkin. The evening before, he'd enjoyed it in pie, and now he tasted it in a custard.

When he left, Hester walked him back out to the barn. "I want you to take the horse back with you. You can board it at the blacksmith's in town. He's a friend of Papa's."

"That's very kind of you but I can't accept it." How to explain to her that he didn't have the funds to keep a horse?

"Don't worry, it's taken care of. I already spoke to Papa about it."

He felt doubly uncomfortable at the offer. Not wanting to hurt her feelings, he tried to explain, "This is not exactly the way to win your father's favor. He already thinks of me as a worthless—"

"Shh!" She put a finger to his lips. "I promise you it's all right. He agreed right away when I brought it up. Maybe he's already beginning to change his mind about you."

Not likely. Gerrit frowned. What trick was the man playing with him? Undoubtedly to see whether he'd accept the easy way out. But Hester looked so hopeful he didn't have the heart to refuse her offer. He'd bring the horse back tomorrow.

She smiled. "I hope Jamie isn't being a nuisance to you. He seems to have developed quite a case of hero worship. A month ago, he wouldn't have been caught dead talking with a 'lobsterback' as we call the redcoats around here."

He chuckled at the name. "I can remember being his age and thinking I could take on any challenge."

"I'm glad you understand. Right now, Jamie's dream is to go on a logging drive and prove himself as capable as the men who work for Papa."

"That's the second time I've heard of a logging drive today. It seems to be an important event around here."

"Logs are our livelihood. They're even used as legal tender. If this city prospers, it's because of the lumber in the woods upriver from us. It's every boy's ambition to go into the forest to chop down trees and float them down the river to the sawmills." Her face became serious. "But it's very dangerous work, and Papa would just like for Jamie to be a little older before he begins."

"How old is he?"

"Only fourteen."

"He seems older."

"Yes, he's tall for his age. He takes after Papa." She smiled. "Papa has a hard time justifying his protectiveness, since he was already on board a ship at Jamie's age, heading for America. When he arrived here in the Maine Territory from Boston, he signed on with a logging crew." She wrapped her shawl more tightly around her shoulders to ward off the cold. "Well, I'd better let you go and get some rest. I know you have hard work tomorrow. I hope you had an enjoyable evening with us."

"Thank you for your kind invitation."

She handed him the reins. "With your own horse now, you have no excuse not to come every evening. I shall come fetch you again if you don't come on your own." She looked down. "That is, if you *want* to come. You mustn't feel obliged."

He lifted her chin with a fingertip, loving the combination of shyness and boldness in her. Grudgingly, he had to admit to himself that she must have inherited the latter quality from her father. "I'd love to come. There is no amusement sitting in a tavern by myself each evening. But I don't want to wear out my welcome."

"You couldn't ever do that." Her eyes held so much promise, again he longed to bend his head and kiss her. But he held himself back. It was premature. With a long sigh, he straightened and took a step away from her. "Until tomorrow then."

When Gerrit arrived at the inn, there were still a few sailors sitting at the tables, drinking from their pewter tankards and playing cards. A couple of them looked up as he passed and he nodded, but they ignored him and went back to their cards.

He walked up the dark stairwell which had a musty odor. The higher it got, the colder it became. Only the ground floor was heated. By the time he reached his door, his steps heavy with fatigue, the air was frigid.

He opened his door and stepped immediately back. The stench was like a thick wall. He used the taper he'd gotten from the taproom to shine it around the dark room.

"What in blazes—" He stared at his bed. The middle held a pile of…he stepped closer. Lobsters! The black shells of raw lobsters glistened in the candlelight, their large claws ferocious. Their beady eyes and long thin antennas made them look like ugly armored insects. But they were harmless, dead at least a week by the smell.

The homespun sheet and straw ticking underneath were soaked with a large round wet spot where the pile of lobsters had been dumped.

Suddenly his blood boiled. Who would play such an ugly trick? He marched back down the narrow stairwell, determined to find the culprit and have it out with him.

He stared at the men at their game of cards then walked to the bar where the tavern owner leaned. "I want to know who had access to my room this evening."

The man looked at him bored. "What's the problem? The maid not make your bed to your liking?"

He heard a snicker behind him. He turned slowly and narrowed his eyes at the group of men. His boots thudded on the wood planked floor as he walked over to them. "Whoever thought it a joke to soil my bed with rotten shellfish can own up to it and we can settle this outside right now." He stared each one in the face, but they all looked away from him in turn.

He heard the innkeeper come up beside him. "What's that you say? Shellfish in your bed?"

One of the men looking down at his cards smothered a laugh.

"Lobster to be precise," answered Gerrit, his words clipped.

A swarthy looking fellow in his forties finally addressed him. "We don't take kindly to lobsterbacks in these parts. I suppose someone was just making that clear to you."

Lobsterbacks, the same term Hester had used earlier.

"The war is over and you've beaten the British twice over. I would think that would be sufficient," he told them quietly. "If not, I hope you're man enough to tell me to my face."

"'Tweren't me that did it. I didn't know nothin' 'bout it," came the mumbled words from a few of the men, none of them meeting his eye. He noticed one was silent, his dark glare malevolent.

"I don't want no trouble in my tavern," the innkeeper said.

"There'll be no trouble if no one messes with me," Gerrit told the men.

The innkeeper turned to the open door to the kitchen. "Liza! Emma!" The tavern maid and the older woman who had first served him came out with a slow gait.

"Get this man's bed cleaned up!"

"It's a bit late for making beds," the woman, whom Gerrit assumed was the innkeeper's wife, began in a whiny tone.

"I don't care if it's midnight. See to this man's needs." With that he strode back to the bar.

Gerrit ordered a tankard from the bar and took it to a lone table. All he wanted to do was sleep. Instead, he sipped at the ale and watched as the women came down carrying the fouled bedding. The smell permeated the taproom as they passed to the back of the inn. The men chortled as the women walked by and more jokes were traded with them.

How he'd love to have it out with the culprit. That's what he needed, a good fight to relieve himself of the mixture of stress, fear, frustration and exhaustion pent up inside him.

By the time he was finally able to retire for the night, the younger woman, whose name he'd learned was Liza, followed him up the stairs. Too tired to give her a setdown, he ignored her as he opened the door and went to inspect the bed. If he so much as sniffed the slightest whiff of rotten fish, he'd demand a new room.

But the bed appeared freshly made. He turned down the quilt and sheet. Everything looked and smelled clean. He turned to the young woman, somewhat mollified. "Thank you. I appreciate all your work."

She sidled up to him and put her hand on his upper arm, and he saw with alarm that she'd mistaken his gratitude for an invitation. He gently pried her hand off his arm. "I'm very tired tonight and am sure to get a good night's sleep on this clean bed."

She eyed the bed. "It gets cold here at night. I know an excellent way to keep warm."

"I'm sure you do, but as I said, I'm exhausted." As he spoke, he steered her towards the door. "And in no shape for anything but sleep."

Her eyes hardened when he managed to maneuver her outside his door. "Think yer too good for the likes o' me, is that it?" She tossed her stringy ringlets, which appeared none too clean, "I know where you've set your sights. You want to catch one o' those Leighton girls. Hah! Bible-toting temperance ladies. All they know is how to keep a man from having a good time. You'll see, and then you'll know what you've missed."

With a flounce of her skirt, she turned from him and stomped down the stairs, her candle the only light illuminating the cold, dark passageway.

With a sigh, Gerrit shut the door and latched it behind him. He hoped for no more intrusions that night. Once he lay between the icy cold sheets, the anger he had felt earlier that evening fizzled to a heavy gloom.

What was he doing in this forsaken land, away from all civilization, performing a menial job for a mere pittance, most likely? He would never amass a fortune this way. He had worked hard to earn the rank of major; he was used to leading a troop of men who depended on him and trusted him in battle. And he'd come to this. Being an underling—a mere sawyer working in a mill, hated by those around him because he'd represented the other side in war.

The only bright spot in his life was Hester. The only thing that kept him going hour after hour at his task of chopping wood was knowing he'd see her for a few hours in the evening. But even those moments were tinged with frustration. They rarely could be alone together, as they had in England. Her family hovered around her like a protective cloud. They were good people and he envied her their love and warmth.

But he despaired of ever amounting to enough to offer for her hand. Certainly not in his present position of lowly lumberer as they called them here.

And there was that even scarier condition. If the offers of a tavern wench like Liza elicited no desire in him, how much less was he confident of his manhood around a pure, untouched lady like Hester?

What if his abilities as a man were finished for good?

Chapter Sixteen

Jeremiah Leighton tossed and turned in his bed. It had been a fortnight now since Major Hawkes had arrived at his office. He'd never thought the man would last more than a week.

But the man was still here, working at the sawmill. The foreman had no complaints about him. Although inexperienced, he'd known how to follow commands and seemed to have learned how to handle an ax and saw. Jeremiah punched down his feather pillow. Well, there was more to wielding an ax than squaring a few timbers. He who'd spent many a season in the woods could tell him that.

So, Hawkes was a diligent worker. Still, he couldn't be satisfied working as a lumberer at a low wage, sleeping in a lowdown tavern. That was another thing. Jeremiah turned onto his back, his hands behind his head, seeking a more restful position. He hadn't heard anything negative about the major's behavior at the inn. With all those sailors berthed there for the winter, the waterfront could be a rowdy place on a night. But the major seemed to be a very quiet guest, who kept to himself.

Of course he could keep out of trouble. He was at Jeremiah's table most nights of the week! And that was another thing. For a womanizer like Hawkes, Jeremiah hadn't seen any untoward behavior with all the young ladies who'd surrounded him at the house. Not even casual flirting. His wife and daughters had organized several parties, and his wife had obediently invited many a comely young lady.

But the major hadn't seemed overly interested in any of the young females. He might talk with them a few minutes, or dance one dance with each girl, but he always came back to Hester's side. The major even attended services with Hester each Sabbath!

Jeremiah should be pleased. Wasn't this what he wanted for his daughter? Wasn't this the kind of man who would make her happy? Steady in his work habits, moderate in his appetites, and most of all, attentive to the woman he'd chosen?

But Jeremiah wasn't convinced. Not yet. He'd always hated the British aristocracy, seeing them as useless parasites who kept the majority of the population landless and near starvation. Major Hawkes epitomized what was worst in that privileged class—a selfish disregard for anyone beneath them.

What would happen a year or two down the road, once Jeremiah gave his blessing and the major had what he wanted? What would keep him true to Hester? Jeremiah finally got up from the bed and went to stand by the window. He pushed aside the heavy velvet drapes and looked at the dark night. The moon cast a luminescent glow onto the white snow. He spied a fox slinking across the field. He'd have to organize a fox hunt with some of the men before it got into the henhouse.

Sighing, he rubbed the back of his neck. Jeremiah feared for his eldest daughter. She was innocent and always thought the best of people. How little she knew of men! Jeremiah was well acquainted with what beasts they could be. Hadn't he been one himself in his youth? Drinking, wenching, gambling. It had taken a series of strong setbacks to bring him to his knees before the Almighty and make him change his ways.

A thought he'd been avoiding since it had first come to him a week ago now pushed its way to the fore. The logging camp. He let out a breath. Soon the river would freeze up and there would be no more access to the camp until spring. Sending Major Hawkes upcountry might solve two problems pressing on him. If Hawkes survived the next few months at the logging camp, and still wanted to have Hester, well, that would certainly bespeak a depth of feeling and a strength of character Jeremiah hadn't credited him with up to now.

And if he sent his only son, Jamie, along and asked the major to look after him...

Jamie had pleaded with him all summer and autumn to go along with the lumberers to the camp. Jeremiah had been adamant up to now in his refusal. He well knew the dangers to even the most experienced loggers. He shuddered to think of his impetuous son.

But he knew he could only postpone the danger a short time longer. If not this year, then next year he'd have to face letting his only son go. If he didn't, Jamie was liable to run off without his permission. He'd have done the same at his age. Hadn't he run off and shipped aboard an America-bound vessel?

But if Jamie went along with the major… The way the boy hung around him every time he came to the house attested to the admiration he had for the major. Whatever else he might be, Hawkes was an officer used to being responsible for the men under him, some of whom were probably Jamie's age.

The thought of *the blind leading the blind* filtered into Jeremiah's mind. What if he were sending his only son, barely out of babyhood, to his doom? And what of the major? Was Jeremiah being reckless and cruel, playing with another man's life like that? Could he ever forgive himself if anything happened to the man his daughter loved? Would she ever forgive him if he caused her that kind of pain?

He remembered the teamster at the camp. Orin Barnes. He was a good man. If Barnes kept an eye on the major… Jeremiah left the thought unfinished as he turned back to his bed. Instead of getting beneath the covers, he lowered himself to his knees at the edge. He clasped his hands together and bowed his head onto the thick coverlet.

Dear God, show me the way…

It was the week before Christmas. Instead of spending that holiday in Hester's company, Gerrit had just been told by the foreman to get some gear together because he'd be leaving the following morning for the logging camp a few days' journey up the river.

"Who else is going along?" he'd asked, having thought that the loggers were already all at the camp and wondering what this new twist meant in his life.

"Young Jamie and your guide, Pierre Portneuf. You'll take supplies up to the camp before it gets snowed in and while the waterways are still passable."

It sounded as if he was going to penetrate the vast wilderness he'd seen edging the horizons of this outpost. He felt a glimmer of excitement. Then he remembered who was sending him. Mr. Leighton. Was this his method of getting him out of the way for good? He thought of Hester and of being parted from her yet again. "How long will I be gone?"

"Till spring," Baxter replied, "when the ice melts."

His heart sank. To be separated from Hester so long? How would he survive it? She was the only one keeping him going day in and day out.

"What'll I need for the trip?" he asked the foreman, a man he knew he could trust to give him adequate information.

The older man eyed him up and down. "The warmest garments you have. A stout pair of boots. Go down to the cordwainer on East Market Square and get a studded pair. A rifle if you have one, with enough shot for a few months. Tobacco. A flask of rum, for medicinal purposes. Your ax."

"What about a bedroll?"

"You'll get your own fir boughs once you're up there. We'll supply you with blankets."

After work, Gerrit went to the bootmaker and got outfitted. Returning to the inn, he repacked his few things in a knapsack and settled his bill, then headed to the Leighton place, his heart heavy at the thought of leaving Hester again so soon after he'd found her.

"What are you saying, Papa?" Hester didn't want to believe what she'd just heard from him.

Her father leaned forward in his armchair. The two sat in the little room off the front parlor that he used as his home office. A warm fire burned in a small iron stove in one corner. Her father sat in front of the rosewood tambour desk he'd brought over from England a few years back.

"What I'm saying is simply that I think it would be good to have Major Hawkes accompany Jamie up to the camp."

"B-but I thought Jamie was too young…." How could her father have decided to do this? Neither one was prepared for this kind of work. Her heart plummeted at the thought of not seeing the major again for at least three months…and if anything should happen to him… No! She wouldn't think such a thing. The Lord had brought him to these shores for a purpose.

"He *is* too young. But with the major here, it might be the best thing for both of them." He covered her clasped hands with one of his own. "I haven't come to this decision lightly, my dear. Believe me, if there were a better way…" His gaze slipped past hers to the window beyond. "I know what a winter of logging means, especially for an inexperienced man."

"What do you mean, 'a better way?'" she asked, almost afraid of the answer. How many tests was Gerrit expected to pass?

Her father blew out a breath, removing his hand from hers and using it to rub his face. "Even though Baxter has given me a good report of Hawkes's performance at the mill, I can't help but wonder how long he'll be satisfied with the most menial tasks assigned to him. Don't forget, Hester, he's a man used to being in charge of no small thing."

She considered her father's words, realizing what he said was true. Even though Gerrit had seemed perfectly content when he'd visited at her house, he rarely mentioned his days. She had preferred not to think about his situation, trusting that everything would come right eventually. But now her father's words threw her into doubt. "Do you think he'll want to go…back to England?" She voiced the question she most dreaded to hear the answer to.

Her father looked at her steadily. "It's possible. To be perfectly honest, I expected him to have hastened back there by now." He glanced at the items on his desk. "But it's early yet."

Hester stifled an impatient sigh. "Why do you think so little of him?"

Her father looked startled for a moment. "Well, I've told you the obvious reasons before we left England. Now…I can't say I haven't seen things to admire…and yet, I am doubtful of a person's ability to change overnight…not unless the Lord takes a hold of a body as He did in my case.

"I admit I have some prejudices." He pursed his lips, his expression thoughtful. "I can't help looking at him from the point of view of someone who rose from the lowest ranks of British society by sheer hard work and sees a person who was given the command of men just by benefit of his birth and the payment of some coin. The major comes from a class to whom everything comes easily. And what does that lead to?" His eyes demanded an honest answer from her.

He replied for her. "It leads to wasteful living. Don't forget the parable of our Lord Jesus—God will require an accounting of what we do with the talents He's given us."

Hester looked down at her clasped hands.

"I've prayed long and hard about this decision, my dear. My heart is heavy at the thought of sending your young brother into the wilderness. But I think it will do them both good. If a man is to be stripped down to the point where God can reach him, there's no better place than in the wilderness of our woods.

"I have to trust them to the Lord and trust that He will complete the good work He's begun in your major." His brown eyes looked earnestly into hers. "If after he comes back he still wants to ask for your hand, I won't withhold my permission."

"Oh, Papa!" She leaned forward and put her arms around his neck. The two embraced for a moment, saying nothing.

"There…there," he said, giving her back a pat before letting her go. "The months will pass quickly, you'll see." He sighed. "More quickly than I'd like, unfortunately."

"When…is he…leaving?" she asked, hesitating.

"Tomorrow morning. I'm sending them with the Penobscot guide, Portneuf. He's one of my best, you know."

So soon! Would there never come a time when she and Gerrit could be together for always?

That evening, Hester had to endure Jamie's enthusiasm at his chance to prove himself in the woods. He regaled Gerrit with all sorts of tales of bravado and danger he'd heard over the years from the lumberers.

"Every spring, there are a few that drown on the log drives down the river," he told them. "They lose their foothold on the logs and go toppling into the icy rapids."

"That's enough of that sort of talk," his father said sharply with a look toward his ashen-faced wife.

"They'll never put you on the logs," Adele told her younger brother. "You're so clumsy, you'd probably drag a few men down with you."

"I'm sure they'll choose me to rescue a few. I can swim like a fish and am as nimble as a squirrel."

Hester turned to her father. "Papa, Major Hawkes won't have to go on the drive, will he?"

"I imagine not. They don't put inexperienced men on the river. He'll probably help maneuver a bâteau or help with the oxen team. The camp boss will know when he's ready for which task."

Before they left the dining room, Mr. Leighton called Gerrit back. Hester turned, but seeing her father's nod of dismissal, left the room with a reluctant step. What could he be telling Gerrit? Last minute advice?

To Hester's gratitude, her mother had made a fire up in the front parlor—the one only used when they had a large gathering of company. "You and the major can spend some time there before he has to leave tonight," she told Hester. "I'll keep Jamie and your sisters in the back parlor and have Meggy bring in some tea."

"Thank you, Mama." She gave her mother a quick hug.

She paced the spacious room as she waited for Gerrit to come back from her father.

When he finally passed through the parlor door, she practically ran to him, unable to forget that this was their last evening together. He held out his hands and smiled down at her. How she loved his smile, which dimpled the rugged planes of his cheeks. She joined her hands with his. "What are you looking so pleased about? Was it something Papa said?"

He shook his head. "I was smiling at how lovely you look."

She felt herself blushing. These were the first romantic words he'd ever given her. "I bet you say that to every young lady."

His eyes lost their humor and he let go of her hands, turning away from her.

"What did I say?" She touched his arm. "Gerrit?"

He glanced back at her at the sound of his name on her lips. "Perhaps that's why I've never given you any compliments."

She drew her brows together. "I don't understand."

"Because what you say is true. Compliments come very easily. They cost nothing." He raked a hand through his hair, as if finding it difficult to express what he wanted. "I don't…want you ever to think I'm merely flattering you when I tell you something."

She took a hesitant step toward him again. "I didn't think that just now. It…just sounded nice to hear that from you and perhaps I had to make a joke because I felt…shy." Her face felt warm at her admission but she didn't back down from his gaze. He was leaving on the morrow and she didn't want there to be any silly misunderstandings between them.

"Oh, Hester, you are too good for me," he murmured, taking her in his arms.

She reached up and put her hands around his neck, hugging him tightly. How was she to endure being parted from him again?

He lifted her up on her toes and buried his face in her shoulder. "Why didn't I just turn around and walk away that first evening when I saw you at the masquerade in London?" he said with a groan. "You'd probably be engaged to a nice young fellow by now and make both your parents happy."

She laughed aloud, never wanting to be separated from him. "It was our destiny to meet."

He looked down at her face, his eyes both humorous and tender. "Destiny? You mean your doom?"

She smiled. "My future." Before he could say anything more, she continued. "The Lord permitted us to meet and He brought you here. He has a purpose for you once you stop running from Him."

Gerrit didn't dispute her words. "I don't think I've been running from God as much as from myself."

"He's the only one who can give you peace."

"I came across the ocean because—" he swallowed, looking away "—because you seemed the only one who could save me from myself."

She reached up and smoothed the hair away from his

temple. "What you saw in me was my love for Jesus and the light of His love for me burning in my heart. But He loves you, too, and wants to save you if you'll invite Him into your heart."

He looked down, his shoulders drooping. "My heart is too black," he murmured in a heavy voice.

When he finally met her gaze again, Hester's heart twisted at the look of absolute dejection she read in his eyes. Slowly he disengaged himself from her arms with a false laugh. "I don't think your father would approve of our position right now," he said. "I won't repay your parents' trust with ungentlemanly behavior."

"Come and sit with me," she said, inviting him to the settee which was near the crackling fire in the grate.

When they were both seated, he at one end, she noted, instead of close beside her as she wished, she decided to risk the question that had bothered her since she left the dining room. "What did Papa want to say to you?" she asked softly.

His look sobered again. "He told me I wasn't obliged to make this trip tomorrow. He left the decision up to me and told me I could still work at the mill for the rest of the winter if I chose, with the chance at promotion when the opportunity arose." He turned to gaze at the fire, his dark brows creased in a frown.

Hester watched the glow of the flames reflecting off his profile. "Why didn't you take his offer?"

His lip curled in an ironic smile. "What makes you think I didn't?"

She reached over and took one of his hands in hers. "I know you."

He gave a silent chuckle. "Not as well as you should. If you did, you'd go running in the opposite direction."

She rubbed her fingers along his palm, loving the feel of his callused skin under her fingertips. Even that small part of him was beautiful and rugged, worthy of admiration. "You say that only because you haven't been reborn. You haven't shed your old man and he's weighing you down."

He laid his head against the back of the settee, his fingers tightening on hers, and glanced sidelong at her. "What makes you so wise?"

She answered without hesitation. "God's Word."

They sat silently for long moments, each wrapped in his own thoughts, their gaze fixed on the crackling fire. Then Hester scooted across the space separating them until she sat against him. Instead of pushing her away, he brought his arm up around her, and satisfied, she nestled close, taking courage and heart from the warmth of his strong body.

"Promise me you won't go treading on those logs during the spring drive," she said.

"Since I'm not sure exactly what it entails, I can't very well promise anything," he answered her quietly. "I can promise you I'll take care of my hide. I'm used to looking after myself." Humor laced his words.

"I shall be praying for you that this time it's the Lord looking after you as well."

He squeezed her shoulder. "Thank you for your prayers, Hester. I can't imagine the Lord denying you anything."

"That's because you don't see the old me. I'm a new

creature in Christ and that's the one whose prayers God is heeding, the one who's in His Son."

He said nothing more, but she felt the pressure of his lips, kissing the top of her head. She sat still, her only movement her hand pressing his.

When Meggy came in with a tea tray, Gerrit stood. He tended the fire in the grate, while Hester poured the tea.

They spoke about his preparations for the journey, and she offered what little advice she could, based on her own experience traveling upcountry.

"Even though I wish you weren't going for so long, I'm glad you'll see my woods. It's part of who I am." She giggled remembering their time in England. "You can tell me if you think it's sublime or merely picturesque."

He smiled in recollection. "What a bunch of fools we must have appeared to you in England."

"Not at all. I will never forget all I saw and experienced there." She laughed again. "Besides, my sisters are so jealous I can lord it over them when they become insufferable. They'll give Papa no peace until he gives them each their trip abroad."

Gerrit took a sip from his cup and set it down in its saucer. He leaned forward on the settee, his hands on his knees. He wore plain workmen's clothes—dark corduroy jacket, fustian vest, rough linen shirt and leather breeches—but he'd never looked more handsome to her, not even in his decorated uniform.

"I'd better get going," he said softly. "We'll get an early start."

She nodded, not wanting to think about tomorrow.

He still hesitated. Then he slipped off the ring he wore on his finger.

"This is the only thing of value I have left," he told her, holding it out to her. "It's my family crest." He looked away again. "I…I want you to have it…as a pledge of my fidelity to you."

She took the ring from him. It was a heavy gold signet ring. She wrapped her hand around it, unable to speak for the lump in her throat.

He looked at her then. "I don't ask anything of you. I want you to consider yourself free of any pledges to me. If you should meet someone else…"

She shook her head, unable to speak.

"No, don't take offense at my words. I need to know I'm not holding you back in any way."

"You have my heart, Gerrit," she whispered.

"Shh…" He brought his finger up to her lips. "Don't say it. I want to hear it more than I can say, but I can't go and do what I have to do if I think I'm tying you down in any way."

She pressed her lips together to keep from contradicting him. She knew in her heart that she needed to let him go, and she knew she could not join herself to him until he had been set free by the Lord's redeeming grace.

"Why does Papa have to make it so difficult for us?" The plea escaped her lips.

"It's not him. Whatever happens, don't let me cause a breach between you and him. Believe me, he loves you very much."

"I know." Her voice broke.

"There, don't make it even harder than it already is for me to leave you."

She managed a smile. "I'll be here when you return."

"I'll keep that thought." He stood finally and gave her his hand.

Together they rejoined her family where he bid them all farewell.

"I'll see you bright and early," Jamie said with an eager smile. "Wait until you meet Pierre. Have you ever met an Indian?"

Gerrit shook his head.

"You'll like Pierre. No one better to be with in the woods."

Hester's father shook Gerrit's hand. "Don't forget, if you change your mind, I won't hold it against you."

Gerrit looked him in the eye. "I won't change my mind."

"Very well. God go with you."

When Hester stood alone with Gerrit at the front door—he'd refused to take the horse back with him— she said, "Thank you for entrusting your ring to me. I shall keep it safely for you until you return."

"Thank you." He looked down. "Maybe then I can exchange it for another one for you."

She smiled even though he couldn't see her face. "Yes," she replied softly. She sighed. "Are you sure you want to go? Papa said you didn't have to go. I know he meant that."

"I'm sure. Although he has given me a way out, I know he'd like nothing better than to see me fail and head back to England." His teeth gleamed in the dark. "Don't worry. I don't intend to fail."

* * *

It was still dark the next morning when Mr. Leighton and his son came for Gerrit at the tavern. The three of them trudged down the block to the waterfront. Another man waited for them there.

Mr. Leighton introduced him to Pierre Portneuf, a tall dark man with a braid down his back. After a brief handshake, he turned to load Gerrit's and Jamie's bags onto the canoe tied to the wharf.

After Jamie had climbed aboard the canoe, Mr. Leighton took Gerrit aside. For the first time, the older man seemed unsure of himself. He didn't quite look Gerrit in the eye. "Keep a cool head on your shoulders and you'll be fine," he finally said.

"Yes, sir."

"I want to ask you…for something."

Gerrit waited.

He met his eyes. "Look after Jamie for me. He's a bit reckless at times. I…heard how you saved his neck on the wharf here when you first arrived. I'm much indebted to you for that."

Gerrit shook his head. He didn't want a man's gratitude for that. That had been a stroke of luck.

"If you do half as much for Jamie on this trip, I'll…" The man cleared his throat. "Well, you can ask what you will."

"No!" Gerrit softened his tone and said more slowly, "I can't be responsible for another person. I don't even know if I can save myself. I don't know what awaits me."

"You've been in more danger than most men will

ever be in. I think you know how to use your wits and act quickly and coolly when there's danger. Look after my only son, and I'll be forever in your debt."

Gerrit couldn't take his gaze from the other man's. What he had said filled Gerrit with dread. The man didn't know what he was asking, nor of whom. The dead French cadet's face rose before him and he felt sick.

If Mr. Leighton had any inkling of how many young men had died at Gerrit's hands, he wouldn't be asking this of him.

With a heart weighed down by this new burden, Gerrit gave only a nod and turned away from Hester's father. If anything was destined to keep him from Hester, it was this commission. If he failed, how could he ever face her again?

The journey by canoe took three days. Gerrit soon learned to handle the paddle, holding it in what first seemed an awkward position—one hand gripping the top shaft, the other the haft—and reaching down into the water with each stroke. When his arm ached with the motion, they would switch sides, and he'd begin the same motion on the other side of the craft.

The canoe itself took some getting used to. Made of white birch bark, which he was able to see once the sun had risen, it rode low in the dark turbulent water. What looked like a small, fragile craft in danger of capsizing any moment in the midst of the broad river, proved to be a very maneuverable and buoyant vessel. Soon they had to leave the river at the rapids above Bangor. They carried their supplies on their backs and the upturned canoe over their heads, its gunwales resting on their shoulders. Pierre pointed out his village of Old Town, where his people had first settled before the Europeans had arrived.

That evening, Pierre taught him how to make a simple tent of fir boughs and blankets. They built up a large fire at the open mouth of the tent and slept after a simple meal of salt-pork strips cooked on a stick over the fire, boiled tea and sea biscuits.

As the next day wore on, Gerrit acquired the same rhythm he'd developed as a young ensign on the marches through the rugged Portuguese and Spanish countryside. When they branched off the wide Penobscot River onto a narrower waterway, they again had to lug the canoe onto the banks where the rapids were too rough. Here he came to appreciate its lightweight build as they hefted it onto their shoulders.

They traversed through thicker and thicker forest, the dark fir trees lightened by the slim white birch trees and the white carpet of snow. They crossed wide lakes, their edges already rimmed with ice.

At last they arrived at the logging camp. It proved to be a rough log structure with a fir-bough roof held down by crossed timbers. Beside it stood another log structure for the oxen. The crew, with the exception of the camp cook, was out in the forest.

Inside the log cabin a long bunk made of logs ran all along one wall. Dividing it from the rest of the room was a half-split log serving as a bench. This faced a large fire pit in the center of the dwelling. A hole in the roof allowed the smoke to escape. The fire was built up with massive logs and the cook sat on a three-legged stool tending a kettle and pan hanging over it. He stood to greet the new arrivals.

"Mr. Leighton sent two more men," Pierre told him. "His son, Jamie, and Gerrit Hawkes, lately from England."

The thick-set man with black hair and beard nodded at them, a twinkle in his brown eyes. He held out a large hand. "Got your way at last, Jamie?" Giving the young man a pump of his hand, he turned to Gerrit. "A Brit, eh? We got another o' your kind in the company."

His hand kneaded Gerrit's for a second before letting it go.

"Cookee here is the most important man in the camp after the foreman," Pierre told him.

"I'll remember that," Gerrit said.

The cook indicated the far end of the bunks. "You'll have to make room for yourselves down yonder. The rest of the men will be along soon and you can have supper. There's tea on the fire if you want something hot."

They accepted the offer. After drinking down the strong tea liberally laced with sugar, they went back out into the biting cold to unload the provisions and put away the canoe in the ox hovel.

"We'll need to cut some fresh fir to place on your bunk," Pierre told them. "It's best to use the sweet-smelling balsam." He showed Gerrit how to identify the fir tree by its needles and scent. "Camp'll get mighty smelly after a short while and this will help ward off the stink."

That night when the hungry men came back from a

day of chopping, the small cabin became a noisy, tumul-
tuous place as they shed boots and wet clothes. Soon
every nook of the roof was hung with drying pants,
shirts and coats, and boots were grouped around the
roaring fire. The men sat in their underclothes as the
cook passed around the few plates. Most men shared a
dish. Gerrit sat by Jamie and Pierre and spooned up the
hot dish of beans and broke off pieces of Johnny Cake—
a crumbly yellow cornmeal flat bread that he found
coarse and gritty but not unpleasant. The beans, too,
were different from what he was used to and he found
out it was the molasses they were cooked in.

"Bean-hole-beans," one of the loggers told him with
a satisfied smack of his lips. "Best food on earth.
Cooked all day in the ground," he said, pointing with
his spoon to the pit dug by the fire, where the bean pot
had been buried under coals.

Gerrit soon met the other Englishman.

"They call me Weasel," the slight, slim man with red
hair and darting green eyes told him. "Cause I can
shimmy up a spruce so fast."

Gerrit learned most of them went by nicknames. The
foreman was named Bull, after a bull moose. An Irishman was Carp.

"So, where you 'ail from?" the Englishman asked him.

"London."

"You ever been in the woods?" He eyed him with the
superiority of someone who is confident of his abilities.

"Never."

Before he could stop him, Jamie blurted out, "He's
been fighting the French." Then he stopped, his face red-

dening, remembering that Gerrit had asked him not to say anything of his military career.

Weasel's shifty eyes roved over him. "In the army was ya?"

Some of the other men, ranged on the long log that Pierre had told him was called the deacon seat, stopped their conversation to listen. Gerrit set down his spoon. "Yes."

"Ye sound like a gent," Weasel said, disdain edging the words. "What rank?"

Gerrit eyed him steadily. "Suffice it to say I was an officer."

"A redcoat," a man beside them grunted.

Jamie turned to him. "But he fought the French, not us."

"A redcoat is a redcoat," another spat out. "We don't need any 'round here."

"What's Leighton mean putting a lobsterback in our midst?" the first man demanded.

Jamie stood. "My father thinks highly of Major Hawkes and so you'd better treat him right."

"Sit down, Jamie," Gerrit said quietly, but the boy didn't heed him.

Jamie fisted his hands. "Anyone that wants to make trouble with him will have to answer to me."

The men roared with laughter. "Ready to take us all on?" a large man at the far end of the deacon seat asked.

The foreman brought his plate up to the fire for a second helping of salt pork. "The only proving ground we have here, men, is the forest. Remember it's how many logs we bring in for Leighton that counts. Nothing else. When we total our logs down in the boom in spring, that'll prove the worth of our crew compared to every other crew in the territory."

The men cheered his words, their hostility forgotten, at least for the moment.

Gerrit resumed eating although he had no more appetite. He wondered if this first evening would foretell his reception in the woods. Would he be thwarted out there because of his background?

The other Englishman soon moved away from him, muttering, "We don't need no Mayfair maidens here in the woods."

Gerrit noticed a large man who said little, sitting in a far corner of the room, but who eyed him from time to time. After the dishes were cleared, the task of washing fell to him and Jamie as the newest of the crew. The other men sat telling stories, smoking their pipes and sharpening their ax blades on the grindstone.

When the talking died down, one of them started singing. Most of the men joined in the logging song. When a few songs had ended, the man who'd sat observing Gerrit began to sing. The others fell silent as his strong bass filled the cabin.

Come, Thou Fount of every blessing,
Tune my heart to sing Thy grace;
Streams of mercy, never ceasing…

Gerrit sat at his end of the deacon seat, caught by the man's melodious voice. When the hymn ended, the man stood and stretched. With murmured good nights, they watched him don his coat and exit quietly into the night.

Gerrit asked Pierre, "Who was that?"

"The teamster. He usually beds down with the oxen."

Later as the men began claiming their bunks, a massive log was placed onto the fire, sending sparks flying. "That should last us through the night," Cookee declared, standing back with satisfaction.

Gerrit put his coat on and opened the flimsy wood door. He stepped out into the frigid night. His breath immediately crystallized into a cloud of white vapor. He looked above him; the sky was pitch black, the blanket of stars bright pinpoints in the night.

Instead of silence, the air was filled with the sound of the cold-frozen trees crackling, branches creaking.

He didn't dare wander far from the cracks of light visible through the door. The rest of the logs were chinked to keep in the warmth of the cabin.

After relieving himself, he paused a moment, glancing at the other building, the hovel. He walked toward it, his boots crunching on the dry snow. A thin line of light peered through a sliver in the door. His hand lifted to push open the door, but then he stopped and let it fall back to his side.

Shaking his head at his foolish need to seek out this quiet man with the deep, soothing voice, Gerrit turned back to the cabin. Perhaps tomorrow he'd have a chance to speak to him. For now, however, he had a few moments of quiet, alone with his thoughts of Hester.

Chapter Seventeen

The weeks that followed were filled with the hardest work Gerrit had ever known. He was made a swamper, a position he soon discovered was the lowest of the team. He spent the day whacking off the bark from one side of the great logs that were felled, so that they could be easily skidded across the snow and down to the lakeside.

He didn't know whether to be relieved or disappointed when Jamie was assigned to the forest with the choppers. He wouldn't be able to keep an eye on him and he knew that was the more dangerous work, bringing down the great pines that sometimes reached up to a hundred and fifty feet. The ground shook beneath him whenever one came down.

From Jamie's stories around the fire at night, the greatest danger came when the tree toppled. Although the experienced choppers could bring down a tree exactly where they wanted, without breaking any of the smaller trees in their midst, there was always the risk the tree would fall in another direction and those beneath it would be crushed.

Each night Gerrit listened to harrowing stories of accidents other men had seen in their years in the forest. Although the men hardly talked to him, he heard from their accents that they were a mixed bunch: a few French, the Irish and Englishman, a couple of Penobscots in addition to Pierre, and the rest Mainers—proud men of English or Scotch descent but with little regard for their mother country.

The cabin became a steam-filled lodge of dirty clothes, with only the smell of frying salt pork to relieve it. One evening, about a week after they'd arrived, Gerrit contemplated another lonely few hours until bedtime. Only half-heeding the talk and song from his place at the fringes of the group, he decided he needed to fill his evenings with something more than sharpening his ax and washing up the dishes. The days stretched out before him as if they had no beginning or end. The hope of seeing Hester at the end of this sojourn seemed slimmer by the day. Finally, he rose and stretched, retiring to his bunk earlier than the others.

As he lay against the logs, softened only partially by the scented fir boughs, his hands clasped behind his head, he wondered for the dozenth time why he had come to these strange shores. He'd left behind a civilized life in London. Why hadn't he done the sensible thing and married an heiress as Delia advised him? Right now, he'd probably be enjoying a plum pudding after a lavish holiday meal on some country estate. The men around him, following the tradition of their Puritan forefathers, hardly acknowledged the Christmas holiday.

Instead Gerrit was breaking his back to gain the approval of a lowborn tradesman, whom he'd never have give a second glance to in London, in the hopes that the man would allow him to court his daughter. Gerrit shifted on the bed, trying to dispel the negative thoughts. No matter what her father was or wasn't, it didn't matter to him. He'd do anything to win Hester's love.

Gerrit blew out a breath, watching it form a white cloud. Despite the great fire in the center of the cabin, his bed at the very end of it already felt cold from the frigid temperatures just beyond the six-inch logs forming the walls.

Would he ever see Hester again? At the rate he was going, he thought it unlikely. The winter days seemed endless. He sat up. He had to have some kind of link with her if he was going to be able to see it through. His gaze fell on his pack. He reached for it, remembering what Crocker had given him. With a thought of dropping his old valet a line, he'd stuffed the writing paper into it at the last moment. A useless thought. There was no mail in and out of the camp until spring. Pierre had brought up the last link to the outside world, and the men had pounced on the letters and newspapers he'd carried with him.

Now Gerrit took out the folded, slightly crumpled sheets of paper. If he couldn't see her or talk to the woman who had brought him to these shores, at least he could write to her. She might never get his letters, but that didn't matter. He only needed to feel a connection to Hester to be able to keep going in this inhospitable land he found himself in.

He took out his small bottle of ink and his quill pen. He shook the bottle. Good, it hadn't frozen. He didn't relish sitting closer to the fire to warm it. He placed the bottle on the deacon seat.

He needed a hard surface to write upon. His glance fell on the Bible protruding from his pack. A parting gift from Hester's mother. At least he had an ally in her. He hadn't even taken it out of his pack since he'd packed it. He took the book out now and placed his hand on the smooth leather cover. He flipped it open and read the flyleaf.

Be strong and of a good courage; be not afraid, neither be thou dismayed: for the Lord thy God is with thee whithersoever thou goest. Joshua 1:9

8th December, 1815

The words comforted him. He needed all the strength and courage he possessed right now. He'd needed them, too, when he'd first gone as a young soldier to the Spanish peninsula, but then he'd had the fellowship of other officers, men, like him, of high birth. He'd had, in addition, his ambition—and like young Jamie, that belief in himself and his own prowess.

Now, he had only the knowledge of what a weak and worthless individual he was. He might be able to kill and defend himself, but for what? He had no power to wash away the guilt of having survived when so many had perished. He sighed and closed the book, knowing he must stop the direction of his thoughts. He opened the bottle of ink and dipped in the quill. Placing a sheet of paper on the Bible, he wrote:

My dearest Hester, I wonder what you are doing at this moment. It is only eight o'clock here. You are doubt-

*less sitting with your sisters, making yourselves useful
with your sewing or quilting, chatting about the day's
events. You probably spent the day at some worthy
endeavor with your mother—visiting the sick or taking
food to some widow or to an old sailor living out his last
days near the wharf.*

*How I wish I could be near you right now. I wish
I could hold you and tell you what's in my heart. I
have never in my life felt so lonely. Not when I was
far from home on the plains of Spain. Not when I
stood contemplating a field littered with broken bodies
after a battle.*

He blotted the last words. He must take another tack.
This line of thinking wouldn't do.

*The days have been long and hard. Your brother is
acquitting himself tolerably well, I've heard. He's had
the distinction of being among the choppers. I know
your father would be proud of him....*

He continued writing, finding a curious release in
being able to pour out his heart, knowing his words
would never be read by anyone. When the other men
began to stand and stretch and make their way to the
bunk, Gerrit quickly blotted the last page and folded the
letter. As an afterthought, he placed it inside the Bible
and packed it away again.

Jamie crept into the bunk beside him. "What're you
writing?"

"Nothing. Just a letter."

"You know there's no mail," he said in concern.

"I know. It doesn't matter." Gerrit stretched back out
on the bed, under the blankets this time, his head pil-

lowed by his boots like the other men. Soon the candles were doused and only the fire remained.

"Are you sweet on my sister?" Jamie asked from his side of the bed.

Sweet on? There was an expression. What did the frank question from the naive young man beside him mean? Had Gerrit ever been sweet on a young woman before? It was much too bland an expression to describe the lusty thoughts he usually entertained toward women.

And it certainly came nowhere near to describing the heart-wrenching yearning he felt for Hester. He turned to look at Jamie in the firelight. "Which one?" he asked, cracking a smile.

The boy looked at him in shock for an instant, before he understood Gerrit's teasing. He punched him in the arm. "You're bamming me."

Gerrit reached over and ruffled the boy's hair. "Get to sleep. You've still got a lot of growing to do."

"All right, if you want me to mind my own business, just say so. Just don't treat me like a kid." His voice held no offense.

"Mind your business. Good night." Gerrit faced back up at the fir roof.

"Good night, Gerrit." Jamie yawned. "I can't wait till tomorrow. The head chopper said I could go with him to the new grove of pine. You should have seen him today. He brought down a tree four-feet wide at the base." His jaw stretched open in another yawn.

"You'd better get some sleep then," advised Gerrit, glad he couldn't witness firsthand the risks Jamie was taking.

"Yeah. I want to be alert tomorrow." With a contented sigh, the boy turned around, resting his head on his elbow. Soon Gerrit heard his even breathing. One by one, the men down the line fell asleep. Deep breathing and snores mingled with the crackling fire.

Oh, to have the peaceful slumber of youth or the deep sleep of hardworking men who had little on their minds but facing hundred foot trees in the forest. Gerrit closed his eyes, picturing Hester's smile. It was the only thing that kept the other images from surfacing.

Gerrit was working on his fifth tree of the morning. The snow around him was littered with gray bark. Suddenly, a man ran out of the forest.

"A man's been hurt!" he yelled before banging open the door of the cabin. "Cookee, Farraday's down! Get your kit ready!"

Gerrit threw down his ax, his thoughts immediately on Jamie's safety, and joined the man when he came out again. "What happened? Where is he?"

"Up in the new grove. Bleeding all over the place. It's his leg," he panted.

The cook joined them, his jacket thrown on and a satchel in one hand. "Take me to him."

The two took off into the woods. Gerrit followed after, along with the other swampers. The pine grove was about a mile away through a forest covered in a foot of snow. A path had been trodden down enough with the dragged logs so that snowshoes weren't needed.

They were all breathless by the time they reached the area. Gerrit stopped short at the great red blotch on the snow. The pure white snow readily absorbed the blood and spread it out like a scarlet carpet.

The man called Farraday was writhing on the ground holding his knee. A deep gash perforated his foreleg. Gerrit approached slowly. A double-bitted ax lay on the ground beside the man. The wound on his leg went clear to the bone.

Gerrit had seen worse injuries—from heads blown off to holes leaving a man's insides spilling onto the battlefield. But his reaction now was like a maiden soldier's. His stomach lurched, wanting to cast up his breakfast.

It was happening all over again. From the trampled grass sticky with blood across the fields of Europe to the wild forests of Maine, it was the same. Suffering and death.

The men were all talking at once and hovering around Farraday. "What happened?" Cookee asked, crouching down and examining the leg.

"Ax flew the wrong way. Landed in his leg." The foreman frowned. "Think he'll make it?"

The cook didn't speak right way, but took his knife and cut away the pant leg. Then he began binding the wound with the roll of bandages from his sack. He glanced at Farraday. "Looks like a clean wound," he said as he tied the ends together. "You'd be dead by now if your ax had severed anything important." He turned to the group of men. "All right, let's get a pallet made to carry him back."

Relieved to have something to do, the small group of men quickly set to work cutting a few spruce and balsam saplings and stripping them of their branches. These thin poles were lashed together and covered with the boughs. They laid a moaning Farraday upon it and four men carried it back to the camp.

"All right, the rest of you back to work!" Bull called out. As Gerrit hesitated, the foreman pointed to him. "Lobster, you stay here and take Farraday's place since we're short a man." They'd given him the nickname since the evening they'd discovered he'd been a British soldier.

"I have to go back for my ax."

The man grabbed up Farraday's by its helve and tossed it to Gerrit who managed to catch it in the upright position it was thrown. "Use his. He won't be needing it for a while," was all he said before turning and marching back to the tree he'd been working at before the accident.

The few remaining men split into two groups, one with the foreman, the others following another man back into the forest.

"Come with me." Jamie motioned to Gerrit to go with him with the second group. They walked about a quarter of a mile deeper into the grove of pine. These trees grew higher than the other fir trees surrounding them.

"We found a tree that's gotta be a hundred and fifty feet high," Jamie told him barely able to contain his excitement, the injured Farraday seemingly forgotten by the youth. "At least six feet across. We've been working at her for half an hour and hardly made a dent in its trunk."

Gerrit couldn't get the picture of Farraday's agony from his thoughts. He trudged through the snow alongside Jamie, remembering that once he'd been as carefree. He'd quickly block out the aftermath of each battle and remember only the excitement of victory. When had it gotten impossible to forget the agony of the dying?

When they reached the three other men standing by the pine, Gerrit saw that Jamie hadn't exaggerated. The tree was wider across than Gerrit was tall. He craned his neck and tried to see the end of it. Its first thick branches didn't appear until the height of the younger trees around it, seventy or eighty feet up.

"We each take an area and begin chopping. It'll take at least another half hour before we feel the tree begin to move."

"What do we do then?"

Jamie grinned. "Move to the opposite side from where it's heading."

"All right then," he said, hefting the ax in his hand and choosing a side of the trunk where no one was standing.

"Don't worry," Jamie said. "Deke there'll yell when it's time. He's aiming it to fall over yonder." The boy indicated a swath slightly wider than the tree where other trees had been cut down and only a few stumps remained. "That's why he's put the felling wedge on the other side."

The wood chips went flying as the men settled in to chop in earnest. By now Gerrit's body had become accustomed to the rhythm of chopping. He found working at an actual tree instead of logs on the ground a vast improvement. He wondered how old a tree so large could be. He'd never seen such girth in a pine, not even in some of the ancient oaks back home.

What seemed like an hour later, the tree did indeed begin to move. Gerrit sensed the trembling around the widening wedge the men had made around its trunk.

"Stand back, men!" Deke shouted. When they stood together some feet away, they watched silently as Deke peered up at the very summit of the tree. "Yes, just where we want her," he said. "All right, back to chopping. It won't be long now."

Hoping he wouldn't end the day flattened under the towering tree above him, Gerrit went back to where he'd been chopping. He tried to ignore the occasional shaking of the tree until finally Deke called for them to stop and get away from the tree.

Again they grouped themselves several feet away around Deke. In horrified fascination, Gerrit watched the monstrous tree begin to sway. After interminable seconds, the last fibers of its trunk gave way and it began its descent. As the lumberer had predicted, it began to fall away from where they stood.

The thud was an enormous thunderclap against the ground, causing Gerrit to jump. The boom echoed in the forest. The silence afterwards seemed absolute by contrast.

They were given only a few moments to absorb the victory of the fall.

"Come on, let's make some logs."

The next hours were spent cutting the great tree into five lengths. Gerrit was astounded to see the hollow space at the base of the trunk. The entire trunk was taller than he, and he was six feet tall.

Soon the oxen were brought and one by one, the great sections of trunk were dragged through the forest to the landing by the river, where the logs were being kept until spring.

That evening, when they returned to the camp, to

another supper of baked beans and fried salt pork, Gerrit stripped off his damp garments like all the rest and sat on the deacon log to eat his dinner. His attention was drawn to the man lying on the bunk. Farraday's leg was propped up on a mound made of folded blankets.

The men stopped by and asked him how he was doing.

"I'll live, I guess," he said, his face strained.

The men were subdued that evening over the fire, whether to keep from disturbing their companion or sobered by the fact that it could easily have been any one of them, Gerrit wasn't sure.

As soon as he'd cleaned up the dishes, he retired to his pallet and took out his writing things. Although physically spent, his mind couldn't rest.

My dearest girl, How I hope you are safe and well.

Today I witnessed an accident in the woods. Because of one man's suffering, I have been promoted from swamper to chopper.

He stopped writing and rubbed a hand over his eyes. How he wished he could run somewhere—far from pain and death. But there was nowhere.

I think of your beautiful eyes, so full of light and life, and it is the only thing that gives me a reason to keep going.

Knowing she would never read these words, Gerrit found himself able to write freely. At one point he heard the teamster begin a hymn. Although he sang softly, the deep timbre of his voice resonated through the cabin. As the last time, the words of the hymn arrested Gerrit.

There is a fountain filled with blood drawn from Emmanuel's veins; and sinners plunged beneath that flood lose all their guilty stains.

Lose all their guilty stains, lose all their guilty stains; and sinners plunged beneath that flood lose all their guilty stains...

The quill sat idle in Gerrit's fingertips as he pictured the words. *Lose all their guilty stains.* What would it feel like to lose all one's guilty stains and feel as pure as the untouched snow surrounding these rough cabin walls?

The man went on to sing another hymn and Gerrit returned to his letter. But he no longer felt like writing. He put away his things and stretched out on the bed of fir, listening to the soothing words of the hymns.

That night, he kept waking to the soft moans and shifting of the wounded man. Gerrit was back on the battlefield, listening to the cries around him. He'd always visited his men in the surgeon's tent after a battle, holding a hand, offering words of comfort even when he knew the man would never make it. He'd closed countless sightless eyes; he'd written letters of condolence to grieving mothers and widows, and he'd always felt he'd done his duty as a good commanding officer.

Whom had he been fooling? What had made him feel so invincible against death?

By the next evening, when the men returned to camp after another long day from sunup to sundown chopping down trees, they discovered Farraday had developed a fever. The cook shook his head, telling them they'd have to wait and see if the wound festered. The camp was even more subdued that evening.

Gerrit once again noticed the teamster sitting in the shadows. Before he left the hut, he bent over the wounded man and laid a hand on his leg and closed his eyes. Gerrit watched him, realizing the man was praying for him.

Each day the men trooped back to camp, their immediate inquiry being after Farraday's condition. By the third day he was delirious.

Gerrit began his usual letter to Hester.

I don't know why this man's condition shakes me so. I've seen so many bloodied faces, so many bodies blown up. Sometimes I find myself imagining it was these same woodsmen on the battlefield with me. What if it had been them there on the battlefield blown up by the cannonballs? Some of these men fought against the English here on their own shores.

Who chooses who will live or die? I saw so many men suffer agonizing deaths, cut down in their youth. Why was I permitted to live? I was the least worthy to be chosen to live. I've done so many things I wish I could undo.

Here I am stone-cold sober, with nothing available to me to mute the visions or silence the memories that hound me.

I ask myself so often what I am doing in this godforsaken place. This man, on the verge of death, hasn't even a simple surgeon to tend him, only the camp cook. You would doubtless say God is here, even here. But I don't perceive Him. Am I so lost that I cannot perceive your God? I feel so utterly lost.

It's only my dreams of holding you in my arms that sustain me.

That night he exited the cabin before retiring. He paused again outside the hovel. This time, before giving himself time to turn away, he pushed open the door.

The interior smelled of cattle and hay. A large fire burned in a center pit, just as in the men's cabin. A lantern, hung from a hook set in a ceiling log, cast a golden light over the interior. The six oxen lined one side of the interior, harness and smithing tools the other. The teamster was bent over an ox, examining his shoe. When he was satisfied, he set the leg down and looked up. Seeing Gerrit, he gave a brief nod before bending over the animal's other front leg.

Gerrit took a few more steps into the warm interior.

When the teamster had finished, he turned to Gerrit, wiping his hands on his leather apron and approaching Gerrit. "What can I do for you?"

Gerrit stood and held out his hand. "Gerrit Hawkes."

The man accepted his hand in his large calloused one. "Orin Barnes."

Gerrit stared into the man's eyes. He'd never gotten such a sense of peace in a person. The man's dark eyes— black in the dim light—looked at him in an acceptance so complete that for a moment, Gerrit felt overwhelmed.

Barnes gestured to two thick tree trunks set on the log floor. Gerrit took a seat on one. They sat silent for a while by the fire. Gerrit wondered what it was about the man that had drawn him. Like most of the men at the camp, this one was big and brawny, and his face was covered with a bushy beard. This man's was black, his hair long and straight, combed back and tied with a leather thong. He had a paunchy gut and his hands were thick and blunt.

"Do you think Farraday's going to make it?" Gerrit's abrupt question broke the stillness.

The man showed no surprise at the question. He took

out a pipe from a pocket of his waistcoat and tapped it against the side of the trunk. "Could be."

Gerrit blew out a breath in frustration at the answer. "Doesn't it mean anything to you?"

The man glanced sidelong at him, amusement evident in his deep-set eyes. "'Course it does. But whether now or later, is immaterial."

"I've seen too many young men die to remain as casual about it as you seem to be."

The man proceeded to fill his pipe from a small bag of tobacco he had in another pocket. The sweet aroma of the tobacco leaves filled Gerrit's nostrils, reminding him of nights spent in tents under the Spanish sky, the aroma of pipe smoke carried on the air.

"It's not the hour of our departure that's as important as where we're headed," he said, looking at him from under his shaggy black eyebrows. "And it's not the length of our sojourn here, but how we use the time allotted us."

Gerrit fell silent, the words punctuated by the crackle of the fire. He could say nothing. How had he lived his life?

Orin lit his pipe with a piece of straw he set afire in the burning blaze. Then he took a puff and sighed in satisfaction.

"I've squandered most of mine," Gerrit said softly.

"Most of us do," he replied, as if Gerrit's confession held no surprise. "By the time we realize it, it's too late." His dark eyes measured Gerrit. "Be thankful if the Lord is pricking you now while you still have time."

Gerrit's hands lay idle between his knees. "It doesn't

matter whether I realize it or not. There's nothing I can do about changing my life. What's done can't be undone."

Orin puffed a few more times. When Gerrit thought he wouldn't respond, the teamster said, "I killed a man once."

Gerrit stared at him. This man? What he'd observed of him at the camp was a man whom everyone respected, a quiet man, a man both strong and gentle at the same time.

"You never forget the look in a man's eyes as his spirit is leaving him," he continued, as if his words were having no effect on Gerrit.

Oh God, please forgive me! Things Gerrit had tried to contain for so long began spilling over. "I've killed hundreds," he finally gasped, looking down at the rough-planked floor.

After a moment, he continued in a broken whisper, "But the one I'll never forget is one of the last…" He bowed his head into his hands and kneaded his skull. There. He'd said it aloud. He'd confessed his sin. In a voice hoarse and somewhat incoherent, he told this stranger about the young French cadet who wouldn't leave his memory.

The man let him talk without interruption.

When he'd finished, Gerrit felt drained. He daren't raise his head, too ashamed of his confession. As long as he'd kept it bottled inside him, he could almost pretend it hadn't really happened.

He started when a pocket of sap snapped in the fire.

"What do you think it would take to make you feel clean again?" Orin asked him.

Gerrit raised his head and looked at the man. He'd voiced what Gerrit had never dared articulate even to himself. He thought a moment. "A thousand baths wouldn't make me feel clean." He sighed, a sound deep from his soul. "Would that I had never been born."

Orin nodded with understanding. "To be reborn. That would take care of a lot of things in one's past." He shifted his girth on the makeshift stool. "You know, in ancient times, men took care of their sin by slaying goats and bulls and sprinkling the blood of these beasts upon themselves. Then they'd burn the carcasses and sprinkle the ashes over themselves and their altars to purify themselves."

He considered Gerrit. "But it was an outward cleansing. It didn't clean their consciences." He nodded, as if reading Gerrit's deepest thoughts. "That's your real problem, isn't it? Your conscience. How to purify your conscience."

Funny, he hadn't said to *silence* his conscience, which is what Gerrit had been desperately trying to do. He'd said *purify your conscience.*

"A nasty thing, a conscience. Keeps a man from sleeping at night."

"It refuses to be still," whispered Gerrit.

"There is a cure."

Gerrit waited, feeling as if his entire existence depended on this man's next words.

"Only one thing will clean a conscience. It won't just cover up your sin or forgive it. It will wash it completely away." The man's gaze penetrated him. "The blood of Jesus."

The words reverberated in the room. They echoed the words of the hymn. *And sinners plunged beneath the flood lose all their guilty stains....*

"Jesus is able to wash away our sin because He doesn't overlook what you've done. He acknowledges it then takes it from you and lays it on Himself. When He accepted His death on the cross, He accepted all the punishment and retribution you deserved. He's lifted the sin from off your shoulders, so you never have to drag it around after you anymore."

He tapped the end of his pipe against Gerrit's knee. "It's called *redemption*. It's more than absolution, which is what I think you've been seeking. Absolution means being freed of the consequences of your sin. When you're redeemed, on the other hand, you're set completely free as if you'd never committed it. A priest can offer you absolution. Only the Son of God can redeem you. He takes the penalty for your sin. He pays the price you would have paid."

Orin nodded. "It's simple really. A life for a life. A life free from sin. It's that rebirth you were seeking. It's yours for the asking." His gaze twinkled with understanding. "But you have to ask for it."

A life free from sin. Gerrit could hardly imagine having the weight of his guilt removed. *Freedom.* He tasted the word that for the first time seemed within his grasp.

It was the middle of February. To Hester, it felt longer than any winter she'd ever known. Gone was the time in her youth when winter had been a time to frolic and play in the snow, and she'd fail to understand why her elders would sigh over the length of cold days and the long stretch still remaining until spring.

She put down her crewel work and gazed out at the snow-filled fields edged by dark fir trees. For weeks, nay, months, she'd tried her best to fill her days with worthy occupations, but she was weary of embroidery, sewing, cooking—tired of putting on a busy front before everyone, pretending to be her bright, cheery self when all the while she was dying inside.

She tried to maintain her conviction that the Lord was at work. He had brought Gerrit this far and He would continue the good work He'd begun.

But to have no word from the man she loved with all her heart—no sign that he was even alive—and to know it would still be weeks before she heard anything.

Would he still love her when he returned from the wilderness? A love he'd never articulated but which shone warmly from his blue eyes? Could such a love which wasn't nurtured endure over months of silence?

She read her Bible and clung to the promises in it every day, but lately, it was getting harder and harder to fight the sense of defeat that threatened to engulf her.

That evening as they sat around the supper table, her father turned to her. "Hester, I need your help."

She put down the dish of Indian pudding she was serving herself from. "Yes, Papa, what is it?" Did he need a button sewn on a coat?

"There's a report of wolves in the forest a few miles up. Would you like to join me on a hunting trip?"

She stared at him. It was always Jamie he took with him. A trip into the snow-covered woods? Maybe it would help her feel closer to Gerrit. "Yes, Papa, I should like that very much."

"Good. We'll be leaving the day after tomorrow." Her father turned back to his pudding. "Perhaps you'll come back with some bloom in your cheek."

So, her pallor hadn't gone unnoticed.

They left two days later on snow shoes, their camping things piled onto a sled. Hester turned to wave a final goodbye to her mother and sisters who stood at the barn door. One of their dogs barked his farewell.

The air was crisp and cold, but she felt cozy in her thick layering of clothes. She'd borrowed a pair of Jamie's breeches and a fur-lined cloak covered her down to the knees. She hadn't felt so alive…since she'd last seen Gerrit.

She and her father trudged through the woods for some miles, their snowshoes supporting them on the surface of the snow. Hester loved the silent forest with its hoary trunks rising toward the sky, their scented boughs looking black against the vivid blue far above.

Her father straightened from the prints he'd been studying in the snow. "They've been here. I shouldn't think they'd be too far. Let's make camp."

Hester shivered, knowing how dangerous a pack of wolves could be.

They fashioned a tent beside a gurgling brook, its flow almost obscured by a cap of ice and snow.

Leaving the camp, they took up their rifles and followed the trail of prints as the shadows began to lengthen.

Hours later they returned from an unsuccessful foray

into the woods and now sat around the campfire. Hester felt satisfied and warm after a supper of roast rabbit and some of her mother's still fresh biscuits.

Her father poked at the fire with a long stick. "They'll probably show their noses here tonight." He patted the rifle leaning against the tree trunk at his side. "We'll be ready."

She hugged her knees, glad for her father's company. Darkness surrounded them. Only the fire and the guns kept the dangers at bay. The Lord's presence would protect them, she reminded herself, with a glance at the black branches forming a canopy above them.

She had felt abandoned in a sense by Him in late weeks and was now glad she'd come on this trip. Witnessing the wild beauty around her had heightened her awareness of God's silent presence.

"You're very quiet, my girl."

She roused at her father's voice and smiled at him. "I was thinking of the verse, 'Be still and know that I am God.'"

"That He is. Even when one cannot hear His voice or perceive His presence."

She gazed in wonder at him. "Ho-ow did you know?"

Her father poked at the burning logs once more. "I know a lot about the girl I've raised for the last twenty-three years. I know when she's downcast about something. My heart goes out to her, even when I can't seem to help her." He sighed heavily, his eyes both tender and sad. "I have to trust the Lord at those times to see her through."

She pressed her lips together, her chin against her

knees. Her father saw so much about her, and yet…
how could she make him understand her despair over
the separation with the one she most loved on earth?
"Papa?"

"Yes, dear?"

She sighed. "Nothing."

"You're thinking about him."

It was a statement, and she knew whom he meant.
"Yes. Gerr—Major Hawkes is never far from my
thoughts, even when he seems so far away. Just the way
I've felt the Lord so far away, and that has made it all
the more unbearable. I'm glad I came on this trip. Being
here in the woods has helped me feel closer to both of
them. Thank you, Papa."

"You have seemed a little lost of late." He set down
the stick and clasped his hands between his knees. "It's
made my heart heavy."

"It's not your fault." Her gaze returned to the fire.
"It's no one's fault."

"Nevertheless, I do feel responsible." His mouth curled
upward in a bittersweet smile. "It's my burden to carry as
your father." When she said nothing for a few moments,
he grunted. "You shouldn't let that major trouble you.
He'll be back soon enough." His voice was grim.

She swallowed, unsure how to explain, knowing
whatever she said would add to her father's burden. "I
worry how he is. It's hard to keep one's faith when there
is nothing but silence." She paused and in the crackle
of the fire, whispered, "I miss him."

Once again, her father took up his stick and prodded
at the remnants of a log. It cracked in the middle and

fell into the fire in a shower of sparks. "You love him." The words held no pleasure.

She raised her eyes to meet his troubled ones. "Yes, Papa, very much."

Chapter Eighteen

April 1816

Gerrit stood high on a ridge overlooking a lake. The sun was just edging the tall firs on the horizon, casting them into black silhouettes of rising and falling jagged points. The opposite side of the lake was bathed in the golden glow of the rising sun. It lightened the trees to a gray green. Here and there, a birch tree's slim trunk broke the mass of thick green in a startling flash of white. The sunlight began to transform the black surface of the lake to a deep blue. Chunks of ice floated in it and edged its border, but slowly the ice was losing its battle to the sun.

His gaze roamed over the scene, captivated. The place where he'd spent the entire winter was untouched, wild, inhospitable, but so excruciatingly beautiful it caught his breath. Forgotten for the moment were the days of backbreaking labor, the barely disguised contempt of his fellow logging mates, the biting cold, the filth of living in suffocatingly close proximity in such primitive conditions. During the peninsular campaign, Gerrit had had to endure many rough conditions, but usually an officer was bivouacked with some regard to his higher status. His batman would set up his camp bed, procure some local provisions, see that his linens were washed and his boots polished to a high glow.

But here he'd had to fight just to prove himself an equal. For the last four months, Gerrit had endured the crudest conditions among men. He tried to picture one of the lumberers reclining on his sister's gilded Grecian chaise longue or another handling all the silver plate and Sevres china at an evening's dinner party. He had to smile; everything they touched would probably be broken within minutes.

Gerrit felt the sun on his face. A deep sense of satisfaction welled inside him. He'd endured the winter. He'd made it. He looked to the near edge of the lake far below him. A thousand logs covered that curve of the water, displacing the remaining ice floes on the lake's surface. Today, some of the men were moving out, taking back the first load of provisions from the camp. Tomorrow, the rest of them would follow, beginning the annual log drive.

Gerrit drew himself up. One more test he must pass before he could stand before Hester's father and ask for his daughter's hand.

He spent the rest of the day helping to roll the remaining logs from the stacks at the lake's edge, into the water. He could feel the men's excitement at the prospect of soon going home.

That evening, after his last supper eating off a shared tin plate, Gerrit retired to his bed. He opened his satchel to dig out his writing things.

His heart lurched. Nothing was there! He pulled out his clothing, his hands searching the deepest recesses of his bag, yet he found nothing but his ink bottle and a couple of feather quills. He looked around his bed and under the deacon seat. What had happened to all his letters?

"Lose somepin, Lobster?" Deke asked from his place by the fire.

Gerrit turned around slowly to face the remaining men. He noticed they'd all fallen silent. One of the larger men sniggered. Gerrit dropped his hands from the satchel he'd been about to search through again. It would be pointless. He heard a chuckle from another part of the cabin.

"Whatcha' spend all that time writin' anyway?" Weasel asked him.

"Love letters?" Another logger picked at his teeth with a sliver of pine.

"You'd put a woman to sleep with so much writin'!"

The men laughed as each one offered his opinion.

So, someone had taken his stash of letters—letters which he'd never intended to mail and which no eyes had a right to see. Well, he'd have to put up with a lot of ribbing on top of everything else. Gerrit threw down his pack in disgust. Fitting end to his time among these uncouth, unwashed barbarians. He wouldn't give them the satisfaction of letting on that he cared a whit.

He thought their teasing was the worst he'd have to endure, until he heard Cookee say, "The men should reach town in a few days if they don't run into any trouble. They'll post any mail we've given to them."

One of the men who'd left that morning had taken his letters! The thought made him sick to his stomach. Well, there was nothing he could do about it now. For all he knew, the letters would probably fall into Leighton's hands.

The next morning, the crew set out. Gerrit sat in one of the bateaux, long, slim double-enders carrying their provisions. A man stood at either end with a pole to guide it over any rapids. When the logs jammed against anything, they'd bring the boats alongside so the men could use their pikes to loosen them.

They left the placid lake and guided the logs down the wide stream. Soon they encountered their first rapids. Gerrit watched how the men beside him wielded their metal-pointed pikes. Whenever the jam was too difficult, some of the men would have to leave the bateau and jump onto the logs, leaping nimbly from log to log with their spiked boots, jabbing at the stubborn logs with their pikes.

Gerrit glanced over at Jamie. He could see by the boy's eager countenance and rigid stance that he was itching to join them. "Easy, Jamie. Just stay in the boat. These men know what they're doing."

Jamie huffed. "But I'm lighter and quicker than most of 'em. I could get that jam cleared in no time."

Gerrit could feel the tension rising in him. He would not only have to keep his own body from drowning but also try to ensure that Leighton's offspring made it home in one piece.

Soon, they were soaked to the skin from the icy rapids, but they didn't stop their labors until nightfall. The men who had traveled with the team of oxen had made camp and Cookee had a hot meal waiting for them. Among them was Farraday. His wound had healed, but he'd spent most of the winter helping the cook or the teamster with any chores they had. Gerrit was still amazed each time he saw the other man walking, remembering Orin's bending over him and praying for him.

At the evening's camp, the men changed into dry clothes and ate their meal before bedding down under tents. The next morning the day was repeated. At one juncture they had to guide the logs over a falls. The bateaus couldn't approach the falls too closely, so they had to rely on the men who jumped from log to log to guide the logs down. Gerrit watched in fascination as they jumped aside just in time to avoid being hurtled down the falls. The great logs fell with resounding crashes below and were once again swept downstream toward another lake.

Five days after leaving the woods, they arrived at the Penobscot. The great river flowed swift and black, wider than any of the smaller waterways they had traversed so far. Other loggers had joined them at different points, adding their logs to the growing drive. Each log had been carved with the owner's mark. They'd be sorted once they were placed in the booms at Old Town, where buyers would come to negotiate a sale.

Gerrit marveled at the sight of the logs floating down the wide river. The entire surface was covered with them like a brown pavement.

Their last challenge would be the rapids at Old Town.

As they neared it, the roar increased. Gerrit could see the first logs piling up against the rocks. He stood in the bateau and wielded his pike, breaking up jams, but it was in vain, as more and more logs became stuck at the mouth of the rapids. It was useless to stay in the boat. As the bateau neared the area of logs stuck fast, he took a decision and turned to Jamie.

"You stay put. That's an order!" Then before he could rethink his decision, he stepped out of the bateau onto a log. Thinking he'd roll off immediately, he was surprised that his boots held fast. This log was securely wedged between others, so it was stationary, which helped his balance. He'd watched enough of the other lumberers so he knew what he had to do. He had to get as near the head of the rapids as possible, where the first logs had jammed.

Using the pike as a walking stick, he trod onto the next log and then the next until reaching one that was bobbing free. Now would be his test if he could stay upright.

He was deafened by the thunder of the river and the shouts of the men. He managed to jump from a rolling log back onto a jammed one. Finally he reached the head of the logjam. Coming alongside another man, he helped him pry the logs apart with his pike. He strained to lift and push the logs away from each other, all the while aware of the plunging rapids only yards away. When two great logs suddenly broke free and were carried downstream by the current, Gerrit felt a surge of triumph. He looked across and smiled at the other man and was surprised when the man lifted his pike in victory.

"Come on, I see another one!" the man shouted and indicated a pile-up ahead. The two men sprinted across the logs until reaching the area.

After clearing the jam, which took a lot more maneuvering and all the strength he possessed, Gerrit glanced back from where they'd come. Panic rose in him as he saw Jamie out in the water, his pike in his hand, sprinting from log to log.

He was going to shout at him when the name died on his lips. He'd only endanger the boy even more if he called out to him now. Futile rage rose up in him at the boy's deliberate disobedience. Didn't he know how dangerous this was?

Well, he'd go to his side and carry him bodily back into the boat if he had to. Resolved, Gerrit began making his way back up the river. This proved much harder than going with the current. Before he reached Jamie's side, he had to assist another logger in breaking up a jam.

He looked with relief to see Jamie closer to him by this time. His relief was short-lived as he saw how much nearer the boy was to the rockiest part of the rapids.

Gerrit jumped a few more logs, this time coming dangerously close to falling into the icy water. He looked at the frothy black current, knowing if he did, it would be minutes before he'd be carried over the side and onto the rocks below.

A shout rang out above the raging noise. Gerrit whipped his head up to see Jamie lose his balance and topple from his bobbing log backwards into the water.

Rivers of fear rushed through Gerrit's veins. "No!" he shouted, his own stance on his log faltering. Jamie's terrified face and upraised arm was the last thing he saw. *Dear God, the boy was going to drown.* Gerrit leaped off his rolling log into the river.

The raging flow of icy water sucked him under immediately. Pushing his arms forward, he managed to surface. He grabbed onto a log, hoping Jamie had been able to do the same. He couldn't see him past the log the boy had been treading. The log was too heavy to use as a raft, so shoving himself off it, Gerrit began swimming toward the place he'd last seen Jamie. Glad he'd learned to swim as a boy, he fought the current with every ounce of strength, his limbs growing numb, his muscles pulled taut, but he refused to admit defeat.

Reaching the log Jamie had stood on, Gerrit gulped in air before diving under and searching the dark water. *Jesus, don't let him die. Please, God, don't let him die.* Frantic, his lungs beginning to burst with the need for oxygen, Gerrit strained his eyes, looking for his charge. Imagining the worst, having to bring the boy's father back the dead body of his son, Gerrit begged God for a reprieve. *Let him live, God, let him live!*

The logs above him obscured the sunlight which would have helped him to discern the objects under the surface. He swam deeper then surfaced again, taking in more air.

Again he dove under. Then he saw a bulk ahead of him. Swimming for it, he experienced such overwhelming relief when he felt the heavy wet clothing of a man.

Locking one arm around his torso, Gerrit made his way to the surface again. *Let him still be alive! Please God!* His face broke the surface, and he heaved Jamie's body upward. The boy's face looked deathly pale.

By then, a bateau rocked alongside him. Strong arms lifted Jamie's body from him, then others came to grab Gerrit by the armpits and bring him over the side and into the boat. Blankets were wrapped around him. He watched, his heart pounding in fear and exhaustion. One of the men laid Jamie facedown and pressed his stomach in. A gush of water came out of his half-opened mouth.

A second later, Jamie began to cough and sputter. A cheer went up around him. They turned Jamie over and covered him with blankets.

Gerrit slumped over in such profound relief he could hardly breathe. A hard slap on the back brought his attention back to the men around him. "Well done, Lobster. Thought you were both goners there."

The other men in the boat came over and thumped him on the back as well. "Few men can swim against that current…. If you'd been a second later, you'd both have found yourselves thrown against the rocks…. Leighton's gonna kiss your feet!"

Jamie looked up at the mention of his father. He coughed a few more times, then gasped out, "Do—don't tell my—my father."

One of the men wrapped his brawny arm around the boy. "Don't fret about it, lad. The old man's gotta know. But it could'a happened to any one of us. There's a rare log drive when one man doesn't go down. Even the most experienced of us." He looked across at Gerrit. "Thank the good Lord, Jamie, he sent you that guardian angel sitting there at the other end of the boat."

Jamie looked at Gerrit. "I'm sorry, Gerrit. I shoulda' listened to you."

Gerrit met the boy's frightened eyes and couldn't find it in his heart to be angry. Only grateful. "Forget it. I'm just thankful you made it." His teeth began to chatter in the cool April river breeze. His clothes stuck like wet clay against his skin.

The boat had arrived at the banks of the river. An oxcart driven by Farraday was waiting for them. He helped them aboard and piled more blankets on them. "We'll get you to the camp and in front of a good fire," he told them.

"I thought I was going to die for sure," Jamie said, huddled beside Gerrit on the jostling wagon. He gave a weak smile. "I saw my life pass before me, as they say. Mama, Papa, Hester, Katie and Adele—I saw all their faces and wanted so badly to live. I just prayed so hard to live. I promised God I'd never disobey you or Pa again."

Gerrit glanced sidelong at him, his body still shaking from the cold. "I hope God understands that's one promise sure to be broken." He grinned as much as his frozen lips would let him.

Jamie looked at him, his face still pale, his expression scared, then recognizing the teasing in Gerrit's tone, finally managed a small smile. "I meant it then… it's just sometimes hard to obey."

"I know…I know."

"I felt so useless sitting there in the bateau."

"I understand. You don't have to explain. Save your strength. I'm just thankful you made it." As they both fell quiet, Gerrit began to go over what had happened.

He'd cried out for God's mercy and the Lord had heard his prayer. Whether He'd heard his prayer or

Jamie's, or one of the other men's, Gerrit would never know, but the fact remained, God had seen fit to let Jamie live—and had allowed Gerrit to rescue him. Gerrit bowed his head, overwhelmed by the fact that he'd be able to bring Leighton's son back to him in one piece.

He remembered Leighton's words to him. *It's easy to destroy. It's much harder to build something.* He could just as well have said, *It's easy to kill. It's much harder to save life.*

Was God giving Gerrit an opportunity to build and not to destroy? Would his past sins be outweighed by a new beginning? He tried to picture the French cadet, but the memory seemed dimmer now.

He'd spoken many evenings with Orin, the teamster, during the cold winter nights at the logging camp and thought long over the man's words. But he hadn't been able to believe that the promises could really hold for him. He'd wanted so much to believe, but couldn't.

Was God showing him today that He was giving Gerrit a second chance?

Hester's mother entered the warm kitchen where Hester stood rolling out pastry for a pie crust.

"What's that?" she asked, indicating the dirty-looking bundle in her mother's hands.

"I don't rightly know. I thought I heard a thump on the door and when I went to look, I found this on the stoop." She began to undo the string that held the package together. She sat down across from Hester and began to unwrap the parcel.

"Why, they look like letters… I wonder why they

weren't sent by the post…" she murmured as she took out the top sheet and unfolded it. After only a glance at the writing, she refolded it and looked at Hester. "They're for you." Her eyes looked troubled.

Hester stopped what she was doing. "For me?"

"They're addressed to you. I think they're from Major Hawkes."

Hester's heart began to thump. He'd written to her? But how had the letters…?

"I know from your father the first men from the camp were due to arrive any day. Do you think one of the men delivered the letters here for him?" her mother asked, then immediately answered her own question with a nod. "I'm sure that must be the reason. That would explain, too, why they didn't come by post." She placed the letter back onto the pile in the parcel. "Why don't you let me finish your pie and you go somewhere you can read these by yourself before your sisters get home from their visit to their cousins."

Hester was already heading toward the sink to wash her hands.

She bent to give her mother a hug. "Thanks, Mama."

Her mother handed her the packet, and Hester took it and held it to herself as if it were the most precious thing in the world.

It had been so long with no word from Gerrit that she'd wondered sometimes if she'd ever see him again. What would the long winter have done to him? Would he be ready to return to England without a backward glance at Maine? How had he survived the harsh world of the logging camp? Would he have news of Jamie?

Hester's mind whirled with questions as she climbed the stairs to her room. A late-afternoon sun warmed her rocker by the window. She sat down and took the first letter off the pile. Glancing at its date and seeing it was April, she unfolded the bottommost one of the pile. December twenty-third. She began with that one.

Dearest Hester...

Hours later, Hester looked up, tears long dried on her cheeks. She glanced past the chintz curtains framing her window to the fields and forest beyond. She felt as if she'd lived a couple of lifetimes since she'd begun to read Gerrit's letters.

There was so much she hadn't known about the man she loved. And now he'd opened his heart to her and she discovered the pain and loneliness and overwhelming guilt he carried around inside him. Behind that teasing smile and that look of amusement in his blue eyes, lay a pain she had only had an inkling of. But most of all, she now knew he loved her. *He loved her.* She articulated the words in her mind as a revelation. She'd thought it so before, but now she was certain of it.

She took out her handkerchief and blew her nose. Then she bowed her head. *Thank you, Lord, for allowing me to see past the front he displays to everyone. Thank You for the privilege to love him and offer him the hope that is in You alone.*

Feeling a stronger urge than ever to pray for him, she sank to her knees at the rocker and laid her head on its seat, the bundle of letters still clutched in her hands. She lifted Gerrit's name to the Almighty, pleading for his salvation.

Only You can set him free! I pray for Your mercy and

*grace to envelop him. Let him feel Your loving arms
wrapped around him.... Keep him safe....*

By the time Gerrit arrived in Bangor, the men were
treating him like a hero. The name Lobster was no longer
used in derision but in endearment. He realized that, for
all their bantering, they held Mr. Leighton in high regard
and would have dreaded the loss of his only son.

When they reached Old Town, their arrival was filled
with confusion as the logs had to be dammed into an
area of the river called a boom. In the distance Gerrit
saw Mr. Leighton on the quay.

It took most of the day to sort the logs and put them
into the booms. It was almost evening before they could
take their bateaus the rest of the way downriver into
Bangor. By that time, Mr. Leighton rode out in a skiff
to meet Gerrit and Jamie.

"Hi, Papa!" Jamie's face beamed with pride. "I'm so
glad to be home." Before he could say anything more,
his father indicated to him to join him aboard his boat.
Once he stood with his father, Mr. Leighton took him
in a strong embrace, which the boy eagerly returned.

Gerrit averted his gaze, feeling a pang at the undis-
guised display of love between father and son. When he
sensed their drawing apart, he turned back. Mr. Leighton
was eyeing him. When he saw Gerrit's attention on him,
he held out his hand. Gerrit's met his across the space
between the two boats.

Leighton pressed his hand firmly, bringing his other
hand to cover Gerrit's. "Welcome back."

"Thank you, sir."

"Thank you for saving my son." Leighton's eyes misted over, saying more than any words could, and Gerrit couldn't speak. What would it feel like to have a son to love as this man did?

"Come to the house when you get to Bangor," Leighton told him. "Do you mind if I take Jamie from you?"

"Not at all." Gerrit managed a smile. He gave Jamie a salute and turned back to continue downstream. He could hear Jamie chattering away telling his father all about his adventures until Gerrit was too far away to hear more than the sound of the river.

Gerrit allowed his thoughts now to turn to Hester. His heart beat in anticipation at the thought of seeing her again. He hardly dared think about it. Too many months had gone by. Months in which she had probably been in the company of the many young gentlemen and farmers that frequented the Leighton household.

He brought a hand up to his heavy beard. He knew first of all he would have to stop by the boarding house and get a bath and shave.

When he entered the tavern, he almost didn't recognize the place. The taproom boomed with the sound of loggers' voices, the tables echoed with the bang of tankards. He had to press through the crowd of smelly lumberers to make his way to the bar. Halfway there, Liza, the barmaid ran into him, her hands full with a couple of tankards in each one. As soon as she recognized him, her mouth split in a wide smile.

"You're back, major."

He couldn't help returning the smile. At that moment he felt happy with all the world. "Here, let me help you with those," he offered, taking the tankards from her. "Where do you want them?"

She smiled in gratitude and pushed past him, her body pressing against his. "Follow me."

She led him to a table filled with bearded, unkempt lumberers, who yelled in glee when they saw their drinks. One of them took Liza on his knee. She laughed and slapped his hand.

Gerrit set down the ale and turned away, eager to bathe and change. There was only one person he wanted to see.

It took some time for him to get a few buckets of hot water to his room, but at last he was able to soak in a tub. Deciding he needed both a haircut and shave, he headed out for a barber's.

By the time he left the barber's, he was feeling like a new man with his cleanly shaven cheeks. Every nerve ending in his body thrummed with impatience. All he wanted now was to look into Hester's eyes and see if she still cared about him at all.

He walked through the muddy streets of Bangor, the tension growing in him the closer he approached her house. The snow had melted, but few signs of spring were evident. The grass was still brown, the deciduous trees bare. A few crocus and snowdrops blossomed at the edges of the street.

Gerrit was coming today! Hester sat at one of the front bedroom windows, watching for him. When her father had sent a boy up to the house to tell her the log drive had arrived in town, she had stationed herself by the panes of glass, her gaze unmoving, as she'd done each day for the past few days. Today, however, she knew her wait wouldn't be in vain.

He was coming! Her heart beat an erratic rhythm each time she thought the words. Her fingers tapped an impatient tattoo against the windowsill. She tried humming a hymn of praise but the lines of the verses got mixed up and she finally gave up.

Lord, I thank You for bringing them home safely. She bowed her head for the dozenth time and uttered the same prayer, then quickly shot her head back up again, afraid she'd missed his arrival.

Finally, as it was nearing supper time, she spotted a lone man walking up the dirt road. He turned into their long, lilac-edged drive.

She didn't wait any longer. She raced down the stairs and out the door, not bothering with a cloak. She kept running until she reached him and flung herself into his arms.

After his first look of surprise and joy, she buried her head in his neck. To her delight, he swung her around in his strong arms. She clung onto him, as her feet lifted off the ground.

They stayed wrapped in each other's arms a long time, words unnecessary. She breathed in the fresh clean scent of him, felt the smooth skin of his cheeks, the soft hair at the nape of his neck. He was back. At long last, he was really there.

"You're finally home!" she cried. "The closer the time came, the slower each day seemed to be. I watched for you every afternoon this month."

He lowered her back onto the ground, though he

didn't let her go. "It was no faster for me, believe me, dearest Hester," he said, as he looked at her warmly, his hand coming up to touch her hair as if he didn't believe she was real.

"I wasn't sure…" he began.

"About what?" she asked.

"If you'd still…"

She watched him swallow. "Be here?" she finished for him, her eyes searching his with a new knowledge of the man he was.

"If you'd still want to…see me."

She remembered his outpourings of love in each letter, his anguish and utter loneliness, and her heart constricted at the doubt in his tone. "I counted each day. I've never wanted to see anyone more." Her own hand reached up and drew out the chain she wore around her neck under her fichu. She smiled as she showed him his ring dangling from it.

He looked at it in wonder, then at her and a slow smile graced his lips.

"I kept it for you, as I promised I would."

"Thank you, Hester." His hand came up and skimmed her face the way he had when he'd said goodbye to her in England. "Just hold on to it until I can replace it for you. I know it's in safe hands."

She smiled at the implication of his words. "You're not going away again are you?" she asked. "I know you love me."

A shadow passed over his blue eyes. "I've used so many words with so many women—words of love and fidelity, of not being able to live without them…so many promises I'd no intention of keeping." He sighed, passing a hand over his eyes as if the recollection pained him. "I didn't mean any of them." He looked at her. "I'm afraid to use any words with you. All I know is I couldn't have made it back without knowing you were here, waiting for me.

"I *need* you…" His voice cracked, and she saw tears welling in his eyes. "I need you so much," he whispered, his arms tightening around her as he buried his face in her hair.

"You have me. I'm here."

"I need you more than life." His eyelids closed and, as if unable to hold himself back, his face neared hers, and she held her breath waiting for his lips to join with hers.

She had longed for and dreamed of this moment for so long that she wasn't sure if it was really happening or if she was still dreaming it.

When he kissed her this time, it was nothing like the soft brushing of his lips against hers the last time. This time it rocked her to her very toes. He kissed her like a thirsting man. There was no politeness or gentleness in the kiss, only hunger and want.

Hester gave herself, sensing his need and praying that he would understand that it wasn't she whom his spirit sought, but God's spirit residing in her. Her mouth parted beneath his and she longed to give him all her love in that one expression.

Finally, as if trusting that she wouldn't run away from him, he softened his touch, raining featherlight kisses all along the edges of her mouth. She melted against him, her fingers caressing the hair at the nape of his neck. When they finally broke apart, he looked at her so tenderly she was afraid to breathe.

"I missed you," he said, repeating the words she'd once given him, his lips smiling as his fingers smoothed back her hair.

"I hope I won't have to say goodbye to you again," she managed.

"Your father didn't seem too displeased at seeing me back."

"Come," she said, her arm tugging his waist. "Everyone's anxious to see you." Together the two walked arm-in-arm the rest of the way up to the house.

It was only later, when Jamie arrived home with his father, that she heard about Gerrit's heroic rescue of her brother. She looked at Gerrit, not surprised by what she heard from Jamie, but grateful once again for their safe homecoming.

Gerrit seemed more at peace than she'd ever seen him. She thanked God again for whatever He'd worked in his heart during the long winter months in the woods. When they said good night to each other on the front porch under the evening sky, Gerrit kissed her again, this time tenderly and gently.

"I still have nothing to offer you but…my heart," he said.

Her fingers cupped his face. "That's all I require."

"I don't know what your father will say." He sighed. "I told him when he first hired me that if I succeeded in proving myself to him, I wanted to ask for your hand in marriage."

She drew in her breath then slowly smiled. "I think you've done that and more."

"He told me this evening he wants to talk to me tomorrow. We'll see."

"I'm sure he wants to thank you again for rescuing Jamie."

"I didn't do anything any other man wouldn't have done." His eyelids flickered down. "If anyone is to thank, it's God. When I thought I would drown alongside Jamie, He answered my prayer." His voice sounded awed as if still disbelieving that it could have been so. "It was a miracle that I found Jamie under the water and was able to bring him back up. Then it…" his voice thickened "…it looked like there was no life left in him. Then he sputtered and began to cough and he came back to us."

"Oh Gerrit, God is so merciful. But He used *you* to rescue Jamie. You never have to doubt yourself again."

Instead of saying anything more, he kissed her before slowly drawing away. "I'd better get going. I'm not sure what awaits me tomorrow."

Hester stood on the porch until he'd reached the front gate. She waved a final goodbye as he disappeared into the night.

Gerrit whistled on his walk back to the waterfront. The night was chilly but it felt balmy to him after the frigid temperatures during the winter months. He glanced up at the stars. The whole world felt wonderful to him at that moment.

He drew in a deep breath of the fresh-scented air.

For the first time in his memory, he felt hope of a new start. He'd done it. Hester's father had thrown him into the lion's den, and he'd emerged unscathed. He uttered a whoop of triumph to the darkness around him. *He'd done it!*

Suddenly all those awful times in the woods, when he'd despaired of coming through, took on a humorous tint. He pictured the faces of his fellow lumberers—large, uncouth men—they'd shunned him, mocked him, disparaged him, but he'd shown them. He hadn't caved. In the end, with Jamie's rescue, he'd even gained their respect.

His lips tugged at the corners, remembering his stolen letters. No more mention had been made of them, so even that hadn't proved the humiliating incident he'd feared. Who knew where they'd ended up? Probably dumped in one of the lakes or streams between here and the woods. Good riddance!

He picked up his pace, feeling the kind of exhaustion that came from a hard day's physical labor. He knew he'd sleep well tonight, dreaming of Hester and her warm welcome. Even the rest of her family had greeted him like a long-lost member of the clan. He smiled, remembering their welcome of Jamie. He'd been treated like a prince.

Gerrit arrived at the tavern. Although the crowds had subsided somewhat, it was still filled with lumbermen. He probably wouldn't get much sleep with their noise. On an impulse he turned into the taproom. Maybe a tankard of ale would settle his own high spirits before going upstairs.

"Hey, Lobster, see your lady love?" Carp, the Irishman asked, looking up from his drink at a crowded table.

Gerrit slapped the man's shoulder as he passed him. "Jealous?"

The others laughed, but it was a companionable laugh. Gerrit proceeded to the bar and gave his order to the boy standing behind it. When he had the tankard in his hand, he looked for an empty bench. As his eyes scanned the crowd, another lumberer from the camp called him over.

Gerrit walked toward him and the men made a place for him. The table was covered with pewter tankards and green bottles of rum.

One of the men raised his glass. "To Lobster—the man you'd want at your side on a log drive!"

"Hear! Hear!" All the men raised their tankards and glasses and took loud gulps. Only one man seated at the end of the table didn't raise his drink but stared with the same hostility as the first time Gerrit had been in the taproom. He wasn't one of the men from the camp. Gerrit recognized him as one of the locals who'd frequented the tavern before he'd left for the camp. To him, he was probably still just a redcoat.

Gerrit ignored him and raised his own tankard to his lips.

"So, what are you going to do with your earnings?" one of the men squeezed in beside him asked. "You've earned as much as the rest of us." They each received a portion of each log sold, and their harvest had been good this year.

"I know what I'm gonna do," another man answered before Gerrit had a chance to reply. "I've had my eye on a little parcel of land just out of town at the end of Broadway."

"I know that area. Good land. Smith has a farm out there. Good yield of corn and oats. Got your woodlot beside it and a plentiful supply of water." The men nodded their approval.

A parcel of land. A pipe dream in England, but here, it was within reach of every hard worker. Gerrit had heard the men talk often of their ambitions during their time around the campfire. A piece of land, a farmhouse, a good woman and eventually offspring to help them in their labors.

He took another long draft from the tankard. Not a bad ambition. He watched the man at the end of the table stand and amble over to the bar. Glad to be rid of his oppressive presence, he turned his attention back to the men's conversation.

A while later Liza came over to their table. "Evening, gentlemen," she said with a smile which included them all but which came to rest on Gerrit. "Anyone still thirsty?"

"We all are!" Deke roared. "What are you waitin' for, woman? Get us another round!"

"And bring another bottle of rum," shouted a man farther down.

She swung her towel at him. "Ask like a gentleman or I'll ignore you and wait on those that treat me right." She leaned over the table with the excuse of removing an empty tankard and brought her face close to Gerrit's. "Anything you need, Major, and I'll bring it straightaway."

Gerrit backed away from her as much as the crowded bench permitted. "Thanks. Just another ale along with the others."

She gave him an assessing look, bringing her gaze to rest on his mouth. "Very well, Major." Slowly, she straightened. "If your thirst keeps up, I know a sure way to satisfy it."

"Thanks. I'll keep it in mind." He shifted his gaze away from hers, thinking he'd need to find a new rooming house. The last thing he needed was an over-eager tavern wench and a bunch of men who would probably soon spread a tale that had no basis in truth.

"Come on, Lobster," a lumberer called out from the other end of the table, "tell us how you learned to swim against the current the way you did today on the Penobscot."

He turned to the men and let out a breath of relief as Liza moved away from him. When she came back a short while later with a tray laden with their drinks, he didn't glance her way except to murmur "thank you" when she thumped his tankard down in front of him.

The men raised their glasses in another toast. "To another successful river drive!" Ale splashed on Gerrit's wrist as the tankards clashed against each other. Then he tipped his head back and took a long draft like the men around him.

"Aarggghhh!" Gerrit awoke to an icy dousing of water over his head. "What—?" He brought his hands up to his eyes. Rubbing away the water, he peered in shock at Mr. Leighton, holding the pitcher from Gerrit's washstand over him. The last drops of water dripped from its wide mouth.

"So this is how you spend your nights after bidding my daughter a good evening?"

Leighton stood over Gerrit's bed. Gone was every shred of the gratitude shining from his eyes the afternoon before.

Chapter Nineteen

Gerrit gripped his throbbing temples. What had happened? He felt like a leaden cannonball. Suddenly he became aware of a warm body pressed against him. He flinched in alarm. There beside him lay Liza, the sheet drawn up to her chest, but her bare shoulders making it clear to everyone present in the room that she was naked.

It was only then he became aware of the two other men standing around his bed.

What was going on? How had Liza ended up in his bed? He pushed himself away from the woman, the half-formed questions whirling in his mind. Even as he did so, the full weight of his offense swept over him, enveloping him as powerfully as the Penobscot current over his head. In a matter of seconds, he saw all of his hopes, his strivings since reaching America, pulverized into nothing.

He struggled to sit up but his limbs wouldn't cooperate. He became more entangled in the twisted bedclothes. He realized then his own nakedness. As he became aware of his condition, his thoughts went from dazed to horrified to confused. What had happened to his nightshirt? What had *happened* last night?

The evidence pointed to only one conclusion, which threatened to crush him. If someone had handed him a pistol at that moment, he would have blown his brains out.

Instead, he let his head sink into his hands, the questions hammering at his temples. *How could he? How had he? Why?*

"So, you're only sorry to be caught." Leighton's voice, thick with scorn, shot a barrage at Gerrit's aching head. "You vile, sorry excuse for a man! Pretending to be a gentleman! Courting my daughter while you're nothing but a filthy, lying scoundrel. I knew it all along! I knew it!" As the accusations grew in volume, he lunged at Gerrit, grabbing him by the shoulders and dragging him out of the bed.

Gerrit fell with a thud on his knees onto the hard wooden planks. Leighton's companions managed to pull him off Gerrit before he could do him further harm.

"Don't bother with him, sir." Gerrit recognized a man from Leighton's office. "He's not worth it."

Leighton looked down at Gerrit's crouched form. "You're right. Look at him there in all his manly glory. He's nothing but a fraud." In a steady, unrelenting tone, he spoke to Gerrit directly, "I want you out of this town today. Don't try to see Hester. If you have any sort of conscience, don't hurt her any more than you already have."

Without another word, he turned and stalked out of

the room, followed by his men. The door banged shut, echoing in the room. Then it was quiet.

"Don't mind them. They're nothing but—"

Gerrit started, having forgotten the woman's presence. He turned and looked at the bed and received a second shock. There she sat in his bed, shameless, actually smiling.

He scrambled for something—anything—and landed on a shirt—his own—on the floor. He threw it at her.

"Cover yourself!"

"You should talk," she drawled, making no effort to do as he commanded.

Realizing once again his own state, he grabbed his breeches and pulled them on. He walked across the cold, bare floor, wanting to put as much distance as possible between himself and the evidence of his iniquity. He hated the sight of that knowing—almost malicious—smile on her face.

In those moments, staring at her, he knew the full, crushing weight of despair. If he'd thought himself lost to all hope before, it was nothing as compared to this.

Then, he hadn't gambled it all. He'd always had a few reserves left; another trick up his sleeve. Now, he'd done everything he knew to do. He'd used everything up, given all he was worth.

Now, he knew there was nothing left.

Liza finally rose from the bed, leisurely donning the shirt he'd thrown her.

"My, but some people are cross in the morning." She clucked her tongue. "You sang quite a different tune last night. So amorous you were. Bragging how you'd prove that redcoats were better than lumberers at pleasing a girl." She chuckled as she rolled up the long sleeves. "You even claimed you'd father a child in one evening."

Gerrit wanted only to shut out her words. How could her words hold any truth? His mind was an entire blank. Why couldn't he remember anything of the night before? He recalled drinking a tankard—or was it two?—with the lumberers, then nothing.

He sank down on the edge of the bed, recalling other occasions in London when the previous evening contained blanks. But last night? He hadn't intended to down more than a tankard of weak ale then go up to his room to sleep. When had he changed his mind? Why couldn't he remember? There had to be someone who had been there who could fill in the pieces of the puzzle.

Like a man possessed, he tore through his belongings for a clean shirt and waistcoat. As soon as he'd finished dressing, he hurried from the room.

Hester shook her head at her father, refusing to accept what he was telling her.

"Don't look like that," he pleaded. "He has hurt you terribly, but know that he'll be punished for his deceitfulness. Oh, my darling daughter, I know you don't want to believe what I'm telling you." Her father took a step closer to her and put his arm around her.

She pushed him away. "I—I'm sorry, Papa, but it can't be true. I know Ge—Major Hawkes, and he wouldn't do something like this."

Her father gave her a look full of pity.

"I know he would have in the past," she amended, "but not now. He's changed."

"My darling Hester, as much as it pains me to tell you this, you have to know the truth. I walked in on him. There was no misinterpreting the scene in his bed. Women like that don't share a bed with a man innocently. Oh, Hester, Hester." He shook her gently by the shoulders. "A man like that, after being in the woods all winter, will take any woman offered to him. Put him out of your mind, out of your heart. I should never have given him work. I should never have let you keep seeing him in London. I kept hoping you'd see through him." He smiled sadly at her. "But you're so young and innocent. You don't know the wicked ways of men."

Hester's lower lip trembled. Her father's words sounded so much like Gerrit's when he'd kept trying to warn her against himself. But no! She knew he hadn't done what her father accused him of. She broke away from her father.

"Excuse me, Papa, I—I'm going to go to my room."

Her father only nodded, seeming to understand her need to be alone.

Her mother, who'd been in the same room with them and had heard everything, followed her. Once in Hester's room, all she said was, "Let's pray."

Hester nodded, unable to get any words past the lump in her throat. Her mother took Hester's Bible off a small table and brought it with her to Hester's bed. Together, the two knelt. Her mother opened the Bible and read, *"For the word of God is quick, and powerful, and sharper than any two-edged sword, piercing even to the dividing asunder of soul and spirit, and of the joints and marrow, and is a discerner of the thoughts and intents of the heart. Neither is there any creature that is not manifest in his sight: but all things are naked and opened unto the eyes of Him with whom we have to do."*

As soon as she finished reading, Mrs. Leighton looked heavenward. "Lord, God, we lift up Gerrit Hawkes to You and ask that Your light shine into his heart. Pierce him asunder with Your word, with Your love. Reveal truth to his spirit."

Her mother took hold of Hester's hand. "Reveal truth to my daughter. You know her heart. Show her if this man is worthy of her love and esteem. Bring all things to light. We ask this in Your dear Son's name."

When her mother had left the room, Hester felt her spirit renewed. She took up the Bible again and along with it the packet of Gerrit's letters which she'd put away in her bedside drawer. She sat on the rocker, and after reading some more of the Scriptures, she opened the packet and began reading Gerrit's letters again.

A long while later, when she'd finished, she looked up and stared across the room, not seeing the cross-stitched sampler hanging there. Instead, she saw her beloved's face. After re-reading his words—words written in anguish and with the honesty of someone who has nothing left to lose—she resolved in her heart that she would not receive these evil tidings.

She weighed her father's accusations—no doubt he reported everything accurately. She didn't doubt for a minute her father's words. *A man like that...will take any woman offered to him.* She remembered the ferocity of Gerrit's kiss. Would he have kissed any woman the same way? She looked down at the packet in her hand, weighing her father's words against them and against Gerrit's behavior with her from the time she had first met him until the day he'd returned. She remembered Gerrit's pledge of fidelity as he'd given her his ring. She clutched it now through her gown. He wouldn't have left everything behind in England for her sake, he wouldn't have undergone the grueling test of the logging camp or the derision of the men around him to come back and fall so easily.

She knew in her heart that God had brought Gerrit to these shores for a reason. Nothing would convince her otherwise. She'd been obedient on her part. She'd bidden Gerrit goodbye on the London docks, though it had broken her heart. She'd returned home like a dutiful daughter and had not had any communication with her beloved or looked back in any way.

And then he'd appeared on her doorstep, and she'd known deep inside that the Lord had brought him there.

She stood and addressed the empty room. "Gerrit must tell me himself if there is something I must know. I won't receive anyone else's report. So, you can keep your calumnies to yourself, Satan. You are a liar and the father of all lies. I rebuke you now in Jesus' name. I rebuke every device you are bringing against Gerrit Hawkes!"

With her words, she grew more confident. Her faith renewed, Hester left the room and went in search of her brother.

* * *

Gerrit reentered his room, the room he'd quit that morning and to which he hadn't returned all day. It was now early evening. He surveyed the room with disgust. The bed was still unmade, the sheets pulled half off from Mr. Leighton's violence that morning. Some of yesterday's garments still lay on the floor. He bent wearily to pick them up and set them on a chair. He stopped in mid-action, seeing a woman's stocking lying like a slithering snake across the floor.

He shuddered, picking it up and fisting it in his hands. He looked back and forth, seeking a place to be rid of it—evidence of his perfidy. Then he slumped his shoulders once again. Who was he fooling? He could burn it in the grate, but it wouldn't erase last night's actions.

He sat on the bed, letting the offending item drop from his hands. He'd spent the day on a futile chase, tracking down anyone who'd seen him last night, to try to piece together what had happened, to try to discover what had possessed him to behave so. But he'd found no answers. Most of the men were feeling sicker than he was. The others had laughed, telling him they'd seen him walking arm-in-arm out of the taproom with Liza. They hoped he hadn't been too drunk to remember an enjoyable time.

He still didn't remember a thing. Nothing. Not a shred of memory had returned, which was odd. Usually by this time, bits and pieces would emerge. Gerrit rubbed the back of his neck wearily. He hadn't felt so bad since he'd been a greenhorn having his first experience with a bottle of blue ruin.

Well, it was finished. He could do nothing to undo what he'd done last night. All those months of working, striving, trying so hard to be someone else.

It had all been in vain. Last night had proven he was the same man who'd tried repeatedly to warn Hester away. He stood, too restless to sit still, and began pacing the confines of the room. He'd never wanted to fall in love with Hester. He'd recognized her goodness and hadn't wanted to taint it the way he'd tainted other's.

He remembered Gillian—sweet, innocent Lady Gillian, willing to give herself to him out of her girlish love for him. And he'd taken it and used her and never felt the slightest remorse until…

He stared into the distance, remembering that day when her new husband, Lord Skylar, had fought for his wife's honor. He remembered the humiliation of being bested by a man still weak from illness. But that had been nothing compared to the look Lord Skylar had given him at the end of their match.

A look of the deepest contempt for a man who would compromise a lady's virtue and then not offer for her, a look mingled with compassion. *Compassion!* It had shocked Gerrit to the core to read compassion in his rival's eyes. It had been as if for a second he had been able to read Gerrit's deepest secrets—his own self-contempt—and pitied him.

Gerrit scrubbed his hands across his face, remembering a similar look in Leighton's eyes. It said more than any words how beyond hope Gerrit's condition truly was.

Ever since that day in London when Lord Skylar had bested him in a fight for Lady Gillian's honor, Gerrit had been running. He'd tried to drown the memory in drink, in daring exploits, in women, and then, grasping at straws, he'd tried to save himself through a ridiculous attempt to preserve Hester's innocence by staying away from her.

But he'd needed her too much. He swallowed the bitter taste that rose up in his mouth. He'd been fool enough to think he could actually change by going to a new land, working harder than he'd ever worked in his life, striving to gain the respect of Hester's father, in some vain hope to some day be worthy of his daughter. All along, it had been a fool's dream. God had known Gerrit was the same inside as he'd always been.

Gerrit glanced up at the ceiling as if able to discern the Almighty.

Gerrit was the same man he'd started out as…the same man he'd always been…always looking for the easy way out. Willing to deceive, seeking only the pleasure of the moment and leaving before he'd have to pay any consequences. And God had known it all along. He must be laughing at Gerrit's futile attempts to change the facts.

"You were right," he whispered to the smoke-stained ceiling. "You were absolutely right. If You knew so much, why didn't You take me on the battlefield?" The words came out broken. "Why didn't You take me then and save those more worthy?"

He collapsed to his knees, bringing his hands to cover his eyes. "I'm nothing but a miserable sinner."

In the silence which answered him, the words of that hymn which Orin had sung so often in the cabin came back to him.

There is a fountain filled with blood drawn from Emmanuel's veins; and sinners plunged beneath that flood lose all their guilty stains....

"Oh, God, if you can really wipe away these guilty stains…" He held out his arms, crossed at the wrists, palms up. He couldn't finish the sentence, but bowed his head further, shame crushing him, and sobbed for all he'd never been and never would be.

Hester grasped Jamie's hand. "Will you do this for me? Papa wouldn't let me near the waterfront now with the lumberers back in town."

"Of course I'll do it. I don't believe for a moment any of those lies against Major Hawkes."

She squeezed his hand, smiling for the first time since she'd heard the awful things about Gerrit. "I don't either. I know he wouldn't—" She pressed her lips together, not even wanting to repeat the things. "But be careful, Jamie. It's dangerous on the waterfront now, especially in the evening. The men are drinking something awful."

"Of course I'll have a care! Who do you think I am? Don't forget I spent the whole winter with them."

She smiled at her brother's lofty tone. "But they did no drinking then."

"I know." He released her hand and took her by the shoulders and leaned his face toward hers. "Don't worry. I know what I have to do. I'll stay out of sight and just go to the major's room."

"Do you remember what you need to say to him?"

He chucked her on the cheek. "I remember."

"I'm so afraid you won't get there in time. What if he's already left Bangor?"

"Then I'll follow him wherever he's gone to."

"But come back for me first. If he's left town, I'm going with you."

He nodded his head. "I promise."

When Jamie left his sister, he hurried down to the center of town. The streets were deserted at that hour of the evening, everyone safe in their homes. But as he neared the waterfront, signs of life reappeared. Here, men flush with money were just rising from their afternoon slumber, ready to enjoy themselves of all they'd been deprived of during the long months in the woods.

Jamie skirted a group of loud-voiced men and slipped down an alley. He knew a quick way to the tavern where Gerrit was staying. A couple of blocks more and he'd be there. He slowed his steps before turning a dark corner.

Voices indicated someone in the alley just at the rear of the tavern. Jamie stopped, hardly breathing. A man's and a woman's voice.

"I did exactly what you said and it didn't work," the female voice complained. "The Major just passed out on the bed. He was useless!" Her voice was filled with scorn.

Jamie sucked in his breath. It was she! The woman Gerrit was accused of having spent the night with!

"Well, that isn't any of my fault. If your charms aren't enough to woo the lobsterback, that ain't nothin' to do with me."

"You told me if I went along with your plan, I'd have my reward. It's not my fault if you drugged him so much, he collapsed on the bed and didn't wake up till the next morning when he had a pitcher of cold water thrown on him."

The man chuckled. "Wish I coulda' seen that."

She laughed. "It was a sight all right. Poor man didn't know what hit him." Her tone resumed its petulant note. "But I did what you wanted and it didn't work. So, now I say I deserve something for all my trouble."

His voice hardened. "You did what you wanted. Ever since the major arrived, you been eyeing him. Well, you had your chance and if you couldn't rouse him, don't come blamin' me!"

"Why you, lowdown, conniving—" A scuffle began and Jamie regained his wits enough to back quietly out of the alley and retrace his steps to the front of the tavern. He had planned on entering through the back, but thought it more prudent now to come directly by the front. The last thing he wanted was to be detected by the two in the alley.

His heart beating in excitement, he avoided the noisy taproom, only glancing in quickly to make sure the major wasn't there. There was no sign of him, so he hurried up the stairs and pounded on the major's door.

When no one opened the door, he knocked again. "Major Hawkes, it's me, Jamie. Are you in there?"

A muffled voice replied, "Go away, Jamie."

"I've got to talk to you, Major, it's important. Please open." He rattled the latch but the door was bolted. "Please, Major. Please. I'll stay here all night if I have to."

Finally, he heard the bolt being drawn. The door

opened and Jamie stared at Gerrit. His face was un-shaven, his eyes bloodshot, his hair disheveled. Jamie glanced down at his clothes. It looked as if he'd slept in them, but then his face reddened, remembering the con-dition his father had said the major had been found in this morning.

Jamie cleared his throat. "Thanks. M-may I come in?"

The major said nothing, just moved back a step. After another second's hesitation, Jamie entered the room. The major shut the door behind him.

Jamie immediately noticed the portmanteau on the bed and the clothes beside it. "What are you doing?"

"What does it look like?" The major approached the bed and resumed setting clothes into the bag.

"Packing."

"You're very observant, Jamie. You'll make a good businessman like your father."

"Hester sent a message for you."

At those words, the major's hands stilled but he didn't turn around. "Did she?"

He could read nothing from the major's tone. Could the stories really be true? No! He'd just heard about what had been done to the major. He cleared his throat. "She said to t-tell you that she loves you no matter what. She said if you were going away, she'd go with you anywhere." The major slowly turned around at his words. Jamie delivered the last part of Hester's message directly to his face. "She said that you were the only one who could tell her if you didn't want her."

The man brought a hand up to his face and covered his mouth, rubbing his unshaven cheek. "Oh,

Jamie…" He could say no more, and turned away from him.

Jamie quickly went up to him and touched him on the arm. "Gerrit, we know you didn't do what they say—even before, but—" his voice rose in his excitement "—when I was coming here tonight I heard a woman and a man talking about what they did to you. They drugged you. Nothing happened. Do you understand? They made it look like you spent the night with her, but she said as soon as she had you up here you passed out and didn't come to until this morning!"

The major had turned and his look had gone from confusion to incredulity to an intensity that frightened Jamie. The major gripped his shoulders. "Slow down and tell me again. You say I was drugged?"

Jamie repeated what he'd heard.

The major walked away from him as he spoke, running a hand through his hair. "No wonder I can't remember a thing. Not one blasted thing about last night after my first tankard of ale. It must have been something in the second one. She brought it to me. After that, all I remember is waking up to a dousing of cold water."

He came back to Jamie, his face breaking out in a smile. "Jamie, I can't tell you how grateful I am to you for coming here and telling me this." He sobered. "You'd better get back home. I'll take it from here. Tell Hester—" He paused. "Please thank her for me. Tell her her words meant more to me than she can ever know. Tell her I love her and will come for her."

Jamie nodded his head, grinning. "I'll tell her word for word. She'll be glad to hear that."

As soon as Jamie had left, Gerrit collapsed on the side of his bed. His heart was too full for words. Slowly he slid to the floor again, once more on his knees though this time no longer in brokenness, but in joy and gratitude.

He clasped together both hands and bowed his head. "You have revealed Your grace to me. I am yours, Lord, to do with as You will."

He knelt in quietness. And then he felt it. A warmth invaded his body, filling him and covering him. He felt washed clean.

Washed by His precious Savior's blood. The precious blood of Jesus.

Later that evening, Gerrit went in search of Liza, but not finding her, he returned to his room. The next morning, he again went looking for her. He found her in the kitchen.

"I need to speak to you," he said with no preliminaries. Her smile of greeting died and she thrust out her chin.

"What's a matter, Major? Conscience bothering you?"

"If I'd done something to wrong you, it would be. But I haven't done anything, have I?" He looked at her until her gaze slid away from his.

"Doesn't look to me like you didn't do nothing."

"Appearances can be deceiving, can't they? Especially when people put things into a man's drink."

She looked around frightened. Then she hurried out the back alley where no one could hear their conversation. "I don't like what you're saying, Major. I didn't do nothing to you but try to please you."

"You and whoever put you up to it spiked my drink

then made it look as if you'd spent the night with me. But it was all a lie. I want you to go to Mr. Leighton and tell him the truth."

Her eyes hardened. "I don't know what you're talking about."

"I give you my word, you won't be punished for it. Please, Miss Liza, tell Mr. Leighton the truth. This isn't worthy of you. The man who put you up to it hasn't even paid you for your part in it, has he?"

She didn't meet his gaze and her hands twisted in her dirty apron. Suddenly Gerrit felt pity for her. He shoved a hand through his hair. How many times had he taken what a tavern wench had offered him?

He turned away from her, realizing he wouldn't get anything more from her. She was too scared to own up to her part in it. With a final attempt, he turned back to her and said, "Please, Liza, tell the truth." He softened his voice. "I love Hester Leighton and want to marry her. I'd like her father's good opinion of me. Please do the right thing." Then he walked away from her.

He collected his belongings and settled his bill, knowing he needed to find a new place to stay before he did anything else. On an impulse, he asked where Orin lived. Getting directions, he made his way out of town to a log cabin surrounded by a fringe of firs.

The man didn't seem surprised to see him. He invited him in and seeing Gerrit's bag, told him he had an extra bed if wanted to stay a while. Gerrit thanked him, and over a cup of coffee and some breakfast, told him what had happened.

"I feel different. A whole new man, even though Mr.

Leighton still thinks I'm the scum of the earth. Before, I would have agreed with him heartily, but now, even though I know I don't deserve Miss Leighton, I feel differently inside."

Orin nodded over his pipe. "You've been redeemed. You're no longer your own. You're a new man in Christ."

"Yes." He smiled at the older man. "Redemption. You were right."

After he bid Orin goodbye, he headed up to Hester's house. He rang the bell. When her mother answered, part of him was tempted to look away in shame, but then he remembered who he was. He looked her straight in the eye and asked, "May I see Hester?"

She looked at him keenly then gave a slight nod. "Please come in. I'll fetch her for you."

He waited in the front parlor, the same room he'd spent that last evening with her before heading up to the camp.

He turned at the sound of her step. She looked pale, but as soon as she saw him, she smiled, a tentative smile, but when he returned it, she ran toward him. He caught her up in his arms.

"I got your message from Jamie," she breathed, her gaze searching his. "Did you mean it?"

"I meant it, if he told you that I love you." He smiled into her beautiful hazel eyes. "Was your brother able to deliver that simple message? That I love you and was coming for you?"

She nodded, her eyes shining in delight. "Perfectly. Where shall we go?"

His heart swelled at her readiness to go with him wherever and whenever he'd say. "Hester, even though…" he hesitated, then took a deep breath before continuing "…even though it seemed as if I'd broken my word to you, I didn't do what it looked like. I'm glad Jamie discovered the truth, but what makes me even gladder is that you believed in my innocence before then."

Her eyes were bright with her love. "How could I not, after reading all your letters?"

He looked at her, gradually understanding what she was telling him. "You read my…letters?"

She nodded. "A few days before you came home, someone—no doubt a lumberer—dropped them off here."

He remembered his confessions. Things he'd never tell a soul. He could feel a flush stealing across his cheeks and he loosened his hold on her. "I…never intended to send those letters," he finally managed.

She frowned at him. "What do you mean? I read them. Each one was addressed to me. Weren't they meant for me?"

He dropped his arms and stepped back from her. "In a manner of speaking they were." He shoved a hand through his hair. How to explain it? "I…needed…to feel you close to me during those awful days when it seemed as if I'd never see you again. But I never wanted you to actually see those pathetic outpourings of a man consumed by self-pity and guilt…"

She touched his arm. "Don't be ashamed of what you expressed. I feel honored that you felt you could tell me what you were going through inside." She took a step closer to him. "Don't you see? I love you and want to know everything about you."

He stared at her, hardly believing she could actually

still look at him with admiration in her eyes after reading what he'd written.

Her words came forth more rapidly as she spoke. "If I hadn't had those letters, I might have doubted when my father told me what he'd seen. The Lord knew I'd need to know the real you, so I would be able to discern the false accusations that were being brought against you."

He gazed at her in wonder. Even what had appeared a catastrophe then had worked out for his good. "I never meant for any eyes to read those silly letters…" he said with an embarrassed laugh. "Someone stole them out of my pack and brought them back here to you." Slowly he shook his head, marveling. "I'm glad now you received them."

She smiled at him. "I am, too. They certainly weren't silly. They were the most beautiful words I've ever read in my life." Her fingers touched his face. "They brought me so much closer to you. They allowed me to see your heart. I hope—" She looked down. "I hope you'll never be afraid to tell me your deepest thoughts ever again."

He took her back in his arms and rubbed his knuckles against her jaw. "I won't. I promise," he whispered, still in awe over what the Lord had done.

At that moment, they heard someone clearing his throat in the doorway. They both turned to see her father standing there, a scowl marring his features. Though he loosened his hold on Hester, Gerrit didn't let her go.

"Good morning, Mr. Leighton," he said.

"What are you doing in my house?"

"Your wife let me in."

"Papa, I love Gerrit."

Before Hester could say anything more, Gerrit disengaged himself from her and took a step toward Mr. Leighton. "When I first arrived here, I asked your permission for your daughter's hand."

"*If* you satisfied my requirements."

"I believe I've fulfilled my part of the bargain…until the other evening." Before Mr. Leighton could say anything, Gerrit continued. "I did nothing wrong with that barmaid. I was drugged and made to look as if I'd used her."

Mr. Leighton made a sound of disbelief. "I cannot believe you have the temerity to come here, to my house, and tell me I didn't see what I saw."

"I stand by my innocence. I was drugged and knew nothing of what happened that evening. The last thing I remember was drinking one tankard of ale in that tavern."

Her father turned to his daughter. "Hester, don't believe this man's lies. He's used to deceiving women."

"You can ask the tavern maid herself," Gerrit interrupted him, although he had no hopes that the woman would admit to the truth. "Jamie overheard her and the man responsible for the dirty trick talking about it last night."

"Now you dare to bring Jamie into this? He worships you to the extent he'd be willing to say anything for you—"

Hester broke away from Gerrit and went toward her father. "Papa, that is not fair. Take a moment to listen to Gerrit. What he's saying is the truth. Talk to Jamie."

"Hester, go to your room. Leave this man."

"No, Papa. I'm going with Gerrit." Her shoulders

straightened. "We are going to be married and if you won't welcome us here, I shall go anywhere he goes."

Gerrit's spirit soared at her words.

Leighton's tone, however, turned pleading. "Hester, don't make this irrevocable mistake."

Instead of answering him, Hester came back to Gerrit and took one of his hands. "I shall be ready whenever you come for me."

He squeezed her hand and smiled in encouragement, knowing how difficult it must have been for her to go against her father. "I'll let you know." Then he bent down and kissed her lightly on her lips, knowing he needed the memory of them to get him through the time until they could be together for good. "I'll see you very soon."

He walked toward the doorway. Leighton just barely moved out of his way. Gerrit gave him a curt nod. "Good day, Mr. Leighton. I'll be back for Hester."

The next day, Gerrit faced the doors of Leighton Lumber & Shipping once again. He wasn't much better off than he had been last November when he'd arrived. He still didn't have much money in his pocket. He had no employment and no other assets except himself and his willingness to work. He wouldn't have come by here, except he needed his earnings from the winter. Yesterday he'd been willing to forgo them, but not today. He had earned them, and he and Hester would need them for wherever they'd be going.

He'd thought about it a lot last night. He'd slept little, although his insomnia hadn't been due to a guilty conscience or to worry about the future. Instead it had been due to the excitement and anticipation of what would come next.

Should he return to England with Hester? He didn't think so, although he hadn't ruled it out entirely. He wanted to discuss it thoroughly with Hester first. He thought it more likely they would stay in this Maine Territory, although Bangor was probably out. But there were many settlements surrounding it. He didn't want to deprive Hester of the rest of her family.

Well, delaying the moment wouldn't make it any easier. He squared his shoulders and opened the heavy door. Maybe he wouldn't even need to see Mr. Leighton.

He went up to the same clerk he'd seen the first day he'd arrived. "I've come for my wages from the logging."

"Oh, yes, Mr.—Major—Hawkes, sir." The man immediately slid down from the stool and made his way toward the back office.

Gerrit drummed his fingers on the dark wood counter. He could feel the glances of the other clerks. Had news of his scandalous behavior traveled here? No doubt. Well, he'd have to endure the knowing looks, at least until he and Hester could leave and make a fresh start.

A fresh start…isn't that what he'd attempted once before when he'd left England?

But this time it was different. This time the Lord was on his side. It made all the difference in the world.

The clerk interrupted his thoughts. "He'll see you now, Major Hawkes."

"Who? What?" He pulled his thoughts back to his reason for being there.

"Mr. Leighton, sir."

"I don't need to see him. I just came to collect my wages."

"But he wants to see you."

Gerrit frowned, then sighed. He really had no desire to stand and be insulted again by his future wife's father, but he supposed he could endure it one last time. "Very well."

He followed the man back through the door, again remembering the last time he'd passed that way.

Mr. Leighton rose from his chair this time and came around to the front of the desk. "Good morning, Hawkes. Thank you for coming in."

Gerrit raised his eyebrows. The man's tone certainly didn't sound belligerent. Why the change?

Leighton cleared his throat. "I won't beat around the bush. I want to apologize for thinking the worst of you."

Gerrit stared as the older man extended his hand. "Can you forgive me for believing what was utterly untrue? My only excuse is that I love my daughter very much. Someday you may very well be a father and know how much a parent wants the best for his child."

Gerrit hardly heard the words. He extended his own hand in a daze and felt it enfolded in the other man's. "What—?" Gerrit began again. "What happened to make you change your mind about me?"

Leighton's eyes flickered away from his briefly. "The tavern maid was waiting for me this morning as soon as I arrived. She confessed the whole plot to me. It seems Anderson, the man who put her up to it, has had it in for you ever since you arrived. He had a brother killed by a redcoat and couldn't abide the thought of you. When you came back a practical hero from the drive, that put him over the edge. I hope you'll forgive him, if you can." He ended on an embarrassed note.

"Never mind about him." Gerrit was still trying to adjust to Leighton's kinder tone. "What about Hest— Miss Leighton? Do I have your permission to court her—to marry her?"

The older man nodded. "You have it and you both have my blessing. You've proved more than once the kind of man you are. I know you'll make her a good husband."

"Thank you, sir." He tightened his own grip on Leighton's hand.

The two walked out of the office together after Leighton had personally given him his wages, with a hefty bonus for "looking after my wild son." Gerrit had tried to refuse the money, but Hester's father had insisted. "You'll need the capital if you're going to set up housekeeping. Speaking of which, we need to talk about what kind of work you'll be doing in the company now." They stepped back into the front office. "That is, if you care to continue working here…"

His words were cut off by a commotion. They turned in unison at the loud voices, one vying with the other for dominance. The clerk was trying to reason with a well-dressed man who was gesticulating in growing agitation.

"Ce n'est pas possible que personne ne me comprenne. Je veux seulement acheter quelque bois—"

"Sir, if you slow down, perhaps I can—"

Gerrit immediately recognized the man as a Frenchman trying to purchase some lumber. He hurried forward. *"Pardonnez-moi, monsieur. Peut-être je peux vous aider. Combien de bois souhaitez-vous acheter?"*

The man turned to him in surprise then relief before he let loose in another rapid string of French. Gerrit replied to his questions, turning to the clerk and Mr. Leighton for any questions he needed answers for.

After about twenty minutes, the Frenchman agreed to meet at the wharf in the afternoon to go with them to the boom up the river to select the lumber he wished to buy.

"Merci beaucoup!" He shook hands all around, a smile creasing his face this time as he finally backed out of the office with a final *"à bientôt."*

As the door closed behind him, Mr. Leighton asked Gerrit, "Speak French pretty well, do you?"

Gerrit shrugged. "School…then fighting the French, I picked up some more."

Leighton nodded. "Any other languages?"

"Latin, Greek, a smattering of Spanish and Portuguese."

For the first time since Gerrit had met Hester's father, a look of admiration touched the older man's features. "Come over to the house for dinner. Maybe we can discuss your future in the company. I could use someone with your abilities. An agent, if you will. Now that the war is over, we're going to expand…"

Later that day, dining with the Leightons, Gerrit felt himself once again fully welcomed by them. Afterwards, he sat a while with Mr. Leighton, discussing the opportunities in the shipping firm. However, through it all, Gerrit wanted only one thing: to be alone with Hester.

He finally got his wish when most of the family had turned in for the night, and he and Hester could sit together in the front parlor. He told her about the conversation with her father.

"So, I won't have to give up everything and follow you to the unknown with only a small satchel holding all my earthly belongings?" she asked in a playfully wistful tone.

He kissed her nose. "Knowing your penchant for the unconventional, I hate to disappoint you, but it looks like the farthest you have to go is to our new house, with perhaps an occasional trip with me to England or France."

She latched onto the first part. "New house?"

"Your father wants to give us a parcel of land not far from this one as a wedding gift." He reached for her hand, squeezing it gently. His heart was barely able to contain its joy. He smiled. "Speaking of which, when would you like to be married?"

She returned his smile and slipped her hand from his to place her arms loosely around his neck. Her delicate fingers played with the hair falling over his collar, one of the best feelings he'd ever experienced. "I hadn't thought about it," she murmured. "It seems you've been gone so long…to actually talk about a wedding seems too good to be true."

"What about this summer? Will that give you time to accustom yourself to the idea of having me always underfoot…?"

Her smile widened, her eyes sparkling. "I like the idea of having you underfoot."

"Let's hope you continue saying that once it's a reality." To silence any more words, he bent his head to kiss her.

She sighed with deep contentment. "I could grow to like being kissed all the time by you."

"What, don't you like it now?" he whispered against her lips.

"Can't you tell?" she whispered back, pressing her own lips closer to his.

As their kiss deepened, Gerrit felt a surge of desire such as he hadn't felt since…he couldn't remember when. He realized with a growing sense of wonder, that this, too, was a gift of God. He vowed he would never again misuse this gift.

Gently he disengaged himself slightly from his future wife and stroked her cheek, replying to the question he saw written in her eyes. "Nothing is the matter. Everything is wonderful, in fact. I'll explain it to you on our wedding night," he said with a smile to the lingering question in her gaze.

He sighed deeply before drawing her back into a tight hug. "God is gracious." Then he reluctantly let her go. "I want you with all my heart." He placed her hand to his heart. "My heart belongs to the Lord first, and then to you."

She smiled, taking his hand and resting it against her own heart. "It's in good hands then…as is mine."

He could feel the heat rise in him and slowly removed his hand, vowing he would honor her by waiting until their union was sanctioned by God.

Epilogue

July 1816

"I baptize you in the name of the Father, the Son and the Holy Ghost," the preacher declared before guiding Gerrit backwards into the cold waters of the lake. He had wanted to be baptized before his marriage, but had had to wait until the lake water was warm enough.

With this public display, Gerrit was announcing his new birth.

Although still cold, the water refreshed him on that hot July day. As he came out of the water, he wiped the water from his eyes and hair. He searched for Hester in the applauding crowd and smiled.

She looked beautiful in her white muslin with the wide band of lace at the hem and neckline. It was a new dress, especially made for the occasion. In her hand was a bouquet of delicate white roses.

As he left the lake, well-wishers shook his hand or

patted him on the back. When he reached Hester, he touched her soft cheek. "I'll be right back. Don't go anywhere."

She smiled, her eyes warm and glowing. "I'll be here."

After he'd changed into dry clothes—a new suit— he rejoined Hester and the pastor.

"Dearly beloved…"

Together the two repeated their wedding vows before all their family and friends.

"You may kiss the bride," the pastor said.

"At last," Gerrit murmured for Hester's ears alone as his face neared hers.

Then their guests clustered around them to offer their congratulations. Among them was Crocker, who had sailed all the way from England to be at Gerrit's wedding. He'd told Gerrit the evening before that he intended to stay in the Maine Territory.

Now with Gerrit's permission, he kissed Hester's cheek, then turned to the groom. "I brought you something." He fumbled in the pocket of his new frock coat.

Gerrit took the small cloth packet from him. As he unfolded it, wondering what it could possibly be, he saw the edge of the blue and silver badge. His Waterloo medal.

"I got it out of hock for you. Cost me a pretty penny," Crocker told him.

As Gerrit started to tell him he'd repay him, Crocker stopped him. "Consider it a wedding gift. Got the rest of your medals, too."

Gerrit smiled. "Thank you, Crocker. You're a good friend." Together the two men shook hands.

"I'm glad you found yourself a good woman," Crocker

said. "About time you had someone else to look after you instead of me." His gaze wandered over the crowd. "Wonder if there's another single lady for a lonely bachelor…"

Gerrit laughed. "There are plenty and it'll be my pleasure to introduce you to some, but right now, if you'll excuse me, I'm going to join my married one."

He approached Hester and showed her the medal. She squeezed his hand, telling him she understood how much Crocker's gesture had meant to him.

As the afternoon waned and the heavily laden tables of food were emptied, a band of fiddlers began to play. After several dances, Gerrit leaned toward Hester where the two sat on a bench to catch their breath, and said, "As much as I'm enjoying being accepted as one of your family, I wonder if I'll ever get you all to myself?"

She met his gaze. "We can leave whenever you wish."

He searched her face. "Do you mean it?"

"I want more than anything to be with you." He read unconditional love in her eyes—the same love that had steered his course since the day he'd met her.

The smile on his face grew. He took her hand in his and brought it to his lips. Then he stood, bringing her with him.

"Come, then, let us bid your parents farewell, and go to our new home."

"Our home." Hand in hand they walked together as husband and wife. Gerrit felt the joy surging through him, knowing she was his, and he was hers, and together they were God's children.

* * * * *

QUESTIONS FOR DISCUSSION

1. *Opposites attract* is an obvious literary device for romance writing. What are some of the things that make Hester Leighton and Gerrit Hawkes opposites? How will some of these elements be advantages or disadvantages to any future relationship they have?

2. What is it about Hester that attracts Gerrit, a man used to attracting all kinds of women?

3. How does the war change Gerrit? How does it reinforce (or aggravate) his bad habits? How does it make it difficult to fit into civilian life back in London?

4. Even though Hester is not Gerrit's type physically, what makes her grow more and more attractive to him the longer he knows her?

5. Why is it so ironic that Gerrit is forced into a protective role regarding Hester's virtue during the house party?

6. Why does the notion of trust unnerve Gerrit, especially when Hester keeps insisting that she trusts him? Why does Gerrit mistrust himself so much?

7. Why does Hester feel like a fish out of water in British society? During the house party, for example, she is forced to confront her own moral convictions. She is thrust into a world where there are a lot of

gray areas. In the long run, how does this episode in her sheltered life affect her faith? Does it weaken it? Strengthen it? Why is it important that she leave her safe haven and be confronted with this other world for a season?

8. Why is Gerrit so obsessed with death? Why does the Scripture comparing love with death convict him so?

9. At one point the oxen teamster, Orin Barnes, tells Gerrit about the two terms *absolution* and *redemption*. Think of these two phrases: "He was absolved from that crime." "He was redeemed of sin." The first phrase means he was found innocent of a crime. The second implies a person is guilty but that someone paid the price for him so he wouldn't be liable for the punishment he deserved. What do you think about the two sides to this coin and why does Orin feel Gerrit needs redemption instead of simple absolution?

10. Jeremiah Leighton prides himself on his ability to read a person's character. Is Hester's father always fair to Gerrit? Why or why not? What things from his own background color his opinion?

11. Hester doesn't fight her father to remain behind in England but returns home to Maine even though it means saying goodbye to the man she loves. Why does she leave so dutifully? Is she right to leave Gerrit?

12. When Gerrit returns from the log drive in seeming victory, he believes things in his life are finally changing for the better. The morning after, he discovers all the reverse, when he is brought to the lowest point yet. Why is it essential that he come to the end of himself and all his resources?

HARLEQUIN

More Than Words

"The transformation is the Cinderella story over and over again."

—**Ruth Renwick,** real-life heroine

*Ruth Renwick is a Harlequin More Than Words
award winner and the founder of **Inside The Dream.***

Discover your inner heroine!

SUPPORTING CAUSES OF CONCERN TO WOMEN

HARLEQUIN

WWW.HARLEQUINMORETHANWORDS.COM

MTW07RR1

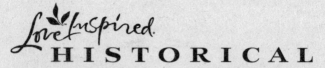